Beyond World's End

Mercedes Lackey &
Rosemary Edghill

BEYOND WORLD'S END

This is a work of fiction. All the characters and events portrayed in this book are fictional, and any resemblance to real people or incidents is purely coincidental.

A Baen Books Original

Baen Publishing Enterprises
P.O. Box 1403
Riverdale, NY 10471
www.baen.com

ISBN: 0-671-31855-1

Cover art by Steve Hickman

First paperback printing, December 2001

Library of Congress Cataloging-in-Publication Number 00-046736

Distributed by Simon & Schuster
1230 Avenue of the Americas
New York, NY 10020

Typeset by Brilliant Press
Printed in the United States of America

MEN WITH GUNS, OR DARK LORDS—
CHOOSE NOW!

Eric had time for one last coherent thought—
*if any of these things gets past me into the City,
there's going to be a bloodbath even the Guardians can't stop*—before he raised his flute and let
the music take him, shutting out everything but
the battle before him.

As Aerune's Hunt eddied about the edges of the
human warriors seeking an opening, the Unseleighe
Lord suddenly heard a bright waterfall of music—
Bard magic. Here was power enough to play all
of Aerune's dark dreams into reality. "Take him!"
Aerune roared, gesturing toward the Bard. He blew
his horn, summoning back his Hounds and
creatures.

The monsters he'd been fighting melted away
like ice in a blast furnace and Eric stopped playing, feeling the magic he'd been following
simply . . . stop. He became aware of his surroundings. Searchlights. Gunfire. Elves on horses. Men
with guns.

What the hell have I stumbled into?

Eric risked looking away from the Unseleighe
Lord on the horse. Behind him were half a dozen
guys in commando suits. Some of them were wearing chain mail and carrying spears. All of them had
guns.

"Choose quickly, Bard!" the leader of the Wild
Hunt called to Eric, holding out his hand. "I think
your shields will not hold against their weaponry!
Choose! Them or us!"

The hell I will! Eric thought. He reached inside
himself, to where the music ran like a deep underground river and pulled up a melody for which
there were no earthly terms.

And he vanished.

IN THIS SERIES

DEDICATION

To all the folks at the Arlington Pak-Mail, John Giardi, Amy Bombardieri, Stephanie Cole, and the divine Murphy (woof!), for last-minute copies, shipping, and cold wet noses far beyond the call of duty.

And to my esteemed co-authoress, who is as fond of elves as I am.

—Rosemary Edghill

CONTENTS

"By a knight of ghosts and shadows
I summoned am to tourney
Ten leagues beyond the wide world's end
Methinks it is no journey."

—Tom O' Bedlam (traditional)

ONE:

THE PARTING OF FRIENDS

"Are you sure you really want to do this?" Beth asked Eric for roughly the five hundredth time in the past month.

As a long-time stranger to big cities, it was hard for Eric to believe that there was anywhere in New York City where she could have been heard without shouting, but this strange little tree-shaded court was somehow as quiet as a desert canyon miles outside of Los Angeles—and just about as hot. It was September, but there was no hint of fall in the air, and the leaves on the slender maples growing in their squares of earth allocated in the sidewalk were still green. Today was one of the shimmering-hot days that persisted well into October here, and the stone of the buildings surrounding them seemed to hold and reflect back every degree of heat. The buildings also shut most of the traffic noise out, making a private oasis in the heart of the city. Beth and Kory—and their motorcycles-cum-elvensteeds—were the only creatures on the street besides Eric.

Eric looked up at the old apartment building that was going to be his home for the next year or so, and nodded.

"I'm sure," he replied firmly. "Things couldn't go on the way they have been—and none of us wanted them to." Then he grinned. "Besides, you aren't going to be that far away by Underhill standards. And I'm a fully functional Bard now, remember? I can come visit you any time I want to—or any time you guys are getting stir-crazy."

Beth looked as if she might want to argue that point for a moment; then, instead of saying anything, she just sighed.

"You certainly aren't the same Eric Banyon anymore," she admitted. "You not only have feck, but you know what machine to buy your clues from," she said, grinning proudly.

"And I brought my own roll of quarters to put in the machine," Eric shot back, grinning.

Earlier this morning, the three of them had packed up the last of their stuff from the friend's place they'd been crashing at between Faire weekends. The Sterling Forest RenFaire ran every year from July to September at a site about an hour north of New York City. There was even a Nexus there, Elfhame Everforest, the only one on the

East Coast, tucked away in the State Park that surrounded the Fairesite.

The three of them had been working the Faire together, just like old times. Only this time it was a farewell performance, and they'd all known it. It had added a certain sweetness to the music. But all good things must come to an end.

He put down his two bags to hug her. "No worries, pretty lady. I'll be fine. The kids at Juilliard are already calling me 'old man,' and taking bets on who's going to win the confrontations between me and the administration. Odds are in my favor, by the way." Classes started on Monday, but he'd already been up to the school several times, for Registration and Orientation. It hadn't changed much in all the years he'd been away—schools had a lot in common with Underhill in that respect.

Beth traded places with Kory, who was not at all ashamed to bestow as hearty a hug on Eric as Beth had. "You do know the way Underhill, if you need to come," Korendil appealed. There was an unspoken plea in the elf's emerald-green eyes. "Do not allow pride to keep you from seeking your friends if you need help."

Eric shook his shaggy head; haircuts had not been a priority either Underhill or at the Faire, and he didn't want to do anything about the length of his mane just yet. "Believe me, Elfhame Everforest is the first place I'll head for if I get into trouble," he promised. "Now, you two—go! If you don't make some tracks, you won't reach Sterling Forest before sunset, elvensteeds or no elvensteeds, and this is going to be your last Renfaire gig before the baby comes. I think I can manage to move my last two bags into an apartment without help—and take care of myself once I've settled in."

They'd been staying with Bonnie and Kit up in Inwood—a comic book writer and a Witch that Beth knew from years ago—while Eric and Beth made the many purchases necessary to turn a rented apartment into a home—*and* waited the several weeks for delivery of the furniture! Eric wasn't displeased to have the transition time: living Underhill for an extended period made returning to the World Above a distinct shock. And no place else, in Underhill or the World Above, was quite like New York City. It made even the Chaos Lands seem quiet.

Beth paused to hug him once more. "You know, I think you can," she admitted, looking just a little tearful. "And maybe that's the scariest part of all. You don't need us anymore."

There wasn't any reply he could make to that statement—there was enough truth in it to sting— so Eric didn't bother to try. Instead, he picked up his bags and moved away from the curb, walking backwards, as Kory and Beth mounted their sleek, exotic motorcycles.

A third bike already resided in the tiny parking lot behind the building, and Eric had no fear that anyone was going to steal it. For one thing, they wouldn't be able to find a starter or a place to hotwire it. For another, *she* wouldn't let them. Lady Day was an elvensteed, and could take any form she chose. Eric didn't really ride her, she carried him; he could go to sleep while riding her and she would get him safely to his destination no matter what the conditions were. She could take any shape he wanted her to—he'd heard that there were even elves in other Elfhames that had elvensteeds the shape of racing cars, though frankly Eric would believe *that* when he saw it.

His mind was already running ahead, into his future here. He preferred her as a motorcycle, and Lady Day preferred to take that form, but as soon as the weather turned, she was going to have to take on the form of a little econobox car, unless he intended to take the subway across town to Juilliard. She wasn't looking forward to that, and frankly, neither was he, but that was the price he paid for returning to Juilliard—East Coast winters.

Maybe I can have her clone a Kia, a Neon or a sporty little Isuzu 4x4 instead. That wouldn't be too out-of-keeping with my cover story, Eric thought hopefully. It had been so long since he'd had to worry about money at all that he wasn't too sure he remembered the gory details. *I can always say I put the bike in storage for the winter. Nobody at Juilliard is likely to know enough about cars to wonder how I can keep a maintenance hog fuelled and running!*

Eric paused at the front door of the building for a last look back. Beth and Kory had donned their helmets, and "started" the bikes, thus making further conversation a moot point. The elvensteeds not only knew enough to counterfeit the roar of powerful motorcycle engines, they seemed to enjoy doing so. The two riders, anonymous now in their matching helmets and leathers, pulled neat little reversal moves that got them going in the right direction on the street with an appropriate amount of tire spin and smoke. They waved, and Eric tucked one bag under his arm and freed up a hand to wave back. He kept waving as they roared out of sight.

That didn't take long in the city; they were out of sight as soon as they turned the corner. He evened his load again, and walked soberly up to the door of the building.

Home. Sweet home? Well, home is what you make it, I guess. This is as good as any. And a lot better than some. Good thing I'm not on a starving student's budget.

He could have had any apartment in any building in the city, of course: as an adult student, Eric didn't have the same residence restrictions that the minors and first-year students did at Juilliard, and a fellow with a safety-deposit box full of gold Krugerrands could pretty much afford whatever he wanted. But he'd gone out walking one day when he and Beth and Kory first arrived here, and found the old building as if he'd been drawn to it. It'd had a name once—most old New York apartment buildings were named—but time had eroded the carving above the door, until all that remained was a florid "G" and a barely legible "ouse." Something-house. Maybe Gargoyle House, for when Eric had looked up—he was enough of an out-of-towner to do that frequently—he had been surprised to see the hunched winged forms of classic medieval gargoyles perched on the building's four corners. New York was rich in such hidden sculpture, he knew. Art for birds, someone had once called it.

There'd been a discreet sign in the building manager's window—the only "For Rent" sign he could remember seeing anywhere, actually—and the building itself had attracted him. There were three apartments available. One was a corner apartment on the top floor, and when he saw that there was a gargoyle perched right outside the living-room window, he'd been sold.

That had been the good part. The bad part was the age of the building. Old buildings had old building problems. Still, it had a lot more heart to it than some of those high-rise condos that were going up everywhere. And a place like this would be a lot easier to explain if anyone ever asked.

For a wonder, the building manager—her name was Toni Hernandez, a middle-aged Latina woman—had been ready to show him around right then. The building was of about the same vintage as the Gunfight at the OK Corral, which meant that the ceilings were high and the bathrooms were ancient—which meant very cool lion-footed bathtubs, but teeny sinks and plumbing he wasn't altogether sure about. The kitchen cabinets and counters looked like originals from when the building was new, and forget central air—if he wanted to be cool during the summer and early fall, he'd have to buy a window AC, and hope the wiring could stand it. He was going to have to swelter for the rest of this year, though—by the time he could get a window unit delivered and installed at this time of year, snow would already be falling.

As for the heating, it was all by ancient steam pipes, and those didn't function until the super decided it was cold enough—and Eric knew all about the way steam pipes sang and banged at night. He'd probably need to supplement the radiators with space heaters, given how far away his apartment was from the basement boilers, anyway.

He'd been assured that the wiring was modern, though—and looking the apartment over, seeing all new cover plates and plenty of grounded outlets, Eric had felt fairly sure he wasn't being lied to. If the wiring was modern enough to accept the load of a computer, a microwave, and an air conditioner, he felt he could put up with steam heat and ancient plumbing. He'd accepted the top-floor apartment on the spot, and the rest had been mere formality.

The building might be old, but it had some nifty modern amenities where it really counted, and considering its West Side location, Eric was surprised that the building hadn't gone condo a long time ago. A security system mounted discreetly in an etched brass plate beside the door had a code for every tenant—and with ten digits, it would take a long time for someone to hit a correct one at random.

He punched it in now—a little slow, but he'd taken care to pick a string of numbers fairly easy to remember—and walked in through the front door. The coolness of the lobby was welcome after the heat outside, and as he usually did, he paused to admire the foyer—very Art Nouveau, and all of it original. Even the opulent brass faces of the mailboxes were vintage. Of course, that meant that the elevator was pretty vintage too—hydraulic, and in mint condition, but very slow. Ms. Hernandez told him that when the building had been built, people had been afraid of fast elevators. So it rose gently and serenely at a less-than-walking pace, but hey, if he was in a hurry, he could always use the stairs.

The elevator took its time in arriving on the top floor, but that wasn't bad either. He wasn't as frisky as he'd been when he first came to school at Juilliard, himself. He liked the folding bronze safety-gate; it reminded him of an old hotel he'd once stayed in that actually had an elevator attendant, little red uniform and all. Fortunately the building didn't come with a doorman, like some of the posh places along Park Avenue did. He didn't think he could quite handle that.

The long elevator ride up to the 10th floor gave Eric time to think and to probe his feelings as if they were a newly filled tooth. Did it hurt, Beth and Kory going off like that and leaving him behind? Should he reconsider?

Nope. It doesn't really hurt, it just feels different. It stopped hurting a long time ago. And the decision isn't really new. It's old.

He remembered the day Beth had first told him she was pregnant. She and Kory had looked so happy—Beth wanted a large family, and elves were crazy about children anyway—but all Eric had felt was fear, as though he'd made a disastrous mistake in fathering this child. It had been Beth who'd gently broken it to him that she already knew what Eric had only that moment discovered: that while he'd been growing into his magic, she and Kory had been growing into a couple. Without him.

Only not really. After what we've been through together, we'll be friends forever. Only it's a different kind of friendship now. In some ways it's better.

Better, because it lacked the element of sexual anxiety that had flavored the earliest days of his relationship with Beth . . . and Kory. This was something strong and deep that didn't need sex to fuel it, something that would last as long as the pillars of Underhill.

The elevator creaked to a halt on the top floor, jarring him out of his reverie, and Eric opened the safety gate and the door. His apartment was a corner apartment, which had been another selling point. Its location meant that there would be less noise from fellow tenants, and no noise from the elevator itself, as well as a cooling cross-breeze on most days. He still wasn't used to how *noisy* this city was—even in the middle of Central Park you could hear the sirens and the traffic noises.

New York, New York, it's a wonderful town. The Bronx is up and the Battery's down. And the city never sleeps.

Like the lobby, the hallway decor had somehow survived being "modernized"; it was original, and for a wonder, no one had ripped off the vintage *paté verine*[1] light-fixtures. Then again, maybe that was why the owners had put in the security system in the first place. Architecture thieves were only one of the problems of life in the Big City.

The only concession to the modern world was in the carpet running the length of the hall; it was standard grey-beige industrial stuff, but it didn't clash with the Art Nouveau wallpaper and frosted-glass fixtures, not all of which were lights. There were cameras in some of those wall fixtures, and

---

[1] Glass-paste.

smoke and heat detectors too, and sprinklers in the ceiling—everything the heart could desire from a safety and security standpoint. Another selling point, not that a fully trained Bard had much to fear from human thugs. Magical attacks were another matter, but frankly, Eric wasn't expecting many of those.

At the end of the hall was his door. No hollow-core flimsy barricade or scary metal portal this, but a solid slab of oakwood, polished deep brown with the passing of years, with brass lockplates and doorknob that gleamed brightly against the old wood. Here was the building's second concession to the modern age—there were two key-operated deadbolts plus the door key, and a final key pad on which once more to enter his ten-digit code. If he didn't enter it, or keyed it wrong and didn't correct himself when it beeped at him, the system would alert Ms. Hernandez—she'd check the cameras and maybe call the cops.

I wonder why this place has got so much security? Or maybe this is normal for New York? After all, I have been away for a while. . . .

Like about 20—no, closer to 30—years. Though he'd spent a lot of that time Underhill, where time flowed more slowly than it did in the World Above. That was one of the reasons he'd been willing to risk coming back so openly. Anybody who was still looking after this long would be looking for a guy in his forties—not a sassy young dude still in his twenties.

He negotiated the three key-locks—here was a moment of fumbling with the ring of unfamiliar keys (Eric hadn't carried keys in years, and had kept losing them for the first few weeks)—punched in his code, and watched while the light went from red to green. Then he was inside and locking the door of his new home behind him. Beth's friends said it would soon become second nature, but for now it was an effort to remember the actions involved.

At last he turned away from the door and looked around with a sudden feeling of hesitancy. Even with as much work as Beth and Kory had already done while he'd been getting squared away with Juilliard, there was a lot still to unpack and arrange, and most of it was brand-new untouched-by-human-hands stuff. This was the first time in his life he'd had this many *things*.

Immediately before him was the living room, a huge space (so Bonnie had said) by New York standards. A new leather couch and matching recliner in the sort of oxblood brown that reminded him of Old English clubs sat cozily in front of the fireplace—this place was retro enough to have fireplaces, (with terrific white-marble mantels, though he didn't think the fireplace still worked). To the right of the sofa and behind it were the tall sash windows, and if he looked up, Eric could just see the back of the gargoyle on the corner of the roof. Against the blank wall was his new rack system and a television and laser-disk player. In the corner farthest from the windows was his desk— light cherry, from Levinger's—which mostly held a brand-new computer with a music keyboard and speakers as well as the usual techie stuff.

Sheepskins covered the worn wooden parquet floor, and the glazed-chintz curtains in an archival

William Morris pattern—mostly deep greens, with a hint of orange—that Beth had picked out were pulled open to display the view. There were flowers in a blue glass vase on the mantlepiece—moonlilies, so that was Kory's touch; they didn't grow anywhere but Underhill, and a daily little touch of magic would keep them alive forever. The heat made the apartment seem stuffy, and Eric moved around opening windows. Though there was a six week wait for delivery of an air conditioner, he'd been able to pick up a couple of wall fans. He lifted them into the kitchen and bedroom windows now and switched them on. A cooling breeze began to waft through the apartment, and Eric sighed with relief. He could manage to be pretty comfortable, so long as he didn't get into any heavy lifting.

Eric still had a faint feeling of trespassing when he moved around the place. It looked like an apartment belonging to a moderately (okay, let's admit it: more than moderately) prosperous classical flautist—at least, until you got to the CD collection, which was currently still in boxes waiting to be unpacked. He'd had one heck of a time putting that together, and the look on the clerk's face at Plastic Meltdown over in the East Village when he kept coming up to the counter with another stack of disks had been worth every penny. Thanks to a little help, both magical and non, Eric Banyon had an A-1 credit rating and an AmEx Platinum card to prove it. Thanks to the Krugerrands in his safe deposit box, he even had a way to pay the humongous bill that was going to arrive!

Beside the empty bookshelves—more light

cherry from Levinger's—were boxes of books, also waiting to be shelved. He'd had almost as much fun in the Strand as he had in the record store. More, in a way, because he kept straying over to the children's sections, picking up volumes he'd read as a kid and wanted to get reacquainted with. This place was as unlike his L.A. apartment as possible—and just as unlike the house he'd shared with Beth and Kory in San Francisco. That had been due to calculated effort on all their parts. He was starting over, in a sense, and he should start fresh.

Beth had stocked the kitchen, so he wasn't going to starve, and she hadn't loaded it down with equipment he didn't know how to use and food he didn't know how to cook. Mostly microwave stuff, he suspected, to go with the mother-of-all-microwaves sitting in silent splendor on the white-marble kitchen counter.

It was too quiet, suddenly, and he walked over to the rack and turned on WQXR, the local classical station. Stravinsky's *Pulcinella Suite* filled the room; not his first choice, but not bad, and more to the point, not reeking of Omens and Portents. He'd had about enough of those for a while.

He took his bags into the bedroom and once again was confronted by newness. The bedroom was small, only 14x14, with just enough room for a double bed with a bookcase headboard. The bed, covered with a thick, red, silk-covered goosedown comforter—another of Kory's touches, Eric suspected, because elves liked color and weren't shy about using it—was a classier version of one of those adjustable beds you saw on late-night TV commercials. He hadn't wanted a waterbed; that would have come with too many memories of Beth and Kory attached. The headboard had built-in lamps and his new alarm clock (retro-Deco to match the building) nestled cozily in a nook that would be difficult to reach if he wasn't awake. On top of the matching bureau was a smaller television, and one of those nifty-keen Bose Wave radio/CD players. The curtains were the same glowing red silk as the comforter. There was another sheepskin rug—dark brown this time—on the floor in front of the bed; it reminded Eric slightly of a large flat dog.

He carried his bags over to the walk-in closet and opened it. It was the old-fashioned kind with drawers in the back and several tiers of shelves reaching all the way up to the ceiling, and it was full of bags of brand new clothing that he hadn't yet opened. Eric slowly unpacked his bags and hung the only things he owned that had any wear on them on polished cedar hangers at the back. The clothing was nothing if not flamboyant; Faire garb, all of it, and all of it made by magic. That was Kory's forté: he could produce clothing at the drop of a pointed ear. It wasn't likely that Eric would need any of this at any time soon, but he wanted to have it around. A link to his past—to the Faires and Underhill—to the only part of his life that Eric thought of as real.

Everything else in the apartment had come by way of the efforts of Eric's mentor, who was as skillful at producing gold as Kory was at producing clothing—and as Beth was at knowing where to shop. Thanks to Master Mage Dharinel's work,

Eric was not going to have to worry about where his money was coming from for a very long time, if ever. The rest of his tenure at Juilliard was already paid for in advance. His rent was paid up for the next year in advance. Utilities, phone, cable, ditto—all handled out of an escrow account administered by a "friend of the family" down in Wall Street somewhere, just so Eric wouldn't have to worry about them. And in addition to everything else, Eric had a bank account again, besides that excellent credit rating and the emergency stash of Krugerrands.

As for the inevitable IRS agents (if nothing worse)—well, he'd found a way to handle them. They'd stopped in DC before coming up here; Eric had set up shop outside the agency, put out his hat, and played his flute until he found one agent that was susceptible. A little Bardic magic, a sob story about being out of work in Mexico for the last couple of years, a tale of winning an unspecified lottery outside the States, and an expressed eagerness to pay his rightful share of taxes (and a check for the amount the nice agent deemed appropriate), and his record with the IRS was as clean and shiny as Lady Day. He could use his own social security number without being afraid it would red-flag every Federal computer from here to Ultima Thule . . . in fact, his entire record was so clean and shiny that anyone checking on him might suspect he was in the Federal Witness Protection Program. Eric's name, his real name, was on the mailbox, the apartment lease, the utilities, in the phone book, and on the driver's license and bank and credit cards in his wallet. He wasn't hiding, he wasn't Underhill, and he didn't have to start thinking of ways to escape whenever he saw a cop or someone in a too-perfect suit. *I'm a person again,* he thought with wonder. *I'm real. Whatever I do will go with me; I can't shed my past like a snake with an old skin.*

He went back into the living room and sat in his new chair, the glossy leather chilly through the back of his damp shirt. He listened to the Moonlight Sonata wafting in courtesy of the radio station. It all felt—odd. Very odd. Not luxurious, no—strangely enough, although this was luxury by all common standards, it did not match the level of sumptuousness Underhill, or even the standards of comfort Kory had established in their old San Francisco townhouse. But it was all Eric's, chosen to please only his taste and no one else's, and it was real and solid, not something conjured up out of energy and thin air like goods of elvish making.

It might have felt restrictive after the bootless freedom of the past few years, but somehow it didn't. It felt solid and comfortable and good. And when the Krugerrands ran out, and the account that covered his rent and utilities expired, he'd have to have a job to pay for all of this.

Not that he had any doubt that he'd be able to do that when the time came. He was probably one of the few people, if not the only person, who ever quit Juilliard and then returned to finish what he'd started.

Returned to finish . . . that had been a recurring theme lately. It wasn't the first time the thought had crossed his mind over time—but the first time, it hadn't been his thought at all.

"You have unfinished business."

When he closed his eyes he could hear that stern voice saying those words even over the strains of Beethoven in the here-and-now. He didn't have to think about it; the scene played out behind his eyes without effort, as clearly as if it had happened yesterday.

Underhill. He'd been Underhill, at Elfhame Misthold, and he hadn't known what day, week, or even month it was. Time moved strangely Underhill; light came and went, but there was no telling if it was the end of a day or if the Queen of the Hill had decided she was tired of light and wanted some darkness for a change. Beth—Beth needed not to be Above, in the mortal world, where there were law-enforcement people who thought she was responsible for some very unfortunate occurrences. And she was—but not in the way that they thought.

Besides, as the elves with the ability to See into the future had said at the time, at some point Real Soon Bethie was going to show up preggers, even more reason not to go back into the World Above. So he and Kory were living Underhill with her, and in that strange timeless land Eric had thrown himself into his music—which meant his magic—fully and completely for the first time in his life.

After the Loma Prieta almost-disaster, the Nightflyers, and the absolute proof to everybody involved of the madness of allowing a half-trained Bard to run around leaking magic and going off unexpectedly, he'd had little choice. It hadn't been ambition that had driven him, it had been desperation. Beth was slipping away from him more every day, and he knew it. Things were changing in his life, even in the timeless world of Underhill, and he didn't like it. Maybe he'd thought that being a real Bard, one with full control of his powers like the old Druidic Bards—Merlin, Taliesen, Gwion—would lure Beth back and put him on an even footing with Korendil, Elven Knight of Elfhame Sun-Descending. Heck, Kory didn't have all that much magic by elven standards, surely Eric could catch up!

But before long, the music and magic stopped being a crutch, or a means to an end, and became the end itself.

One day—a day much like any other, here—he had finished playing and put his flute down, waiting for Dharinel to give him the usual critique. Dharinel was a Magus Major and one of the most powerful of Elven Bards in any Elfhame, anywhere, and there was always a critique. Either Eric's control over the magic energy was not firm enough, or it was too grasping, and he didn't let it flow. He went too slowly, or too fast. There was always something wrong, and Dharinel was always correct when he pointed those things out.

It had all felt right when he played, completely and utterly right, but it had felt right in the past, too. But this time when he stopped, Dharinel said nothing for a very long time. The perfumed mists of Underhill drifted past them both, and the birds that had stilled out of politeness while Eric played resumed their song. There was no sunshine, of course: there was no sun Underhill, only a perpetual twilight, except when the Prince or the Queen deemed it appropriate to deepen the twilight to something like true night, so that the fireflies, Fae Lights, and Faerie Illuminations could enliven the darkness. Eric held his breath and wondered what he had done wrong this time. Was it that horrible?

Finally Dharinel had let out his breath and opened his jewel-toned eyes. "I have nothing more to teach you," he said in his controlled, utterly perfect voice.

Eric had shaken his head. "What?" he blurted. "Was I that bad?"

"You were that good," Dharinel corrected. "I have nothing more to teach you. The rest will come with maturity and practice, and it is a pity that you are not of the Blood, for you would be a force to reckon with in a hundred years or so." He had actually smiled then; a thin smile, but the expression so seldom crossed Dharinel's sardonic lips that Eric had nearly fallen off his bench. "As it is, in a mere handful of mortal years, you will be a force to reckon with in the mortal world. And that is where you must go now. You have unfinished business there."

The moment Dharinel said those words, all of the vague discontent that had been in Eric's heart attained an object. Once music had become his All again, he had been able to come to terms with the fact that Beth and Kory were an Item and he had been slowly eased out of that side of their relationship. They would always be friends, the three of them, but—Kory and Beth were a pair, and he wasn't part of that structure anymore. He'd allowed it to happen without trying to fight. And once those last pieces of the puzzle had fallen into place, like the tumblers in a lock, he'd known what he should do.

Besides, Beth had a lot of Things she needed to deal with. She and Kory wanted kids, and while Eric liked kids in the abstract, he wasn't ready to play daddy right now, even though he'd fathered the child she was carrying. It had seemed like a good solution at the time—call it a kind of parting gift. Kory and his cousins were very pleased with the idea of raising a baby-Bard from scratch in Underhill where she could be properly taught. Though Eric knew that Beth wanted more children—and with Kory—an elf couldn't father a child on a mortal woman without a lot of high-powered—and very dangerous—magical intervention. Halfling births could be arranged in a number of ways, but most of them involved stealing life-energy from another source to allow the woman to conceive—and that meant wholesale slaughter of the innocents who donated that energy. There were rumors that there were gentler ways, but no one in Misthold was really certain what was involved, actually, though Kory had the elven librarians searching the most ancient records and sending to the other hames for hints of the ancient Seleighe quickening magics.

But unlike Eric, Beth really didn't have much choice about staying in Underhill. Those very unpleasant people from the "alphabet agencies" were still looking for Beth. This was bad. It meant that Beth Kentraine could never live in the real world again, unless she concocted a whole new identity or moved to another country where no one would ask her about her past. She could visit—with care and constant vigilance—but she couldn't live in the States anymore. And babies and the Faire circuit didn't coexist well, at the best of times. . . .

And if the two of them didn't have enough problems, there's the fact that if Beth spends long enough in Underhill, she CAN'T come out, ever. She'll die. And before that happens, even if she does find some way to live Outside, she gets older. And Kory . . . doesn't. Or not fast enough, anyway. He's young by Sidhe standards. He has centuries ahead of him. Bethie has less than a century. There are spells that can slow her aging, but they'd tie her and Kory together for the rest of their lives—and shorten his. And even if she were willing to take that kind of responsibility, she won't even let Dharinel try anything like that while she feels responsible for me!

It all had come together in that moment. Eric wanted his life back—his life in the World Above. There were things he needed to finish, like his degree, if only to prove to himself that he could. And he just didn't like Underhill all that much, to tell the truth. He had at first. He'd enjoyed the timelessness, the tranquility. But after a while, what was sweet had become cloying, what was tranquil seemed stale, and a growing restlessness brought it home to him that nothing ever changed here.

"You're right," he'd told his mentor. "I have unfinished business. And I don't belong here." He'd looked around, for a moment. "Maybe no mortal belongs here—"

"Unless they're sorely wounded in heart or soul, lad," Dharinel said softly, so softly Eric had to strain to hear him. "Only then, when mortal sunlight brings pain, not gladness, can they bide happily with us. Or if they're so heart-bound to one of the Blood that losing the sun of the mortal lands seems no kind of sacrifice to make."

Eric opened his eyes in the here-and-now and sighed. Well, if anyone qualified as "wounded in the heart or soul," it was Beth. Hell, she still couldn't even sleep at night unless someone had her sandwiched between him and the wall—except when she was Underhill. Living at Kit and Bonnie's during the week, doing the Sterling Forest RenFaire on weekends, was one of the rare situations when she relaxed outside of Underhill—it would be next to impossible for a government goon to insert himself into the organization of Rennies. Rennies all knew each other, or knew people who knew each other, and the habits and mannerisms of a Rennie were something it would take a long time for a government agent to master. Not to mention the esoteric skill-sets it took to get hired on at the Faires in the first place! Beth could feel safe there, and at night, surrounded by other campers (and guarded by her and Kory's elvensteeds) it would be pretty hard for anyone to get at them. Impossible to do it quietly.

Unless you're a ninja, and I don't think they take government contracts. At least I hope they don't.

The three of them had already planned the trip to the Sterling Forest Faire before Eric had made his decision—he'd just expanded the trip to include his reentry into the human race. It hadn't been easy, but the biggest hurdle had actually been getting an audition to reapply at Juilliard in the first place. Convincing Beth that this was something he had to do had been child's play. Kory hadn't objected at all, largely because Dharinel, who was his superior as well as his Elder, had made it quite clear in his quiet but implacable way that this was something he felt Eric had to do.

After that it was just a matter of lining up the ducks, and shooting them down. And here he was.

He shook his head, levering himself up out of the chair with a sigh. He had a lot to unpack, so he might as well get to it. He could always brood later. There'd be a lot of time for it. And it wouldn't get much cooler even if he waited: the stone and concrete of the city held heat for hours after the sun set, unlike both L.A. and San Francisco, where temperatures tended to drop sharply once the sun went down. Since his apartment was near the Hudson River he could expect a drop of at least a few degrees tonight, but not really enough to count on. Still, there were only three or four more weeks of this hot weather at the very most, and he could always conjure up some cool if he really needed it.

Say . . . there's an idea. He rubbed his sweaty forehead, and then went into the bedroom for his flute.

Music was a handy tool for focusing his Bardic magic, but in most situations it wasn't absolutely necessary. Still, Eric enjoyed the game of fitting the music to the spell. And here in the World Above, where magic didn't fill the ambient air as it did in Underhill, it was nice to have a bit of a framework to work within.

He fitted the pieces of the flute together and blew an exploratory trill before segueing into "Troika," one of the five pieces that made up Prokofiev's *Lieutenant Kije*. A troika was a three-horse Russian sleigh, and you could almost hear the sleigh-bells and the cadence of the horses' pacing feet in the bounce of the main theme. Eric closed his eyes, imagining the crunch of hooves on snow, the clear cold bite of the wintery air—

But not too much. We just want to make it a little cooler in here, not turn the place into an icebox. . . .

As a pleasant chill rolled through the apartment, Eric opened his eyes. He could see a faint shimmer of magic over the windows, where the parameters of the spell he had set turned the air from hot to cold as it passed through the window. In a few moments, the muggy cloyingness of the air was gone. The spell would fade away naturally after a few hours in order to avoid being too disruptive; after all, he could set it again any time he needed to. Eric walked back out into the living room, flute in hand.

Now for a little urban renewal.

He started with the CD collection, although the first things he unpacked didn't go into the storage cabinets, they went on the machine, and when he was done, he had a stack of thirty empty jewel boxes piled beside it.

He set the changer on "shuffle," and let it rip, sinking back down in his chair and thinking amusedly that this was one mix no radio station on the planet would ever match. *Hey, it's K-Banyon radio, all Celtic, all the time!*

Then again, maybe there was one station that could match his CD-shuffle. WYRD, a little station somewhere in the middle of nowhere in North Carolina or Georgia or someplace like that, was allegedly programmed by elves. All he knew was the one or two times he'd accidentally picked it up, it had played things he was only thinking about, as if the DJ were reading his mind. And supposedly, you could count on it to give you omens of what was going to happen to you.

No thank you. And I certainly hope and pray my CD player doesn't start doing so.

Well, he had some pretty esoteric platters in his Celtica-mix today; stuff he hadn't known was back in production, stuff he hadn't known was in production in the first place. Strange little labels he'd never heard of, and some that were clearly self-produced.

"We don't get a lot of call for this—" The clerk had said that over and over, in a bewildered voice, as Eric brought out disk after disk that wasn't in his computer. Finally one of the assistant managers had taken pity on the poor kid and sent him off to help a Gen-Xer find the latest Smashing Pumpkins CD.

"Our owner has a hobby," the assistant manager explained, as he patiently entered the prices and stock numbers manually. "He's independently wealthy; as long as the store breaks even, he doesn't care. His hobby is to make sure that no matter what someone's musical taste is, he'll always find fabulous surprises here. You should see the mail he gets—catalogues from individual artists, even. So—a lot of stuff may sit around for a year or more before anyone buys it. He doesn't care; he knows that someday someone is going to want it, be amazed and thrilled that it's here, and keep coming back to see what else shows up. That's why the store's called 'Plastic Meltdown.' He expects credit cards to go into overload when the right people walk through the door."

Eric just grinned. "Well, I know I'm going to put my plastic through a workout here on a regular basis. Does this happen often?"

"Often enough," the middle-aged fellow said, with a wink. "Yesterday it was someone who collects movie scores—she was funny, kept saying, 'My God! My God!' until I thought the Big Guy was going to show up to find out why she was calling on Him. Today it's you. Tomorrow, probably no one unusual, but next week, maybe an opera buff. The heavy hitters are usually from out of town; the rest of us know we don't have to blow all our savings at once."

If that was a subtle inquiry, Eric didn't answer it quite as the fellow expected. "I just took the plunge on a CD player—I resisted for a long, long time; now that I'm a convert, I put the vinyl in storage and gave away the tapes, and I'm replacing everything with CDs. And picking up stuff I didn't know was around."

The clerk coughed, but didn't comment; it was a Centurion AmEx card on the register.

He probably sees a lot of heavy rollers in here.

"Win the lottery?" the clerk asked instead, as the total on the register continued to mount.

Eric grinned, since that was his original cover story. "Actually," he said, "yes, I did. Low enough it paid out all at once, high enough to let me do what I've wanted to for a long time."

The clerk stared at him for a moment as if to see if he was joking, then said, almost reverently, "Does any of that luck rub off?"

Eric chuckled. "Not that I've ever heard of. You know luck—you always get it when you don't need it. I was pretty happy where I was—playing for tourists down in Mexico. Climate was good, cheap to live down there, and the tourists were pretty pleased to discover people who spoke English, so they always tipped well. But—when I didn't need luck, there it was. And if things don't work out here like I hope, I'll probably go back."

"Why would anyone leave Mexico for New York?" the clerk shook his head wonderingly as he passed the AmEx through the reader and waited for the approval to come through.

"Because the coast of Mexico doesn't have Juilliard, and I want to find out if I'm a musician or only a busker," Eric told him as the approval came across the wire and the receipt scrolled out. The clerk nodded, and might have said something more, except at that moment four more customers appeared behind Eric, and all of them looked in a hurry to check out and leave. So Eric took his bulging bags and got out of their way before they started giving the clerk a hard time.

He opened his eyes and sank a little deeper into the chair, acutely aware of the silence beneath the music coming from the speakers. For the first time

in a long time—a very long time, going back to
even before his last girl dumped him, just before
he met Kory and got really involved with Beth—
there were no other sounds of occupation around
him. The walls and floors of the building were very
thick—which would be a blessing on the whole,
but right now it prevented him from hearing the
sounds other tenants made, noises that might have
let him feel less alone and isolated. The only
sounds within this apartment came from him.
There would be no quiet clatter of Beth putter-
ing about, or of Kory experimenting with modern
human foods in the kitchen—

*On the other hand, that isn't altogether bad. The
kitchen won't have to be hosed down at least once
a week. I'll never forget the day he discovered
microwave popcorn. . . .*

But the place felt like a museum—a stage set,
with no life in it. He sighed. *Maybe I ought to get
a cat. Or a couple of finches. Anything to sound
as if there's something home besides me.* He
couldn't remember what the lease said about pets;
he'd have to look it up.

But a cat would mean more responsibilities, and
having to remember to feed it and change the litter
and be here to play with it. How much time would
he have to give a pet, anyway? Even if the lease
said he could have one (he hadn't read it that
closely), he'd better be careful about what kind of
companion he chose. He'd be in classes and rehearsals all the time, and studying when he wasn't at
the school. It would be cruel to have a pet that
needed a lot of attention.

A dog would be out of the question. So would

a parrot or any other bird bigger than a pair of budgies. With enough toys and each other, a couple of budgies would be all right left alone all day, and so would the right temperament of cat. *If I got an adult cat from the pound, or even rescued one off the street. . . .*

Maybe a tabletop waterfall and some environmental disks might be the better answer. Or canaries? Eric sighed, remembering the birds of Underhill. Now *that* was one thing he *would* miss about the place.

I wonder if Dharinel would let me sneak a couple of those Underhill larks out here? I could leave the cage open so if they got bored or hungry they could go back home. . . .

He watched the clouds pass outside the window, and let his thoughts drift with the music. And at some point he must have actually fallen asleep, because he suddenly woke with a start, to find that the sky outside his window had gone from silvery to indigo, there was a crick in his neck, the environmental spell had faded, and his mouth was dry. *Sunset! I didn't think I was that tired; I must have been working harder than I thought.* By now the Faire was over for the day, and Beth and Kory were—what? Probably gathering with old friends and new around someone's fire, passing around bowls of stew, trading gossip. The Faire circuit really was a world unto itself, upon which the real world seldom intruded until Monday rolled around again.

He got up, stiffly, and wandered into the kitchen to get something to drink.

Beth had loved the apartment's kitchen, which meant, he supposed, that it was laid out well.

There were too many cupboards for his few pots and dishes, though Beth had seen to it that the pantry was filled with things that were easy to cook, even for someone of his limited skills. The cabinets were newer than the building, but not by much: cream-colored metal with black Bakelite Deco motifs, and the floor was those tidy octagonal tiles that no building outside of New York seemed to have. But the stove was modern enough, and so was the refrigerator, and at some time in the past one of the cabinets next to the sink had been sacrificed to permit the installation of a dishwasher, which was a good thing, since Eric never liked to wash dishes. The countertop and splashboards were of white marble that matched the cabinets, and it all looked very unused and perfect, like an illustration in *House Beautiful* from 1920.

Yeah, well, I'll try making an omelet tomorrow, and fix that in a hurry. If I don't slash my hand open chopping onions, I'll drop at least two eggs on the floor and leave bits of potato all over the top of the stove.

He opened the fridge and was confronted with a vast array of crystalline water bottles of various shapes and labels, with a few lone bottles of juices, root beer, cherry, and cream soda providing a little color among the colorless army. There'd be no one to drink it all but him, and suddenly Eric was struck with a sense of loss that brought a lump to his throat.

Kory had obviously, personally—lovingly— stocked the fridge.

Elves couldn't handle caffeine. It was as destructively addictive for them as cocaine was for

humans, and worse: it acted on them like horse
tranquilizers, sending them into a euphoric, oblivious state they called "Dreaming." Kory would no
more have put cola or tea into a fridge than Eric
would have stocked one with heroin and crank.

Bless Kory! Nothing wrong with yuppie-water.
And until I get a filter on it, I'm not sure I want
to trust what comes out of the kitchen tap. Kory's
"allergy" had done Eric a favor. The pipes in old
buildings frequently added a liberal helping of
rust—if not lead from the pipe solder—to the
drinking water. *I've killed enough brain cells on*
my own, I don't need to lose any more! Eric
snagged the first bottle that came to hand, twisted
off the top, and took a long swig of water as he
wandered back to the living room.

As he settled back into his chair, Eric suddenly
had enough of the CD player. He shut it off with
the remote control, and silence rushed in so
abruptly it felt as if his ears had popped.

He waited, straining to hear what, if anything,
the building contained. By now people should be
coming home from work or school; they should be
taking baths, fixing dinner, turning on TVs for the
evening news. And there were some sounds, faint
and far-off, as if from another building, but they
certainly weren't intrusive. In fact, he had to really
concentrate to hear them at all.

He shivered, stood up and started to pace, then
stopped himself and sat down quickly on the sofa,
putting the water down on the floor and reaching for the flute case that lay on a small table in
front of the sofa. Suddenly he wanted the silence
filled again—but not by someone else's music.

For a while he simply played whatever was most familiar, a mix of the tunes he'd used to play when he busked alone. One thing he knew he didn't want to do, and that was to play the things he and Beth and Kory performed together.

But as his fingers warmed up and the notes came as easily as breathing, an idea came to him.

He didn't necessarily have to stay alone. He was a magician, and although he had to be very careful not to meddle, there were things he could do for himself without casting a *geas*. Why not use Bardic magic to hunt out a friend here in this building?

There was no good reason why he shouldn't do just that—now. He had the control; he knew what not to do as well as what to do. Instead of the old sledge-hammer process of using brute force to get something done, his touch these days was the equivalent of a neurosurgeon with a hair-thin laser beam. All he had to do was to send out a call for someone who also needed a friend like him— simply speeding up the inevitable, because sooner or later he'd run into people in the building who had similar interests anyway.

If he did this right, whoever came would hear his music despite the excellent sound-deadening qualities of the building. He—or she—would recognize it for live music, become curious, and follow it to the source. He shouldn't get too specific, though. And he should keep the need on the lighter side of friendship. *Otherwise I could end up with a case of Fatal Attraction. Oh, no; no thank you! We'll keep this casual and innocent. Just the same kind of good times and good fun I had*

with some of my Faire buddies. He knew what that
felt like; friends you could count on, but who gave
you the space you needed. He'd taken it for
granted: first, on the Faire circuit, and then
Underhill, but now that he'd shut himself out of
both worlds, he realized how much he'd uncon-
sciously depended on them.

He set his thoughts in the right pattern,
breathed softly into the flute, and set the magic
free on the wings of the song.

Three times to repeat the song; that was what
Dharinel had taught him. Once to make the pattern, twice to set the pattern, three times to bind
the pattern. For really heavy work, he'd repeat his
melody nine times—or, more rarely, five—but this
wasn't heavy work. There was nothing riding on
whether or not anyone "heard" his call, there would
be no grave consequences if no one answered. He
had been careful in being so completely species-
nonspecific that it was even remotely possible that
something from Underhill might answer the call.
He didn't think any of the Sidhe lived in New York
City—they lived in Los Angeles and San Francisco,
but so much more of New York was man-made
than either of the other cities, layers and layers
of infrastructure descending as far below the surface as the skyscrapers stretched above, that he
doubted they could stand it. He hadn't even specified "in the building," only "nearby"—and for Sidhe
or other Underhill creatures, "nearby" could be
quite some distance away.

Not that he wasn't being cautious; the other half
of his "call" was very specific. Nothing would "hear"
him that didn't have what Dharinel called "good

intentions." These were not the kind of "good
intentions" that the road to Hell was allegedly
paved with—more like a healthy set of ethics and
morals. Nothing would hear or respond to Eric's
music that would harm him, willingly or accidentally.

It was no longer a difficult proposition to hold
all those components of his magic in his mind—
but it was rather like being a skillful juggler. It
required intense concentration, and he kept his
eyes closed to maintain that concentration right up
to and through the final note.

And as the last breath of that note faded, Eric
heard a quiet tapping, just loud enough to catch
his attention.

But not from the door. From the window.

Surprised, he opened his eyes, wondering if the
wind had blown some bit of debris up against the
frame of the open window that was making the
tapping sound. But he knew there were no trees
that close to his windows. Maybe a pigeon? That
was possible. If the last tenant had been feeding
them. . . .

What they hey, there's bread in the kitchen.

He walked over to the window to see, still
thinking of pigeons, so it was with a profound
shock that his eyes met another pair of eyes on
the other side of the frame—dark, wide, and set
in a fanged grey face beneath a pair of waving,
batlike wings. And just to confirm that it was no
accident, beside the face was a claw-like hand with
a single talon extended, tapping once again on the
frame.

TWO:

A CALLING-ON SONG

If this had happened a couple of years ago, before Eric had the unique experience of having an Elven Knight appear in his apartment and scare the crap out of him, been worshipped by Nightflyers, chased by Unseleighe Elves and become a Bard, he probably would have put an Eric-shaped hole in the door on his way out. By now though, he had seen so many arcane and outré critters that having a monster staring at him from his fire escape, wanting to come into his apartment, was not going to frighten him. It was a surprise, even something of a shock, but it didn't frighten him.

If it had happened the last time he was in the

World Above he might still have come at it with either a baseball bat or a sword. He hadn't known how to protect himself, not really, and his grasp of magic had been rudimentary at best. He had tended to assume that anything he didn't already recognize—or which hadn't been properly introduced by someone or something he already knew—was dangerous. And that wasn't an unreasonable way to operate, given all he'd been through. Paranoia was not a bad thing, in the appropriate degree.

But that was then. Now he had the responsibility that magical ability brought. He didn't act without thinking. He observed and thought before he did something. He had enough power and the control over it to protect himself for a limited time against almost anything. And he had the ability to call reinforcements quickly, which was even more important. All these factors gave him a level of calm he wouldn't have had before, but his time Underhill had made some deep-laid changes in Eric's psyche, had made him realize that his mind could work faster than his body, and that there generally was time to take in and process information before doing something, because acting without thought usually led to doing something that might prove to be very stupid.

So he had taken in a lot of information with his first glance at the visitor outside his window. It wasn't as large as shock had first made it appear; only half the size of a human, though that didn't mean it couldn't be dangerous. Still, there were other considerations as well.

First of all, he had noted the eyes; there was no

anger or aggression in them. Granted, a professional killer would probably look just as calm before he killed you, but at the moment, Eric couldn't think of any enemy he'd made Underhill that would have the motivation to send an assassin after him.

Second, the creature was just sitting there tapping on the window frame. And even if the window had been closed, from the look of it, if it wanted to get in to attack him, a sheet of glass wasn't going to stop it.

Third, it appeared to want to be invited in, rather than just walking in through the open window. Now, all vampire mythology to the contrary, most nasty critters could cross a mortal's threshold without any problem; he hadn't had time to set up the heavy-duty wards that would stop it. So there was a very high probability that this thing—whatever it was—was friendly. That it had, in fact, answered his call. So what if it wasn't necessarily the kind of drinking-buddy he'd assumed he would get? After all, he hadn't specified species—just someone he'd like to know, and who'd like to know him.

So, after the first jolt of atavistic fear, Eric carefully put down his flute and walked slowly over to the window. The thing grinned at him as it saw that he was going to let it in, and he noticed a few more things about it.

One, except for its big dark eyes, the creature was a uniform, textured grey, all over, just like granite. Right down to the soot smudges and patches of lichen.

Two, the gargoyle that perched on his corner of the building just outside his window was gone. Or to be perfectly accurate, it wasn't where it had been. It was on the fire escape outside his window, bat-wings, fangs, ape-like arms, and all.

"Hi," he said, extending his hand cautiously (the creature did have some formidable talons, after all). "My name's Eric Banyon—"

"Sieur Eric, Knight and Bard to the court of the Queen of Elfhame Misthold, don't you mean?" the creature asked, in a thick accent that was part Bronx, part Irish, and all cheerful, raising what would have been an eyebrow if it had any hair on its uniformly granite-colored exterior. It took his hand in its for a firm but not overly aggressive handshake, and stepped through the window. Its hand was surprisingly warm and dry, though rough and hard as granite.

"Or is it that you aren't much of a one for titles and all?" It didn't wait for an answer. "I ain't, so that'd be all right with me. Greystone, at your service. Glad you whistled, Eric me fine laddybuck. I was trying to figure out how I could do my job without you noticing that I was moving. Or gone; sometimes, y'see, I got to leave, and I figured you'd catch on that I wasn't there pretty quick."

The gargoyle released his hand, and Eric blinked. "Job?" he said carefully, then woke to his duties as a host. "Please, would you like to sit down? Can I get you anything? A drink? It's pretty hot out there." *So what do I offer a gargoyle to drink? I'd think they'd get kind of tired of water.*

"Yes and yes, and me thanks t'you." Greystone plopped himself down on the floor and stretched his wings luxuriously. "Water—more of yon yuppie-water, if you please. Take the acid taste of the smog-wash out of me mouth."

Just goes to show I shouldn't jump to conclusions. Eric fetched two more bottles of a different (and more expensive) variety of water. The best he could offer would be nothing compared to the waters of Underhill, after all, and any gargoyle he met would be more than familiar with Underhill, after all. At least it ought to be.

Greystone accepted his offering with a grin and an appreciative smack of the lips as he drank about a third of the bottle in a single gulp.

"Ah!" he said with enthusiasm, while Eric took a seat on the couch. "Now that's more like it! Clean, clear—you wouldn't believe what city rainwater tastes like these days."

He drank again and put his bottle down on the floor beside him. "Well, Eric Banyon, and did you think you'd come to live in this grand building all by accident? Not hardly. Yon cold-spell was an amusing little conceit, but I'll admit I didn't think you'd have the balls to make a calling-on song; that took some brains and some moxie, I'm here to tell you."

Eric took a careful sip from his own bottle before replying. He had the feeling that he needed to phrase his questions carefully. "You say I didn't get this apartment by accident?"

The gargoyle nodded.

"So why did I end up here?"

"The building chose you, lad, what do you think?" Greystone nodded wisely. "That's the long and the short of it. No one comes here that Guardian House doesn't want; that's the way it was built. It felt you enter the city, and it made its own calling-on song to bring you here. That's why you went for a walk, and that's why you found the building and saw the sign. The building manager just serves the building's needs. When it has a vacancy, Ms. Hernandez waits until someone shows up who can see the *For Rent* sign—not everyone can, but you've probably guessed that by now. That's why it's called Guardian House. One of the reasons."

A building that picks its own tenants? Boy, that's a new one! "Why choose me?" Eric persisted. He wasn't alarmed; he was quite certain that if there had been anything ill-omened about this place, Kory would have sensed it. And the name— Guardian House—sounded as if it were a force for Good, at least. "Is it because of the magic?"

Dharinel had warned him it would make him visible to all kinds of creatures that didn't have the time of day for an ordinary mortal, but Eric had already had a taste of what that was like.

"A bit." Now Greystone seemed to be picking his words carefully. "Most people who live here aren't witches, sorcerers, or even mages—not the way you are, me lad—they're just people with a very singular talent for living, and certain gifts to be nurtured. Most of 'em are artists, but not necessarily the way most people think of artists. Oh, there is a fair crop of painters, writers, musicians and dancers, but there are others who do things like—like putting exactly the right people together. Or who can make computers do things that'd bug your eyes out. Or who've got the gift of healing the mind and body together. The city needs people like that, and this building—this House—needs them too. They make things and people around them happy, and the House lives on that happiness. It's a living thing, not just a bunch of plaster and stone, and happiness is food and drink to it. So it shelters the special people it finds and protects them in exchange for their happiness—it's like that arrangement with the little fish and the seaflower."

"The clownfish and the anemone?" Eric hazarded, out of his memories of some half-forgotten *National Geographic* special, and Greystone nodded.

"What about the people who live here who are mages. Do they know about the House? About you?"

"Only four of them do. Ms. Hernandez's one, of course. And, no disrespect intended, boyo, but each one of the four of 'em could blow you into powder and not have to think about it."

Greystone waited to see what Eric's reaction was, but Eric just shrugged. It was hardly news to him that there were other magicians out there who were much more powerful than he was. What surprised him was that four of them lived in the same building, as mages tended to be as touchy and egotistical as . . . well, as professional musicians.

The gargoyle seemed satisfied with Eric's response, for he continued. "As for the other four, they know about me, of course, since I—well, we, me an' the lads—are their security system." The gargoyle smiled smugly. "And sometimes guard dogs. Stuff they need to worry about won't even show up on a camera, like as not, but we'll sniff it out before it ever gets within a block of here."

"Why?" Eric asked. "I mean—why do they need you?"

He realized as soon as he asked the question that he really didn't have any right to know the answer, but Greystone didn't act upset. He laid one finger along his nose and leveled his gaze at Eric. "I'm telling you all this for your protection, lad. Maybe those four can blow you into powder, but you're streets ahead of the rest in the House. The four—well, they take care of things Out There, in the city. One's a real cop, the rest, well, you wouldn't know they were special. But when bad things happen out there, bad magical things, sometimes they need to get taken care of, and the four of them do that. That's the real reason the House was built, grown, whatever you like—to shelter the Guardians. There've been as few as one and as many as nine here at once. And that's why we're here, me and the lads, to watch while they're sleeping. But the four of us can't stop everything, and sometimes when bad things come looking for a fight, they don't much care who's in the way, or take the time to sort out the Guardians from the bystanders."

Ain't that the living truth. Eric thought over the possible implications. "So something coming after one of them might mistake me for the right target?" he hazarded. There had to be a reason Greystone was telling him all this.

"Might. Not likely, but might. So you get to know about the House, and about me." Greystone grinned. "You did a calling-on for a friend, you know. I hadn't figured on letting you know about all this so soon, but I couldn't pass up such an open invitation."

Eric grinned back; he liked the feisty little

fellow! In fact, he couldn't think of a better answer to his call. "Do the four mages you mentioned know about me yet?"

"Ms. Hernandez, of course. The other three will figure it out in the next couple of days if she doesn't tell them first," Greystone said complacently. "Now don't you go get cocky now that you know about them, mind! They're not here to babysit you—you're expected to defend yourself against anything you get yourself into. That's only fair—they've got a deal more to worry about than you, any day of the week."

"Oh, believe me, I've learned my lesson!" Eric assured the gargoyle hastily, with a shudder as he thought of some of the things he'd done out of ignorance in the not-so-distant past. *And if I never see another Nightflyer again, it will be just fine with me!* "At least, I hope I have."

"You did all right with your calling-on song," Greystone assured him kindly. "Just keep thinking cautious and conservative, and you'll be all right." He grinned again. "Anything else you want to know?"

He wanted to know who the other three mages were, but he had the feeling that Greystone wouldn't tell him. "You're a sort of magical security system—how do I know if there's trouble around?" Eric finally asked.

"I'll tell you," the gargoyle informed him. "You'll hear me in your head. I'll tell you what the danger is, and give you my best guess on what to do to avoid it. After that, you're on your own. If you don't do what I tell you to, that's your problem, and you handle it."

"Fair enough," Eric acknowledged. They both finished their drinks in friendly silence, then Eric slam-dunked the empties into the trash basket near the kitchen door. "Can you be a security system and hang out with me at the same time?"

"Sure," Greystone replied firmly. "I have to be able to do that—multi-tasking, you mortals call it. Sometimes I sit out there and read a book, if it isn't raining. Ms. Hernandez lets me borrow hers. And P— One of the others gave me one of those little FM ear radios. I used to use a set of headphones until some smart-ass photographer took a picture of me wearing them and it got into the paper, but that little one hardly shows."

Just what I was hoping to hear! "In that case," Eric said, as the gargoyle watched him with a look of expectant anticipation. "How about popcorn and a movie?"

Greystone had good—and sophisticated—taste for someone who sat on the edge of a roof all day every day. After a quick scan of the movies Eric had bought to go with the new DVD player, he chose *Bullets Over Broadway*. "I have to tell you, laddybuck, sometimes it's downright frustrating sitting out there, listening to a line or two from this or that, and not able to even catch all the dialogue." Greystone shook his head sadly as Eric unwrapped the DVD and loaded it. "I can't tell you the number of times I've sat up there and thought about flying down to a window and taking my chances on being spotted."

"Well, if you get bored at night, even if I'm asleep, just come in the window and channel-surf or load a tape or something; I'll leave the window unlocked," Eric promised him. "I guess you'll take care of any burglars that happen by."

Greystone sighed happily. "Somehow we're never bothered with that sort of thing," he said innocently. "Blessed if I know why. But you're sure it won't wake you?" he asked, anxiously. "I've got good hearing, I won't play it above a whisper, I promise."

"It won't wake me," Eric assured him. "Honest. My last roommate never slept to speak of, and he used to run the tube or the stereo all night long. He was pretty considerate about volume, but some of his friends weren't, and they'd drop by any time they felt like it. I learned to sleep through entire parties."

"Ah, the Sidhe are not always thoughtful guests, now, are they," Greystone observed shrewdly, then turned his attention to the screen.

When the movie was over, Eric's sides hurt from laughing. Since it was his choice next, he put in a copy of *Riverdance*, which had Greystone tapping his talons in time to the music almost immediately.

"You could do that," Greystone said when it was over. "You could play with that group, right this moment. You're good enough. Why don't you? Why are you wasting another couple of years going to school when you don't need to?"

Eric was no longer surprised that Greystone knew so much about him. A telepathic gargoyle would be an entire intelligence network all by himself.

"Because I have a couple of things to prove to

myself," Eric told him, as he sat on the floor beside the DVD player and ejected the disk. He cocked his head to one side as he watched to see Greystone's reaction.

"One of them is the laying of old ghosts. Another is that I have to prove to myself that I have the discipline to make it through to a degree; that I have the patience to put up with teachers who are going to put me through the wringer just because they can. I have to know that I can do something alone, without help from anyone else. And there are things I can learn in classes that I'll never learn on my own. The piece of paper I'll get doesn't mean a damn insofar as my passing auditions; it's what it will mean to me that matters."

He hadn't explained any of this to Beth or Kory; Kory wouldn't have understood, and probably Beth wouldn't have, either. Kory would point out that he could study with the finest of Underhill Bards if what he wanted was to learn about music and discipline—hadn't he survived Dharinel's teaching? Beth, who never had graduated from college, had the contempt for the sheepskin that many who drop out or never make it through often have. In Beth's case, Eric was fairly certain it was because she had seen so many overeducated idiots pass through the television studios she worked at. She had a point, but every time Eric had tried to argue the counter-point, he'd had to give it up before he lost his temper with her. Or she with him— Beth had a temper that could strip wallpaper at 600 yards, and the temper that went with it. *And her not even a redhead.* . . .

"In a way, you need to prove you're a man, eh?"

the gargoyle observed shrewdly, and Eric had to laugh. Going back to Juilliard was a far cry from John Wayne heroics.

"Yeah, you could say that. This is kind of my manhood ordeal." He made a face. "And part of it is going to be an ordeal, all right. I'm going to have to keep slapping myself down to keep from using magic to deal with some of those bastards in there that call themselves teachers. Why is it that the teaching profession attracts so many insecure sadists? But I won't do it. That would be cheating—and hundreds of people who don't have magic manage, after all. I just have to remember that my way won't count in there, figure out what they want, and give it to them."

"I don't know. Sounds like knuckling under to me." Greystone examined his talons carefully, not looking at Eric.

"Sometimes you have to knuckle under," Eric replied without heat, though such an implied slur would have had him in a rage as recently as a couple of years ago. "That's life in the mortal world; it's a food chain, and you can't always be top predator." And, a part of him acknowledged, he wouldn't *want* to be top predator. You gave up as much as you got if you became King of the Hill—Above or Below—and there were some things Eric wouldn't give up, no matter what price he was offered for them.

"I suppose." The gargoyle sighed. "Makes me glad I have a simple job, one with no compromises involved."

"And there are plenty who'd envy you," Eric told him honestly, and yawned. "Well, I'm for bed.

Knock yourself out: watch or listen to whatever you like, just shut the window behind you when you leave, okay?" He got up, and offered his hand to Greystone, saying in his best Humphrey Bogart voice, "Louis, I have the feeling this is the beginning of a beautiful friendship."

Greystone shook his hand and, to Eric's delight, then saluted with his bottle of water and responded (in a better imitation), "Here's lookin' at you, kid."

Eric went off to his bed and fell easily and quickly asleep, with the reassuring sounds of British comedy and the gargoyle's low chuckle murmuring through the apartment to keep him company.

In the morning, it all could have been a dream. The disks Greystone had used had been put neatly away, and the gargoyle was back in place, looking like an ordinary stone gargoyle. But as Eric entered the living room, the gargoyle moved just enough to look over his shoulder and wink.

Eric laughed, and waved back. Greystone returned his gaze to the street below.

With that reassurance, Eric sauntered into his warm, pleasant kitchen, and sat down at his own tiny kitchen table. Memories of other kitchens, other wakings, filled his thoughts. *I never used to get up this early,* he thought, noting that the time was only nine A.M. *But then again, I used to drink or smoke myself into oblivion most every night, too. That tends to make for late risings.*

He poured and devoured a bowl of cereal absentmindedly, and considered what he was going to do for the day. It was Sunday, his last day of complete freedom. Tomorrow he'd begin classes and all the rest. While he didn't expect to have a great deal of trouble with actual playing, there would be things like music theory and composition, orchestration, and other technical subjects where his natural gifts wouldn't carry him. *Homework! My god, I'm going to have to deal with homework again!*

At least this time around the drudgery of homework would be lessened by the computer set up on the desk in the living room. Pointing and clicking, and even typing, were all things he could manage on his own, and there were classes at Juilliard in using the same composition software and MIDI interfaces he'd had installed on his box. Then again, the tech he'd hired to install his rig had sworn to him that the MIDI software wasn't all that hard to learn, so maybe he could play around with it himself. That would take up a bit of his time.

And then there was the not-unattractive possibility that he might find some female company somewhere along the way, which would also take up some more of his time. . . .

I guess I've gotten over Beth pretty painlessly, he realized with a pang of surprise.

Then again, he'd have to be careful about letting new people into his life. There were holes in his carefully-patched-together cover story that would be pretty hard to maintain against someone who was getting close to him.

Complications, complications. Oh, well. I guess the first thing I'd better do is go down and 'fess up to the building manager that I've penetrated her little disguise.

Though if he was going to do that, he'd better
fix himself up to look more like a responsible,
respectably cautious mage and less like a Gen-X
slacker who couldn't be bothered to shave.

An hour later, shaved, chestnut hair thoroughly
brushed and pulled back with an elastic tie orna-
mented with a silver plaque inscribed with Celtic
knotwork, and wearing a perfectly proper outfit
of jeans, a good collarless shirt, and a moleskin
vest, Eric Banyon presented himself at Apartment
1-A on the first floor. There was a small hand-
lettered label that said "Hernandez-Manager" over
the bell. After a brief interval, she answered his
ring.

Ms. Hernandez didn't look like a mage. She was
a Latina woman with skin the color of buckwheat
honey; an older woman who wore a harried lifestyle
and a score of responsibilities like an invisible cloak.
She was dressed in jeans and a pink Henley, and
her blue-black hair was pulled back in a tail.

Her eyes showed a flash of annoyance—quickly
hidden—when she saw who was at her door, and
Eric knew what was going through her mind. She
probably figured that he was going to complain
about one of the many features of the apartment
that she couldn't do anything about, because you
simply had to accept a few problems when you
lived in a building that was this old.

He held up his hand in the universal gesture
of peace. "I'm not here to hassle you about anything, Ms. Hernandez," he said quickly. "I just
wanted you to know that I've met my neighbor,
Mr. Greystone. He was kind enough to spend some
time watching movies with me last night, and he

told me that you sometimes loan him books. He told me to say hello to you."

For a moment she stared at him without comprehension, as if his words had taken her by such complete surprise that her mind had gone blank. Then her eyes widened, and she opened the door further. "Please, Mr. Banyon, come in," she said formally, gesturing to him to move past her. "I'd like to talk to you about that, and see how you're settling in here."

He took the invitation, and she shut the door behind him. Her hallway was the mirror image of his, and so was the living room, though the apartment looked as if it had a dining room as well, and probably three bedrooms instead of one. By New York City standards, it was palatial, and any place else it would cost a fortune to get this much space. Most of the people Eric had known from student days here lived in about two hundred square feet of room, and considered themselves lucky if they didn't have to share it with a roommate. Her living room was pleasantly furnished in the usual mishmash of furniture that most people who didn't buy "suites" out of department stores owned. Her color scheme was a mix of golden yellows and browns, and she had a couple of bright rugs on the polished wooden floors. He wondered soberly just what Ms. Hernandez did to earn this place. *If the House rewards these Guardians commensurately with risk—yikes!* Guarding a city the size of New York? He wasn't certain he'd have what it took. *I wouldn't want to get her mad at me!*

"The kids're out at a movie, so we'll have some

privacy. I'll put on the kettle and make us up a nice pot of peppermint tea. I don't do coffee in the morning any more. Makes me jittery. I hope you don't mind."

"Not a bit," Eric said, following her into the apartment with a smile. He'd met Toni's two boys—Raoul and Paquito—briefly when he'd signed the lease. They were eight and ten, and seemed—from Eric's limited experience with that age group—to be perfectly normal kids, if a bit more polite than the average run.

She gestured, and Eric seated himself at the table tucked into one corner of the kitchen. Evidence of Toni's boys was everywhere, from the action-figures tucked onto the shelves along with the dishes, to the promotional glasses for the latest Star Wars movie in the drainer.

"Please, sit down, Mr. Banyon," Toni Hernandez told him, moving over to the sink to fill the teakettle.

"Call me Eric; I'd rather," he replied. "Mr. Banyon is still my father to me, and I don't think I've turned into him yet."

"Fair enough. And I'm Toni. Well then, Eric," Toni Hernandez said, looking into his eyes intently. "Either you have managed to get hold of a name and a fact and put them together with extraordinary skill, or you must have been a bit startled last night. Which is it?"

"Startled," Eric smiled. "It isn't every day that a gargoyle comes to call—but it was my fault, if fault there be. I did invite anyone who might be a friend to come over and say hello."

"Interesting—so that was you, playing?" She

smiled. "I don't think we need to play word games, then, or beat around the bush. You're obviously a mage, and a better one than most of the people in the House who dabble in the Art. You got Greystone to reveal his nature to you by cooperation rather than coercion, so he may know more about you than he's told me. I heard you playing, recognized what you were doing, and admired the careful crafting—and if I hadn't been busy at the time, I would probably have followed the invitation. I knew that it couldn't be a trap or a trick, but it didn't occur to me that it might be the new tenant who was setting the spell."

Eric spread his hands, grinning despite himself at her praise of his magic. "Consider the invitation still open—on weekends, anyway. During the week I have to be a conscientious student."

She made a face. "I wish you could talk my kids into that attitude. All right then—I knew the House wanted you the moment you came in, but it wants a lot of people that aren't the kind to get visits from Greystone. So what are you, besides a music student at Juilliard? You aren't Wiccan, I know that much."

Eric considered his words carefully. "Are you aware of the powers once attributed to Bards?"

"Like that Welsh guy, Taliesen?" she asked. "Magic through music? That what you do? How the heck did you find someone to teach you that? Not at Juilliard, I'll bet."

He smiled crookedly, answering her questions with others—a habit he'd picked up from the elves. "Wouldn't True Bards confine themselves to a single student at a time? And wouldn't any of the old True Bards tell you that no bard can ever afford to stop learning?"

"Touché. Perhaps I ought to be asking, then, why a True Bard is incarcerating himself in Gotham." She raised an eyebrow. "Except that the answer is obvious; Juilliard is here. So I'll try a different angle—is that the only reason you're here? Is there something going on I should know about?"

Eric recalled what Greystone had told him about the four Guardians "fixing" things that needed to be fixed around the city. She was probably thinking that Bard Eric represented someone with a problem that could easily get out of hand, given what some of the ancient legends said about bardic mischievousness.

"Juilliard is the only reason I'm here," he promised. "Or at least, it's the only reason I know about. I am not aware that there's about to be a War of the Trees played out in Central Park, or that the Fair Folk are about to start Wild Hunts through the East Village, if that will set your mind at rest."

She heaved a sigh of relief. "In that case, the interrogation is over, Eric. Here in the House we respect peoples' pasts, so whatever you choose to tell me you can do so socially. And in return for your forthrightness, I'll tell you that the fallout shelter in the basement is proof against magical fallout as well; if Greystone sounds a warning, you aren't certain of your own protections, and you haven't time to get out of the free-fire zone, head for the basement. Punch three, six, and nine all at the same time on the elevator and it becomes an express to the basement."

She held up a warning finger, and he noticed that there was no polish on the well-kept nail. "Be careful not to try it outside of an emergency, though, and keep your knees flexed. It's a jury-rigged override on a very old system, and although it does work, the stop is abrupt enough to drop you to the floor. Fred rigged it—he's the fellow who had the building manager's job before me, and he's the one who installed the regular security system. I know the override works, I've used it and the shelter."

Which means that she lived here before she was a Guardian. Interesting. I wonder if her kids know what she is? I'd think she'd have to tell them, but maybe somehow she's managing to keep it secret from them.

Then again—these were kids. Even if she thought she was running a double life, she probably wasn't.

The kettle was boiling now, and Toni poured the tea into the pot, bringing it over to the table to steep. She took down two hand-thrown stoneware mugs from the cabinet above the sink and brought them over as well.

"Adam made me these. He's one of the artists who lives in the building—a potter. He's got a lot of stuff at Mad Monk, down on Sixth and Nineteenth. If you need any dishes or anything like that, he's got a special rate for tenants."

"Thanks," Eric said. From the look of the mugs, he already had a few of Adam's creations in his own cupboards. Beth had insisted on the hand-thrown pottery, saying that fine china was too soulless—and too easy to break.

When the tea had steeped, Toni poured both

mugs full and added a liberal dollop of wild honey to her own. Eric picked up his cup and inhaled the fragrance. *Fresh mint, no matter what the box said. I wonder if it grows wild anywhere around here? There's a lot of wild herbs and plants growing in empty lots here, if you know what you're looking for.*

"Do you ever worry about your kids, I mean, living here in the city?" Eric found himself asking. *Gods, where did THAT come from?*

Toni checked in the middle of raising her own cup. "All the time, *mi hermano*. I worry about them following in my footsteps—and I worry about them not. Drugs, gangs, stray meteors—life is just one big anxiety-filled minefield when you're a parent," she said, with a rueful note of amusement in her voice. "But I wouldn't have it any other way. I only wish their father had lived to see them grow up. I think he'd be proud of them."

Eric nodded, his thoughts turning to the other things he'd come to ask her about. "I'm wondering—Greystone said there were three more of you in the building? Would it be a good idea if I threw a little private housewarming for the four of you? And anyone you want to bring along, of course. That might be the best way for all of us to get a look at each other." *And for everybody to get the chance to interrogate me at once.*

She pondered that for a moment. "It wouldn't be a bad idea," she said slowly. "Maybe it should be just the five of us and Greystone. Believe me, I know these apartments like the back of my hand, and six people will more than fill up your living room. How's next Saturday night for you?"

It sounded good to Eric—he'd need a break after the brutal first week of classes.

"Sure. I'll get the usual party stuff—ah, except for one thing." He flushed, a little embarrassed, but not too embarrassed to insist on it. "No alcohol. I don't do it anymore, and I don't like having it around me."

"No problem. As it happens, none of us drink, other than the old honey-and-whiskey thing for a sore throat." Toni looked oddly relieved, and explained why in the next sentence. "The House doesn't like druggies and drunks, and it seriously doesn't like addicts of any kind. The House doesn't make mistakes, but people change, especially here. I've had the unpleasant duty of finding reasons to evict some of the tenants in the past who thought that artists had to debauch themselves in order to be artists."

Eric winced, since he had come rather too close to that line himself a time or two. Looking back on it now, he'd been on a collision course with oblivion before he'd stumbled into Kory. *All the freedom in the world, and no place to go but down.* "Right then, I'll see you all Saturday night?" He swigged down the last of his now-cool tea and stood.

Toni Hernandez smiled, and held out her hand and shook his. Her grip was warm and quite firm. "Once you meet them, I think you're going to find that you fit in here quite well, Eric. Even if you actually turn out to be an elf or something."

Eric managed not to wince. "See you Saturday, then."

❖　　❖　　❖

Over the course of the week he found that he had cause, more than once, to look forward to that party on Saturday. Fitting back into the student life was much harder than he'd expected.

His alarm clock jarred him awake at seven A.M. Monday morning. It was set to an all news, all the time station, and a woman who sounded far too perky for this hour of the morning was chattering on about tie-ups at various bridges and tunnels. Eric staggered out of bed, groping for the "Off" switch.

A cold shower jolted him awake, but his brain didn't seem to want to take the hint and join the rest of his body. He dragged a comb through his hair and tied it back with a strip of rawhide, then grabbed the first things out of his closet—chambray shirt, featherweight suede vest in a deep rich burgundy, and well-broken-in jeans.

Not bad, if I do say so myself, he decided, glancing into the mirror.

His stomach was too jumpy for breakfast to seem like much of a good idea, so he grabbed a handful of granola bars and stuffed them into his messenger bag for later. Fortunately he'd made most of his preparations the night before, so his course schedule and the paperwork he'd need for today was already stowed away, along with his flute in its case. With one last look around the apartment—amazing how much it had started looking like home in just a few short days—he headed for the street.

The hot weather had broken overnight—though according to his friends uptown, it would be back a time or two before autumn really came to stay—

and the morning was bright and cool, a perfect early fall day. He hesitated about taking Lady Day over to the school, but then decided against it: the only easy-to-find parking around Lincoln Center was paid parking in garages, since most of the students couldn't afford to keep cars in the city, and public transportation made it really unnecessary. He'd been in the subway a few times since his arrival, and there was a stop only a few blocks away. That would do for now.

The subway station was hot—the trains were air conditioned to the point of pneumonia, but the platforms weren't—but as he passed through the turnstile, Eric was surprised to hear the sound of music echoing off the walls: a busker setting up his pitch to take advantage of the early-morning commuter traffic.

Can't beat the acoustics, Eric thought, looking around for the source of the music. He saw a tall, regal young woman, her hair dyed a surreal cherry-black, playing an electric violin. Its silvery surface gleamed with rainbow iridescence in the florescent lighting of the platform. Her case was open at her feet, and there was already a tidy accumulation of coins and bills—even a few subway tokens. He caught her eye and grinned, giving her a thumbs up. She smiled back and nodded without missing a beat: he recognized Copeland's *Variations on a Theme from Appalachian Spring.*

For a moment Eric thought about joining her for a little impromptu jam session, but decided against it: he'd heard that street musicians had to have a license to perform in New York, and that was something he hadn't gotten around to finding out about just yet. He dug in his pocket and tossed a handful of change into her fiddle-case. With the practice of long experience, the violinist brought her music to an end just as the train pulled into the station and her appreciative audience began moving toward the open doors. Eric joined them.

In a few short stops he reached his destination: Lincoln Center. The Center was essentially the Juilliard campus: the school itself was a tall building tucked off in a corner behind Lincoln Center. Though when evening came this would be one of the busiest parts of the city, there were few people in the plaza at this hour of the morning. Familiar with the layout from previous visits, Eric found his way to his classroom without difficulty.

The halls were filled with students, some new, some returning. Juilliard wasn't "just" a music school. It offered programs in Drama and Dance as well. The dancers were easy to spot, most of them already in leotards and soft shoes from early-morning practice, with their dance-bags slung over one shoulder. A number of the other students were carrying—or towing—instrument cases.

He found the auditorium without difficulty. There were several of his fellow students waiting around outside. One of them—a short blond kid who looked like he should still be in grade-school, waved.

"Hi. You must be 'Pappy' Banyon." He grinned, relishing the joke. "I'm Jeremy Mitchell. Bassoon. You know what they say about double-reed players."

"Hi," Eric said, holding out his free hand. "Pleased to meet you. Back when dinosaurs ruled the earth, they always used to say the pressure on the brain'd drive you crazy. Glad to hear it's still true."

"Some things never change," Jeremy agreed happily. "I'm a musical prodigy—but then, hey, aren't we all? This is Lydia," he added, pulling a redheaded girl forward. "Lydia Ashborn, meet the legendary Eric Banyon."

"Hi," Lydia said, blushing heavily. If he hadn't met her here, Eric would have been sure she was one of the drama students. She had the looks for it—flaming red hair, ivory skin, and the most amazing eyes Eric had seen outside of Underhill, a deep violet color.

"With Banyon here, Rector won't have any time to pick on you," Jeremy promised her. "He's supposed to be a real monster—likes to keep his students from getting too stuck on themselves, from what I hear."

"I know the type," Eric said. "Ashborn. Isn't—"

"Yeah," Lydia said too quickly, looking even more uncomfortable than before. Marco Ashborn was a world-class violinist, and Lydia was obviously his daughter. And equally obviously would rather be anywhere but here.

"But it isn't your fault," Jeremy said. "Nobody's going to hold it against you. *We* won't, anyway. Right, Banyon?"

"Right," Eric said, because it seemed to be expected of him. For all his upstart sassiness, Jeremy seemed to be fond of Lydia and doing his best to put her at ease. It couldn't be easy coming here as the child of a star of the music world. Talk about performance pressure. . . .

At least that was one thing I never had to face: parents who were expecting me to follow in their golden footsteps.

Just then the bell rang. "Time to face the lions," Jeremy said cryptically. "C'mon. Let's sit together."

Before long, Eric knew exactly what Jeremy had meant, and was grateful for the warning.

Professor Rector taught History of Music. He was new since Eric had last studied here, and seemed to be one of those professors who believed in teaching through intimidation. That meant that somebody in the class had to be the scapegoat, and after meeting the sixteen-year-old Lydia, Eric was just as glad it was him. Before the hour was over, he'd already had his fill of sardonic comments about unusual aspects of the work of this or that obscure composer aimed directly at him and ending with, "but I don't imagine that you encountered any requests for his work in the subway, Mr. Banyon."

It was obvious that his history had preceded him, and if there'd been anyone at the school who didn't know that he'd left Juilliard years before and gone out to make his living as a street-busker, they all certainly knew by the end of the first class.

Eric kept his temper, although the constant gibes really began to grate after the fourth time. When Mr. Rector actually phrased his comment as a question, Eric answered it when he could, and when he could not, he admitted it. Otherwise, he ignored the constant stream of barbs—at least that was something at which he had plenty of practice, thanks in no small part to having studied under Dharinel. Dharinel didn't like *anybody*, least of all half-trained ragamuffin scapegrace dragged-up-anyhow human Bards foisted on him by his liege-lord. When it came to hitting nerves, Dharinel had all the accuracy of a surgical laser, and had taken just as much malicious enjoyment in getting a reaction out of Eric as Professor Rector did.

Probably Rector thought Eric was a pushover, and some of the students might, too—but the ones who weren't getting off on seeing Eric constantly slapped down were beginning to see just what a sadistic bastard the man was without having to become a target themselves. So in a way, Eric was giving them a useful lesson in maintaining dignity in the face of adversity. And that was certainly a vital survival skill in the world of music.

I've faced off with bastards who could kill the populations of entire cities, and who got a kick out of the kind of torture that leaves lifelong scars. I can handle a little harassment. And besides, it's still the first week. Maybe he'll get tired of it. It's possible.

Fortunately, none of his other professors were as confrontational as Rector, nor did they seem to want to waste class time busting his chops, and by the end of the day, Eric had figured out a way to take the wind out of Rector's sails if he ever needed to. He'd bought a very nice microcassette recorder with a good microphone in order to tape all of his lectures in addition to taking his own spoken notes. When he got home that evening, he sat down to transcribe his notes—including every word of Professor Rector's lecture, inappropriate gibes and all.

When he was done, he labelled the tape and put it aside—from now on he was going to save every golden word of Rector's lectures, and if the man tried to drive Eric out of Juilliard by any monkey business with Eric's grades, he'd find out in a hurry that Eric Banyon wasn't the pushover he'd thought. Those tapes would be in the hands of the president of Juilliard—along with a neatly typed transcript with the important parts highlighted—within hours, and the good professor would have a hard time explaining away what would look like a really unhealthy negative fixation on a student.

Microcassettes were wonderful things.

But Eric didn't think he'd ever have to use that weapon. He'd eaten lunch with Jeremy and Lydia, and Jeremy seemed to be a clearing-house for every scrap of gossip on the Juilliard campus. He'd told Eric that Professor Rector didn't have tenure—and as a result, Rector didn't have any real power in the Juilliard hierarchy.

So Eric didn't waste any energy fretting over one more bully. Energy and time were two things he didn't have enough of to waste; there was an awful lot to learn, and the structured classes—with their structured expectations—were more of a drain on his energy than he'd thought they'd be. Students were expected to do three things in the course of their studies: learn, perform—and compose original works.

When it came to composition, he'd always worked on pure inspiration and impulse; now he had to learn music theory and be able to explain why certain things worked or didn't. It was a lot like mathematics, and left his head aching with the amount he was trying to comprehend. And this was only the first week, the overviews of what students would be expected to master in the weeks ahead.

It was only when it came to performance that Eric was completely at ease. The years of playing at RenFaires and on the street had taught him how to improvise endlessly on common themes, and playing before the Sidhe—the toughest audience on either side of the Hill—had polished his performances. All of that showed, even when he was playing classical or contemporary music, and so Eric was quickly recruited, not only for the main orchestra, but for the chamber group and a trio.

He wouldn't take any more ensemble groups after that, in spite of the fact that he was repeatedly asked to, and the fact that many of the Advanced Certificate students were carrying a lot more. He was older than they were. He needed a life away from music; he was too old to be able to dedicate himself obsessively the way some of the younger kids could, playing in half a dozen chamber groups besides their regular work. Granted, some of it paid—and that was another reason not to take potential work away from people who needed the money more than he did.

He reflected with some irony that, as with mainstream religion, it was easy enough to dedicate your life to music before you discovered sex—but afterwards, it was a different proposition. The way the kids threw themselves into everything—they had an intensity he'd lost somewhere along the path to growing up. He didn't regret his loss—change was normal everywhere but Underhill—but sometimes he envied the passion the younger students seemed always to carry at their fingertips.

By Friday, Eric had less idea than before if he was going to come out of this experience as a really brilliant musician (as opposed to a Bard) or merely a competent one, like the normal run of Juilliard graduates. If he didn't add magic to the music he played, just how good a flute player was he going to be, anyway? He was way too old to be a prodigy now, but had the years of actual playing been enough to make up for lack of formal schooling?

It was not a question that caused him to lose any sleep—as Greystone had pointed out, he could get a decent-paying professional gig just as he stood, and he could even go back to the Faire circuit with time in between spent Underhill—but it was a question that he pondered in the few moments not devoted to his coursework. Did he really want to be another James Galway? Eric didn't think so—being a True Bard *and* having the high profile of a celebrity musician could be a dangerous combination.

But being very good didn't necessarily mean you had to be very famous. There was always studio work, for instance, if he wanted to stay in one place. And there were a lot more recording studios in New York than most people thought.

The weekend arrived, and he spent Saturday afternoon happily shopping for his party, taking Lady Day rather far afield to obtain some of the things he wanted. After all of the celebrations Underhill and in the house in San Francisco, he had the feeling he would never again be content with potato chips and dip, a platter of cheddar and jack, and boxed crackers, and he was rather proud of the spread he assembled.

I know I don't really have to try to overawe these guys, even if I could, but heck, It sure would be nice if they liked me. Greystone's cool, and I like Toni—and I guess I can judge the rest of them by the company they keep, at least more or less—but it never hurts to make a good impression. And besides, after a week like that one, I'm entitled to a little celebration.

By the time his guests began to arrive, he'd finished arranging the food in the living room and kitchen—not at all bad for a lone bachelor, he congratulated himself. There was something here for every taste—he figured that between him and Greystone, there wouldn't be any leftovers, either. There were two plates of the sushi rolls he'd grown to love on the West Coast; a cheese platter containing brie and neufchatel and other strange or strong cheeses; lox and cream cheese and bagels from the corner deli; a cold hors d'oeuvres tray from Balducci's, with shrimp and miniature quiches and spinach rolls and stuffed mushrooms; fresh-baked, thinly sliced, miniature loaves of bread for the cheese and the handmade Amish jams and jellies he'd found down at the 14th Street Farmers' Market.

Remembering what Toni Hernandez had said, for drinks he had gourmet teas and coffee, his vast assortment of designer waters, Classic Coke, plain seltzer, and a couple of oddball soft drinks. He could hardly wait for his guests to arrive.

Eric found himself going to the mirror nervously, over and over. He'd dressed carefully, in a mix of the clothing Kory had kenned for him and more mundane garb. Tucked into a pair of black suede trousers from a leather store was a deep burgundy silk shirt straight from Underhill, and the pants were tucked into his Faire boots with the burgundy leather pattern laid into the side. Under a side-laced, black suede vest he wore his sword belt without the sword, and wondered if any of the four would notice that omission.

Greystone slipped in the window as he was going to the mirror for the fourth time. "You look simply fah-bulous, kiddo," the gargoyle said, with a wink. "Settle down, you'll like these people, and they'll like you. You've already made points with them, just by being low-key."

"I wish you'd told me more about them," Eric fretted. "At least what they look like! I mean, I'm never comfortable meeting people cold, and you're hitting me with three total strangers! I don't even know how many are men and how many are women—"

"Well, they won't be strangers for long, now, will they?" Greystone countered, scarfing up a plate-ful of food and a bottle of water. "Toni an' me, we didn't want you forming any opinions in advance. Have some sushi and relax."

"As if I could," Eric grumbled *sotto voce,* and just then the door buzzer sounded. He opened it to let in the four "senior mages" of the House.

And as Greystone had said, maybe it was a good thing that he hadn't been told anything about these people, because he couldn't have picked out four more normal folks if he'd tried.

"Everyone, this is Eric Banyon," Toni said, as

they all moved inside and Eric shut the door. "Eric, this is Jimmie Youngblood—that's short for 'Jemima,' and she'll kill you if you use it. Jimmie is with NYPD Detective Division."

Even in her street clothes, Jimmie looked like a female cop; Eric had come to be able to recognize the commonalities with other LEOs[2] he'd met. She didn't have to look tough, it was simply a part of her. In point of fact, if you only looked at the surface and not at the way she moved and the carefully wary way in which she was always checking her surroundings, you'd have said she looked frail—but she wasn't thin, she was whipcord and muscle. It was difficult to identify a nationality for her; she had thick, lustrous straight black hair, very dark eyes, a bronzy complexion under a good, even tan, and cheekbones a model would kill for, though the rest of her face was too strong to be called "pretty." *Maybe some Cherokee in there?* Eric thought.

"Good to meet you, Eric," Jimmie said formally, shaking his hand firmly. She raised an eyebrow, glancing at his waist. "Nice belt, but isn't there something missing?" she asked with a glint of a smile in her amber eyes.

"Now it's my turn to make an introduction. This is Paul Kern: computer nerd by day, gaming addict by night."

"Eric," Paul said, shaking his hand with a grin. Paul was a tall elegant black man who carried himself with the grace of a dancer. Most of the computer nerds Eric had known had moved as if they weren't sure where to put their hands and

---

[2] Law Enforcement Officers.

feet, but Paul moved like a cat turned into a human. Eric noted that his eyes had already flicked to the computer in the corner and back to Eric's face in the brief instant of their introduction. "You get in trouble with that system of yours, give a shout," he said with a grin. His voice held a faint trace of a British/Islands accent.

"I will, if you won't mind," Eric replied fervidly. "What I know about computers would fit in a greeting card."

Paul laughed. "Now I make the last introduction—this is José Ramirez, who leads a triple life to my double one. He's the super—which is less work than you'd think, since the House's systems tend to cooperate rather than break down at the drop of a power surge—he's our fourth Guardian, and when he's not fixing faucets, he's raising African Grey parrots who are probably more intelligent than most of our tenants." There was general laughter at the last remark, which had the flavor of a family joke.

"Pleased to meet you, Eric." Like the others, José had a firm, warm handshake. His bronze skin and strong square features made him attractive— if not as model-handsome as Paul—and he reminded Eric slightly of a darker Charles Bronson. "If you are ever considering a parrot as a companion, please let me know. I can help you decide whether or not you will have the time, and if so, which breed would suit you best." He grinned. "I'm afraid, like most bird people, my conversation tends to begin and end with my little ones."

"So?" Toni put in, gesturing with a piece of sushi. "That's not much different from any other person with an all-consuming avocation. Or a parent, for that matter, but I promise I'll leave Raoul and Paquito out of the conversation tonight. José is night-shift supervisor for any extraordinary problems here at the House; I'm day-shift. We cover for each other if a problem takes one of us outside."

All of them found places in the living room; Eric took the kitchen chair, Toni and José shared the sofa, Paul got the chair and Jimmie stood leaning against the wall where she could watch all of them. As usual, Greystone sat on the floor, since his wings tended to get in the way of using furniture.

Eric had a million questions he wanted to ask, but he didn't get a chance to, for Jimmie, who'd gone and gotten her own plate of food, got her question to him in first.

"So, Banyon—just where did you learn your stuff?" she asked, direct and to the point. "And how come your clothes have magic all over them?"

He'd intended to tell them anything they wanted to know, but he hadn't planned on telling them about Kory and Company quite yet; he'd hoped to warm up to the subject.

"Ah—" he hesitated, then tried to look apologetic. "I'm not sure just how much you people are going to believe."

Granted, Greystone already knew about Underhill, but from his conversations with the gargoyle, Eric had been led to believe that these people had yet to encounter anything like the Sidhe. He'd gotten the impression that their problems had all dealt with the consequences of powerful, untrained amateurs dabbling in magic, or powerful, trained magicians doing very nasty things.

"Hey, they believe in living gargoyles," Greystone said (now around a mouthful of bagel). "How much harder to believe in can your pointy-eared friends be?"

"Pointy-eared friends?" Paul raised both eyebrows. "Somehow I don't think Greystone's referring to Vulcans."

"He's not," Eric said faintly, then gave up and blurted it all out. "Elves. *Seleighe Sidhe.* The Fair Folk. I learned my magic from them."

At first, the four Guardians looked at him as if they thought he was joking. Then they looked at each other, questioningly. Finally, they looked at Greystone, who nodded emphatically.

"Cross my heart, folks," the gargoyle said, making the appropriate motion. "He's not putting you on. I'd never seen a Sidhe before his buddy Korendil showed up to help move him in, but I'd heard about them. No kidding; under the glamourie that made him look human, there wasn't a doubt. I knew what Korendil was the first moment I saw him."

So much for disguises, Eric thought. He'd have to remember to mention to Kory that his Seeming spell wasn't as seamless as it might be.

"Elves." Jimmie pondered that for a moment. "Well, that's not the sort of thing you expect to hear about in the Big Apple, and I've never met anyone before who could say he'd seen elves, but— well, we've seen weirder things than elves, I guess. So, okay. Elves." She sounded as if she were pronouncing a judicial verdict. Luckily, it seemed to be in Eric's favor.

"My impression is that there's too much Cold

Iron around this town for elves to be anything but uncomfortable here," Eric put in, hesitantly. *At least, without a Nexus closer than the one at Elfhame Everforest.* "Kory can stand it only because he wore silk from neck to toes while he was here with me, and because he's been conditioning himself to handle it. I've heard that Sidhe can manage to build up a resistance to what they call Death Metal—kind of like you or I developing a tolerance for snake venom. Most of them, though—at best, they'd be uncomfortable all the time, and at worst, in terrible pain, depending on how sensitive to Cold Iron they were, and how much experience they'd had being around it."

There were more questions about Eric's friends, as his four guests batted the idea around until they got comfortable with it. He was rather surprised that it took them as little time as it did, but then, they were trained professionals.

"If elves taught you magic and took you Underhill, how did you get away from them?" Paul asked pointedly. "All the legends I've heard indicate they tend to grab musicians and keep them prisoner for extended periods of time. Thomas the Rhymer, Tam Lin, Taliesen—" He shrugged, breaking off what promised to be a lengthy catalogue of examples.

"It's a long story," Eric admitted. "Basically, you can't believe everything you read. I wasn't their prisoner. I was an honored guest. And—well, the whole story involves elves in Los Angeles, and elves in San Francisco, some of them Seleighe and some of them Unseleighe, and—it's a long story."

"We have food, drink, and it's Saturday night,"

José said, settling down on the couch as if he was prepared to stay for as long as it took. "So, stranger among us—tell us the story. As you are a Bard, it should at least be entertaining."

Since Eric couldn't think of any reason why he shouldn't tell these people the truth, he did, starting all the way back at the Grove of Elfhame Sun-Descending at the L.A. Fairesite.

"Once upon a time—a very long time ago (more or less)—there was this traveling musician named Eric Banyon. . . ." he began.

And the story did take a very long time to tell, but not as long as he had thought it would, since other than the Sidhe themselves and the existence of Underhill, the four Guardians were quite familiar with magic, nodes, Groves, and other arcanities, including power-mad Black Magicians. And while they were hardly a group of conspiracy nuts, they were also more than familiar with some of the military, governmental and quasi-governmental projects involving psychics that were floating around the espionage underworld—including many that were supposed to be secret.

To Eric's surprise, they even knew about Nightflyers, those terrifying, life-devouring creatures from the Chaos Lands Underhill, and were about as fond of them as Eric was.

"Not my chosen dancing partners," Jimmie said with a shudder. "Not that you really get a choice once they show up. Well, Eric, you just verified your story for us. We knew something about the business in San Francisco—not everything, of course, but nothing you told us conflicts with what we already knew, and most of it dovetails very nicely. You couldn't have done that if you'd been making it all up."

Eric felt himself relax inside. Jimmie Youngblood seemed to be the one in charge of vetting newcomers for the group, and even on such short acquaintance, Eric found himself valuing her good opinion.

"That thing with Project Cassandra's something I don't ever want to have to go through again," Eric told them soberly. He thought of Warden Blair, the madman responsible for hurting Bethie and hundreds of others so horribly. "It would have been so easy for everything to go terribly wrong—as it was, well, people got hurt, and people got killed, and I can't help thinking it was my fault that they did. If I'd realized what was happening sooner—if I'd figured out a better way to handle the situation—"

Jimmie patted his hand and the others murmured sympathetically, but none of them said the kinds of things others had said—about how it wasn't his fault, and that he'd done the best he could. He was grateful for that. Platitudes didn't help, not when he remembered how many people had been hurt or even killed.

"Every time you have a situation, you always think it could have gone better," Jimmie sighed. "And you know what? It probably could have. My partner always says you can only try to keep it from eating at you so bad that you can't learn from it. He might even be right." She grinned faintly.

"So, what about this guy that taught you about being a True Bard?" Paul said, quickly changing the subject to something less painful. "How'd that happen? I thought you said that most of the older elves didn't much like humans."

Explaining Dharinel—which meant trying to explain a little about Underhill—was harder than explaining the last several years of his life, and by the time they were done with their questions, Eric felt like a wrung-out—but content—dishrag. It was nearly four in the morning, all the food was gone, and most of the drink, but he didn't have that dissatisfied feeling that usually came when he'd been raked over the coals. It felt more as if these were four people who really wanted to be friends, but needed to find out everything they could about him and didn't have a lot of time to do so.

That impression was reinforced when Toni called a halt to the "party."

"That's enough. You're tired, we're tired, and we all know for certain that you're all right. Next time, I promise it will be your turn, Eric," she said, for they had all quickly gone to a first-name basis, even Jimmie. "None of us will ask any questions, and you can put *us* through the wringer."

"I'll help," Greystone offered, grinning wickedly, and Jimmie groaned. "Oh, no. *Not* the Jell-O shooters story! If you turn it into another 'Truth or Dare' game, I swear I'll wring your neck," she threatened.

"Who? Me?" Greystone spread his wings and managed to look as innocent as it was possible for a gargoyle to look—which wasn't very.

"Meanwhile, we all need sleep—well, except José," Toni continued, ignoring both of them, and setting a good example by getting out of her seat. "Thank you, Eric; we know what we needed to know. You've got a lot of power, but you're also responsible and mature. We don't have to worry about you getting all of us into trouble by doing something stupid, and we don't have to worry about you messing up something we have going by blundering into it. I think you're going to be a welcome addition to the House."

"Absolutely," Paul seconded, as they all got up, stretched, and took their leave. It was all accomplished smoothly and efficiently; so much so that they were out the door almost before Eric was ready to say good night.

He shut the door behind them and turned to face the suddenly empty apartment. Well, almost empty.

"You made a good impression, kiddo, like I said you would," Greystone told him. "And they're a tough house to play for, y'know what I mean?"

"They aren't planning on recruiting me, are they?" Eric asked, a little anxiously. "I mean, all that about being a welcome addition to the House—I'm not up to taking on other peoples' problems, you know. I have my hands full with my own!" He knew it sounded a little selfish, but it was the plain truth. He hadn't done so well on his last outing as a would-be Worldsaver that he wanted to repeat the experience.

"Naw. If you were going to be a Guardian . . . believe me, you'd'a known a long time ago, laddybuck. Or your elf buddies would've, and pointed you our way a lot sooner. No, they folks're just glad you're smart enough not to attract trouble, and skilled enough to duck anything that comes here. Wish I could say the same about some people

that've moved in. I could tell you stories. . . . And—
I will, but not tonight. Get some shut-eye, kid,"
Greystone said severely. "You're about to go up
with the blinds."

"Yeah, thanks. I will." Eric felt exhaustion drop
over his shoulders like a too-heavy cloak, and
stumbled into the bedroom, barely noticing that
Greystone was courteously picking up the party
detritus. He managed to get undressed and make
it as far as his bed, and all he remembered of the
rest of the night was a deep and dreamless sleep.

THREE:

ON THE SEACOAST
OF BOHEMIA

I can do this. The woman walking down the expensively-carpeted hallway that led from the express elevator to the penthouse boardroom gave no hint that there was anything amiss. From her Manolo Blahnik pumps to her fashionably disheveled ash-blond hair, Ria Llewellyn looked as if she belonged here.

Once she had. The world of mega-corporate high finance had been her element, and she had moved through it as naturally as a shark moved through water. Until the Accident.

Oh, Christ, Ria. Tell the truth, if only to yourself.

81

*Before Beth Kentraine hit you over the head with
a Fender guitar and the backlash from your lov-
ing father's magic scrubbed your brain like a
copper pot.*

Almost against her will, she remembered. It all
began with the Nexus, the rent in the fabric of
Reality that let the power from the World Beyond
seep over into this one, to be tapped by the Sidhe
and others with similar magics. Only a human Bard
could create a Nexus, for Creative Magic was the
human power. Elves could imitate, copy, refine on
the original. But they could not create something
as unique, as powerful as a Nexus.

Since before she was born, Perenor had plot-
ted to steal the Nexus of Elfhame Sun-Descending
near Los Angeles and bring it under his direct
control. He'd created LlewellCo to do that. He'd
created Ria to run it, to deal with the daily grind
that elves had so little taste for. And after years
of plotting, he'd managed to buy the Fairegrove
where the Nexus was—in order to destroy it,
bulldoze the great trees that anchored the Nexus
in the World. The warriors and mages of the Sidhe
Court were powerless against him, lost ages before
to Dreaming and despair. It should have been easy.

But at the eleventh hour, the Sidhe had found
an unlikely champion. A human Bard, living in
ignorance of his true nature and his great power:
Eric Banyon, street-busker and Rennie. Perenor
had ordered Ria to destroy him, but she'd thought
she'd found a better way. She'd englamoured him,
taken him and hidden him away, with her.

And it had worked, for almost long enough. But

then he'd awakened to the danger—come into his birthright of power, driven by dire necessity and danger to his dearest friends. He'd awakened the High Court, stolen back the Nexus from Ria's control to move it to Griffith Park, high above the city, a place where bulldozers and urban development could never come. To protect it and him, Eric's ally and lover, the human Witch, Beth Kentraine, had gathered those humans together who had not quite forgotten the Old Knowledge, and offered battle.

Ria remembered driving like a madwoman in her Porsche, up the twisting mountain roads that led to the park. The sun had been high—a glorious bright L.A. day, the last she was to see for quite some time. Even then she'd thought there would be some way to end the war without bloodshed. With the power of the Nexus at her command, Ria could have sent the surviving Sidhe of Elfhame Sun-Descending across the Veil, to the Faerie Lands beyond. She'd thought that Perenor had agreed to that. But conciliation had never been her father's way. He'd intended to kill them all, in repayment for an eons-old insult.

She remembered the hot smell of summer grass, remembered how glorious Perenor had looked in his armor the color of blued steel, remembered the music that had filled the air, the Celtic rock of Kentraine's group Spiral Dance. Since that day she'd never been able to listen to Celtic music, though she'd once loved it. The memories were too terrifying, too painful—as if she'd been given a glimpse of Paradise, only to have it ripped away before she could reach it. Most of all, she remembered her first sight of the Court in all its glory, gathered around the musicians and the Bard on that sunny hillside. In all her life, she'd never seen any Sidhe other than Perenor. How beautiful they had all been in their silks and armor! Something glorious, out of the oldest dream of strength and beauty there was. In that moment she had hated them, for being something she, by the curse of her half-human blood, could never be.

But she had never meant to kill them.

But Perenor had. By what right? they had asked him. She remembered the defiant words he had shouted in return:

"By the right of the strong over the weak, Eldenor. Of the master over the slave—the right of one who was unjustly banished, cast from his place among you, and has dreamed of the moment when all of you shall lie lifeless in pools of your own blood—"

In that moment, a moment far too late, she had truly understood her father for what he was—a monster, without love or charity, compassion or honor. He had reached out to her, stripping away all her carefully constructed shields and defenses with no more than a thought, making her nothing more than a tool of his madness, a wellspring of Power for him to draw upon in the fight. Imprisoned by his magic, she had been forced to watch as day became night, as the sunlit hillside became a shadowy glen filled with billowing black fog, as the Seleighe Sidhe had clashed with nightmare monsters of Perenor's summoning.

They had died to music, to the clashing of blades and the wild howl of guitars, to the hammering of drums and of sword-blows. The black ground had gone red with blood, and the screams of the dying had melded with the frenzied song of the Bard's flute. The day would have been lost in that moment, save that Terenil, Prince of Elfhame Sun-Descending, had shaken off his despair and challenged Perenor directly.

And all Ria could do was scream silently within her own mind, fighting uselessly against what Perenor had made of her.

She had not seen Terenil die, though die he had. Before that moment, the Witch Kentraine had realized the truth, and had struck her own blow against Perenor and his nightmare allies.

Ria remembered that last moment: Kentraine standing over her, her Fender guitar raised like a club. She had willed the girl not to flinch, to do what had to be done to stop the madness and slaughter. And Kentraine had—striking with all her strength, smashing her guitar down on Ria's head, shattering the magical link Perenor had forged, saving them all. Saving the Nexus, and the Sidhe foothold in this world.

Ria had only learned the details of the end of the battle long afterward—how the dying Terenil had slain Perenor with his last breath, how Eric had reached beyond himself to pierce the Veil and anchor the new Nexus in a place beyond harm, how when Korendil would have slain her, Elizabet and Kayla, healers who had been drawn into the conflict on the very morning of the war, had claimed her life in payment for their help.

Together the two, Healer and Apprentice, had brought her back on the long slow journey from the edge of death, piecing back together Ria's shattered body, mind, and soul. She owed them a debt she could never repay.

Even when she was well at last, it would have been so much easier just to slink away and hide herself forever. As Perenor's heir at law, everything they had built together was hers. She never needed to work another day in her life if she didn't want to.

But when she'd tried to offer Elizabet money, the Healer wouldn't accept it. *"You'll repay me best by taking up your life again, Ria. I don't Heal people so that they can hide from their lives. You have responsibilities in the world. Go see to them."*

So now she was here.

But that was old news, and Ria preferred not to dwell on the past. Perenor was dead, his bid to claim the power of Elfhame Sun-Descending a failure, thanks to a Witch, a Bard, and an elven knight. She'd never figured out by what twisted mercy the three of them had spared her to claw her way back to memory and sanity once more. She tried not to think about it.

Ria had other things to think about.

She reached the end of the corridor, and the uniformed LlewellCo security guard opened it for her.

There was an audible hush as she entered the boardroom. Nine men and three women were gathered around the gleaming oak table. A breathtaking view of Los Angeles and the Valley was visible through the enormous windows that filled one wall of the room, but most of those at the table were sitting with their backs to the view. An oil portrait of Ria—done in Early Hagiography, she'd never liked it—hung over the head of the table. She'd been wearing black when it was painted, but today she wore red. Phoenix red, the color of rebirth.

She shut the door behind her.

"Good afternoon, gentlemen. Ladies. I hope I'm not late?" she asked with a warrior's smile.

Several of the people sitting around the table glanced from Ria to the portrait as if confirming her identity. Ria smiled inwardly. She didn't look a day older than she had when it was painted. One last advantage of her elven-Blood heritage—she wouldn't age as fast as mortalkind, though she didn't share the elves' immortality. In the mortal world, especially in these rarified corporate circles, her prolonged youthfulness would be taken for the work of an excellent plastic surgeon, nothing more.

Jonathan Sterling had gotten smoothly to his feet as she entered—of all those in the room, he was the only one who had been expecting her arrival here today—and stood aside as Ria took his place at the head of the table. The seat at her right was unoccupied—*how had he managed that feat of choreography?* a small part of her mind wondered idly—and he settled into it, trusted courtier to a grand prince. Only a shadow of a smile marred his perfect corporate mask, and you would have to know him very well to be able to see it. An answering flicker of amusement in her own green eyes, Ria took her seat.

She let her gaze sweep slowly up and down the table, taking careful note of who flinched, who looked angry, who looked relieved—and there were one or two—and who couldn't meet her gaze at all.

"I understand that there was some doubt about the extent of my recovery," she said dryly. "Thank you for your concern. Now, if you will all direct your attention to point one on the agenda. . . ."

For the next three hours Ria worked them unmercifully, probing for signs of timidity and unsoundness in LlewellCo's interim rulers. It was primarily a display of power, proving that no matter how long she'd been a bed-ridden basket case, she was back now, and as much to be feared as ever. It was easy enough to know what buttons to push: their minds fairly shouted out their deepest fears and reservations, allowing her to leaf through their eddying surfaces like the pages of a high-fashion magazine. Only Jonathan, beside her, was a still pool of well-organized calm.

There had been lapses and attempted coups, of course. She'd hired the cleverest and most ambitious corporate sharks, and one had to expect a little feeding frenzy now and then. Baker and Hardesty, in particular, had taken advantage of her absence to do things they knew she wouldn't approve of, and that Jonathan would be hard-pressed to discover. Several of the companies they'd bought had been bleeding money for years, with precious little to show for it.

"So we're all agreed on breaking off the courtship of TriMark Pharmaceuticals?" Ria said, looking Sabrina Baker right in the eye.

"Of course, Ms. Llewellyn," Baker said. She put up a good facade, but the TriMark deal had been all Baker's idea, and everyone here knew it. Most of them didn't know that TriMark was substantially funded by certain South American investors, but Baker did, and if she didn't, she should have.

"And the leveraged remortgaging of our Far East assets?" she added, turning to Colin Hardesty.

"Well, with the Asian dollar going soft . . . yes," Hardesty said, capitulating all at once. Ria hadn't quite made up her mind whether he was stupid or just subtle, but what was plain was that he'd overreached himself mightily with this deal. And now he and everyone else here knew it.

"Good," Ria purred. "I imagine this concludes all our current business. I'd like to move our next meeting forward a bit, so that I can get an update on your other projects. So shall we say two weeks from today? I'll have my secretary prepare you a memo."

She did not smile now. Smiling was a sign of conciliation, and she had no need of that. There wasn't any argument—she hadn't thought there would be—and her staff quickly gathered up their papers and left the room. Ria stayed behind, watching the long blue shadows stretch over the L.A. Basin and savoring the moment.

Jonathan remained behind.

"I thought for sure you were going to can Baker and Hardesty," he said.

She smiled then, a genuine smile without edge or malice. "So did they. They know that I know, and they know I let them off just this once." Her expression turned grim. This was not the whole war, just a minor battle in it. Today's victory settled very little. "And from this second on, they are going to be so careful how they operate that if I get run over by a bus the moment I walk out of here, the two of them would still wait a year before making any moves, just so they could be certain I was dead." She heard an echo of her father in her own voice, and steeled herself against flinching. Perenor was a part of her—her blood, her bone—and once she would have exulted in that. Now it was only a fact, and one that sometimes made her tired.

Jonathan chuckled. He'd been the one stuck with riding herd on them over the last several years, after all. "And they aren't clever enough to hide their activities from that suite of computer hackers you insisted I hire. And I know they know that."

"Which puts you safely in the driver's seat for about a year if anything happens to me." Ria shrugged. "If you can't get firm control of LlewellCo by then, you aren't ever going to." She owed Jonathan the truth, and Ria had always valued honesty over kindness. In her world, kindness had always been a feint, a prelude to war.

"And if I don't, I'm not the person to handle it in the first place," Jonathan answered. "Which, by the way, I'd rather not, unless you're going to be around to pick up the reins again."

Ria looked at him quizzically. It was almost an admission of weakness, and Jonathan Sterling was anything but a weakling. If he had been, he could not have survived to rise in the company she had built at her father's orders, much less managed to keep control of it in the aftermath of her . . . injury. All her life, she'd never depended on anyone in quite the way she depended on Jonathan. Theirs was not a romantic relationship—he was quite comfortably married, and she'd never seen any reason to change that—but it was a partnership that was stronger than any bond formed of bodies. He had always been her trusted aide, but the relationship she had forged in the arrogant assumption of her own invincibility had changed when she had come to truly need him. He had given her unswerving loyalty and trust; even in her weakness, he had given as a gift what she could no longer demand, and that gift had changed both of them. In another age, Jonathan would have been squire to her knight, trusted vassal to her prince, a relationship to endure beyond all testing. She'd trusted him, and had been given his trust in return. In the last six months she'd learned more about his family from a few oblique remarks than she'd learned in all the years he'd been her assistant.

"I don't like the feeling of the hounds nipping at my heels," he explained simply.

"And you'd rather be married to your wife than your work. I can't blame you there," she added.

"You would have, once," he replied.

Ria shrugged, getting to her feet. "Now I just envy you, sometimes," Ria said.

She walked to the window to stare out over the Valley. The sunset light painted the scene before her in tones of fire and gold, the light bouncing off the inversion layer that hung over the metroplex. She'd told him the truth. She received truth in return.

"There's something you'll want to know," he said, and something in his voice kept her from turning back, kept her gazing out over the city. Her unacknowledged kingdom, bought with blood.

"Eric Banyon's surfaced. I waited until I had definite word from the PI I hired for you that it was the same Eric Banyon you wanted, but there's no doubt. He's in New York, enrolled at Juilliard. After all this time, the Feds aren't looking for him any more; I checked that too. I suppose he figured that."

Eric! She forced herself to relax, and when she spoke her voice was even, neutral. "And?"

"No sign of his friends. He's there alone."

Jonathan, her trusted champion, knowing what she wanted to know and making certain to tell her those things first. Money could not buy such care. Fear could not command it.

So Eric was back at Juilliard. She had as complete a file on him as money could buy. She knew he'd been a child prodigy, knew he'd dropped out of Juilliard on his 18th birthday to make his living on the street and at Renfaires, a rootless rebel, as shy as a wild hawk. The Eric she'd known would never have gone back to the scene of his failure . . . much less abandoned his friends.

But had he? Or had they abandoned him?

Perhaps the truth was somewhere in between. She'd traced the three of them as far as San Francisco, but there they'd vanished. She'd assumed that meant they'd gone to Underhill—the elves would always welcome a Bard, and Korendil and Eric between them could have sponsored the Kentraine bitch—but why had he come back?

Did she dare go and ask him? His enrollment at Juilliard argued that he'd be easy to find. He must feel safe if he'd been willing to go there. But of course the years in Underhill would have been as good as a disguise.

"Does our set of New York interests need a shaking up as well?" she asked. *No. Leave it. He's the past. Let him stay there.*

But Jonathan came to her side, silently holding out a slim leather pilot's wallet. She took it, seeing the sheaf of paper inside from the travel agency LlewellCo used. Plane tickets. A hotel reservation.

"I think you'll just have time to pack and catch the red-eye," Jonathan said. "Your schedule's there. There's a board meeting scheduled for LlewellCo East the day after tomorrow, which should just give you time to get over jet lag."

He handed her another folder, this one legal-pad-sized and thick. "This is the PI report and contact information. You'll have time to read it on the plane. The reports on our East Coast holdings are there, too. Have a good trip."

She might have kissed him then, but such gestures had never been a part of what was between them. Instead she turned away from the window and favored him with a cool Sphinx-like smile.

"Thank you, Jonathan. You always know just what I need."

His answering smile was only in his eyes. "It's good to have you back. And now . . . your car is waiting, and I've just got time to return a few calls before I hit the freeway."

The old yellow-brick building occupied most of a city block, and dated back to the days when there'd been factories in Manhattan. It faced the

East River, in an area that was sporadically gentrifying. But no matter how many new glass office buildings studded Hudson Street and Second Avenue, old dinosaurs like the riverside warehouse remained, legacies of the past of The City That Works.

And as always, they adapted to circumstances.

The logo in gold on the front door said THRESH-OLD LABS, as did the sign over the loading dock doors. It was a cryptic declaration, that might mean almost anything. Whatever Threshold did, it was clear that the company—and its employees—valued their privacy.

For good reason.

Despite its functional, down-at-heel exterior, serious money had been expended on the interior of the building. The three floors had been remodelled and subdivided into offices, Cray sequencers and the power lines to feed them brought in, microwaves and centrifuges, air scrubbers and clean rooms and serious water purification systems installed, as well as a number of modifications below-street that would never have passed any New York building inspection, no matter how well-bribed the inspector.

The small clandestine lab three floors below the street was bisected by a wall of triple-sealed glass, and could only be entered through an airlock by technicians in full clean suits. The lab was kept at negative pressure, so that in case its seals were broken, the air would flow in, not out. On the other side of the glass was a windowless office. It, too, was dark, but there was someone there, sitting behind the desk with a guitar in her lap, fingers soundlessly stroking the strings. She was working late as usual, mulling over the last run of tests. It wasn't as if she had someplace else to go, after all.

She looked up as the timer cycled the lights in the lab down to sleep-time levels. The sudden darkness in the room beyond turned the thick glass into a mirror, mercilessly reflecting the office's occupant. She met her own gaze unflinchingly, a woman who prided herself on having shed all her illusions.

She'd had plenty of help in doing so. If she hated what she saw at 31, she also knew that wishing wouldn't change it.

Romantic loners of any sex should be tall and slender and dressed in black. Jeanette Campbell was short and sloppily plump, with thin fine mouse-brown hair dragged back in an unforgiving pony-tail, persistent acne, and short stubby fingers that struggled to fit around the neck of a guitar. She was a loner through both arrogance and fate—verbal and opinionated, she had always been the sort of person who, when teased, lashed back viciously, taking no prisoners.

By the time she reached high school, Jeanette was a full-blown social pariah. Through pride, she rejected the few tentative overtures that were made to her—it was very clear to her that those willing to be kind to her branded themselves worthless by the gesture. She'd yearned for romantic isolationism while longing to be popular. She'd dressed in studs and leather, knowing she made herself look ridiculous, but still somehow unable to give up the gesture. She was desperately

unhappy and worse: bright and insightful enough
to know she had woven the tapestry of her sor-
rows strand by strand through the long years that
separated third grade from high school freshman,
but unable to find her way out of the web. She
would not bow down to the pretty and popular
whatever it cost her. She would never admit that
their opinion mattered.

High school was hell, but by then Jeanette had
calluses on her soul as well as her fingers. She concentrated on her classes and her part-time job, intent
merely upon getting things over with: so fixed upon
the destination that she discounted the journey.

Then something happened. Halfway through her
senior year, Jeanette slowly became aware of something that had never been true before.

Nobody cared.

Nobody slimed her locker, tripped her in the
halls, stole her homework, made crank calls to her
house. Nobody mocked her in classes, pasted stupid bumper stickers on her guitar case, cut in front
of her in lines, or stole her lunch. She could read
any book she liked, in public, without being afraid
it would be snatched from her hands and ruined.

Nobody cared about her at all.

It took her a long time to believe it could be
true, and longer to trust her good fortune. She'd
spent more than half her life in a war she'd known
she could never win. Nobody had ever told her
that it wouldn't go on forever. And one day, when
she wasn't looking, it had just stopped. The enemy
had declared peace and gotten out.

She didn't know what to do about it. At first the
relief had been so great that she didn't care about

anything else. And when the truth finally sank in, it made room for an anger as devastating as grief.

That's it? You ruin my life, all of you, and then you just walk away? You don't even pretend it never happened. You just FORGET IT?

Well, I can't forget it.

She tried. But all that left her was the realization that she had nothing at all to say to her former tormentors. The only connection she'd had with her classmates was being their scapegoat, and now she didn't even have that. They had shaped her more than she had ever understood and left her to cope with the result. Freed of constant peer pressures, Jeanette sought new pressure as instinctively as the flower seeks the sun. She drifted into things that appalled her, but she couldn't summon up the interest in her own actions to stop. She couldn't even take refuge in a romantic self-image. She'd always longed to—she dressed the part—but it required a level of self-delusion that Jeanette Campbell had never had. She was not and could never be the thing she loved most.

Unless she found the answer.

That there *was* an answer was something she'd never questioned. She'd read all the books, the ones that told her the human mind had powers which, if she could only unlock them, could transform her life. She'd started studying the mind then, reading the classics in the field. The brain was a biological machine. It could be reprogrammed with the right tools.

She'd grown up at the tail end of the period that considered drugs recreational, and for a while she'd thought that was the answer—the right chemical cocktail could do what she wanted and needed it to, unlock the hidden powers of her mind and make them available. A few semesters at the community college had given her the rest of the tools she needed to pursue what she thought of as her Research, and as soon as she had the basic tools for her quest, she'd dropped out. She already knew that legitimate research wouldn't divulge what she sought. For one thing, it frowned on human experimentation.

And she had experimented—first on herself, then on others—a combination of loneliness and rage pushing her down the easy road from science geek to outlaw chemist. Bills had to be paid, and research took money. But she knew the answer was there, somewhere. If she only had the courage and the discipline to find it.

The answer was in the hallucinogens. She'd always known that, from the first time she'd dropped acid. But LSD alone wasn't enough. It was too diffuse, too variable, too soft. She'd added mescaline, crystal meth, cocaine, trying to come up with the right cocktail that would let her push through all the barriers and claim the lightning for her own. She'd known she was on the right track, but every time she had a compound she was ready to try, it failed somewhere along the way. Sometimes people died, but she hadn't cared. She worked frantically, desperately, knowing her time was running out, because life on the street just wasn't safe, and when you were supplying illegal drugs, the working conditions and your co-workers left a lot to be desired. Sooner or later somebody would sell her out, and she'd go down.

But in her own strange way, Jeanette was heroic. Inevitable arrest and imprisonment didn't faze her. Finding the key was all that mattered.

Then Robert Lintel came, and that changed everything.

She'd been in the back room of a garage somewhere in New Jersey, cooking up a batch of methamphetamine in a makeshift kitchen. She'd had to move three times in the past month because of the Feds, and the last time she'd lost her whole lab. If the Sinner Saints—the bikers who were her protection and distribution network—hadn't tipped her off, she would have lost more than her lab, but her product was pure and consistent, and they knew that if she went down she'd sell out as many of them as she could.

Won't live to see thirty if I do, but I don't think that matters, do you, Jeannie?

Of course, they might kill her themselves to keep that from happening. Even without the psychic powers she coveted, Jeanette could tell that. She could almost hear Road Hog thinking that, when he set her up out here in the middle of nowhere. But the Saints were greedy, and already had a deal in place for this current batch. She was safe at least until it was done, and maybe longer if the heat died down.

When the door of the garage opened, she looked up, irritated, thinking it was Road Hog or Hooker coming back to chivvy her along. But it was someone she'd never seen before, a well-manicured man in an expensive dark grey suit, walking in like he owned the place.

Her hand had crept toward the gun in her knapsack—people in her profession always went armed—but she hesitated for a crucial second, because the room was full of acetone and ether and the muzzle flash from a shot would send the whole lab up like the Fourth of July.

And he'd smiled at her, like there was something that he wanted. Her hand closed over the gun, and she pulled it into her lap, behind the desk where he couldn't see, but she didn't fire.

"Jeanette Campbell? Hi. My name is Robert Lintel. I've got a business proposition for you."

With those inane words he'd changed her life. So that now she could look in a mirror, and not flinch quite so hard.

The lights in her office flared to full merciless brightness, and Jeanette blinked and squinted up at the figure in the doorway, laying her guitar aside.

"Hey, Campbell. What are you doing sitting here in the dark?"

There was an edge to Robert's voice, but there always was. He'd rescued her years ago, but it was for reasons even more selfish than her own, if that were possible.

While she wanted the powers that were hers by right—and god help anyone who stood in her way once she had them—Robert wanted Ultimate Power. She wanted the power for herself, Robert wanted to control the powerful people. He saw himself in charge of a group of perfect psychic spies, assassins, and saboteurs, whose work was undetectable . . . and whose skills were for sale to the highest bidder, though he never said that.

He didn't have to. Jeanette, better than anyone else, knew how his mind worked. Hadn't he sought her out back there in Jersey because he'd gotten to see the research notes she'd left behind in the lab the Feds had seized, and knew she could be a means to his ends?

Just so.

There was no love lost between predators.

"Thinking," Jeanette answered sullenly. She gestured toward the primate cages waiting on the other side of the glass. The experimental animals were only one of the things here that shouldn't be. When she'd been a street chemist, she had to make do with what she could get, with random customers as her experimental subjects. These days things were much more satisfactory: absolute immunity from the law, pure chemicals to work with, the best apparatus, and an unlimited budget.

But no human subjects.

"It's too dangerous," he'd said, and for years she'd accepted that. There'd been too much else to do—first, catching up on all the schooling she'd sluffed off, then re-documenting and refining her previous research, as what good was a breakthrough you couldn't replicate at will?

She'd made do with primates—chimps siphoned to Threshold from other projects or bought on the black market. On paper—and more or less in fact—Threshold was a small pharmaceutical research company. Most of its employees were engaged in legitimate research into the neuro-chemistry of the brain. Few of them even suspected the existence of the Black Labs that occupied the cellars of the building, the place where Jeanette Campbell did research that went far beyond simple cures for ADD, narcolepsy, clinical depression, bipolar disorder, and the like. Some of the hundreds of primates shipped to Threshold every year even went to the careful legitimate experiments of the people in the labs upstairs, but more of them went to the Black Labs.

The brain structure of a chimpanzee was similar to that of human beings, and some of them even knew sign language. Jeanette wasn't interested in talking to them, but language use modified the deep structure of the brain and gave her a benchmark by which to measure the effects of her drugs.

She had three consistent results from her drug protocols to date: dead chimps, crazy chimps, and superficially unaffected chimps. She'd lost count of the number of brains she'd centrifuged, looking for results and reasons. But she was getting closer. That was all that mattered.

"Thinking," Robert echoed scornfully. "You want to get up off your dead ass and do a little more than think? Beirkoff told me you were going to be ready for another trial today."

Beirkoff was Jeanette's personal assistant—somebody had to do the record-keeping gruntwork who was in on Threshold's big secret—but she'd always known he geeked for Robert. It was how the world worked.

"Yeah, well, I am ready," she said, getting up and putting her guitar down. The reflection in the glass mocked her like an evil angel, showing her the hated reality so far from her dreams. "Beirkoff should have the chimps prepped. I can shoot them up and leave the cameras running, then check them out in the morning. It's better to do this sort of thing at night, anyway."

No need to put into words the nebulous feeling, not even a hunch, that something about the drugs would just work better in the small hours of the night when most people were asleep. Once upon a time she'd fancied herself a magician, but in the years since then Jeanette had put both magic and superstition behind her. She worked entirely with what was, abandoning dreams.

"What's your hurry, anyway?" she asked incuriously.

"I'm not paying you to sit around playing that damned guitar," Robert said grudgingly, and Jeanette smiled inside, though she allowed no vestige of that expression to reach her face. In fact, Robert *was* paying her to sit around playing that dammed guitar, and whatever else she wanted to do with her time. Her work was as much inspiration as anything else—and the accidental discoveries along the way had proved her worth. She'd come up with a compound that induced abject terror in its subject and one that destroyed the sleep centers. Both killed the subject in anywhere from 24 hours to a week, but Robert had liked them, even though they'd never be mentioned in Threshold's quarterly report to its parent company. He'd taken them off somewhere and never told her what he'd done with them, but Jeanette knew those discoveries were what had bought her a free pass for the foreseeable future.

"I'm going to go down and inject them now. Want to watch?" she said.

Robert gestured, indicating she should precede

him. It was one of the few things she actually liked about Robert. He wasn't squeamish.

She walked out of her office and down the grey-carpeted corridor to the room that held the airlock that would let her into the primate lab. She didn't bother with a clean suit—the whole fantasy of biological contamination was just a useful fiction for any of Threshold's legitimate employees who might stumble accidentally onto her work area. No one but Robert and Beirkoff really knew what it was she did here, and neither one had the brains to follow her science. Secrecy was power. She remembered that from her magical days.

When she walked in, the full-spectrum lights brightened slowly to their daytime levels, washing every corner of the main floor in pitiless illumination, illuminating the row of cages so brightly that their contents seemed like unliving mannequins. The room was warm, and smelled strongly of ozone, ammonia, and fermenting fruit. She looked up, and saw the blinking red lights of the cameras. They'd record every move that anyone made in this room from half a dozen angles, no matter the light level, and store the images in digital computer memory for instant retrieval, so that later Robert and Jeanette could scrutinize and speculate about every squeal and twitch of the subjects. The oldest files were purged on a six-month rotation, leaving no trace of themselves behind. Robert ran a clean operation.

Her subjects were in the five cages along the wall, brought in from the larger primate lab at the other end of the building. Beirkoff had sedated each of them an hour ago, so that now they were torpid and manageable, but most of the sedative had already been processed, so that chemical residue wouldn't screw up her study.

Satisfied that everything was in readiness, she went over to the big refrigerator at the end of the room—past the stainless-steel exam table with its drains and shackles—and punched a nine-digit code into its locking key pad.

The light at the top of the pad turned from red to green, and Jeanette opened the door. Inside, it looked like any other lab refrigerator, with anonymous bottles and bundles neatly stacked and labeled on the shelves. She pulled out the jar she wanted. It was half full of a sparkling white powder, as pure and anonymous as salt. "Threshold 6/157" was written on the label. Sixth year of trials, test 157.

From the cupboard beside the refrigerator she took a fresh bottle of distilled water, and mixed and measured until she had a seven percent solution of T-6/157. She filled five disposable syringes with the liquid, and then advanced on her subjects.

She'd had a lot of time to get good at wrestling primates in the last six years. Pop open the cage door, make sure the damned thing wasn't lying doggo, find a vein, drop her load, snap the cage door shut again. The chimps' bodies were warm and flaccid in sleep, their muscles relaxed. It was over in less than five minutes, the subjects twitching and restless, rousing to wakefulness under the tonic effect of the injection. The temporary restlessness would pass—T-6/157 was a minute variation on a previous recipe, and she knew the spectrum of effects almost by heart—and the subjects would fall into a brief coma. In about fifteen minutes the compound would begin to take effect, though most of the subjects continued to sleep for several hours. The effects would pass completely within twelve hours. Then they could review the tapes and start again.

"What are you waiting for? Brass bands?" she snapped. This was the part that always got her down, when she injected the drug and nothing happened. She knew she couldn't expect anything to happen right away, but it still depressed her.

Robert had already turned away. As he reached the door, he tapped the switch, and the lights went back to nighttime levels. Jeanette followed him back into the hallway, in the dark.

The sound of the bedside telephone woke her. Jeanette groped for it in the dark, but at her first flailings the night-lights went on, motion sensors activating a strip of illumination all the way around the floor. With that to guide her, she grabbed the telephone. The clock on the bedside said 4:07.

"Get down here. Now," Robert said.

The cab ride down from Central Park West— the posh uptown apartment had been Robert's idea, not hers—took about twenty minutes at this time of night, but it was plenty of time for Jeanette to think. Obviously, something had happened—fire?— break-in? At any rate, something big enough that Beirkoff had freaked and phoned Robert—which was as it should be. Threshold was Robert's baby. He was the CEO, and she (on the books at least) a lowly researcher. She even had a tiny office upstairs, with a window looking out over the river, and attended the monthly staff meetings that were a part of Threshold's legitimate side. But her real work was here, down in the Black Labs, alone and unconnected to the rest of the company.

But in that case, why had Robert phoned her?

She came in through the night entrance, using her passcard, and Beirkoff met her at the doorway. His eyes glittered with excitement and she realized that whatever was going on here, it was really huge. Big enough to get Beirkoff excited, anyway, and most of the time the technician approached his job with all the verve of someone working the counter at McDonald's.

Sometimes Jeanette wondered where Robert found all these people. Beirkoff didn't seem to have any life outside Threshold. The security staff were hardcase mercs like she'd never seen working the sunny side of the law. Dr. Ramchandra, who handled the medical side of the Black Ops project, smiled a lot, but from living outside the law Jeanette knew a stone cold spook when she saw one. And she wouldn't have the first idea about how to pull a crew like this together.

Either Robert had a lot of backing, or a complex secret life, or maybe both.

"Mr. Lintel says you should meet him downstairs—" Beirkoff began.

An unfamiliar emotion filled her—hope—and she pushed past him and headed for the executive elevator. She had to present her passkey again, but once she had, the elevator descended into the secret world beneath the street, the one that most of Threshold didn't even suspect was there. Robert was waiting for her in her office, looking as immaculately corporate as ever.

"Tell me," she said, when she saw his face.

"Look for yourself." His eyes were shining with the same light that was in her own: the glow of pure triumph. He turned off the lights, and in the darkness it was easy to see through the wall of glass into the small lab.

"Nobody's gone in there yet. I gave orders," Robert said. His voice was hoarse with sheer stupefied emotion. "Nobody's gone in there since you left, four hours ago."

For a moment she didn't understand what she was seeing. At last her eyes and brain worked together to tell her what she saw.

This was what success looked like.

The room was a mess. Drawers and cabinets had been torn open, their contents strewn around like a fall of strange snow. The wheeled cages were scattered around the room, as if someone had been shaking them, and blood, urine, and chimp feces were spattered everywhere. But most of all, there were only four cages, and four hours ago there had been five.

Four. Yes. She was sure of it.

There was movement in the corner of the room—since no one had gone into the room, the lights were still nighttime dim—and she saw it was the fifth chimp. He was moving slowly, as if he were ill.

"How did he get out of his cage?" she asked aloud. *And where's the cage?*

"Keep looking," Robert said, his voice filled with unholy glee.

She turned her attention to the other cages. One was empty, its bright yellow plastic security seal still intact. In two of the others, the animals were obviously dead, having ripped themselves to pieces with their own teeth and nails. She'd seen that side effect often enough.

But in the fifth . . .

Its occupant was an older female chimp, obviously once somebody's pampered pet until she had grown too inconvenient. Her body was smeared with red, and for a moment Jeanette mistook it for blood, until her disbelieving mind finally admitted what she saw.

Strawberries. Raspberries. And Godiva chocolate-covered cherries. She knew they were Godiva cherries because the distinctive gold-foil box was still in the cage.

How? cried half her mind, and: *It worked!* said the other half.

She looked at Robert, her eyes alight.

"It was T-6/157," she said.

"Yes," Robert said simply. "It does seem to have been."

"We'll have to arrange for more trials—find out what happened—maybe direct injection into the neurocortex. I'll review the surveillance images— we'll have to prep some more chimps—" she said, almost babbling.

"No need. I told Beirkoff to put the rest of the chimps down, anyway."

All she could do was stare at him, stunned by the enormity of her success. Robert smiled, as pleased by that as by the nearness of his ultimate goal.

"Campbell. We aren't going to learn anything from a bunch of monkeys that can't answer our questions, now, are we?" Robert asked, almost playfully.

"Human trials." She felt a thrill of excitement course through her. There was an exhilaration at watching a drug take possession of a person that all the lab animals and private funding in the world couldn't match. Finding volunteers for this sort of experiment was difficult, but there were ways. Expensive. Unethical. But ways. "I'll tell Beirkoff to get the Large Primate Containment set up. I'll need at least half a dozen subjects to start with."

"But not volunteers," Robert said, as if reading her mind. "Not yet. But that's nothing for you to worry about. I'll have your lab rats for you by tomorrow night. This is New York. You can find them on every street corner."

FOUR:

THE DARK CARNIVAL

He had been born a Lord of the Bright Court when mortalkind was still painting itself blue on a small island off the coast of Europe, and for uncounted years of Man's time what the mortals did had not mattered to him. Among his own kind, Aerune mac Audelaine was a high prince, a Lord of the Sidhe, and his rank and birth had insulated him from the petty squabbles that others of his race liked to fall into, spending eons on a vendetta in retaliation for some petty slight. Strong emotion was the bane of the near-immortal Sidhe, tied as they were so closely to place and kindred. Instead of great wars that could tear Underhill apart and doom them all, their energy

was spent on small battles and long-running spite-
fulness.

Aerune, even as a youth, rejected this code of
cool serenity. Passion drew him as the flame drew
the moth. Grand hatreds, nurtured in secret, had
sustained him from his earliest memories, leading
him inevitably to declare his allegiance to the Great
Queen Morrigan, ruler of the Unseleighe Sidhe.
He was her courtier and most trusted lieutenant—
but in secret. For centuries Aerune was as trusted
a guest at the Bright Court as the Dark, until that
shadow-game began to pall, and he withdrew from
them both to follow his own inclinations. Still he
ignored the race of Men, whose antics so amused
the other Sidhe.

*And I would have left them to their sordid lives
forever, were it not for Aerete. Aerete the Beautiful, my love . . .*

She had been barely a woman when Aerune had
known her: golden as the day, a child of the Bright
Court, filled only with love. She had spent that love
upon the mortalkind, healing their wounds, listening to their woes, ruling over them as their Queen.

It was she who had opposed him, standing alone
before him when Aerune would have taken his
Wild Hunt among the tribes under her protection.
She had stood unafraid in the path of the
Unseleighe *rade*, her child's face stern, telling him
that he and his folk must ride another way.

He might have cut her down, bespelled her,
done a thousand things to remove this obstacle
from his path, for Aerune cared for nothing living. But something in her stern innocence had
stopped him, and he had turned the Hunt aside.

Afterward, he had sought her out. She knew him by reputation, but had accepted him into her hall as a guest. She had spoken to him of the humans, the lastborn of Danu, and had tried to show him the good in them, the spark of magic that they shared with Danu's firstborn, the Sidhe. Aerune felt his dark heart open to her like a flower to the sun. He begged her to come away with him to the World Beyond.

"But how can I abandon my human children, Lord Aerune? They are so innocent, so helpless. Their lives are but a brief span compared to ours. Stay with me, and offer them your guidance as well."

He had not stayed, but he had come to her often, always hoping to persuade her to come away with him. And perhaps, Aerune told himself, he would have succeeded in time.

But time was not granted to them.

War came out of the East. At first Aerune paid no attention to it. Mortalkind's battles were the echo of the Sidhe wars, eternal and unchanging. They could not matter to him.

Or so he thought.

Aerete tried to make peace between the two tribes. It was hard, for the newcomers had the secret of a strange metal far stronger than the flint and bronze weapons of her people, and their losses had been heavy. Aerune had urged her to fight, counselling that only their victory would end the threat. He had not meant for Aerete to take the field beside her war-captain, using her magic against their iron blades.

Iron. It was iron that had killed his love, a spear

thrown to strike her in her chariot, piercing the elvensilver armor that she wore. She had cried out for his aid. . . .

And Aerune had come, with all the hosts of Darkness at his side. But he had come too late.

He cradled her dying burning body in his arms, there on that bloodsoaked human battlefield. And as she died, all there was of kindness and mercy died with him. When he left the battlefield that day, all that lived upon it were the ravens of Morrigan. There were no survivors, and no victors. Only his pain, his loss, remained. He would have vengeance upon everything that had conspired to take his Aerete from him.

He began by seeking to crush the Bright Lords who were his kind's natural enemies—those who had let his golden darling go among Men to find her death. His campaign against them had blossomed secretly, silently, over the course of centuries.

It had failed at last, beyond any hope of success, and finally Aerune turned his attention to the world of Men. Men who, in what seemed only a moment of his inattention, had gone from weapons of bronze and stone to weapons of smith-forged iron—deathmetal, fatal to all who drew their life force from magic. These he could kill, if he was careful, but no matter how many he killed there were always more to take their place. They called him Arawn, Lord of Death—but even as they cowered in terror from his Hunt, they fought back in a thousand other ways, breeding like the vermin they were, challenging the Sidhe in their Groves and high places.

His kindred fought back, of course, trying to retain their pride of place. But Men had magic of their own, and the love of powers far greater than Seleighe and Unseleighe alike. With love and iron, mortal Man bound and banished its elder brothers, the Sidhe, until at last the Courts fled the Old World entirely, searching for a place where they could take up the Old Ways unmolested. And Aerune fled with them, wrapped in his hatred and pride.

But Man—arrogant, presumptuous Man—followed the Sidhe even across the Great Water, destroying the ties the Bright Court forged with the mortalfolk of this new land. Destroying the mortalfolk as well, in a slaughter that would have gladdened Aerune's heart if it had only been his own work. At last elvenkind was banished into the shadows of this world, its foothold a tenuous one, its vast empire shrunken to a handful of *hames*.

From his stronghold Aerune had watched all this, too bitter in his wrath even to ride forth as he had once done. The natives of this new land sensed his presence, and avoided his place, but when Mortals followed the Sidhe across the sea, many of them disregarded the warnings of their brown-skinned cousins, and flocked to settle in the place that Aerune had made his own. Aerune tolerated them. There was much to learn before he could work their doom. Cautiously, Aerune sought allies, but even in this extremity, the Sidhe had battled one another, as if seeking to do the humans' work for them.

He had watched from his tower as the Seleighe Sidhe of Elfhame Sun-Descending had destroyed Lord Perenor and saved themselves from the

Dreaming. He had watched as the Sun-Descending elves had summoned great sorceries and forged a new Nexus that would allow them to flourish safely forever in the lands of the Uttermost West, forging a strong alliance with Elfhame Misthold. They thought themselves safe. They would not swear fealty to him now.

And so, like any good general, he had turned his efforts elsewhere—to the iron-haunted city that had grown up in the World Above. To the world of Men, Men who were kin to those who had slain Bright Aerete.

Underhill was a place composed of all places and none, Chaos Lands given form and substance by magic alone, in which the hames glowed like abhorrent stars, welding all Underhill together into one vast tapestry. The Seleighe Sidhe were the bright threads in this weaving, the Unseleighe were its shadows, and once—long ago—that balance had satisfied him. But within Aerune's memory, Elfhame Everforest, with its Nexus so near the heart of the Lands of Men, had grown stronger as well, and the Dark Sidhe could foresee a time when the Bright Lords' weaving would bind the shadows in an unbreakable net, and the Bright Lords would bow their necks and their pride to a yoke forged by mortal Man.

Aerune planned accordingly.

If he could not defeat his Bright Kindred directly in Underhill, nor bring them beneath his banner, then a flanking attack was needed. Aerune turned his attention once more to the Lands of Men.

Aerete, Aerete . . . if you could see what they have become, surely you would renounce them as well!

Cold Iron was their weapon, and in their hands, it could slay Seleighe and Unseleighe alike. But if the Sidhe of Elfhame Fairgrove could learn to tolerate Cold Iron, why shouldn't he and his be able to do likewise? On his dark throne, Aerune dreamed of a mortal army under his command, bearing the Cold Iron that could allow him to wrest the Nexuses from the control of the Bright Lords and plunge all of Underhill into endless night; a first step before he turned his human armies on their mortal brethren, sweeping aside everything that stood in the way of vengeance, his Dark Queen's rule of all the lands, mortal and Sidhe.

But to summon such an army, he needed a foothold in the World of Iron. He needed a Nexus under his control, one that would allow his followers—boggles and boghans, his bane-sidhes, water-horses, nixies, and the like—to move freely in the world of Men. Without that power source, even opening a Portal between the worlds would drain him, and so he moved cautiously, searching for the perfect time, the perfect spot. And in the concrete canyons of Manhattan, he had found it.

Take this city, and with it such souls as these mortals possess. I shall humble them in the strength of their fortresses, until not one stone remains set upon another.

And at last he was through with waiting. It was time to act. And so, in the sanctity of his greatest stronghold, Aerune began the weaving of his webs.

The place in which Aerune held his Court would have been beautiful to mortal eyes, if any had lived to see it . . . a forest of dark silver, with leaves of shadow. He sat upon a throne forged of darker shadow yet, his hellhounds lolling at his feet, his Court surrounding him, a host of insubstantial wraiths and bound servitors, all of whom owed him fealty, just as he owed it to the Morrigan. From the base of his throne stretched a pool of black mirror, in which Aerune often watched the antics of his future subjects, into which he sent dreams to guide them. Even the happiest mortal carried within himself a spark of darkness, the phantom of Death whose dark wings would one day enfold him, and it was from that phantom and that fear that Aerune forged the chains that bound mortals unknowingly to his service.

Just as the joy of the Bright Lords had created a human land of magic and imagination around their grove, so did Aerune's dreams create a darkness in the World Above his palace—a vast dark iron city that the mortalkind had crafted out of blood and betrayal and the dreams he had sent them, filled with pain and sorrow and suffering enough to glut even a rapacious Unseleighe lord. There was even a place in its heart filled with great trees such as his followers needed to anchor themselves—Central Park, the mortalkind called it.

And so, at last, Aerune made his first move upon the chessboard of war.

He sent for the least of his servants, the redcap, Urla.

"My lord?"

Urla seemed to coalesce out of the mist of the grove itself. The redcap was one of the Lesser Sidhe, shaped by the nightmares of generations of men. It was small, barely the size of a child, but with a distorted, misshapen form . . . and very long arms. It wore a laborer's smock and ragged pants, but upon its head there was a soft cap of bright scarlet, as bright as the blood of men.

It approached the Shadow Throne nervously, bowing low and grovelling as it judged its lord's mood. One of the hellhounds raised its massive shaggy head and growled, red eyes glowing. Aerune silenced the beast with a gesture. Today he had need of Urla, for of all his servants, Urla was one of the few who could move with relative freedom in the World Above, for the redcap preyed upon men, stealing their strength to replenish its own. So long as the blood in which Urla soaked its cap remained fresh, it had the strength of those it had slain.

"Do you love me, Urla?" Aerune asked gently.

The redcap winced, and grovelled more deeply, inching its way toward Aerune's feet. "More than death. More than darkness, Great Lord. All my strength, all my power, are yours."

This was nothing more than the truth, and Aerune accepted it as such.

"Then you are mine, to do with as I choose. And so I choose to send you back to the world of Men. Hunt this city for me. Slay whom you will, hunt whom you will, saving only that you choose those souls who will not be missed in the World of Men. But find me the power to open the door between the worlds once more.

"Find for me . . . a Bard."

Why did I ever decide to do this? Eric asked himself again. He ran his hand down the side of

his slacks to dry it, and then transferred his flute
to that hand and repeated the gesture. He was
wearing the standard "school uniform" for recitals—
white shirt, black pants, dress shoes, and tie. His
long chestnut hair was pulled back in a length of
black velvet ribbon. His feet hurt, and his collar
felt as if it were strangling him. *Look at me. I'm
sweating like a novice.*

He'd already been out there once before tonight,
but that had been with the chamber orchestra, and
there'd been safety in numbers. But now it was
time for his chamber group, and there were only
seven of them. The other six members of his
group—Jeremy, Lydia, two French horns, a violin,
and a cello—were standing nearby, waiting to go
on when the previous group finished playing. He
took what consolation he could from the fact that
they all looked as if facing a firing squad would
be preferable—even Jeremy, who normally carried
ironic detachment to new heights. And Lydia
looked as if she were about to faint.

"Hey," Eric said gently, reaching out to gain her
attention. "Relax. It's just another performance."

She turned toward him, her scared violet eyes
huge. The three of them had become friends in
the last several weeks, though Eric's need to keep
his other life under wraps, and the crushing weight
of rehearsal and course work, had kept them from
becoming as close as they might otherwise have
done. While a part of Eric regretted that, mostly
he was grateful. He wasn't ready right now for any
more of what Toni Hernandez had called "hostages
to fortune."

But right now, it looked as if Lydia could use a

friendly hand. Her red hair was pulled back into a tightly scraped bun and her pale-gold freckles stood out against her skin like a dusting of golden pollen on the surface of skimmed milk. Lydia had real talent, but even in the short time he'd known her, Eric was afraid that the Juilliard pressure cooker would destroy any love she had for the music . . . assuming Marco Ashborn hadn't done that already. Lydia was a technically flawless musician, but with her it was *all* technique, no heart.

"It's a *performance*," she said in a low trembling voice. "People will be watching. Important people. Father's friends."

"So what?" Eric said cheerfully. "Our friends will be there too."

Lydia blinked as his words penetrated. Each student got a limited number of tickets to hand out to recital performances, and empty seats could be filled by Juilliard students on a stand-by basis 15 minutes before the performance. Eric had given his passes to Toni, José, and his other friends from Guardian House, including Caity, a children's book writer (with no magical gift outside her stories, so far as Eric could tell) whom he'd met while doing laundry in the basement of the House. He wasn't sure if they'd be able to attend—Jimmie had the usual last-minute crises that came with an LEO's job, and Toni might run into something that kept her at the House.

He'd only wished there was some way for Greystone to attend as well. At least the performance was being taped, and he could play it for his gargoyle friend later.

Lydia hesitated, about to say something, but just

then there was a wash of applause from the other side of the curtain. The previous group was finishing, and it was time for them to go on.

"It will be fine," Eric said coaxingly. "No matter what happens."

He could see that the girl didn't believe him. If there had been time, he might have used magic to calm her and give her some of the confidence he felt, but the other musicians were moving past them, making way for them on the stage, and he knew better than to meddle with another musician's concentration just before they played. Lydia would be fine once she got on stage—Eric knew that from experience—but he also knew that no matter how well she played, it wouldn't be good enough . . . for her, or her father.

Then he had no more time to consider anyone else's problems, because the septet was moving out onto the stage.

He always forgot how hot the house lights were, dazzling his sight even as they pressed down on him like a heavy hand. The small Lincoln Center auditorium was full—he could tell from the sound, even though he couldn't see the audience—and in the first row sat their instructors, clipboards in hand, preparing to grade the performances of their students.

Oh, sure. No pressure, right? Just a big chunk of your final grade and no way to gloss over any missed notes.

And, of course, the fact that, since he was sitting First Chair, the others were looking to him to set the tempo and carry them along.

Their first piece was a sprightly Mozart

contradance—fast, but not too fast, with a French
horn solo in the middle that Lisa choked on half
the time, even in yesterday's dress rehearsal. Eric
waited for the others to take their places, gathered
them in with his eyes, and smiled encouragingly.

*It's just like leading troops into battle. Act con-
fident, and they'll be confident.*

Then he raised the silver flute to his lips, nodding to set the tempo, and blew the first note.

The little trio he'd formed with Kory and Beth,
Beth's group Spiral Dance, and the pickup jams
at RenFaires were no kind of preparation for
working with a real ensemble. It called for discipline as well as spirit, cooperation as well as
feeling—all characteristics that Eric had grown
used to thinking of himself as lacking. But if the
difficulties were greater, the rewards were greater
as well—the complex surge of melody filled him
like a storm of light, the passion and discipline of
the others creating an ocean that bore him up like
a windjammer upon its surface, its master and victim all in one.

There is nothing better than this, Eric thought,
in the last moment in which words were possible,
before he surrendered to the music and simply
was.

Their first piece ended—there was applause—
and he led them through the second, a sprightly
rondo that called for fast fingering on everybody's
part, five separate threads of melody weaving into
a glorious braid of sound. Moments later—too
soon—it was over, and he and the others were
coming to the edge of the stage to take their bows.

Lisa had hit every note perfectly, the horn's golden mellowness soaring over the brightness of the flutes and the deep echoes from cello and bassoon. Jeremy had regained his usual bland expression, and even Lydia looked radiant.

"It was good, wasn't it? It was good," she said, as soon as they were off.

"It was okay," Eric said, smiling back at her. And best of all, it was a part of himself that he could share with those who could not share any other part of his life—this music was a matter of skill and craft, not magic, though the discipline he'd learned in those long lessons with Dharinel certainly helped here.

In fact, I don't think I could have gotten this far without it. You've got to want it, and work for it, to be able to do it. The first time I was here it wasn't my idea at all—it was Mom and Dad, wanting to add "prodigy" to their list of my Trophy Child accomplishments. But this time it's my idea. My success.

"Are you coming to the dorm party?" Jeremy asked.

"Sure." Eric paused to consult the program tucked into his pocket. "I've got a solo after this, then the reception, then I'm there."

"I'll see you, then," Jeremy said, turning away to go look for his bassoon case. "Good luck."

The others had already wandered off, still giddy with the high that came with performance. Eric smiled. No matter how often you performed, it was always a rush to find yourself off the stage alive and in one piece, and these kids didn't have a lot of experience with performing yet.

"These kids." Boy, does that make me feel old!

There were times when the gulf of years—only a handful by the calendar, but far more in terms of experience—made Eric feel like he came from an entirely different planet than his classmates. Sometimes he just felt like grabbing them and shaking them, telling them to value what they already had, to see how precious it was. The mood, fortunately, always passed. If there was one thing he'd learned from his time Underhill and his experience with the elves, it was that you couldn't pass on wisdom just by talking about it. Wisdom came only from experience.

He hung around backstage while two more groups went on, doing his best to stay out of their way. There was a woodwind trio—the clarinetist faltered badly at the beginning and they had to start over—and a baroque group whose members were already getting outside gigs, they were that good. The wail of the shaum and dronepipe sent shivery hackles up his spine—not Bardcraft, but close, close. . . .

But it was time to focus inward, because his next performance was only minutes away. The evening had started with the full chamber orchestra, moving slowly toward smaller and smaller groups as the stagehands cleared away the stands and chairs during breaks. The soloists traditionally closed out the evening. In the high-stakes world of classical music, they were the heavy horses that everyone was waiting to see, the next Galway or Weisberg.

Tonight there were three of them, including Eric. And the whimsical gods of misfortune had placed him last.

Professor Rector was out there laying for him, Eric knew. Tonight wasn't only a solo for him. It was his first Juilliard performance of his own composition, "Variations on 'Planxty Brown.'" He'd picked the tune not only for its lively melody, but because it had no associations with Bardic Magic or elves or anything else uncanny.

The other two soloists—one piano, one violin—acquitted themselves honorably (as Dharinel might have phrased it), and then—too soon!—it was Eric's turn to step out on the stage again.

He was sure he'd sweated all the way through his shirt, sure the audience could see his nervousness and uncertainty. Some of them, probably, still remembered his last memorable solo appearance on this stage, when he'd unwittingly summoned Nightflyers with his nascent Bardic Gift.

Oh, THERE'S a cheery thought!

For a heartbeat he was filled with panic, and for just that moment he was tempted to call up the magic again—under control this time—to exert just a tiny bit of influence on the professors grading and critiquing his performance. It would be so easy. . . .

No. I came back to do this on my own terms. No magic, no Gift but the music I was born with. I know I'm a good Bard. I'm here to see if I'm a good musician, too.

He lifted the flute to his lips and began to play.

It wasn't as powerful an energy surge as playing with an ensemble. That was like driving a team of wild horses, a swelling power that came from many hearts and minds all working as one. This was more like flying, soaring over the earth on the wings the music lent him. As always, his anxiety vanished with the first note, and he carried his audience with him through all the intricate variations of the old dance tune. And perhaps because it was music made for dancing, he felt his audience caught up in his rhythm, toes tapping and heads nodding to the music.

He brought the piece to an end with a flourish, and there was that one moment of silence as he lowered the flute that was the true tribute every musician looks for.

Then the applause began, and Eric stepped forward to take his bow. The house lights came up, and for the first time he could see the people he'd been playing for all night.

He looked down at the front rows—still bowing—looking for Rector and the other professors. He could just imagine the sour look on Rector's face—he'd been good, and he knew it, and so did they. He was smart enough not to catch Rector's eye—the man looked to be in a towering snit, and his mood wouldn't be improved by knowing Eric had seen it—and glanced around the rest of the house as he straightened.

And froze.

Ria Llewellyn was there. Second row aisle, the critics' seats.

She was wearing something in pale blue, looked just the way she always had, the ice princess who had turned his world inside-out. Only years of professional experience kept him moving, and smiling, and got him off the stage.

Ria! How did she get here?

Backstage was full—friends and relatives coming

back to congratulate the musicians, stagehands, other performers. Several of them tried to stop him, to congratulate him, but Eric tore through them, looking for the stairs that led down into the house, his flute still clutched in his hand. By the time he reached them, the audience was getting to its feet, preparing to leave.

He didn't see Ria.

He shoved through the concertgoers, fighting his way up the center aisle like a spawning salmon. He reached the street ahead of most of the audience, but he didn't see Ria anywhere.

The biting chill of late autumn cut through the damp cotton shirt he was wearing, bringing him back to himself. Even if she had been here, he'd never find her now.

And face it, Banyon. You could have been imagining things. And the only question that leaves, is— why would you imagine Ria Llewellyn coming to Juilliard?

The Sherry-Netherland was the grande dame of New York hotels . . . expensive, tasteful, and with better security than the White House. It kept secrets better than the White House did, too, even with the Joint Chiefs thrown in. If you wanted to vanish in style in Manhattan, you booked rooms at the Sherry-Netherland.

LlewellCo kept a permanent suite here to pamper its out-of-town execs and to provide a perk for visiting guests. It had probably been occupied when Jonathan booked her flight. It wasn't now.

Ria didn't care. She'd had a long day with a killer ending.

Damn the boy! she thought furiously, and then, with grudging honesty: *No. That isn't right. He's no boy. He's a man, now—and how does that make you feel, Ria-girl?*

She didn't know. That was the worst. Not the loss of command of her emotions, but the turbulent swirl that didn't even let her know clearly what they were.

She walked into the bathroom, shedding pieces of her ice-blue satin dinner suit as she went. She kicked off her Ferragamo pumps and tossed her jewelled Judith Leiber handbag onto a chair, standing before the bathroom mirror wearing only a silk slip and enough pale-gold South Sea Island pearls to finance a startup company on the Internet. The bathtub beckoned invitingly—water hot enough to scald away her sins, and bath salts from a little shop down on Chambers Street that blended them to her personal specifications. She turned the taps on full, then, too keyed up to simply stand there, walked back out to her bedroom to pace.

The papers from this morning's meeting were still strewn across the bed, as if she'd have the discipline to look at them any time soon. She felt a faint pang of guilt, knowing that she'd dealt with the New York people a bit high-handedly. She'd pay for that later—if there was one thing years of corporate infighting had taught her, it was that while friends came and went, enemies accumulated. She was sure she'd made more than a few enemies today.

But she hadn't been able to give the meeting her full attention, because more than half her concentration had been on the contents of that folder Jonathan had given her, and on the lunch appointment she'd made to interview the private investigator that she'd hired as soon as she'd started reading the report. She'd taken the woman to Le Cirque to overawe her, but the woman hadn't been overawed, and Ria had liked that about her at once.

Claire MacLaren was an uncompromising woman in her fifties, prosaic as bread. She made no effort to hide either her age or the fact that her figure had long since lost, if it had ever possessed it, the whippet slenderness of youth. She resembled the Miss Marple sort of detective, grey-haired and kindly, her strong Scots bones and pale blue eyes showing her heritage, even without the faint flavor of the Hebrides still in her voice, and was, very simply, the very best at what she did.

"I'm pleased to have the opportunity to speak with you personally on this matter, Ms. Llewellyn," she'd said, after they were both seated and the waiter had taken their drink orders. Ria had ordered white wine. Claire had unabashedly ordered Scotch.

All around them the hubbub of Le Cirque's lunchtime clientele eddied and flowed, providing perfect privacy for their conversation. Mechanical eavesdroppers would be foiled by the background noise, and magical ones would be baffled by the sheer numbers of minds all thinking at once. Even Ria, whose gift was very small, had some trouble shutting them all out. But even with her shields in place, Ria could easily sense the unease radiating from the woman seated opposite her at the table.

"I find it's always best to do this sort of thing personally," Ria said. "There are always some things that don't make it into a report. Things too . . . tenuous? to commit to paper."

"Oh, I wrote it all down," Claire assured her strongly. "Everything I could find. And that wasn't enough—considering. There's the matter of the money, for one thing."

"Money?" Ria said, momentarily at a loss. She knew Jonathan had already paid Claire MacLaren's exorbitant fee in full.

"Money doesn't just appear out of nowhere," Claire said. "And that young man has quite a lot of it. Where'd it come from, is what I'd dearly love to know."

"Oh, that," Ria answered.

She kept a show of interest on her face, but in fact, the source of Eric's money didn't concern her very much at all. A full elven mage could ken and replicate anything—rubies, diamonds, Krugerrands, bearer bonds. She couldn't work that magic, and neither could Eric, but all that meant was that someone Underhill had set Eric Banyon up with a serious stake and the means to finish his studies Here Above.

Why?

That was the question that had occupied her throughout the meal, as she'd fenced with Claire and finally thrown a small glamoure over her to quiet Claire's worries that Eric Banyon was being financed by drug lords, industrial espionage, or worse. It had nagged at her through the round of afternoon meetings with various LlewellCo East department heads. She'd been supposed to have dinner with one of them, but had cancelled at the last minute. That was good luck of a sort. If she hadn't, she wouldn't have given in to the impulse to drive past Juilliard and seen the notices of a student concert to be held that evening. She wouldn't have looked at the list of the soloists and seen Eric's name. She wouldn't have gone inside—gaining a seat by a minor enchantment—and seen Eric soloing up on the stage, performing with a surety, a grace, and an art that he had never had before.

The bathtub was full, and she walked back into the bathroom, shedding the last of her clothes, and turning off the taps. She picked up the bottle of bath salts and shook in a generous helping, watching the crystals dissolve and stain the water a rich living green.

She sank into the water, wincing at the temperature. But the heat did its work, leaching away the nervous energy that filled her, calming her.

Eric is back, and he has Underhill backing. And why is he back? Because he's finished with everything he needed to learn Underhill—that much was clear from tonight. You saw that performance. The old Eric couldn't manage to play "Baa Baa Black Sheep" without some magic leaking. This Eric has as much control and discipline as any Elven Bard I've ever seen.

She closed her eyes, trying to surrender to the spell of the water. In a lot of ways, an Eric in control of his magic was the scariest thing she'd encountered since she'd reentered the world after her coma.

First of all, who taught him? And most of all, who sent him back?

She knew that most of the Seleighe Sidhe didn't blame her for Perenor's attempt to grab the Nexus back in Los Angeles. She'd changed sides at the last minute, at great cost to herself, and that counted for a lot with their kind.

But what if Eric's teacher were one of the few who did bear a grudge against her—either because of her past actions or because of her halfblood ancestry? What if Eric had come into the world as a kind of secret agent, intending to lure her out?

What if, for that matter, Eric held a grudge of his own? She'd tried to kill his friends, after all. Most people tended to take that personally.

She sighed, sinking deeper into the water and inhaling the fragrant steam. She had no idea what Eric was feeling right now, and that disturbed her more than she could express. She hadn't been able to read anything in his face but shock when he spotted her, and after that . . .

She'd panicked, plain and simple. Proof (as if she'd wanted any) that her feelings for the man were too strong to lightly dismiss. There was unfinished business there, and like it or not, one way or another, it was going to be finished. *Before the turn of the year,* she thought, with an undependable flash of Foresight, and shivered.

The bathwater had grown cold while she'd sat musing, and now Ria got to her feet, swirling her long ash-blond hair up into a towel and wrapping herself in another of the voluminous Turkish towels the hotel provided.

It was just too bad the problem wasn't on Eric's side, she thought, rubbing herself dry until her fair skin was pink and tingled. If Eric hated her, it wouldn't matter. Ria had been hated by experts. It made little difference in her life.

The trouble was the fact that *she* wanted *him*. Still. Again. Not as a pet, as she had before, a graceful subservient boy who could amuse her while she used his magic for her own ends. No, if it were that, if her own desires were that simple, it would be an inconvenience, but not a problem.

The problem—the real problem, the insurmountable one—was that seeing him tonight on that stage, assured and totally in control, Ria had realized that Eric Banyon would never again be anybody's pet. Not a boy, not a toy. He was a man now, with a man's will and determination. Her equal, and more.

And everything in Ria's half-Blood Perenor-nurtured soul rebelled against the thought of accepting anyone on equal terms. Conciliation was weakness. Cooperation was only a trap. Only the strongest had any right to survive, and Ria knew that if she matched her power and her tricks against the Eric she had seen tonight, she might very well lose the battle.

And the worst was, she had no heart for such a fight. Unless he truly was here hunting her, he was no threat to her, and unlike Perenor, Ria had never had any taste for empty cruelty. She was ruthless. That was her nature. But viciousness had never been a part of her spirit, and if it had, that part of her was purged long since. So she had no quarrel with Eric Banyon, True Bard of Underhill, and if he were in truth sent here as her foe, mercy would be impossible. For either of them.

I can't be his pet. He won't be mine. Where does that leave us?

Where does that leave ME?

FIVE:

GOBLIN FRUIT

It was cold out here under the highway tonight, but Daniel Carradine tried to ignore it. There was money to be made, and the need to make it. Bobby wanted his money, and Daniel wanted his White Lady, the demanding mistress for whom Daniel had given up everything else.

Not that there'd been all that much. When home was a decaying Pennsylvania steel town and a father who couldn't accept that times had changed, even the underside of the West Side Highway on a freezing December night was better.

The wind came whistling in off the Hudson, cold as memories. If he'd been able to fix before he came out, Daniel wouldn't have minded the cold, he knew, but Bobby didn't sell on credit. *Still*, Daniel told himself hopefully, *it might be a good night*. He was seventeen, and looked younger, and that was good. It was what the marks liked, the guys who came cruising down here with their Mercedes and their Jags, looking for what Daniel and the others were selling. Goblin fruit, like in the Rossetti poem, where no matter how much you ate, you were always hungry for more.

A friend of his—Tony—went by, and he smiled and waved. Bobby had come across for Tony before he left the flop tonight—it was obvious in the way Tony strutted, as if he were living in a warm world where the river wind didn't blow—and for a moment Daniel felt a pang of envy that was shocking in its violence. He quashed the emotion firmly. There was no point. Nothing came free. That was the first lesson growing up in Cartersville had taught him. There was a price for everything, even freedom. And if the only freedom he could buy with the only thing he owned—his body—was the freedom of a derelict flop down in the Bowery that he shared with half a dozen other rentboys, then he'd take it.

A car cruised by—slowly, on the prowl—and Daniel smiled hopefully, arching his back and shaking his head so that a lock of bleached-blond hair fell down over his eyes. But the car moved on, and Daniel hunched back into himself again, seeking what comfort he could.

He wanted to get this over with and go find Bobby. He really did.

❖　　　❖　　　❖

From a few feet away, beneath the body of a burnt-out and abandoned car, Urla watched its victim. The redcap had been about to rush out, but the cruising car had stopped it. The Great Lord had said there must be no witnesses, and Aerune's command sat upon Urla like a *geas*.

He had also said that Urla must take no one who would be missed, and Urla knew that nobody would miss this one. Still young and strong, and filled with such self-hatred and despair that the redcap was nearly drunk with it, all laced through with a yearning, a fiery craving for something that was not food or drink or sex. Urla dismissed its own curiosity. It did not matter what the boy hungered for, for he did not hunger as much as Urla did for the bright warmth of the untasted years, the unspent years the boy would have had if Urla had not come hunting here tonight.

Another car passed, then two more, and each time the boy was assessed and refused. His fear was stronger now, and Urla licked its lips in anticipation. Soon, soon. . . .

At last the boy stumbled away from the pillar by which he stood and began shuffling up the street, his steps uncoordinated. He shivered, wrapping his thin jacket tighter around his starved body as if the thin cotton had the power to grant him the warmth he lacked. In a few moments more he would pass directly before Urla's hiding place.

But the redcap's anticipated feast was not to be. Another great black chariot turned down the street, its night lamps pinning the boy in their beams. Urla saw its prey stop, hopeful once more, as the car drew level with him, and the door opened. The

boy stepped forward, and a mortal—tall, tall, with
the stink of Cold Iron about him—rose up out of
the car and grabbed Urla's prey, dragging him into
the car as he began, too late, to struggle and cry.

The door shut. The chariot moved away, more
quickly now, belching foul gasses that made Urla
cough.

No! They will not have him! He is mine!

Snarling its disappointment, the redcap wrapped
itself in shadows and began to trot after the black
chariot that had taken its prey.

"I said no alkies, goddammit! Which word don't
you goons understand?"

The tall dark man with the sleepy eyes blinked
at her. Jeanette wished she could kick him, but she
didn't dare, quite. She took a deep breath and tried
again, marshalling her hard-won and inadequate
social skills.

"Look, Elkanah." Was the name on the tag first,
last, or even his? Not her problem. "Most of these
people are fine. But you see that one in the corner?"

Jeanette gestured toward the monitor in the
Security Room. It showed the space they called
Large Primate Containment—a euphemism for the
Black Labs and holding cells set up for human
experimentation. Just now it was dressed to look
like a police holding cell—an environment she was
sure all of her guests were more than familiar with.
Junkies, rentboys, and hookers, the lot of them,
and that was fine with her.

Except for the man in the corner, the one in
the tattered vomit-stained trenchcoat, his face long-
unshaven and caved in upon missing teeth and

malnutrition. The others gave him a wide berth, and she could imagine why. He probably stank to high heaven.

"That guy is a juicehead. I can't use him. His liver's already shot to hell—drugs process through the liver, *Elkanah,* did you know that? Alcohol's *legal*—by the time a juicehead gets to the street he's already a walking corpse; all his insides pickled and shot to hell. I told you guys when you went out: no alkies, no crazy street people. Junkies and whores, that's what I told you to get."

The man in the uniform of Threshold Special Security blinked down at her, as impassive as a cigar-store Indian, and for a moment Jeanette didn't think he'd heard her. Didn't any of Robert's hardboys speak English, for God's sweet sake?

"So what do you want me to do with him, Ms. Campbell?" Elkanah finally said. His voice was slow and deep and thoughtful, and despite her fury, Jeanette did not for one moment make the mistake of thinking he was stupid. Stupid people did not rise to key positions in Threshold's Black Ops.

She took a deep breath.

"I don't care what you do with him. Throw him in the East River for all I care. But get rid of him before lights out, because if he's still there tomorrow when my Judas Goat goes in to offer these losers a trip out of this world, I am going to be seriously pissed. And when I'm pissed, Robert Lintel is pissed. Are we communicating?"

"Yes, Ms. Campbell. I'm sorry about the confusion."

He wasn't sorry and there'd been no confusion.

Jeanette knew that perfectly well. But she'd won, and that was all that mattered.

"Okay," she said. "I'll be in my office if anyone needs me."

She turned away and walked quickly out of Security before this Elkanah person could guess how scared she was. When she'd been running with the Sinner Saints, she could have eaten corporation rent-muscle like Elkanah for breakfast, but it had been years since she'd had to face off anything but chimps and wimp lab technicians, and, unlike riding a Harley, some skills didn't stay with you forever.

Security and personnel were Robert's problem. They always had been. She supplied the science. He supplied the money and muscle. That was the deal. So why did she have to do everything around Threshold herself?

She reached the safety of her own private lab and closed the airlock behind her gratefully, irritation and a feeling of narrow escape both fading as she surveyed her private kingdom. Nobody would bother her in here. Nobody would dare.

The room had been cleansed of all traces of the chimps' occupation, though they were still looking for the one that had vanished. The two that had died instantly had been autopsied, and she'd found about what she'd expected: massive stroke and brain hemorrhage, the inevitable side effect of chemical Russian roulette.

The other two—the ones that had manifested the bizarre powers—had also died, but several hours later and of something that looked surprisingly like starvation, though how the old female could have died of starvation with all she'd eaten was an interesting question. She was the one who'd survived the longest, and Jeanette was looking forward to seeing those autopsy results, but right now both bodies were in freezers awaiting their turn. Ramchandra had better work fast, because in a day or so those chimps were going to have a lot of company.

Jeanette fully expected that the people Robert had gotten for her off the New York streets would die of the drug the same way the chimps had. That was what lab trials were for—to find out what killed them and to try to refine the next batch even more. She'd obviously found the right button to push, the one she'd been looking for ever since she was a teenager.

Now all I have to do is keep their heads from exploding. A few more hours alone would clean her test subjects out of whatever they'd been using, then another of Robert's goons would be thrown in with them, the packets of T-6/157 in his pockets looking like any other sample of party dust. He'd say he needed to get rid of it before the police searched him, and if Jeanette knew junkies, they wouldn't ask too many questions when there was free dust on offer. They'd suck the stuff right down, and then . . .

Then she'd finally start getting some answers.

Hell couldn't be worse than this, Daniel thought. And to think, he'd thought his luck had changed when that limo had pulled up.

He could still feel the shock of anger, almost of betrayal, when the big man had seized him and dragged him into the limo. He and his buddy had tried to make it look like they were vice cops bringing him in on a solicitation bust, but Daniel had been through that mill more than a few times since he'd gotten to New York, and he'd never seen a vice cop that rode around in the back of a fancy car—or that put a hood over your head so you couldn't see where you were when they dragged you out of it.

That was weird, and for a while he'd tried to console himself with the fantasy that they were just two kinks looking for a wiggy party, but he couldn't make himself believe it. He'd never seen a co-ed holding tank, for one thing, and no matter how much this place might look like the Tombs, it just didn't smell right. And it was way too quiet. In prison there was always somebody screaming, somebody crying, somebody jonesing for a fix that wasn't going to come any time soon.

That would be him, in a couple of hours. He needed his White Lady, his beautiful lady who made the world all soft and sweet. He didn't know about the other eight people stuck in here with him, and he didn't care. Life on the street was rough enough without caring about other people, and Daniel had jettisoned his emotional baggage early.

They fed him a couple of times, and once the lights went down low and he'd slept a little, but by the second day he was too sick to care about his breakfast. A lot of the others were just as bad off, and when one of them started screaming and wouldn't stop, two guys in black almost-a-cop uniforms had come in and dragged her away pretty quickly. The rest of them sat, huddled in silent misery, waiting for the torture to end.

No lawyers, no bondsmen, no arraignment. This isn't any bullpen I've ever been in. But I ain't gonna be the one to say it. They're probably watching everything. Whoever they are.

The word must have gone out to make up the numbers after the woman disappeared, because a little while after dinner—he'd forced himself to eat, but thrown up again almost instantly—they brought in someone new.

He was dressed better than they were, but still street. Daniel's internal radar prickled instantly. He was pretty sure he knew what this guy was, and he was only hoping that the rest of his guess was right as well. The guy was holding. He could smell it. Nobody had searched Daniel when they brought him in. Why should they search any of the others?

He waited until the lights went out, when everyone was curled up in their bunks. There were twelve bunks—four sets of three tiers each—for nine people, which meant that nearly everyone could have his pick of places to sleep. The New Guy took what was left—a bottom bunk, of course, since anyone with brains wanted a top one.

Daniel made sure he had the top bunk on the New Guy's tier. It wasn't his to begin with, but he got to it first and stared down the woman who'd been sleeping there. She just shook her head bitterly and went to find another bed.

"Hey," Daniel called softly. "Hey, New Guy?"

"That's me." The voice came out of the darkness,

pleased and mellow and unafraid. "You got a name, pilgrim?"

"Danny-boy." It was what Daniel answered to on the street, as if keeping the name he had been called at home a secret could somehow lend him armor against the cruelty of the streets.

"Well, Danny-boy, you can call me Keith."

"Hey, Keith." Daniel's voice was ragged with relief. He knew the moves of this dance, and knew he'd been right. The man was holding, and Daniel meant to cut himself a slice of that pie.

"Now Danny-boy, I got me a problem that maybe you could help me with. I was checking you out earlier, when I came in. You look like an intelligent kind of a guy."

"Yeah, that's me." He wasn't entirely successful at keeping the bitterness out of his voice. If he'd been really smart, would he have ended up here?

"Well, I've got this inventory. And I kind of need to hold a fire sale, as it were."

Daniel dropped down out of the top bunk, quick as a cat, and squatted beside the bottom bunk. Keith was resting on one elbow—looking toward him, though it was hard to see that in the darkness. A gold ring in the shape of a phoenix glinted in one ear, the brightest thing Daniel could see.

He's holding. And he needs to get rid of the stuff before the cops figure that out. Daniel held out his hand.

Keith dropped the small white packet into it. "There's plenty for everyone," he said in his mellow voice, as the other inhabitants of the holding tank began converging on him with a slow tidal movement.

Daniel backed away, defending his prize. In one pocket, along with other odds and ends, was a chopped off bit of soda straw. He tore open the small glassine packet—carefully, oh so carefully—and dipped the straw end into the white powder. It wasn't as good as spiking a vein, but it would do, oh, yes. He snorted hard, pulling the powder up into his sinuses, and from there, straight to the bloodstream. He didn't know what Keith had offered him—coke, horse, one of the new supposed-to-be-legal concoctions—and right now he was too far gone in need to care. Just a little something to quiet the dragon trying to gnaw its way out of his bones.

He felt it come on almost instantly: a velvet-wrapped pile driver that made his heart race, even while it wrapped him in soft clouds of not-caring. He blinked, forced himself to look up, and saw Keith handing out packets to everyone.

"Hey," Daniel croaked. "Save me some for later." The white tide was rising, carrying him off to a place where nothing hurt and no one was cruel.

"Don't worry, Danny-boy." He heard Keith's slow rich voice as from a great distance. "This stuff, nobody ever needs two."

And the heaven and hell of it was, Daniel heard him. Heard him and didn't care.

Five minutes after the last of the meat had gone on the nod, Keith stood up and stretched. The floor of the cell was covered with unconscious junkies. He shivered, looking down at them.

Whatever this stuff was, he was sure as hell glad *he* hadn't sniffed any of it.

He looked up at the main security camera in the ceiling.

"Hey. What are you guys waiting for? An engraved invitation?" he demanded.

There was no response, but a few minutes later the lights came up in the corridor outside, and technicians in white lab coats wheeling gurneys appeared. The one in the lead opened the cell door, and Keith stepped outside hastily, as if whatever had sent the eight people in the cell off to dreamland might be catching.

"Everything go all right?" Beirkoff asked.

"Fine as frog hair. What the hell was that stuff, anyway?"

Beirkoff smiled, and the lights turned the lenses of his tinted glasses silver. "Hey, you know the drill. I could tell you, but then I'd have to kill you."

Keith growled wordlessly under his breath, and stalked off to report.

Jeanette had slaved the security cameras to her desktop PC. She could have been down in the security room, where all eight holding cells were being monitored on visual and audio as well as by a whole spectrum of other devices, but she didn't want to share this moment with some wage slave of a technician. She could see all she needed to from here, anyway. By tapping a few buttons, she could watch as her unconscious subjects were transported to separate holding cells, implanted with transceivers that would monitor their heart and brainwaves. As soon as the pickups were live, she killed the picture and brought up the telemetry. Slow rolling delta waves billowed across her screen like the waves of an ancient ocean.

What are you feeling? she asked the silent screen. *Where are you?*

But the answers, she knew, would have to wait. Until the awakening.

Beneath the edge of the desk, her hands tightened into fists. *Give it to me,* she demanded silently. *Give me something I can use!*

Outside the building, wrapped in a darkness of its own weaving, Urla watched the metal door through which the car had gone. Day had come and gone while the redcap waited. When the sun rode high in the sky, Urla retreated to the friendly darkness of the city's sewers, killing rats to amuse itself while it waited. Their tiny deaths were only an appetizer, though, one that left the redcap restless and unsatisfied. Urla hungered for its stolen prey, taken by the men in the black night-wagon, the one that had burned with such painful inner fire.

There were others like that one in the grimy yellow building, and Urla comforted itself with fantasies of a gluttonous feeding, one that might slake even the redcap's eternal hunger, for there were many within the yellow building filled with terror and such a burning despair that it made Urla's mouth water. When night came again it took up its watching post once more, though by now it had lost all hope that the prey it had tracked here would emerge once more.

Its tiny mind had been occupied for several

hours with the question of whether it would be better to abandon its waiting and go once more in search of the Bard its dark master had commanded it to find, but instinct told it that this place contained many secrets, and secrets were always good to know.

The moon rose high and began to set. And then, just before the sky began to lighten and Urla must once more choose whether to retreat into the sewers again or to admit its failure, something happened. The prey-creatures' lives burned in Urla's consciousness like bright candles, but suddenly several of them simply . . . went out.

Urla crawled forth from its concealment beneath a parked car, leathery brow wrinkling in puzzlement. They had been there a moment before, and now they were not there. It did not sense the tang of death, and sleep alone could not render prey invisible to a redcap's hunger. Urla crept closer to the strange building, wondering.

The riptide of fury that followed the strange quenching was enough to send the redcap sprawling stunned in the middle of the street, visible to any who might look. After the first shock, Urla dragged itself to concealment again, shaking its head as if to ward off the effects of a mighty blow. The rage still keened through its senses—an unhinged fury worthy of a mighty Unseleighe lord, black and all-devouring.

It had to know more.

Forcing itself forward against the tempest of madness, Urla began searching for ways to enter the building.

✦   ✦   ✦

She'd ordered someone to go out for pizza—one good thing about New York, you could get takeout at any hour—and most of a deluxe pie now sat on the corner of Jeanette's desk, cold and forgotten. Styrofoam cups, half full of cold coffee, studded every available surface within reach. Across the screen the readouts scrolled, changing only slightly from moment to moment.

The first effects of the drug should be wearing off now, Jeanette thought. It had been four hours, and her psychoactive cocktail was layered, like a fine perfume, to deliver its effects in calculated stages. So at least some of those loser-freaks should be coming around by now. Jeanette ground her teeth in impatience. They couldn't all just die on her!

Suddenly two of the readouts . . . vanished. Jeanette stared at the screen, galvanized to alertness by the impossibility of it. A moment later she heard the faint hooting of the situation alarm sounding through the building. She pushed herself to her feet and ran.

"What is it?" she shouted, flinging open the Monitor Room door. The technician turned toward her, white-faced and scared. GALLIARD, her nametag said.

"I was watching them every moment," the tech babbled. "Every moment! They didn't go anywhere, they couldn't have, I locked them in myself—"

The denials made no sense until Jeanette looked at the screens. Eight were live. Six showed sleeping subjects, lying on the floors of their padded cells.

Two cells were empty—as in, nobody home.

Well, Galliard, you're going to wish you'd chosen another career when I get done with you.

"Where the hell are they?" Jeanette asked in dangerously reasonable tones. She took a step toward the cringing girl.

A scream from the monitors stopped her. The subjects were awake, going from a comatose sleep to full consciousness in instants. She watched, spellbound, as first one, then another, of her test cases began throwing himself about his cell, violently seeking escape, battering and tearing at the padded walls until streaks and flowers of blood appeared.

After a timeless moment, Jeanette realized that the technician was staring at her, waiting for her to give orders. Jeanette reached out and turned the master audio control on the console to "Off." It didn't totally shut out the screams, audible even through the soundproofing, but it did make it easier to think as she mulled over what to do next.

Sedate them? No, with the dose in their systems, that would be a quick ticket to the boneyard, and even if they were doomed, she didn't want to kill them so quickly. Restrain them? Gazing down at the gyrating madmen, Jeanette wasn't sure there was enough money in the world to pay anyone to enter one of those cells. One of the madmen—the display at the bottom said his name was Nelson—cheated of any other outlet for his rage, had turned his fury on himself. He'd gouged out both his eyes and clawed his skin to bleeding ribbons, and was still tearing at himself, howling in a deep voice as he drooled blood from a mouth from which he'd torn his own tongue.

Galliard was still staring at her, eyes wide and scared.

"Go find Mr. Lintel. Tell him two of the subjects have escaped. Tell him to find them," Jeanette ordered. *That should keep both Robert and this bimbette busy!*

Galliard scuttled out. Jeanette settled down in the vacated chair to watch the show.

Urla was inside the building now, crawling through the ventilation system unseen, making slow progress against the invisible headwind of madness that buffeted it. The presence of Cold Iron was a palpable weight against its bones, but unlike others of the Seleighe kin, the redcap was not affected by its poison. It winced as the first mind was joined by one, two, three others, until the four of them raged in a torment that was almost Power—the rage of a demon lord. What was it the mortals did here to cause such anguish? Urla desperately wished to learn their secret, for it would make the redcap's kind a rich banquet. Some there were among the Unseleighe Court who fed on emotion as Urla fed on lives, and did it own the secret of such cosmic despair, it could trade it to them to its advantage.

But then something happened that thrust all thought of self-interest from the redcap's mind. For the last of the mortals prisoned here awoke, and the uprush of true Power nearly blinded his Sidhe senses. Here was the power of Bard or Elven mage trapped in mortal flesh—a wellspring of such Power as the dark lord Aerune had sent him to find. It was here, somehow here where it had not been a moment before, in mortals who had not possessed it before this instant.

Daniel Carradine awoke with a sudden start, shivering and sweating, his strongest emotion a cheated anger that whatever it was that Keith had supplied, it hadn't taken the edge off his need. The long-unslaked craving, stronger than he had ever known it, filled him now like a wild thing desperate to be free.

His Lady . . . his beautiful White Lady . . . . Somehow Daniel could sense her somewhere near, somehow certain that this was Truth, and not some withdrawal-fuelled hallucination. His hunger was strong enough to tear down walls, to see into all the hidden places of the world as if they were made of glass. He knew she was here, knew that all he had to do was reach out for her, and he could have her.

Daniel reached. The first attempt brought pain, enough almost to blot out the fire in his bones, but it also carried a teasing promise of certainty. If he could only try a little harder . . .

He reached out again, whimpering as he did it, his whole body shaking and drenched in a greasy sweat. The pain flared again, blinding him, but behind it he felt a strange cool flexing of senses he'd never known before, and abruptly there was a hard roundness in his hand—the object of his desire, summoned to him through all the walls and barriers that separated them. In his surprise, he dropped it, and then crawled frantically across the padded floor after it until he'd grabbed it in both hands.

He looked down at the stoppered jar half filled

with glistening white powder. He didn't need to open it to know what it was. His Lady. The White Lady. Pure, pharmaceutical-grade heroin.

He could have taken her that way, opened the bottle and snorted its contents or spilled it across his tongue, but now Daniel knew he didn't need to. The rest of what he needed to make everything perfect was out there. All he had to do was imagine it, and its location appeared in his mind. Then all he had to do was . . . reach. This time, when his hand was filled, he clutched the bottle tightly, chuckling with success. Here—and here—and here. *And wilderness is paradise enow,*[3] he quoted out of some half-full store of memory.

He broke the seal on the pint of distilled water, and slopped a little into the Pyrex beaker. The powder dissolved into the water easily, turning it a milky moonstone color. The rest of what he needed was here, summoned from the same place as the water and the beaker. He syringed the mixture up with the ease of long practice.

Now everything will be all right, he thought, tapping his arm to find a vein.

And it was, for those few moments before the massive overdose of uncut heroin—far more, far purer than any fix he'd ever known—carried Daniel down into the darkness and the safest place of all.

Ellie Borden woke suddenly out of a long confused dream. Her whole life the last few months had been a dream—a bad one—as she lost first her job, then her health insurance, then her

---

[3] The *Rubiyat*.

apartment, ending up on the street doing whatever she could just to survive one more day.

It wasn't supposed to be like this. The automatic protest no longer held either fury or grief, only a weary resignation. She'd paid her taxes, obeyed the law, been kind. She was supposed to be safe, protected by Society from cradle to grave. But that hadn't happened. All the social services' safety net that was supposed to be there to catch people like her had melted away the moment she needed it. The programs that were supposed to help had waiting lists months long, and Ellie didn't have months. She'd discovered that the halfway houses were not for people like her, that the only place that would take her in on that terrible day she'd gone home to find everything she owned piled on the curb in front of her former apartment was the street.

She'd quickly learned there were ways to take the edge off the pain, to gain the minimal money that would buy her a room in a flophouse she'd never have dared enter when she'd had a life, to buy her the things that would let her live with the sickness that was eating her life away, but the things she'd had to do to get them were best forgotten.

When she'd been arrested, it had almost been a relief, because you got medical care in prison, didn't you? Only that had turned out to be another grim joke like the rest of her so-called life, because all they'd done was dump her in a cell with a bunch of other street people and forget about her. She'd taken the packet from the dealer the way a starving man would take food, not caring what

it was, half-hoping it would kill her if it would only
end the pain.

But it hadn't.

She awoke in a strange room, not the holding
cell, all by herself. The pain was gone. Gone! She
felt better than she had in almost two years. The
evil shadow that lived in her bones had vanished
forever, she knew it. She felt reborn.

What have they done? she thought in slow-
growing wonder. *What did they do to me?* She
stared at her hands, marveled at the soft brown
skin. No longer cracked, scarred, covered with
sores. New again, reborn.

Just as she had been reborn.

Thank You, God, Ellie thought silently. *I won't
forget this. I won't throw it away.*

One was dead, killed by his overreaching appe-
tite, but the other remained, still connected somehow to the magic so very like that of Underhill.
In the air ducts, Urla gnashed its teeth, hating the
choice it must make, the choice of gluttony
deferred.

This was not the answer that its dark master
sought, the news of a human Bard who could form
the Nexus Aerune sought to build, but it was news
worth the bringing, regardless. The redcap abandoned its own hunt and turned back the way it
had come, hurrying back to the door in the air that
led into Underhill and the road that led to the
Dark Court.

Jeanette glanced at the clock on the wall of her
office. The digital readout said 11:36 in glaring red

numbers—a 24-hour readout, so it was a little before noon of some damn day or other. She rubbed her eyes. She hadn't slept all night—she hadn't left the lab for two days—and the strain was beginning to tell on her.

It had been a busy morning, full of new discoveries. And mistakes, but those happened in any research program.

The first mistake she'd made had been in assuming that all six of the surviving test subjects would react the same way. Obviously they hadn't. The four that had gone psychotic had fixed everybody's attention on them until it was too late . . . sort of. And by the time they'd gone catatonic, what was going to happen, had happened.

For the thousandth time, she replayed the tape of Cell One on her computer screen. That had been a young white male, early 20s. Keith said he'd given his name as Danny-boy. She watched as Danny-boy awoke, agitated but obviously not as crazy as the berserkers. She watched him reach out and pluck things out of the air—a jar of white powder, a bottle of water, a beaker, a syringe. He'd teleported them all from her lab—she'd been able to tell by the inventory number engraved on the beaker, and the bar codes on the stock—but how had he gotten them through a locked door and a solid wall? And how had he known they were in her lab in the first place?

If we'd been watching, could we have stopped you? she wondered. She watched as he fixed, hands shaking with his addiction, and watched as he slumped a moment later, dead in a heartbeat from an overdose of pure heroin.

Stupid boy. Don't you know street drugs are stepped on six or seven times—if you're lucky— before they get to you? This was the pure stuff. You should have cut back the dose. You should have WAITED, you blockhead.

She sighed, and rubbed her tired eyes. Now, dammit, she had no way of knowing if her mix would have killed him without the heroin, and an autopsy probably wouldn't be able to sort it out either.

"Campbell?"

She looked up from the screen with an effort as Robert came into the office. If he'd spent as many sleepless hours as she had, it didn't show. He had an ulcer, too—she'd hacked into his personal files once out of idle curiosity—and that didn't show either. Robert Lintel was the original Teflon boy. His three-piece grey suit was immaculate, and he was wearing the particular smug expression that Jeanette liked least. But Robert always had only seen the possibilities in her work, the ultimate goal, and not the long process that led there.

"What?" she said sullenly, knowing that letting him see her mood was weakness, and weakness had always been the thing she defended herself hardest against showing.

"Hey, Campbell. *Smile*. We're almost there, you know. It worked!"

"Two missing—have you found them yet?—four crazy, and of the two qualified successes, one dead. Some success," she grumbled.

"We're looking for the two that vanished, but frankly, I think they went to the same place the chimp did. I had Elkanah dump the other four out on the street. They should be dead by now, or at Bellevue. Either way, not our problem." He walked into the room and stood over her desk, beaming down at her paternally.

"So that leaves—what's her name?—Borden? And her readings have gone back to normal. Whatever she had, it's gone," Jeanette said.

"But while she had it, it was enough to get her clean. I had Dr. Ramchandra give her a quick once-over. According to his interview with her, she'd been diagnosed with terminal cancer. But she doesn't have it now. In fact, she's in perfect health. What do you think of that?"

"I think you aren't paying me to find a cure for cancer," Jeanette answered, but Robert's smug smile only grew wider.

"That's right. But actually, I don't think you need to work on refining your formula any more. We know it works on ten percent of the population. We just have to find the ten percent it works on." He sat down in the chair opposite her desk, the big comfy leather one that only Robert ever sat in.

He was talking about mass trials.

"So where are you going to get enough people to put together a profile for that? Carradine and Borden both manifested Talent, but other than that, they have nothing in common. He was white. She's black. He was a teenager. She's in her thirties. They were both users, but we don't even know they were using the same things."

"Campbell, Campbell, Campbell. When are you ever going to learn to trust me? I have this all figured out." He leaned forward, and she caught a whiff of soap and expensive cologne.

"I want you to go into production with this. Whip me up a few kilos of Batch 157 and portion it out into single-dose packets—we'll call it something like T-Stroke. I'll put it out on the street—we'll sell it of course, but we'll undercut everything else—crank, Mexican brown, snow, the whole menu. They'll buy it, and you'll have your test pool—cheap, easy, and nothing for us to clean up after. We'll rope in the ones that survive, run them through the mill, and find the common thread. Once we have that profile, we can use it to find volunteer subjects."

Jeanette had always been serenely convinced that nothing could shock her, that she didn't care about all those faceless drones she shared the world with. But the butcher's bill Robert was proposing so guilelessly startled even her.

One out of the eight in the first group had survived. Statistically, that meant the odds were that if eighty people received T-6/157, seventy would die. And if you took those numbers out to the thousands of doses that Robert was recommending they spread across the streets of New York . . .

"There's going to be dead junkies stacked like cordwood on every street corner," Jeanette said slowly, trying to decide how that made her feel. She knew she ought to like the idea, but instead she felt curiously numb inside. How confident must Robert be, how eager for his results, to suggest a plan that held so much possibility of . . . unforeseen consequences.

But Robert didn't even seem to notice her lack

of enthusiasm. He bored in, eyes glittering like a high-pressure salesman closing a big deal.

"And your point is? C'mon, Campbell, we're looking for results here, not scientific validation. If we generate the Survivor Profile, nobody's going to care how we got it."

"You're right," she said, knowing it was true. Who cared how a lot of junkies died, anyway, so long as the deaths couldn't be traced back to Threshold? She got to her feet, making Robert stand also. "Look, I've got to crash. Beirkoff knows the stuff to order to make up about ten keys of T-Stroke. I'll come back tonight and put it together."

"We could take care of that," Robert said, too casually. "The formula's in your lab notebook, isn't it?"

Jeanette smiled at him, the street predator that had been hidden beneath a veneer of years and good living suddenly stark and plain in her eyes. It wasn't that she didn't trust Robert—she didn't, that had never been an issue. But T-Stroke was an entirely bigger deal than the other compounds she'd handed over. She intended to keep control of it until she was satisfied.

Of what, she wasn't sure.

You're hoping you'll fit the Survivor Profile he'll come up with, don't you? The Survivors—Robert's new race of psionic hitmen. What're you going to do if you do, Campbell? What are you going to do if you don't?

"Aw, c'mon, Robert. You don't want a numb-nuts like Beirkoff to futz this up at the eleventh hour, do you? You don't want to be wondering if he got the formula exactly right and have to do it all again to be sure? Give me a couple of hours. It'll take him that long to get the stuff here anyway. You can call me when it comes in. And meanwhile, you gotta make up your mind what you want to do with the Survivor bitch you've already got."

She didn't wait for him to reply. She grabbed her coat and headed out the door before he'd quite rearranged his face into whatever expression he'd chosen. She knew he'd go looking for the formula. He always did. She knew that.

And she always left one ingredient out of her notes.

He knew that.

SIX:

TO CHAIN THE PHOENIX

If it was her, so what?

Mechanically, Eric Banyon went through the motions at the après-concert Artists' Reception, standing around an overheated room with a glass of seltzer in his hand along with the other soloists, featured performers, and those who'd paid money to meet them and each other. Politically, it was the most important part of the show—at least if you were aiming for a paying gig in the hothouse incestuous world of classical music. There were many other job openings besides Featured Soloist or Touring Superstar—to name just one example, there were chairs in any number of orchestras, from the Boston Philharmonic to the Hudson Valley Symphony Orchestra, that always needed to be filled with the best, the brightest, and the most underpaid. Music scouts made careers out of tracking the progress of new young talent the same way other talent scouts cruised college athletics. Eric had already been approached about a few spots—Composer in Residence in an artists' retreat in someplace called Glastonbury, New York, various "sure-thing" grants from one program or another, even a booking agent who swore to him that Juilliard had nothing to teach Eric and it was time to look at professional gigs. *As if I haven't heard that song a lot lately, with all of its verses. . . .*

Eric had turned them all down politely. For one thing, none of his reasons for returning to Juilliard were about worldly fame and power—as a Bard, he already had more of both than most people could imagine. For another, he couldn't get Ria out of his mind enough to give any of them serious attention.

He was glad he hadn't been pressured into wearing a tie to the concert tonight. He'd already unbuttoned the neck of his tab-collared shirt—it was that or strangle in the tropical heat of the reception room. He hoped he looked raffishly artistic—it was one of the reasons he'd left his hair long. *Image isn't everything. It's the only thing. Or so they say.*

His flute in its case was slung over his shoulder; Eric didn't delude himself that everybody at Juilliard loved him, and a musician's instrument was an easy target for jealousy. Better to keep it with him than bespell it to keep it from sabotage and risk harming somebody unintentionally.

Once I never would have worried about that. Give me the power and I would have used it any time it benefited me, and de'il take the hindmost, as my old Irish grandma would have said. I guess this is maturity—taking the responsibility of protecting idiots from themselves.

I bet Ria wouldn't think twice about something like that. She'd say it was their own fault for messing with her in the first place.

He frowned. That had been true once. Was it true now? He gave up trying to ignore the inevitable and devoted some serious thought to the question of the hour. It wasn't impossible for Ria to have been here tonight. She wasn't either dead or in a coma—in fact, the last time he'd talked to Kayla and Elizabet (though between juggling Underhill and World Above time zones, he wasn't quite sure when that was), they'd said Ria was on her way to making a full recovery.

They also said she'd acquired a conscience and morals, but dammit, what does that MEAN in real-life terms? They said she was still Ria—memories, Gifts, and all—so it's not like she's been Touched by An Angel *or something sappy like that. She's still the same Ria I knew, and the Ria I knew was ruthless.*

But not vicious. She didn't care what happened to other people, but she didn't go out of her way to hurt them. Not like Perenor. Not that it mattered a lot if you happened to be the person who got in her way. . . .

All the while his brain kept turning over that

unanswerable question, he smiled and made meaningless conversation with men and women in expensive clothes. Lovely concert, yes he was very pleased with his performance tonight, no he hadn't really made plans for what he'd do after he graduated. Round and round they circled, drawn to Eric by something they probably didn't even understand—the aura of Power that a fully trained Bard wore like an invisible cloak—though the other performers got their fair share of attention as well. It was a little like being in a shark tank—but Eric wasn't afraid of any of these particular sharks.

There's nothing they can do to me. None of them is pointing a gun at my head or offering to torture any of my friends. They're all just looking for some way to use me. Once upon a time that would have driven me crazy with righteous indignation. Now it just seems kind of sad.

He circled around behind the buffet. It was pretty well denuded by now—only some cheese and fruit remained—and the ice-sculpture centerpiece was so melted it was now impossible to tell what it had originally been. Eric reached out and placed his hand against it, savoring the coolness. You'd think they could just open the doors and let some December in, but apparently nobody'd thought of that.

"I'm not going to let you ruin your future over some silly girlish tantrum."

The voice was low and furious. Eric glanced up in surprise. Lydia Ashborn was standing backed into a corner by a tall man in a very expensive suit and an even more expensive haircut. Eric recognized Marco Ashborn, Lydia's father.

"Do you want to be a bit player all your life, just some faceless unknown musician without even a separate credit? You should have had a solo tonight, and you know it. Don't you want to record and tour in your own right? Why are you trying to piss it all away? Is this about me? Is that what this is all about, Lydia?"

Man, does it all have to be about you? The uprush of anger was automatic, stemming from still-unhealed scars. He'd been in Lydia's position once: a Trophy Child, treated as nothing more than a playing-piece on the parental chessboard. An accessory. A *thing*, not a person. And that was wrong on so many levels.

Eric saw the glitter of tears as Lydia ducked her head and fought to control his anger. Discipline above all things, Dharinel had told him. A Bard's displeasure could wound. A Bard's anger could kill.

"Don't you look away from me, dammit!" he heard Marco hiss. Marco grabbed his daughter's arm roughly, and Eric saw Lydia's face go white with the pain.

That's enough.

Eric reached for the *stillness within* that Dharinel had created in him with all those long months of training, and composed his face into a simple harmless expression of hero worship as he walked over to the two of them.

"Hey, excuse me, but aren't you Marco Ashborn, the violinist?"

The burly man turned toward Eric, irritation warring with the game face that every public performer learns to assume at need.

"It's an honor to meet you, sir," Eric went on,

blithely ignoring the emotional undercurrents swirling around Marco and Lydia. "I've enjoyed your
work so much." That, at least, was true—though
how much he'd ever like Marco's playing now that
he knew what a goon the guy was in real life was
an interesting question. "Lyd's certainly inherited
your talent—I'm in some of her classes as well as
her chamber music group." Eric held out his hand,
still radiating peaceable obliviousness. "Eric Banyon."

Marco's face cleared. He recognized Eric, and
more, he responded to Eric's calm confidence, his
assumption of being someone whom the famous
Marco Ashborn would want to know. It was the
simplest sort of magic—and not really magic,
because in its own way, it was true.

"I saw your performances tonight. Both of them.
That solo was most impressive," Marco rumbled.

"Thank you, sir," Eric said. "I was pleased with
our ensemble work. Lydia made me look good," he
went on, deliberately misunderstanding the other
man's words. "You must be very proud of her."

He could almost see the conflict between the
desire to administer another put-down to his
daughter and the instinct to appear praiseworthy
chase themselves around Marco's face, but the
older man, as Eric had expected, went with political expediency. You didn't get to where Marco was
on talent alone. A career was built on a network
of relationships. Prima donna attitude might make
good news stories, but professionalism and tact
built a career that lasted.

"Yes, I am," Marco said, gazing into Eric's eyes
with deep sincerity. "I only wish her mother could
have been here to see her."

Eric felt rather than saw Lydia dart an angry glance at her father, hating him for his hypocrisy. Eric sent out the tiniest tendril of Power, willing someone to appear who could end this deadlock before Marco could resume taking Lydia apart again.

"Marco—darling! I've been trying to get you alone all night. Hello, Eric—you were wonderful this evening. You must come and play for us some time soon. Now, this won't take a moment—" The tall grey-haired woman—Eric had spoken to her earlier, but didn't remember who she was—expertly claimed Marco for her own and led him off. As Eric had hoped, Marco was too much a manipulator to want to carry on abusing Lydia with witnesses present. That sort of emotional torture worked best when no one suspected it.

Well, I suspect it. For a moment he was tempted to cast a *geas* on Marco that would keep him from ever being cruel to Lydia again, but Dharinel had emphasized, over and over, that use of the Power was like a stone thrown into a still lake—ripples spread out from every action, and the smallest uses of Power could have the largest—and most unforeseen—consequences. Unless he was certain of what would happen, he'd better leave the matter alone—at least magically.

Eric glanced at Lydia, who favored him with an effortful smile before turning blindly away. He knew he hadn't done much to help, but at least he'd done something. And undoubtedly Marco Ashborn would be jetting off to some exotic foreign city soon to leave his daughter in peace.

For a while. But maybe a while will be enough.

❖   ❖   ❖

After a few minutes more, Eric was able to make a graceful exit from the Artists' Reception and head over to the student party in the dorms. The celebration there was a lot noisier and a lot more honest—everybody was blowing off steam, filled with relief at having gotten through the all-important Winter Concert without absolute disaster.

There was a "No Alcohol" rule for the dorms, honored except by those few who simply had to break any rule just because it was there. But this party was proctored, and after the performance high of the concert, nobody really needed anything other than soda and fruit juice to get really rowdy anyway.

"Hey, Eric!" Jeremy shouted, waving. The young bassoonist was balanced on the end of the battered couch in the Student Lounge, his pale hair damp and standing up in spiky cowlicks. He looked like a goblin-child from a Victorian children's book.

Now where the hell did THAT simile spring from?

"Hey, Jer," Eric said, coming over. There was a big cooler beside the couch. Trust Jeremy to take up a strategic position by the refreshments. He was as savvy in his way as Kayla, Elizabet's young Healer-apprentice, was in hers.

"Have a drop of the pure," Jeremy said, lifting the lid of the cooler and pulling out a bottle of Glacéau.

It was spring water flavored with various fruit essences, and was a great favorite with the elves: Eric's refrigerator at Guardian House was full of it. Eric twisted the cap off and chugged the bottle, relishing the shock of cold. The reception had taken more out of him than he'd thought it would. He felt grimy, like a window so covered with smudged fingerprints that the light barely shone through.

Dharinel told me there'd be days like this. "Nothing comes without a price," he always said. *Being a Bard makes you vulnerable to influences most people never even notice, while at the same time it gives you power most people can never imagine.*

Jeremy handed him another bottle without even asking. "You looked better backstage before we played. So. How many propositions did you get?"

Eric stared at him blankly. *Do you mean that the way it sounds?* Jeremy was 17, but he was short and round-faced, and looked much younger. The boy's face twisted, and for a moment it wore a bleakly cynical expression that Eric had never seen before. "You know. The 'I could do so much for your career with just a little private tutoring' line?"

Funny. Isn't that the phrase Ria used once?

"Oh, you know," Eric said lightly. "The usual nebulous job offers. But nothing like that."

"You're lucky," Jeremy said, then looked guarded, as if he felt he'd ruined his Captain Cool image by saying too much.

If he'd been someone else, Eric would have urged Jeremy to tell him more, to report incidents like that to his Student Advisor. But Eric already knew that offers like that were rarely made openly. It was all interpretation and innuendo, impossible to prove. And the act of bringing the accusation could bring an end to a promising career before it even started.

"Yeah, well," Eric said. "Nobody rides for free. Isn't that what they say?" *Everything comes with a price. Too bad they don't always tell you what it is going in.*

"That's what they say," Jeremy said, obviously relieved that Eric wasn't going to go all over Adult and Role Model on him.

"Hey, Eric!" someone called. It was David, another of the soloists, calling him over to congratulate him on his playing. Eric turned away, the second bottle of Glacéau still in his hand.

He'd only meant to look in at the after-concert party, pick up his jacket, and then go on home. He didn't have any classes tomorrow, or even any rehearsals, but he did have a big assignment in Music Theory that had to get done Real Soon Now, and that meant making time for work instead of socializing.

But the next time he thought to look at a clock—watches didn't work well Underhill, and Eric had never been much for timebinding at the best of times—he realized it was after midnight and the party was starting to break up.

By the time he stepped out onto the street, Lincoln Center was deserted, the cafes and restaurants that abounded in this high-living area mostly closed for the night. If someone wanted a set for New York After The Bomb Dropped, they couldn't pick a better place than right here, right now. Eric shivered, even in the dark-red leather jacket he wore, as he juggled his options. He had to get home somehow. It was too cold to walk, and he hated the subway. The Center was usually a good place to pick up a cab, but since the Mayor's new policy on medallion licenses, cabs were in short supply everywhere. He looked up and down the deserted street, and decided to chance it.

Putting his fingers to his lips, he whistled loudly and shrilly, a few bars of her signature tune forming in his head as he summoned his elvensteed to him. The tune was "God Bless The Child," a Billie Holiday song. He'd named Lady Day for The Lady of the White Camellias, and the song was his surest link to the elvensteed. He felt her acknowledge the call, and a few moments later—far too quickly for a vehicle that had been paying any attention at all to the posted speed limits—he heard the deep growl of Lady Day's engine and saw the gleam of her lights as she suddenly popped visible.

The elvensteed pulled to a stop in front of him and waited, engine thrumming. She looked almost smug, and so she should, having figured out all by herself how to get here while drawing the least attention to herself. If any mortal had enough Talent to manage to glimpse her as she drove by, he wouldn't have seen a riderless motorcycle—and if he had, well, people had a way of editing what they saw until it made sense.

Eric patted her gently on the gas-tank, and heard a ghostly whicker of amusement inside his mind. He climbed aboard, retrieving his helmet and gloves from the back of the saddle and putting them on. As he settled into the saddle, Eric realized that he'd been neglecting Lady Day these past few weeks, taking cabs and subways to school and even walking, and a good run was just what they both needed. A little magic would take care of the cold, and there was nothing on earth more sure-footed—or sure-wheeled—than an elvensteed.

"What do you say, girl? Want to go for a run?" He squeezed the throttle experimentally, and was rewarded with a wail of glee from the elvensteed's engine.

A few turns, and they were headed up Riverside Drive, going north. The enormous bulk of the George Washington Bridge towered above him, and for just a moment, riding through the night, Eric felt a flicker of temptation to just keep on going, let the road take him away from all pressures and responsibilities and everyone he knew. But the thought quickly vanished—not out of any artificial sense of other-imposed responsibility, but because he'd already done that dance in all its many variations. The footloose existence of the open road no longer held any enchantment for him.

I've already done that. It's part of the past, not who I am now. But the past doesn't go away neatly, does it? It's always there, like the key the music is written in.

All unbidden, an image of Ria as he'd seen her—or thought he'd seen her—at the concert tonight rose up in his mind, vivid as a Sending. Unlike the rest of his old life—the drinking, the drugs, the running away—she still had power over him. That was what had been nagging at him all evening, driving him to do everything but think his problem through. Like it or not, he and Ria Llewellyn had unfinished business.

But what? And how? And is all this—seeing her and the rest of it—just what Bethie's old therapist would have called "displaced anxiety"? Juilliard is rough—no secret about that—so maybe I'm just trying to come up with reasons to quit without having to blame myself for quitting.

It was a valid point, and Eric realized he needed somebody to talk it over with. Someone he could tell the whole story to, without editing out the magical parts—a sounding board of sorts. Right now he felt as if an invisible trapdoor had opened up beneath him and left him standing on air.

:Eric. Bard, do you hear?:

It was Kory's voice in his head, and if Eric had actually been driving a motorcycle rather than being a passenger aboard an elvensteed, Lady Day would have gone down and he would have been kissing asphalt.

:Kory?: Eric Sent back. *:Kory—what's wrong? Is it Bethie?:*

:She is well, Eric. But come to us here. We must speak.:

Unbidden, an image formed in his mind, and Eric knew where to go. Lady Day continued northward, much faster now that Eric had a true destination in mind.

Sterling Forest State Park was larger than just the few acres the Faire covered every year. The park was nestled in the gently-rolling Ramapo Mountains—known for centuries to be filled with haunted places and strange creatures, and for good reason. If he hadn't known that NYC was 90 minutes away, Eric wouldn't have been able to guess from the surroundings. He rode through the gates of the park, heading away from the long-gone

Faire encampment—the Faire had already closed two months before—and a few moments later saw the pale flicker of a Portal open before him.

Kory and Beth were waiting for him just inside. At a quick glance, the place where they stood looked just like the park—grass, trees, dark sky above. But the air here was warm and perfumed, the trees were in full leaf and the grass was green and soft and lush. He could see clearly, even into the darkest shadows, and nothing in the mortal world had the rich perfection of the meadows and forests of Underhill.

Kory had shed the glamourie which protected him in the World Above. Now he appeared as himself—an elven knight and Magus Minor, with pointed ears and jewel-bright eyes, dressed in the silk and gold and baroque armor of a warrior of Faery, with a faint glowing nimbus of magic all around him.

Beth was dressed in elven-kenned clothing that was a mix of Earthly and Underhill styles in soft deep greens and russets. She was visibly pregnant now, though the baby wouldn't be born for some months yet—her cheeks were rounder, and in the magic-laden air of Underhill she glowed with the power of Life and Creation. When she saw him she gave him a cocky "thumbs-up" salute, looking pleased.

"Looking good, Banyon."

Eric grinned back. Whatever the reason Kory had summoned him here, the trouble couldn't be as bad as all that if Beth was in such a mood. Of the three of them, Beth had always been the one to see the trouble from farthest away, the one who planned for the future, even when a future for any of them seemed most unlikely.

He glanced toward Kory, and his attention was almost immediately captured by the Sidhe Lord standing beside Kory—one whom Eric had, quite frankly, never expected to see again once he'd left the halls of Elfhame Misthold: Dharinel, Master Mage, Elven Bard, and Prince of the Sidhe. Dharinel looked about as happy as a wet cat.

Eric swung himself off Lady Day's saddle, pulled off his helmet, and bowed formally to his teacher—however much you could let slide in the World Above, in Underhill proper form and due courtesy were absolutely indispensable—before turning back to Kory and Beth. He'd said there was nothing wrong with Beth, which meant the baby was okay too, and Beth's cheeriness seemed to underscore that, but seeing Dharinel here, Eric desperately wanted to know why he'd been called.

"There is trouble in your city," Kory said, looking pretty troubled himself. "We have come to warn you."

"Warn me?" Eric risked a glance at Dharinel. *My city? New York?* Try as he might, he could not imagine his teacher caring whether or not Manhattan sunk into the ocean or flew off into space. There weren't any elves there, and Dharinel thought mortals were a waste of time. "About what?"

Beth started to answer, but Kory put a hand on her arm, silencing her.

"First you must know its history," Dharinel said, glaring in a way that warned Eric not to interrupt, no matter how impatient he got. "As you know,

many centuries ago as mortals reckon time, the
World Above and the World Under Hill lived
together in harmony, until elvenkind was faced with
a harsh necessity: either to seek new lands beyond
the sunset, or to withdraw from the world altogether into the Fairy Lands Beyond.

"This necessity fell upon both Courts, the Dark
and the Light, equally, for all that many believe
that the Unseleighe Sidhe draw much of their form
and power from mortalkind, being shaped in the
image of your fears and hungers—" Dharinel didn't
quite sneer, but Eric was used to that. The ori-
gin of the Dark Court, and the reasons for its
difference from the Bright, was a topic of endless
discussion among the elves, and Dharinel's theory
was a common one.

"And so it was that the Sidhe, Seleighe and
Unseleighe alike, came to the West, planting their
Groves and shaping their Nexuses as they had in
the Old World, gracing the tribes of Men with their
puissance and their strength—in the case of the
Bright Court—and shaping mortals in accordance
with their own base nature—in the case of the
Dark."

Eric fretted, trying not to let it show, but
Dharinel would not be rushed, as he knew from
bitter experience.

"But there were always places that all the Sidhe
avoided, for good and sufficient reason. Places
belonging to neither Court. In some of those places
mortals have built great cities, where their own
natures flourish without influence. Others, mortals
had the good wit to avoid, until recent times. You
have gone to such a place."

New York? Eric thought, even as he boggled at the thought of calling the city "recent"—the Dutch had first settled Manhattan back in the 1600s. Still, he supposed almost four centuries was recent by Underhill standards.

"Yet before you did so, another came here before you, and now, he seeks to take this mortal place and make it his own. This Unseleighe Prince is subtle and patient, and did we openly oppose his works, it might be . . . inconvenient."

"Inconvenient," Eric knew, meant that the network of treaties and promises that bound the Elfhames, and even the Dark and Light Courts, together in an unbreakable web of favors, customs, and obligations, would be severely strained by such interference, maybe even broken. And that would mean a war that nobody in either Court wanted.

"Elves are invading Manhattan?" Eric asked, just to make sure he had it clear. Beth snorted. Well, it did sound kind of funny when you said it out loud.

"One elf," Kory corrected, looking unhappy. "But he is very powerful, very old . . . and very Unseleighe."

"He wishes to build a Nexus there," Dharinel said shortly. "As you know, it requires great power to open a Gate between the Worlds. It is his way that he will seek others to provide it."

"Others like me," Eric said, and surprised a chilly smile on his old teacher's face.

"There are no others like you, Sieur Eric, and I trust that after all I have taught you, you would recognize the traps he would lay for you, and have the mother-wit to run for your life. Others will not, for our legend has become less than a nursery-tale for mortals in this time, and as you know from your own experience in the World Above, many will not believe the evidence of their own senses . . . until it is far too late. And so it has been decided in Council that in order to protect the mortals from the consequences of their own folly, you will carry this warning to the Guardians, and instruct them to take steps to save the mortals under their care from this threat."

"I— But— Wait—you know about the Guardians?" Eric floundered.

Again that look of amusement from Dharinel, as though he were greatly enjoying Eric's discomfiture. "Once we knew them quite well, Bard, though undoubtedly they will have forgotten over the years. Humankind has always had its defenders, paladins of the Light. Some are great warriors, whose exploits are known to all: Launcelot, Roland, Beowulf. Others work in secret, for the knowledge of the forces that they fight would do as much harm to the mortals they choose to protect as those forces themselves. Once we fought side-by-side, brothers on the field of battle. Now they fight alone. But we remember those days, even if they do not. Tell them what you must to arm them against this foe, and warn them well."

Eric sighed, knowing that babbling more questions would only irritate Dharinel when he was in a mood like this, and not get Eric anywhere. Neither Dharinel nor Kory had named the Unseleighe enemy that was causing all this trouble, but Eric knew that to do so in Underhill—and even in some places in the World Above—would be like shouting a warning of their intentions in the Unseleighe Lord's ear. And it wasn't as if Eric would be confusing his new enemy with some *other* Sidhe Lord trying to turn Manhattan into his own private fief.

"Do only that, send them fair warning, and nothing more," Dharinel warned. "Do not let yourself be drawn into the battle against this opponent. It might well be that this is the very thing he looks for to complete his plans, and that your involvement could spell disaster."

"I'll remember that, Master," Eric said.

Dharinel grimaced. "And you will follow your irresolute mortal heart despite anything I may say. I am finished here," he said abruptly. A moment later, he was gone.

Eric blinked at Kory. The young Sidhe smiled, and shrugged sheepishly—a human gesture he'd picked up from Eric—as if to say "you know how he is."

"C'mere, Banyon," Beth said, now that the three of them were alone. She enfolded him in a fierce hug. He could feel the baby pressed between them, a daughter that somehow belonged to all three of them at once.

"God, I've missed you!" she said, letting him go at last. "How are you?"

"I— Well," Eric said, and stopped. How to compress the last two months into a comprehensible tale? He wasn't sure how to bring up the topic of Ria to Beth, either, and he wasn't at all sure this was the right time, anyway. Beth had other things on her mind right now.

"How's the baby?" he asked instead.

"Impatient," Beth said with a grin. She took Eric's hand and placed it against her belly. He felt a flutter of movement against his hand, and stared at Beth, eyes wide.

"Yep, that's her," Beth said proudly.

Hello, little one, Eric Sent gently. He felt a flurry of unfocused response—happiness, eagerness, amusement—and withdrew his hand. Beth's eyes were shining.

"You see how she is," Beth said. "Just wait till she's born—we're going to throw the biggest party Underhill's ever seen!"

And she'll have Power. I can already tell that. And she'll grow up in a world where that kind of thing is understood and accepted. She'll never be an outsider, never have to wonder if she's going crazy because she can see and do things most humans can't.

"Be sure to send me an invitation," Eric said. The thought brought his mind around in a tight circle to the reason Dharinel had called him here. "But right now, this thing with Dharinel . . . it must be something pretty important for him to come all this way," Eric said. *And to care about what happened in the World Above at all.* Another threat, this time not a quarrel between the Sidhe that humans blundered into, but one of the Fair Folk seeking out humans to use them in some plot of his own.

"Yes," Kory said. "It is a matter that is not a new one, I fear. This Lord is very old, and very cunning, and has long blamed humankind for his own misfortunes. But if he seeks human allies now, it is a matter for great concern. But Master Dharinel is right in this, Eric: this must not become your fight. We think he seeks to work through human agents, and so it must be the Guardians' work to protect them. I know you must warn them—but once you have, won't you come back to Elfhame Everforest with us? Surely you have spent enough time in the World Above?"

"Hey, I haven't even gotten up to mid-terms yet," Eric said, trying to downpedal Kory's plea by turning it into a joke.

"Aw, he just doesn't want to leave his new girl-friend, whoever she is," Beth said. "What about it, Banyon? Had any hot dates lately?"

Of all the times for Bethie's erratic Sixth Sense to kick in! It's true there's a woman in my life . . . sort of. But not the way she thinks.

"Too busy studying," Eric said lightly, turning it into a joke once more. "But I've made some new friends. One of them's a gargoyle."

Beth stared at him for a moment before deciding he was serious. "Only you, Banyon!" she said. "A gargoyle? That's a new one on me."

"His name's Greystone. He's a friend of these Guardians. Did you know that my whole apartment building's, well, sort of the equivalent of an Elfhame, only for humans? Everybody who lives there is special in some way, and some of them are actually magicians. Like these Guardians."

"You learn something new every day," Beth said wryly. "But hey, no reason to stand around here like strangers waiting for a bus. Kory brought a picnic. Kick back for awhile and tell us all the news. We've missed you. Not that you were ever the world's best letter-writer, as I recall, and anyway, e-mail doesn't work that well Underhill."

"As if I could figure out how to use it," Eric groaned. "I can barely get the thing to spit out my classwork assignments."

He looked around. Lady Day was getting reacquainted with Beth and Kory's elvensteeds. Since the other two were Underhill most of the time, they'd reverted to their "natural" form as horses. Bethie's mount was a glorious palomino, with a silvery mane and tail and a coat like dark gold. Its mane and tail were braided with tiny silver bells, and Eric remembered the old tales that the Seleighe Court would braid bells into their horses' manes when they went out riding.

Kory's elvensteed was a little more startling—it had the form of a horse, but still retained the markings of its motorcycle form, maroon with black and silver lightning bolts along its sides. Both of them watched Eric with a certain amount of equine amusement.

When he looked back to the others, there was a blanket spread out on the grass, and Kory was kneeling beside a picnic hamper, unpacking savory dishes. The odor made Eric's mouth water—he'd been too nervous before the performance tonight to eat much, and his stomach was reminding him that he'd missed dinner, lunch, and midnight snack as well.

As Kory spread the feast before them, Eric helped Beth to sit down—the pregnancy made her a little awkward at things like that—and for awhile everything was like the best of the old times Underhill when the three of them had been happy together. But the present merriment only served to underscore how much things had changed, as well.

"And after the baby's born," Beth was saying, "we're kind of thinking of taking her around on the Faire circuit. Of course, that depends on . . . things," she finished awkwardly, glancing at Kory.

It wasn't hard for Eric to interpret that glance. Beth had talked about it with him in the time just after she'd first known she was pregnant. Beth wanted a large family, and she was hoping to have more children—*Kory's* children. But even full-blooded elven children were rare occurrences among the Sidhe; it was one of the reasons that the elves were so fond of human children, after all, and spent so much time among them. And children born to a human and a Sidhe were even rarer still. Eric feared that Beth had set her heart on something that was almost impossible, and the worst part of it all was that she knew it.

And being Beth, refused to believe that *anything* was impossible if you wanted it badly enough.

Kory took Beth's hand silently, looking wistful. There was an even greater problem that the young Sidhe Lord faced than the problem of children. Korendil had centuries of life ahead of him—and Beth did not. Right now, it was easy for her to move back and forth between Underhill and the World Above, but eventually she would have to stay Underhill full-time, because humans who stayed in Underhill for too long didn't age . . . until they stepped once more into the World Above. Then, all the years they'd cheated by living in elven lands caught up with them instantly, killing them. So in a few decades—a short time by elven standards—Beth would no longer be able to do the Faire circuit without instantly aging. In fact, Beth wouldn't be able to come back to the World Above at all. But Kory loved the human lands . . . he'd hate to give up visiting them.

And he wouldn't want to visit them without his human lover.

As if he knew what Eric was thinking, Kory glanced hopefully at Eric. They both wanted children. Kory didn't want to lose Beth to death and age in an elven eyeblink. Both problems seemed equally insurmountable.

And the impossible was supposed to be his specialty.

A reputation is a terrible thing, Eric thought, looking back at Kory. *When nothing's ever been done before, how come everyone looks at me? But I'll find a way*, Eric decided, with sudden determination. *I'm supposed to be this great magical Bard. What good is that if you can't help the people you love?* And then, a wisp of inspiration: *I bet Ria would know about the children. . . .*

Eric forced a smile. He clasped Kory's shoulder companionably. "Don't worry so much about the future, Kor'. It gets here no matter what you do."

"Yeah," Beth said. "And *I'm* the one that's going to be having the baby. All you have to do is pace outside the delivery room door looking worried. And think of names for her."

"She will be a great warrior and Bard," Kory said seriously. "We should name her Maeve. Queen Maeve was a great warrior in the human lands of long ago."

Beth laughed, and the moment of sadness

passed. "Maeve, it is, then. Who knows? Maybe someday Maeve Kentraine will have her own rock and roll band!"

At last it was time for Eric to go. Time in Underhill ran parallel to World Above time this close to a Gate, and though tomorrow—today, rather—was Saturday, Eric still had studying to do over the weekend. He ought to make time to check in with Jeremy to see how Lydia was doing, too.

He called Lady Day back from frolicking with the other elvensteeds, and reluctantly prepared to depart. He walked Kory a few steps away from Beth, who was gathering up the remains of their picnic and tucking them tidily back into the basket.

"I don't want you to worry about me—or anything," Eric told Kory. "I promise I'll stay out of this Sidhe Lord's way. And who knows what tomorrow may bring?"

" 'Don't borrow trouble, they give so much of it away free'?" the Sidhe quoted wistfully. "A true saying, O Bard. But the future is where mortals live."

" 'Never their minds on where they are, what they are doing,' " Eric misquoted, smiling. "Yeah. I heard all about that from Dharinel, lots and lots. But it's the way we are."

"And I would not change you," Kory said seriously. "Even if I could. Fare you well, Eric. Visit us again soon."

"I will," Eric promised, hugging Kory forcefully. Kory raised his hand in salute, stepping back. Beth blew him a kiss from where she knelt beside the picnic basket.

Eric swung his leg over Lady Day's saddle and reached for his helmet, settling it on his head. The

elvensteed wheeled and turned back the way she'd
come, taking Eric through the Portal and back into
the park once more, into the sudden darkness and
wintery chill.

It was nearly two in the morning when Eric
arrived back at the apartment house, so it was no
surprise that Toni Hernandez's first-floor front
windows were dark, but what surprised Eric was
the sense of *absence* he felt as he walked into the
lobby, as if all the building's tenants—not just the
Guardians—had packed up and left while he'd
been gone.

That's ridiculous. After all, he'd seen a few lights
on the upper floors as he came up the walk. Artists
and writers tended to be a solitary, nocturnal
bunch, given to working in odd scraps of time
stolen from day jobs. So he knew that there were
still people here. Had to be. It was just that . . .

*It's just that this place feels like Sleeping Beauty's
Castle, all of a sudden.*

It had started to rain on the ride back—thick
slow drops on the edge of becoming snow—and
Eric rode Lady Day right into the courtyard, leaving the elvensteed to find her parking spot while
he rushed inside. His leathers had turned most of
the rain, but his dress slacks were soaked and his
shoes were wet as well.

Impatient with the usual glacial pace of the
elevator, Eric elected to take the stairs at top
speed. He was panting and out of breath from his
climb by the time he reached the top, but he'd
shaken the fey humor that had possessed him in
the lobby. No matter where his other friends in

Guardian House were tonight, Eric knew someone who was always here and never slept.

"Greystone? Hey, buddy?" Eric called, flipping
on the lights in his living room. He kicked off his
shoes and tossed his jacket aside. It was still the
same mess it had been when he'd left for the
concert at four this afternoon: clothes, CDs, and
empty bottles of designer water scattered around
like the debris of a small whirlwind. Housekeeping
had never been Eric's strong suit, and he supposed
if he was going to keep on living here he'd need
to hire some kind of cleaning service, assuming he
could find one that would pick up and put away
his things . . . before he needed to hire an archae-
ologist to find the bedroom.

*Maybe a house-brownie would like to live here
and do the dishes. They're supposed to come if you
put out a bowl of milk for them, but with my luck,
I'd probably just end up feeding half the neighborhood cats.*

Despite the season, he'd left the living room
window open so that his gargoyle friend would
know he was welcome to come and go as he
pleased when Eric was out. "Hey? Greystone?"
Eric called softly. The curtains billowed, and Eric
heard the soft click of stone against iron as the
gargoyle climbed down from its perch.

"Well, if it ain't O'Banyon," Greystone said, in
his odd mixture of Irish and Bronx. "And how was
the concert, laddybuck? Hmpf—you smell like
you've been rolling in magic." The gargoyle
wrinkled its nose and looked disapproving, much
as if Eric had come home reeking with beer from
the corner speakeasy.

"I took a little trip through the looking glass." Eric shrugged. "The concert went okay, but the ending was a real killer. I'll have the tapes in about a week and you can hear it then for yourself. At least I didn't screw up my solo, so Rector must be spitting nails; half the school saw me on stage and there's nothing he can do about it but give me a fair grade. And something really weird happened tonight—I saw Beth and Kory, and Master Dharinel asked me to pass on a message—and now that I get here, it looks like something really weird has happened here, too. Where is everyone? I kind of need to talk to Toni, but I'm not sure what I'm going to say."

As he spoke, Eric walked into the bedroom. He pulled off his slacks and shirt, and shrugged into one of Bethie's finds: a bathrobe of heavy cashmere. He began to feel warmer almost at once. From there he went into the kitchen and came back with two bottles of spring water. He offered one to his guest—Greystone was already crouched in his favorite spot in front of the TV—and flopped down on the couch, exhausted.

"What sort of a weird thing?" the gargoyle asked, ignoring the rest of Eric's speech.

"Two things, actually. First, I ran into an old friend of mine," Eric said. "Or else it was a really convincing hallucination. Either way I wanted to run it past some friends I could trust. *It's not that I think Ria's out to get me. It's just that I . . . well, I don't know. It's Ria. I never could think straight when I was around her the last time.*

A sudden tactile memory, vivid as a kiss, intruded in Eric's mind: Ria in bed, wearing nothing but a seductive smile, her blond hair fanned out against the red silk sheets as she reached for him. . . .

"Yeah, well. . . ." The gargoyle seemed oddly embarrassed. "Toni and the guys . . . they're going to be out for a while."

Eric looked at him, jolted out of the unbidden erotic reverie by the tone in Greystone's voice. " 'Out.' Is this one of those things that Bard was not meant to know, or can you tell me something more? Dharinel sent me to warn them, so I'm wondering if this is tied up with that." *And did Dharinel pass on his warning too late?*

Greystone shrugged noncommittally. "Might be a false alarm. It just seems that Something's loose in the city, and they're out there trying to find out what. I've seen a lot of cases like this before. Sometimes you never do find out what spooked you. Other times, it's Gotterdammerung with a full orchestra." The gargoyle shrugged again, unable—or unwilling—to tell Eric anything more. "But tell me what your mentor said. Ms. Hernandez will want to hear it directly from you, but it can't hurt to tell me as well. And that way, I can tell her the minute she comes in. You might be asleep, you know."

"More than likely," Eric admitted with a yawn. Now that he was feeling more relaxed, the tension and stress of the earlier evening was catching up with him in the form of an urgent need for sleep. "Well . . ." Eric marshalled his thoughts. "You know how there are Good Elves and Bad Elves?" Unbidden, a scrap of one of his old movies came to the surface of his mind, Glinda the Good, in Oz, asking, *"Are you a Good Witch or a Bad Witch?"* "Well the short version is, it looks like one of the Bad Elves has the idea of moving into New York and setting up a Nexus here."

"Can't be done," Greystone said promptly. "Too much iron—and everything else—here. New York goes down as far as it goes up—did you ever take a good look beneath the surface of the streets? There's a whole city under the city!"

Eric shook his head. "I know. That's why the closest Nexus is up in Elfhame Everforest in Rockland County. But what Dharinel told me is that this guy—he didn't give me a name, but I guess that doesn't really matter—really doesn't like anybody very much, elves or humans, and thinks he can use humans to take over the local territory. To top it off, he's supposed to be pretty powerful. So I'm supposed to tell Toni and the gang to be on the watch for something . . . er, unusually elvish."

"Hrumph. Been down to the Village lately?" Greystone snarked. "But what has this got to do with that old friend you said you ran into tonight? From what you've said, this Master Dharinel of yours doesn't exactly qualify as an old friend."

"Not quite," Eric said, grinning as he tried to imagine his mentor here in his living room hanging out with his new friends. "I don't think the two events are connected, but you never know." Although he doubted that Ria's presence in the city, even if she did mean harm, would be enough to set off the Guardians' alerts in the way that something obviously had. "I told you about a woman named Ria Llewellyn, right?"

"The half-Blood that kept that elf-lord from doing in all the Sun-Descending elves and ended up in a coma?" Greystone asked helpfully.

"That's the one, yeah." Suddenly he couldn't even keep his eyes open. He leaned his head against the back of the couch, half-mumbling with tiredness. "Only I saw her at the concert tonight, and I'm wondering—if I didn't imagine it all—what she was doing there. All her corporate stuff is out in L.A."

"I take it she isn't a music lover?" the gargoyle said drily.

"No. I mean yes—I used to play for her. But . . . I don't know." Eric sighed, and reached up to pull the tie out of his hair. He shook his head, making the long chestnut strands—his natural color, restored by the same elven magic that had once turned it black as a disguise—spill across his cheeks.

"Yes, you do," Greystone said unexpectedly. Eric opened his eyes and looked at his friend in surprise. "You're a Bard. You see into people's hearts. You know whether she's a threat or not."

"But what if I'm wrong?" There, at last, was the thing that had been bothering him all evening, brought out into the open. *What if I'm attracted to her for all the wrong reasons? What if I can't trust my own judgment? Leaving aside, for the moment, what HER reasons were for coming to the concert tonight. What if she's working WITH this Unseleighe guy?*

"Do you think she could fool you that easily?" Greystone asked.

Yes. No. Maybe. Dharinel once said that stage

illusionism and true magic have this much in common—that the glamour only really works if the subject WANTS it to on some level.

I guess it's not really that I don't trust her. I guess, deep down inside, I don't trust myself. Maybe all this growing up makes me nervous. Maybe I'm looking for some way to pack in all this maturity and adulthood and go back to being what I was. Even if that isn't what I want on the surface, who knows what I want underneath? Caity's always saying "your mind is not your friend." Maybe this is what she means?

"No," Eric said with slow reluctance. "Not if I don't want to be fooled."

"You're a Bard now," Greystone pointed out unnecessarily. "That might not have been true the last time you two tangled, boyo, but it is now. 'Trust your feelings, Luke.' "

"So you think I should believe in myself?" Eric asked, yawning again. "Is that the answer, Master Greystone?"

"I think you should go to bed," Greystone said. "You look all in. You can tell me the rest of your troubles tomorrow. Because if there's one thing I *do* know about mortals, it's that they don't function well without sleep or food."

You can say that again, buddy. Eric got to his feet, conscious of how tired he was. Sleep sounded like the best idea anyone'd had in quite a while.

"Don't wait up," Eric said, stumbling toward the bedroom. He heard Greystone chuckle as he closed the bedroom door.

❖   ❖   ❖

He discovered that he was walking through a forest. No, not walking. Almost like swimming; pushing the branches out of his way and pulling his body along afterwards. The slippery black bark was cold and silky against his fingers, reminding him unpleasantly of polished bone. The association was so peculiar that he stopped, holding the branches away from his face as he tried to clear his thoughts. How had he gotten here, to this weirdwood, anyway?

I'm asleep, Eric realized. *Dreaming.*

With the ease of practice, he held himself in the lucid dreaming state, not intending to wake up until he found out what had summoned him here. Was this another warning message from Underhill? Half the elves he knew would have just sent him an e-mail, and Master Dharinel had already told him everything he was going to.

So this must be something else—one of those odd visions-cum-premonitions that Bards apparently got from time to time. But who was warning him . . . and about what?

Ria? But even as he thought the name, Eric realized this was none of her doing. Ria had always been more straightforward than this in her dealings with him. This was something else, and he'd better find out what. Feeling a great reluctance to do so, Eric forced himself to study his surroundings.

The bonewood he was in was lit with the source-less silvery illumination that Eric associated with all things Underhill, but there the resemblance to the familiar Elfhame Misthold ended. Everything around him was in shades of silver—even the bark on the trees was not truly black, but the deep grey of tarnished silver. Swags of what looked like Spanish moss festooned their bare branches. Mist lay on the forest floor like a thick carpet, and in the distance the bone-trees faded to a pale grey in the hazy air before vanishing entirely.

There was no life in these woods. No birdsong, no small scuttling forest creatures, none of the playful life he associated with Underhill. Yet this *was* Underhill, his instincts told him, even if it was an Underhill much different than any he'd ever known.

This must be what Underhill would be like if the elves were all dead. But that can't be. Dharinel and Kory both told me that without the elves, there is no Underhill, just Chaos Lands, so some of the Seleighe Sidhe must be around here somewhere or this place wouldn't have any shape at all.

Cautiously, but with renewed determination, Eric forced himself onward through the dreaming wood. The sense of artifice—of being an actor moving across a well-dressed but artificial stage—was very strong, and Eric wondered once again what purpose had summoned him here. It wasn't that he was in the least worried about being able to defend himself. If things got hairy, he could just force himself to awaken. The dream had only as much power over him as he allowed it to have, but he did feel the need to find out why he was having it, especially coming as it did on the heels of Ria's appearance and Dharinel's warning.

It seemed as if he had walked for hours, when slowly Eric became aware that the character of the weirdwood had changed. He began to hear faint scuttlings behind him—they stopped each time he turned around—and now there were faint ghostly shapes flitting about at the edges of his vision: things with eyes that gleamed like faint red embers. And at last Eric realized why this place seemed so familiar to him.

"The sedge is withered by the lake/and no birds sing."

This was Keats' haunted wood, home of La Belle Dame Sans Merci. With a lagging sense of danger, Eric remembered that the Bright Court weren't the only elves inhabiting Underhill who might be sending him messages. The Unseleighe Sidhe had their home here, too . . . the Dark Court that had been the stuff of human nightmares ever since humankind had crawled out of the caves.

Okay. Fun's fun, but this isn't going anywhere I like. Time to wake up now, Eric told himself.

But he couldn't.

Jeanette Campbell came back to Threshold late that afternoon, and spent several hours in her private lab mixing up enough T-Stroke to waste a large percentage of the population of New York and the five boroughs. When it was finished, she trundled the cart and its several pounds of white powder—all neatly packed in large brown plastic pharmaceutical jars—to the Dirty Lab, where Threshold drones would have the unenviable labor of packaging it up in five-gram doses for the street. There was little need to bother with laboratory protocols or sterile conditions down in the Dirty Lab; it was used mostly for scutwork and mass production, and the people who administered the drugs Jeanette made weren't overly concerned with sanitary conditions or the safety of their users. By tonight, T-Stroke would be the new hot ride in everyone's pocket. By tomorrow morning, Robert would be able to start harvesting the Survivors.

And then they'd start getting an idea of how it worked.

Afterward, too keyed-up to sleep, and not willing to go back to her high-priced high-rise crackerbox, Jeanette went down to her office. Her guitar was waiting for her there in its shiny black case. She sat down in her chair, not bothering to turn up the lights, and took it out, running her fingers over the strings. Maybe a little time spent here would help her shake the headache she'd been running all day. Like many former users, Jeanette scrupulously avoided everything, even aspirin. She forced herself to concentrate on her instrument.

It was acoustic, strung with silver, just like the instruments in all the old legends. Once upon a time she'd thought that would make a difference. Now she knew that all she could reasonably expect from silver strings was a brighter sound and a little decoration. But maybe that was enough.

Music had always been her refuge. When the pain got too bad, when even thinking hurt, she could turn to the discipline of music and wipe it all away. She'd even transposed some old Celtic Harp pieces to guitar, and her fingers moved automatically into one now. Silvery rills of music filled the office, painting a vision of a future in which she could be happy and free, where the person she'd always wanted to be and the person she was would match. Where she wouldn't have to brace herself every time she caught sight of herself in the mirror.

If T-Stroke works . . . if we can figure out how to keep it from killing people . . . what happens then?

Would she take it? It was a long way from 16 to 31. She'd always thought her dreams hadn't changed, but that was before they'd come within reach. Now the thing she'd hoped for most was about to happen, and the thought both frightened and delighted her. The goal that had obsessed her for more than half her life—having Power, real power, invincible power—was almost in her hands. She'd done what she'd always dreamed of doing. She'd found it. She'd found the key to do what the fantasy novels she'd devoured as a teen only hinted at—a way to unlock the Talent that would set her apart from everyone else, make her special.

Give her revenge.

The music in her hands turned darker, mocking and warning at the same time. What revenge would ever be enough for all the disasters of her life? Where could she begin?

A sudden flood of light blinded her, and she pressed her hand against the strings, stifling the music into silence. Past and present jangled against each other, and she almost flinched before she remembered where she was. Jeanette had a lot of problems these days, but getting ambushed and beaten up wasn't one of them.

"I thought I'd find you here."

"It's customary to knock," she said icily. She winced at the light, squinting up through the glare to find Robert standing in the doorway of her office. She'd used to respect Robert in a way—he was so much more ruthless than she'd ever dared to be—but lately that respect had faded. She'd never really trusted him to protect her from prosecution the way he'd promised he would back at the beginning, but now she didn't even trust Robert Lintel to have his own best interests at heart. He was in danger of believing his own publicity, she realized with a flash of insight.

But he was still a dangerous man. And right now, he wanted something from her. She knew the look on his face, the one that told her he was going to try to talk her into something—but so close to her goal, Jeanette was feeling a little bit forgiving, and was pretty sure she'd agree to whatever he came up with. It was the easiest thing to do, and in her own peculiar fashion, Jeanette had always taken the easy way.

"They're packaging the stuff up now," she said before he spoke. She set her guitar back in its case. Robert always made fun of her music. There wasn't any power to be gained from music. Or so he thought.

But a protest song can start a riot. End a war . . . or start one. Great musicians live forever.

"That's great," Robert said warmly, oozing false charm from every pore. It must work on his bosses, whoever they were, but it'd never worked on her. And Robert was too self-obsessed to see that. "We'll be able to start distributing the stuff tonight, and have our next batch of subjects rounded up by the end of the week. I wanted to talk to you about developing protocols for the second round of tests, the ones on the Survivors."

"Sure." Jeanette grinned without mirth. "But don't you think it should wait until we have guinea-pigs to test it on? Anyway, I'm not sure what re-dosing the Survivors will do. Maybe it'll just kill them. In terms of practical applications you've got to remember that this stuff wears off fairly quickly. Twelve hours and it's out of the system—and from what we've seen with the chimps and the first round of people, the overt effects only last for an hour or two."

Robert smirked at her, sure he knew things she didn't.

"Well, that's just the thing. We could get started on that second round right now. We've still got that live one from the last round, and we've got plenty of T-Stroke. Why don't you shoot her up again and see what happens?"

The sadistic glee in his voice made her wince inwardly. Jeanette knew that all their human victims were going to be TTD—Tested to Destruction—and that none of them were going to be allowed to survive, but down deep inside somewhere she also thought that they should be treated with respect. Whether they'd chosen to be lab-rats or not, they were heroes. But Robert saw them as nothing more than toys.

And Robert liked breaking toys. She already knew that.

"She's the one who healed herself, right? Fat lot of good that is, for your purposes," Jeanette said grudgingly. She couldn't resist slipping the needle in, even if only a little. What if the only thing this stuff was actually good for was healing impossible-to-cure diseases? Not much power for Robert in that. *Too bad if that's true, party-boy.*

"Yeah. Ram says she had stomach cancer. I was thinking a higher dose might, I don't know—do something else," he said, too casually.

If there was anything Life had taught her, it was that trying to save anyone else only got you hurt. She'd sold folks down the river before. One more couldn't matter. Jeanette shrugged. "Worth a try, I suppose. And if her head explodes we can dump her somewhere like all the others. Okay. Tell Beirkoff to get her prepped and bring her down to my lab and we'll see what we can do. Oh, and Robert? Strap this one down real good, okay? I don't want to spend tomorrow cleaning the place up."

Robert grinned and saluted her from across the room, a faux-macho gesture he'd picked up from some movie or other. Jeanette grimaced—she'd always particularly detested it. But Robert didn't notice. He'd already gotten what he wanted.

After he left, she rummaged through her paper files until she found the one she was looking for: the intake report on Ellie Borden, the sole survivor of the first run of trials. The black hooker'd had the lowest body weight of any of the test subjects, and so the dose she'd gotten in the cells had been proportionately higher.

Was that the reason she'd survived? Would a small dose of T-Stroke kill, but a large one liberate the mind from its fetters?

We're going to get a chance to find out, aren't we? Jeanette thought with grim humor. Her headache was worse than it had been all day. *See? You're going to do someone else down. And it doesn't hurt at all, does it?*

❖   ❖   ❖

They had to let her go. God had given her a second chance, and Ellie Borden didn't intend to waste it.

She knew she was in some kind of trouble. Her head was clear for the first time in many, many months, the disease wasn't hanging over her head like a flaming sword, and she knew that wherever this place was, she was not in the hands of the police.

Everyone she'd met here had treated her with distant kindness. A little while after she'd woken up whole and well, alone in that padded cell, a woman wearing a black uniform had come and escorted her to a bathroom with a shower, given her a rolled towel that contained a toothbrush and soap, and told her to wash. When she'd stripped, she found two disks glued to her skin—one under her ribs, another high on her back—but try as she might, she could not pick them free, and the guard had ordered her to get into the shower and stop wasting time. The water was hot, and beneath its stream Ellie had luxuriated in being clean, really clean, for the first time since she'd been turned out onto the streets.

She might still have been in the shower if the woman hadn't told her to come out. When she had, she'd found her clothing was gone, and she'd been given a set of blue surgical scrubs to wear, and a pair of soft slippers for her feet. The connection between these clothes and those given to prison inmates did not escape her.

"Where am I? Can you tell me that? I know this isn't the Tombs[4] . . . I need to get out of here. I promise I won't cause any trouble."

[4] The Manhattan Security Detention Facility.

But the woman had only stared at her with hard-eyed pity, and refused to answer any of her questions.

After her shower was over, Ellie was taken down a long white corridor to yet a third cell. It was an improvement on the first two: it had a fold-out table, a chair bolted to the floor, a bunk, and a sink and toilet, like an upscale designer version of a prison cell. There were cameras in all four corners of the ceiling, and an overhead fluorescent light protected by a metal grid. The room had no windows, and she heard the heavy sound of multiple locks being thrown as the door closed behind the guard.

That was when she really began to be afraid. Because this place was like a prison, but it wasn't a real, official prison. And that meant that the people running it could just make people . . .

Disappear.

After awhile—not more than an hour, Ellie thought—an Indian man in a white lab coat came in, accompanied by another guard and a trolley full of medical equipment.

"Where am I?" she'd asked them, hating the sound of terror she heard in her own voice. "I know this is . . . could you just tell me what you want? Please?"

"If you'll just cooperate, I'm sure all your questions will be answered later. This is just a routine medical examination, Ellie. We want to know how you're doing," the doctor answered. His voice was soothing, professional, but Ellie had taken a look at the sleepy-eyed guard standing behind the man in white and stopped asking. The guard was a tall bronze-skinned man, in the same black uniform the guard who had taken her to the shower had worn. The nametag on his shirt said ELKANAH—a Biblical name, a good name, but she didn't think Elkanah was a good man. He had a full equipment belt—nightstick, walkie-talkie, gun, pepper spray, handcuffs—and there was something about him that made Ellie submit to the doctor's examination in passive silence. It had been very thorough and puzzling to her, though she was drearily familiar with medical procedures from the time she'd started getting sick. The doctor removed the two silver disks—spraying the places they were stuck to her with something very cold first—and somehow that frightened her even more, as if she'd suddenly lost whatever value she might possess in these strangers' eyes.

Once the doctor was finished—he'd taken blood samples, hooked her up to an EEG and an EKG, and a few other things—he let her dress again.

"Someone will feed you soon."

The words were meant to be kindly, she knew. He hadn't had to say anything, after all. But they'd only made her feel even more like an animal in a cage. She hadn't been able to look at him when he left.

In a few minutes, another of the hard-faced guards had brought her a sandwich and coffee, obviously from a local deli. She'd taken one sip of the creamed and sweetened coffee but found it gaggingly bitter and poured it into the sink, using the cup for water instead. She'd thought she was too frightened to eat, but instead she was ravenous, finishing the sandwich in only a few bites and wishing there were more.

Then all there was to do was pray, huddled up on her bunk with the blanket wrapped around her shoulders, hoping against hope that what she feared so much wasn't the truth.

The sound of her cell door opening jarred Ellie awake—somehow, despite everything, she'd fallen asleep. What she saw in the doorway made her cringe back against the far wall. Elkanah was back, this time with a white guard who looked just as intimidating. They were wheeling a hospital gurney with them. Four thick leather straps were laid loosely across it.

"Please . . ." she heard herself whimper.

"Get on the table." The white guard spoke. His voice was harsh and indifferent. Ellie shook her head, too frightened by the sight of the straps to comply. "Do it," he said, a thread of irritation coloring his voice.

"Hey, Angel. You gotta understand people's limitations," Elkanah said. "Now, Miss," he went on, speaking to Ellie for the first time. "Nobody's going to hurt you. We have to take you somewhere. You have to get up here on this gurney. Can you do that?"

To Ellie's horror, she began to weep. She shook her head, trying to explain how afraid she was, how unfair it was that this should happen now, just when a miracle had turned her life around—had given her a life instead of the death she had expected.

Elkanah took no notice of her tears as he approached her. He pulled her gently to her feet and removed the blanket from her shoulders, then led her over to the gurney. Before she could react, he had scooped her up in his arms and laid her down on it, and the man he'd called Angel was buckling the straps across her legs.

She began hopelessly to struggle, but Elkanah held her shoulders down and stared into her eyes. "There is no point to this," he said firmly. "Do you understand?"

She'd turned her head away then, giving up, letting them do what they would. Uncontrollable shudders racked her as all four straps were buckled tight. The leather creaked as she breathed. She knew better than to ask for mercy. The streets had taught her that much.

Once she was strapped down, the two men wheeled her quickly through a disorienting series of corridors, until she arrived at a brightly-lit room that smelled of chill and disinfectant. There were two people there waiting for her.

One was a white man in his forties. He wore an expensive three-piece grey suit and looked to Ellie like a lawyer, one of those irritable important people who had inhabited the fringes of her world in the days when she'd been a good citizen. He was frightening, but his companion scared her even more— a short dumpy woman with mouse-colored hair wearing a rumpled lab coat, sneakers, and jeans. She had the pasty complexion of someone who spent all their time locked away from the sun. The woman's eyes were the flat pale blue of the winter sky, and there was no humanity in them.

"Well, this is an improvement over chimps," the man in the suit said. His companion smiled thinly and ignored him.

"Hello, Ellie," she said. "I'm Jeanette Campbell. Do you know why you're here?"

"Oh, for God's sake, Campbell. You don't need to talk to her," the man snarled.

"Of course I do, Robert. That's the whole point of this, isn't it? Lab rats that can talk? If you want data from her, she's going to need a context."

Campbell turned back to Ellie, coming closer to the side of the gurney. Elkanah and Angel had backed away like respectful servants, going to stand beside the door.

"When you were brought in here, you had cancer, and you were addicted to something. What was it?"

"P-Percodan," Ellie managed to stammer. Her mouth felt dry as salt.

"Okay. Percodan's a good drug. Highly effective, highly addictive. But you haven't had any in about four days. How do you feel now?"

"I feel—oh, *please*, let me go! I haven't done anything!" Ellie pleaded, hating herself for begging when she already knew it would change nothing.

"But you *have* done something, Ellie. You've contributed to Science. You see, when you were first brought in, you were given an experimental drug. And now you don't have cancer any more. And you don't need Perc. And we want to know what happened to you. So we're going to give you some more of what we gave you before— intravenously this time. And I want you to tell me everything about what happens to you then."

"If I— If I do that, will you let me go? I won't tell anybody about this, I promise, oh, just let me go, please, let me out of here and I'll never tell, I *swear*—"

"Now, Ellie." Campbell's voice was remote, faintly chiding. "You know we aren't going to let you go. But you don't have any place to go anyway. That's why we picked you. If you cooperate you'll be well treated for the rest of your life. That's more than you could expect on the streets."

But I'm well now! I have my life back! Helplessly, Ellie began to struggle against the straps. Campbell reached into her pocket and produced a needle and a bottle of milky fluid. She swabbed down Ellie's arm with cool efficiency and began probing for a vein.

"How do you know you'll get the same effect with an injection?" Robert said.

"I don't." Campbell sounded almost amused. "What I do know is that this will work faster and more of the drug will reach the brain. And that's sort of the whole point here, wouldn't you say?"

The needle stabbed into Ellie's arm with a lancing pain that seemed to strike at the roots of her soul. Eyes tight shut, she could only moan in protest as Campbell gently squeezed the plunger home, injecting the drug directly into her bloodstream. She felt a rush of warmth so intense it was as if she'd been lowered into a hot bath, and when she tried to open her eyes again, she couldn't.

Once Ellie passed out from the drug, Jeanette glued contact pads to her temples. Their wires led to an electro-encephalograph—an EEG—and instantly the displays lit up, displaying the rhythms of deepest sleep, a sleep verging on coma.

"What do we do now?" Robert asked edgily. "Wait six hours for her to wake up?"

Jeanette leaned back against the counter, watching the green waves of Alpha, Beta, Gamma, and Delta roll across the EEG display behind Ellie's head. Something was happening there, down inside where she couldn't see.

"It should go faster this time," she said absently. "And I gave her twice the dose. What I want to know is, what's she going to be able to do when she wakes up?"

Less than fifteen minutes later, Ellie's eyes opened. She stared around herself wildly, as if she'd forgotten where she was.

"Ellie?" Jeanette leaned over her.

She saw Ellie's eyes widen, as if she were seeing things no one else could. Jeanette reached out to touch her forehead, and in that moment a *pulse*—Jeanette had no other word for the sensation—passed between them.

Jeanette recoiled, and suddenly realized that the nagging headache she'd been fighting since she got up this morning was gone as if it had never existed. "Robert," she said thoughtfully, "come over here. Touch Ellie."

"Why?" Robert said suspiciously.

"It's an experiment." *Because you've got an ulcer and I want to see what happens.*

He did as he was told, clasping her wrist above the strap, then jerking away as if he'd been burned. "What the hell?"

"I bet your ulcer isn't bothering you now," Jeanette said sweetly. Robert shot her a narrow look, not pleased.

"My headache's gone, too. It makes sense. Ellie, what do you feel?"

"Hurt," the woman moaned, in a tranced petulant voice. "It hurts. I can't let it."

"First she heals herself. Now she can heal others," Robert said thoughtfully. His eyes were alight with a dangerous fervor. "We have to test this." He turned to the waiting guards. "Go find Dr. Ramchandra. Bring him here."

He could not wake himself up—and worse, he'd lost all control over the dream. Helplessly, Eric's dream self pushed on through the forest, surrounded by slinking red-eyed shapes out of nightmare and the Chaos Lands. Where he was going—and what would happen when he got there—were questions he found himself unable to answer, and that powerlessness fed a sort of angry fear.

This isn't right. I'm dreaming and I know it. Why can't I wake up?

At last the unchanging forest of stark bonelike trees began to thin. Eric found himself drifting to a halt at the edge of a clearing. The open space ahead was perfectly round, and the bone trees that circled it gave it the appearance of some sort of temple. The floor of the clearing was carpeted with a silvery moss, as thick and smooth as an expensive carpet, and at one end of the clearing was the first artificial thing Eric had seen in this tulgey wood—the back of an enormous throne, its high back blocking the occupant (if any) from Eric's sight.

The strange throne was as black as the trees, and

seemed at the same time to be both insubstantial and terribly solid, as if perhaps it were forged from something alive that hadn't finished growing yet. Eric knew now that this dream was a message, a warning—but of what? And from whom?

Or was it a trap that had somehow penetrated Guardian House's defenses instead? The fear he'd begun to feel when he lost control of the dream blossomed into outright panic. As he struggled to wake, the throne began to turn, slowly, so that in moments Eric would be brought face to face with its occupant. Somehow, Eric knew that would be a disaster of an even greater magnitude than his present situation, one that he must avert at all costs.

With all his strength he called upon the Bardic Gift within him, setting the bright humanity of his music against this ghostly moribund wood of silver and shadows. He built in his mind an image of his own safe bedroom in Guardian House, its walls garlanded with the invisible wards of familiarity and good wishes.

You have no power over me! I reject you! I dismiss you! Go AWAY!

It worked.

Eric struggled upright in his own familiar bed, gasping with relief. Not a trap, not a warning, it had been a particularly vivid nightmare, nothing more after all. He stared around at the walls of the familiar bedroom, imprinting its images on his mind, forcing himself to breathe deeply and slowly, banishing fright. It was still night outside. Despite the fact that he seemed to have spent hours in the dream-wood, he'd probably only been asleep for a few minutes.

Can't sleep after that. He flung back the covers and swung his legs out over the side of the bed. His feet sank into the fluffy flokati rug and he wriggled his toes appreciatively. He remembered that sometimes in the old days, Bethie'd had nightmares like this (though nothing, a small voice inside told him, could be quite like this), and when she had, they tended to come in chains that destroyed a whole night's sleep. Elizabet had always said that the best thing to do was make a clean break with the dreaming state—get up, move around, have a cup of tea, connect with the waking world—before trying to sleep again.

Tea sounded like a good idea right now. He wondered if Greystone were still in the living room. Maybe the gargoyle would like a cup as well.

Eric had left the curtains open when he went to bed, hoping that the morning sun would wake him before he slept the day away. As he headed for the kitchen, he glanced casually back that way, wondering if it was raining outside. There was an odd glow shining in; probably the reflection of one of the skyscrapers off the clouds. . . .

It wasn't.

He ran to the window and stared out, unable to believe what he was seeing. New York was gone.

No, not gone. Worse. Blasted to rubble, the twisted remains of the familiar Upper West Side buildings looking like the Judgment Day aftermath of nuclear war.

And out of their midst, a glowing tower, impossibly tall, rose in evil triumph over the ruined city. He felt a wrenching shock—

And then there was brightness, and Eric was

struggling against something that wrapped him in inexorable unbreakable bonds. . . .

Eric awoke again—this time for real. The sun was high in the sky—that was the light—and he was wrapped tightly in the sweat-soaked bedsheets that had wound around him during his nocturnal struggles.

A dream. It had all been a dream, the weirdwood forest and his first awakening. Still gasping with the dream-induced panic, Eric struggled free of his bedclothes and ran to the window. All was as it should be. Everything was normal—wintery trees and pale December sky. No devastation. No dark elven tower raised by Unseleighe power to rule over what was left of the New York skyline.

Unsteady with relief, he staggered back to the bed and sat down heavily, waiting for his heartbeat to slow from its frantic racing. The dream and its aftermath of false waking faded, its insistent nightmare reality becoming less urgent by the moment. He was safe. New York was safe.

But if Toni and the others saw—felt—anything like my dream, no wonder they're all out running around trying to round up the unusual suspects.

But had they? Did the dream—vision, premonition, whatever—have anything to do with whatever was alerting the Guardians? Or was it a message meant for him alone?

Of course, like Freud says, sometimes a cigar is just a cigar.

The joke fell flat, even in his own mind. Whatever it was that had happened to him, Eric couldn't afford to just shrug it off. In the world of elven magic that he lived in, such things were never just innocent nighttime fantasies ralphed up by the collective unconscious. They were warnings—even if the warning came muddled and coded in symbols he couldn't decipher just yet.

He'd have to pass on Dharinel's warning to one of the Guardians as soon as he could, and do his level best to convince the Guardians this was something really serious. Somehow Eric knew that *that* wasn't going to be a lot of fun.

The trouble was, the employees of Threshold were a generally healthy bunch. All Dr. Ram could come up with to test Ellie on were some mild allergies, a cold, a few strained muscles.

At Jeanette's insistence, they'd unstrapped Ellie's chest and legs and raised the back of the gurney up into a sitting position: Ellie could hardly escape, and her new powers seemed to have no aggressive capabilities. In the face of human pain—or even mild distress—Ellie could do nothing but react, healing the injured party as quickly as possible. She seemed entirely without the capacity of self-preservation, a totally vulnerable creature.

It'd be funny if it weren't so flaming annoying. I finally get a lab rat who CAN talk, and she won't say anything! If Ellie Borden had any insight into the process that had gifted her with these powers, she was doing a good job of keeping it to herself. In fact, the second dose of T-Stroke seemed to have reduced her to little more than an animal . . . an animal who could work miracles.

Robert was insistent that they find something that could really challenge Ellie, and they lucked out with one of the lab techs—Donaldson had spilled industrial solvent all over his arm the previous week. Fortunately he was at his desk, within easy reach, so Jeanette sent the two guards up to escort him down to the Lab. When Dr. Ram unbandaged his arm down there in the lab, the ulcerated skin was purple and weeping, an ugly sight. If Donaldson hadn't been such a Type-A control freak, he'd have been home on medical rest with an injury like that.

As soon as he'd come through the door Ellie had started to whimper and reach for him. Jeanette was fascinated. The girl reacted to the presence of the sufferers as if someone were jabbing her with a red-hot poker—as if, in fact, she felt their pain more keenly than they did.

There was a word for that, Jeanette knew. Empathy. But what Ellie had was light-years beyond healing touch. Whatever was wrong, she fixed it. When they brought Donaldson over to her, all Ellie had to do was touch him, not even near the injury, and within seconds the skin on his arm was pink and healed.

"What's all this?" The tech looked bewildered, staring from Ellie to the healthy new skin on his arm.

"Just an experiment in Healing Touch," Jeanette said quickly. Donaldson was a good soldier. He wouldn't ask questions. "You've been a great help. My department will get in touch with you later about filling out an incident report. It'd be great if you kept this to yourself until then, okay?" With an arm around his shoulders, she urged Donaldson from the lab and back into the arms of the Security who'd walk him back to his own turf. There'd be some gossip, she knew, but it wouldn't go far. Threshold's corporate culture didn't encourage idle gossip about its projects.

"This is great—great," Robert muttered, ignoring the byplay with Donaldson completely. "How much more can she do?"

"Do you want me to shoot someone so you can find out?" Jeanette asked, closing the door behind the tech.

She saw Robert start to agree, then catch himself. Yes, Robert would like that just fine, but Jeanette suspected it would play hell with employee loyalty.

Just then she had an idea.

"Does anybody know where Lawanda is? She ought to be here now. One of you guys," she said to the hovering Security. "Go get her."

Lawanda Dupre was Jeanette's personal charity case. She had terminal ovarian cancer, and had come to Threshold through one of Robert's other test programs—Jeanette didn't know where he'd found her and had never actually cared enough to ask. When the test had run its course, Robert was going to cut her loose, but something about the woman had struck a spark in the wasteland of Jeanette's soul, and she'd offered to continue running a private test program of her own with Lawanda, strictly under the radar. She was the one who'd come up with the idea of Lawanda working as a cleaning lady in the Black Labs, and Robert had no complaints of the arrangement.

Neither did Lawanda. Without the morphine,

heroin, and methamphetamine cocktail Jeanette provided, she'd be lying somewhere in a welfare bed, dying in agony. With the twice-daily injection, she was still able to work. Robert thought the research might be a way to produce another kind of super-soldier: impervious to pain, oblivious to wounds. Jeanette didn't really care. Treating Lawanda was one of the few things she did at Threshold that made her actually feel good about herself.

There was no denying that the drugs Jeanette gave her shortened the woman's life. But they improved its quality, and let her die with dignity. That was more important, though Jeanette knew the FDA would hardly agree.

After a short wait, Angel appeared, herding Lawanda before him. The woman moved at a painfully slow shuffle. She was in her early forties, and looked sixty. The injections could mask the symptoms, but all the drugs in the world couldn't cure the disease.

Ellie began to moan and keen before Lawanda had even gotten all the way into the room. Interesting. Jeanette knew that the cleaning woman was in very little pain—if any—but Ellie seemed to feel the presence of the cancer itself, not the pain of its victim.

"Did you want me for something, Dr. Campbell? It isn't time for my shot yet. You aren't going to stop those, are you?" Lawanda asked anxiously.

"No, Lawanda. Of course not. We just want to try something new in addition to the shot. It won't hurt, I promise you. I just want you to come over here and let Ellie touch you."

Lawanda Dupre laughed cynically. "You trying faith healing on me now, Doctuh Campbell?"

"Maybe." Jeanette smiled. "Just come over here."

Ellie strained against the restraints that still held her to the bed, reaching out toward Lawanda. The older woman approached her cautiously. "Sistah, what are you doing here?"

"Let me—just let me—please, it hurts so much," Ellie groaned. Her hand darted out, fastening over Lawanda's emaciated wrist like a clamp.

There was a sudden spark where the two women's flesh met, an ozone-like tang in the air. Lawanda's face had gone slack, as if in a sudden rush of ecstasy, while Ellie's was contorted like that of a saint seeing God. Everything but Lawanda had ceased to exist for Ellie. That much was plain. But what did that *mean*?

"Something's happening," Robert said in a low excited voice.

"No force, Sherlock," Jeanette muttered back. Whatever was happening now, it was on a much greater scale than the previous healings. This time, Ellie's struggle was something Jeanette could almost see—a palpable force conjured into the little room.

Jeanette tore her gaze from the tableau of the two women and looked at the clock. The long red second hand swept magisterially around the dial. A minute passed. Ninety seconds. Longer than any of the previous healings.

There was a faint groan from the bed. Ellie fell back, limp, releasing Lawanda's hand. The cleaning woman staggered away from her, blinking in astonishment. Jeanette could see that Lawanda's eyes were clear, the yellow tint gone from the corneas. She looked years younger, and even stood straighter.

"Lord have mercy! I— What did she *do*, Dr. Campbell?"

"I don't know," Jeanette said slowly. Ellie had healed Lawanda—but how? Cellular degeneration at that level couldn't be reversed. This wasn't like the burn—not a case of speeding up what the body had the power to do anyway.

This was a genuine, bonafide miracle.

Or to put it another way, Jeanette had just seen magic. Real magic.

Robert made an impatient gesture, and Angel stepped forward again to usher Lawanda from the room. She went quietly, glancing back a few times at the woman on the bed.

Ellie still didn't move. Filled with a sudden awful suspicion, Jeanette moved over to the gurney. Gingerly, she reached out to touch the girl.

Ellie's skin was already cold to the touch, and the skin beneath the blue coverall lay slack over withered flesh. There was no pulse.

"She's dead." And oddly, the realization gave Jeanette a faint pang of guilt.

"Well, hell." There was only self-centered regret in Robert's voice.

SEVEN:

LIGHTNING IN A SIEVE

Aerune hated the Iron City, hated the World Above, hated the Mortal Kind, even as he planned to bend it and them to his will and his vengeance. His flesh crawled in the presence of the ferrous metal that the humans filled their world with, diminishing his powers considerably and making the use of magic an uncertain thing. But there were some prizes worth any amount of suffering, and the ability to own the Gift of a human Bard was one. Urla had told him that somewhere within this city mortals who lacked the Gift were given it. Now Aerune wanted to see for himself.

The cloak of silk and shadow that concealed him

from mortal eyes also gave him some protection from the iron that clogged the very air, but he could not long remain here without dwindling away to a wraith. Some elven gifts, however, were not hampered by the world the mortals had fashioned for themselves. A darker shadow among the shadows, Aerune sifted through the minds within the building known as Threshold Labs.

Once he had the power to open his own Nexus, he could spend as much power as he needed to in shaping this city to his ends, conjure serpents and nightmares to feed upon its populace. At the hem of his cloak, even now, a faceless chittering mob of his servitors waited to do his bidding.

At first he found only deception and fear, which pleased him, though the first minds he touched held only small malice. But though they knew little, they knew there were secrets to find, and so, patiently, Aerune sifted through their witless babble.

At last he found what he sought. A mind dark and fragrant with overreaching ambition and sublime cruelty: *Robertlintel.* Through this mind, Aerune learned of an elixir which could wake the dreaming spark of magic in mortal hearts, raise the Power that Urla had told him of and make mortals into living Nexuses. Aerune learned with approval and delight of *Robertlintel's* adventures in discovery—how the elixir had killed or maddened all but two upon whom it was tried, one of whom had died by his own hand, and yet this mortal lordling still persevered. He meant to spread his drug throughout the streets of this city, and harvest for his own any who displayed the Mage-gift.

But that cannot be. Such useful mortals are mine.

Drawing upon his power, Aerune summoned all those creatures of his Dark Court who had the power to walk these streets: the gaunts and boggins, the redcaps and phookas, trolls, goblins, Bane-Sidhe, all the dark fellowship of the Unseleighe Court, those creatures twined closer to mortal man than any lover, for Man was their prey.

"Go," Aerune said to his followers. "Follow those who go from this place with the Mage-elixir. Find those in whom the Power kindles brightly, and bring them to me, for they are mine. Feast as you will, slay whom you will, so long as you succeed in this one thing."

There was a swirling in the air as the infernal host Aerune had gathered about himself vanished to their task. The business of following a handful of men through a city of teeming millions was a simple one to creatures with powers such as they possessed. No one of the human lordling's minions would escape their hunters, nor would any to whom they gave the elixir be overlooked. Aerune turned his attention back to the curdled minds within the building's walls.

Robertlintel's alchemist now administered her elixir to the last survivor for the second time, and Aerune relished the victim's despair, as well as the more subtle bouquet of emotions in the mind of the alchemist. The power the elixir had woken was one of healing, and Aerune watched as, ignorant of the necessities of the gifts that had been woken so powerfully into life within her, *Ellieborden* let herself be sent down into death by the mortal lord and his minion.

Aerune smiled, reconciled to the discomfort of the Iron City by the sight of the triumph almost within his grasp. The children had broken their toy. That was good. Because like all children, they would soon want a new one. . . .

His day having been thoroughly spoiled for him by his unsettling nightmare and the prospect of explaining things to Toni Hernandez, Eric moped around the house until he realized that was what he was doing, then went for a walk. He tried Toni's door on the way out, but she was still out, or else not answering it.

When he hit the street, the cold was a shock, and he slitted his eyes against the light. The raw December day at least gave him something else to focus on besides the assignment still lying undone on his desk. The end of the semester was in two weeks, and the coursework was piling up with all the time he'd been spending on rehearsals. He was going to have a lot to keep him busy over the next fortnight.

And after that? His imagination shied away from the thought of the holidays like a skittish colt. For too many years, Christmas had been a cheap apartment and an expensive bottle: a holiday that everyone else but him seemed to celebrate with their families, whether biological or otherwise. Eric hadn't seen his own parents since the day he'd left home, and for years he hadn't felt any lack there. But the sense of unfinished business that had brought him back to Juilliard was tugging at him there, too, and he knew that sometime soon he was going to have to work up the courage to face the last of his personal demons. *One way or another.*

He still had the next month to get through first, though. Christmas . . . alone again. For a time, Kory and Beth had changed all that, though neither Christmas in hiding nor Christmas Underhill was anything like a Charles Dickens novel, the Sidhe having no concept of Christmas and very little of seasonal festivals. He *could* go back to Underhill for the holidays, but managing the temporal transitions back and forth from here to Underhill with any degree of temporal accuracy was often difficult; if he went to visit Beth and Kory in Elfhame Misthold over the holidays, he had no guarantee that he'd be back before Groundhog Day.

And this is something I've got to do on my own, or I might as well just chuck it now and go back to Underhill for good. That meant Christmas alone once more, and it was surprising how much it hurt. No wonder the suicide rate went up in December.

None of which solved his even more immediate problems. Seeing Ria at the Winter Concert seemed as if it had happened a million years ago, not last night, and somehow, she—or her doppelganger—didn't seem like quite so urgent a problem in the face of astral sojourns to the Night Lands, an invading elf-lord, and a bunch of wizards on Yellow Alert.

He rambled down familiar streets, past Korean groceries, Italian delis, boutiques and antique stores. The streets were full of his neighbors—as much as any place in New York could be said to be a neighborhood—and if the faces weren't familiar, the dogs were. Everybody in New York seemed to have dogs—he saw the woman with the three enormous German Shepherds (all bouncing around and tangling their leashes together), the professional dog-walker managing two Great Danes and half a dozen little fur-balls with ease and efficiency, and the man in the grey suit who walked his Himalayan cat twice a day. Eric stopped to greet her; she sniffed his fingers with ladylike disdain before continuing on her way.

New York is really like a village, I guess. A really big village with about twelve million people in it. A few thousand years ago there weren't that many people on the entire planet. There hasn't been a city this big and this complex since the time of Ancient Rome.

But Rome was long gone, and if he were a pessimist, Eric would think that New York was going the same way. In his dream, there'd been nothing left but ashes . . . and the goblin tower.

Don't think about that. It was a dream, nothing more.

The walk cleared his head, and after an hour or so he turned conscientiously back toward Guardian House. He decided to stop along the way to pick up a peace offering—though why he should feel the need to make peace with Toni was something he didn't really understand.

Maybe I feel guilty for adding one more thing to her workload? I know this Unseleighe Lord isn't my fault, but sometimes it seems that wherever I go, trouble follows.

He spotted a familiar sign on the street ahead, and turned toward it. Sanctuary. And a chance to warm up—he'd gotten thoroughly chilled on his ramble.

Bread Alone was one of Eric's favorite places in his new neighborhood. It had the look and feel of one of those old Lower East Side neighborhood bakeries from the turn of the century, the kind of place where you could stop in for coffee and a bagel and to catch up on neighborhood gossip, with a painted pressed-tin ceiling, black and white marble floor, and a few antique cast-iron tables and chairs nestled into the corners.

He'd just walked inside and taken a deep lungful of the warm heady vanilla-and-baking-bread smell when a familiar voice hailed him.

"Well, if it isn't the Pied Piper."

Eric turned toward the voice. Jimmie Youngblood was sitting at one of the tables, a large styrofoam container of coffee in front of her. She was off-duty, dressed casually in jeans and a black leather jacket worn over a plain white T-shirt. She waved him over, smiling.

"Haven't seen you since the party," she said when he'd sat down. "How are you settling in?"

"Some days are better than others," Eric admitted. "I never realized how much time and energy school can take up. It's different when you're a kid, I guess."

She studied him critically. Though her flawless bronze complexion was more forgiving than lighter skin might be, Eric could see that Jimmie was tired—bone tired.

"You're not much more than a kid yourself," she said. "Or are you using a little of that Bardic Magic to shave a few years off?"

"I'm older than I look," Eric admitted cheerfully. "At least inside. And I'm starting to think that's where it counts. If your body's twenty-five and your mind . . . isn't, the mind is what counts, I guess."

"Ain't it the truth," Jimmie admitted with a long sigh. "Double-shifts and all-nighters were a lot easier when I was twenty. Places like this . . . I come here to re-charge. Look around. Have you noticed that everyone's happy here?"

Eric looked around the tiny bakery. Jimmie was right. The girl behind the counter, the older man (probably her father) transferring pastries from the cooling racks to the case, the patrons waiting patiently for their orders to be filled, even the Gothamites seated at the other tables with morning papers and breakfast, all looked contented.

"Maybe it's the Christmas spirit?" he suggested.

Jimmie grimaced. "Christmas spirit is overrated. Take it from someone who's on the streets eight hours a day. No, this place is like this year round. It sounds kind of stupid and New Age, but this is a happy place."

"You're right," Eric said with surprise. He'd found places like this in the human world before, but they'd usually been places touched by at least a hint of Sidhe enchantment. He lowered his shields cautiously and took a peek, but found no trace of elven magic here, only the happy contentment of people honestly enjoying simple pleasures. "I guess that's one of the reasons I ended up here today."

"Rough week?" Jimmie said sympathetically. "I know you had that concert thing last night. How did that go?"

Eric thought back to the hot lights and the watchful audience, remembered the soaring feeling of *rightness* as he wrapped them all up in his music, the joy of playing with an ensemble of talented musicians. There was no way to put those feelings into words. It almost made up for the downer the reception had been.

"It was okay," he said with a bashful smile. "What really gets me, though, is how people can start out in music because it's something they love, and then forget why they did it. Something they loved just becomes a grind—a duty. It's like they twist all the joy out of it."

"Way of the world, my friend," Jimmie said. "When I started out on the Force— Look, I'm up for another round—let me get you some coffee and something to go on with. You look like you could use it." Before he could answer, she got to her feet and headed over to the counter.

I wonder what she was going to say? Eric thought. One thing that Beth—who'd been Wiccan for as long as Eric had known her—and the Elvenmage Dharinel both agreed on was that there were no coincidences, especially for those who were the least bit sensitive to magic. The more you attuned yourself to the invisible currents of Power that underlay everything, the more you moved in harmony with them. *And the more you end up in places like this, having coffee with your fellow magicians.* Though it was hard to remember that Jimmie—practical, down-to-earth, New York street cop that she was—was a magician as powerful as any in Underhill. A line from one of his favorite Gilbert and Sullivan operettas came back to him

suddenly: *"Things aren't always what they seem/
Skim milk masquerades as cream . . ."*

A few minutes later Jimmie was back, balancing two tall containers of coffee and a couple of
Danish wrapped in bakery paper. They were still
warm from the oven.

"I got you decaf, because of what you said at
the party about not drinking coffee much any more
because the Sidhe can't tolerate it."

"You're right there," Eric said. "Before I met
Kory, I couldn't even get up in the morning without that first cup, now I hardly ever touch the stuff.
Caffeine in any form acts like the worst kind of
drug for them—like a combination of cocaine and
LSD. If you're ever having problems with a mad
elf-lord, just pitch a can of Coke at him."

"I'll remember that," Jimmie said, sounding
tiredly amused. "You never know; it might come
up. But they roast and grind their own beans here.
It's a special blend—you won't miss the caffeine.
And Papa Lombardi only makes these pastries at
Christmas. It'd be a crime to miss them."

She handed one to Eric. The golden crust was
fragrant with almond and cinnamon, and when he
bit into it, Eric could taste citrus and currants as
well. His stomach awoke with a growl, reminding
him he'd missed breakfast by several hours, and
he had to restrain himself from wolfing the whole
thing in a few bites. He set the pastry down and
took a sip of the coffee. As Jimmie had promised,
it was rich and fragrant. No sugar, but it didn't
really need any.

"Oh, man," Eric said, around another mouthful
of pastry. "This is heaven!"

"When you're out on the front lines, it's important to remember the little pleasures. Without them, sometimes we forget who we are," Jimmie said gravely.

"Do you have that problem often?" Eric asked. He hadn't meant to ask such a direct question—it seemed almost hostile—but Jimmie didn't seem to mind. She smiled gently.

"I've lost my way a few times," she said. "Even after I became a Guardian. I've seen too many good people go down into the belly of the beast and not come out again. Out here—on the streets—every day good people die, and bad people walk away smiling. And sometimes there's nothing you can do about it."

"Is that why you became a Guardian?" Eric asked.

"That's why I became a *cop*," Jimmie said, correcting him gently. "Being a Guardian came after—sort of a natural extension of the badge, don't you know? When I was a kid, I always wanted to grow up to be Batman. Well, sometimes I wanted to be the Green Hornet, but usually it was Batman. Fight crime and evil, always come out on top. It didn't hurt that my dad and my—my brother were both cops. I just sort of always knew this was where I'd end up. Not the Guardian part, of course."

"Do your folks still live around here?" Eric asked idly, still thinking about Christmas.

Jimmie sighed and shook her head. "Dad caught a bullet about fifteen years back. El—my brother, well, we kind of lost touch. A long time ago."

Even through his shields, Eric could feel the flare of raw pain when Jimmie talked about her brother. She'd said he'd been a cop, and she hadn't said he was dead. But a lot of things could happen, some of them worse than being dead.

"I'm sorry," Eric said, meaning it.

"Don't be. He made his choice, and I made mine. You can't undo the past. But I didn't mean to bring you down. When you walked in here, you looked like you'd lost your last friend."

"Not quite," Eric said. *More like I remembered how few of them there were.* "I had kind of a rough night, and so I went out for a walk this morning to try to clear my head. And from the look of things, I'm not the only one who had a rough night."

"Can't put anything over on you, can we, Banyon?" Jimmie asked with a rueful smile. "Actually I haven't been to bed yet—Toni and I were chasing around the city all night like Starsky and Hutch because of some stuff, and I'm back on shift in another few hours. I do hate working nights. City gets crazy then. It's like it turns into a whole 'nother place, you know?"

You don't know the half of it . . . or do you? Eric thought.

"What kind of stuff?" he asked aloud. "I got— well, I don't know if you want to talk about it here. But I was going to try to get ahold of Toni. There's some things I need to tell her. But she was out when I came downstairs."

"Probably up in East Harlem, seeing if the *santeros* know anything about what's going down. You don't have to worry about talking here, Eric. I told you. This is one of the Good Places. And nobody's going to overhear our conversation unless

I want them to. Sort of one of the fringe benefits of being a Guardian," Jimmie said.

"Okay." He liked Jimmie a lot—and more, he trusted her judgment. When you spent a lot of time on the street and the RenFaire circuit, you got to develop an instinct that helped you tell the good cops from the bad. And Jimmie was definitely one of the good ones.

"So shoot. What's got you walking the streets on a day like this?"

"Well . . . ." He was stalling, and he knew it. But one of the things that Dharinel had drummed into him during his magical training was that words had power, and it almost seemed to Eric that by telling Jimmie the problem he'd be making it more real than it had to be.

"I've already told Greystone most of it. And, well, it's a lot of different things. Some really personal. Some I've been told to stay out of at all costs."

"Too bad that's the kind of advice that nobody ever takes," Jimmie said. She sipped her coffee, and for a moment her eyes were cold and far away, focused on some secret pain. He noticed that whenever she was thinking intently, her black eyes lightened almost to yellow. It was a startling effect. "The good people . . . they always try to help. And sometimes they get killed. But that's what *I'm* here for. If anybody takes a bullet, it should be me. I chose to put myself on the line, knowing the risks ahead of time." She took a deep breath, consciously shutting away the pain. "But that's old news. Anyway, it's one of the reasons I'm kind of touchy about civilians on the fire-line, if you hadn't noticed already. Good people, who just want to help. But it's my job to protect them—even to take a bullet if I have to. They never asked to be in the kinds of situations I run into. All they want to do is live their lives. And it's my job to make sure they can. I don't want any more deaths on my conscience."

Eric met her gaze squarely, thinking of his own dead. Of the people who hadn't gotten out of the way in time when the magic got loose. Or—worse—had been dragged into situations by people who didn't care who they hurt.

"Understood," Eric said. "I don't like it either." He shook his head.

"Yeah," Jimmie said, with a long sigh. "Looks like you know how it is. I lost a partner once, a long time ago. Because my gun was loaded with silver bullets and his wasn't. Because I knew what we were chasing and I couldn't find any way to tell him that it wasn't his fight. Never again! I guess that's one of the reasons why I never married—though the old joke about being married to my work has some truth in it. What about you, Eric Banyon? Any hostages to fortune?"

"I guess not." The answer sounded wrong, and he examined it. "I have—I mean, I'm going to have—a daughter. But she isn't really mine. She's Beth and Kory's. They just can't have one together, so it's more like—I mean, she'll be theirs, not mine."

"No one else?" Jimmie asked.

Ria. "No. At least, not that I know of. I mean, other than everyone. I'm not going to walk away from a problem just because nobody I know is involved."

"Good answer. Or a bad one. Some things you've just got to walk away from, Eric. It hurts, and you feel horrible, but if you got involved all you could do would be to make things worse."

Eric shook his head stubbornly. On one level, he knew what she said was true, but in reality he didn't know if he had the detachment to just walk away from people in trouble.

"I'm not sure I could ever do that," he said slowly.

"Then be glad you're not a cop, because we have to do it every day," Jimmie said fiercely. "But I didn't mean to lecture you. You look just about all in."

"Bad night," Eric said. "One of the worst, actually, but not really relevant to the business at hand." Once more he hesitated about conveying Dharinel's warning. He'd told Greystone. Surely that was enough?

Thinking like that is what gets people killed, Eric told himself roughly.

"Anyway, here's the deal. I talked to Greystone when I got home last night. He said you were having kind of a situation, but I didn't know about that until I got home from the concert. Before that, I got a warning from my friends that they wanted me to pass on to you."

"A warning?" Jimmie asked, suddenly alert. "For me by name?"

"No. For the Guardians. In general. Dh—my teacher seems to know a lot about you folks. Anyway, he said this was your kind of problem, something that you were equipped to handle. He didn't tell me much, but I'll give you all the help

I can. Apparently, Manhattan Island is one of those places that Sidhe just don't go. Only last night I heard that an Unseleighe Lord—that's one of the Dark Sidhe, and pretty much bad juju all the way around—is planning to move in and take over here. They say he's going to try to open a Nexus to Underhill here in New York City. If he can do it, he'll have quite a lot of power to play with, and from everything I've heard the Unseleighe Sidhe tend to play pretty rough. My friends said I should warn the Guardians, let them handle it."

"That's what we're here for," Jimmie said with a sigh. She held her cup near her face, inhaling the steam. "And since you've been so open with me, I'll pass on a little information in return. The reason we were out last night is that a bunch of people are turning up dead—street people. More than usual, even in this weather, and all with something kind of . . . funny about them. Paul thinks it might be a case of serial possession, but it doesn't quite feel right for that. And then there was this kind of . . . blippy thing. Like somebody was powering up and then just . . . stopping. Kind of hard to figure out—not really like anything any of us has seen before, and if Paul can't pull a parallel out of his books or the Internet, it's got to be some kind of really exotic mojo. So we were trying to run down leads half the night, and coming up with nothing. This helps a lot. Now we know one of the things we should be looking for." She finished her coffee with a flourish and tucked the last bite of pastry into her mouth.

"The important thing from your point of view, I guess, is that my guy's going to be trying to get his hands on anyone with Power to draw on them to build the Nexus, and my teacher thinks that means he's going to be going after humans with the Gift, but from what you're saying, what you folks were following doesn't sound like Sidhe work. Even if he does have a way to find the Gifted, he'd have to drain—kill—thousands, maybe millions, of ordinary people to get enough power to open a Gate here, and I know it sounds awful to say, but that's just too much like gruntwork for their tastes. And . . . the other thing is, last night I ran into an old friend. Only I don't know for sure whether she was there or not—and if she *was* there, I'm not sure what she wants—or if she's tied up with him."

Briefly Eric sketched the details of Ria Llewellyn's appearance and disappearance from the concert, explaining that while it wasn't impossible for Ria to have been there—or for her appearance to have been a coincidence—he wasn't completely sure of what it might mean.

"It's just that she's, well—ruthless. And pretty self-involved. She isn't the type to count casualties if you get in her way."

"Sounds like a real executive type," Jimmie commented. "But not like the type who'd want to be a street soldier for someone else from all you've said about her. At least from what you say there isn't already a local Nexus, so she isn't likely to be out there trying to buy it up to bulldoze it. Not that anybody'd notice if she did. This is New York, after all, the land of Donald Trump and combat-strength urban renewal."

"Yeah. I'd kinda figured that out for myself." Eric thought about telling Jimmie about his dream, and hesitated. Just what could he say? He'd had a vision? A premonition? A guided tour of a place that he wasn't sure existed outside his own mind? He knew it had been a warning, but the Guardians were already on alert, and he'd passed on Dharinel's warning. They wouldn't be any more careful just because he told them he'd dreamed of a New York in ruins, presided over by a baleful elvish tower.

And Greystone hadn't sounded any warning when he'd had the dream. That was the main thing. So whatever had been the source of his dream, it hadn't come from outside Guardian House.

Or Greystone hadn't considered it a threat. . .

"Well, I just thought I'd mention, and to let you know that if there was anything I could do to help out," Eric said hesitantly.

"No!" Jimmie said, too quickly. "I mean, you're a nice guy, Eric, and a helluva magician from what Greystone tells me, but you didn't come to New York to join the Guardians and fight evil. You know what they say about old age and treachery overcoming youth and skill? We've got a few tricks up our sleeve that'll probably come as quite a shock to somebody from the Old Country," she said, sounding just a bit pleased with herself.

"And most of all, if four Guardians need help, Eric, the people of New York are in more trouble than we thought. But I'll pass the word to the others," Jimmie said, smiling at him. "Maybe the two cases'll end up tying in together. Sometimes they do. But I hope not." She glanced down at her watch, and got to her feet in a hurry. "Aiee! Two o'clock already and I'm on duty at four—that leaves me just about enough time to get downtown and get suited up." She held out her hand, and Eric took it, standing as well. "I've enjoyed this, Eric. It isn't that often I can find somebody to talk to. You know how it is."

"Me, too," Eric said. "Meanwhile, I've got a paper to write, and I guess I ought to be writing it. Thanks for the coffee. And the conversation."

"We'll do this again," Jimmie promised.

"It's a date," Eric answered warmly.

He walked the few blocks back to his apartment in a far better mood than he'd been in when he left it. Jimmie Youngblood was definitely a nice lady and a good cop, and Eric hoped he'd be able to see more of her. Not romantically—Jimmie'd made it clear she wasn't looking for anything like that—but as a friend. How many people were there, after all, that he could talk about the magical part of his life with and have them accept it so matter-of-factly? Not many, and you could take that to the bank.

The phone was ringing as he opened the door to his apartment, and Eric dived for it without thought.

"Hello? Hello?" *Just my luck this will be someone trying to sell me aluminum siding or* The New York Times. . . .

"Eric? This is Ria Llewellyn."

Pure surprise held him speechless for a moment. He had almost managed to convince himself that the Ria he'd seen last night had been a ghost, some kind of illusion, or at the very least a non-recurring phenomenon. But the rich sultry sound of her contralto was like a blast of concentrated yesterday, whirling him back to his mooncalf idyll—in her home, in her bed—when she had tried to turn him from a knight to a pawn, nothing more than a reservoir of Power to be tapped . . . just as Perenor had meant her to be.

Or maybe into something more?

"Hello, Ria," Eric said, his voice slightly cool.

In her own way she had cared for him, Eric knew. Fought for him, tried to protect him, turned on her father in the end. For him? Or for her own freedom?

" 'Hello, Ria,' " she echoed, her voice languidly mocking. "After all this time, that's all you have to say? I admit, I'd expected more."

"I saw you at the concert last night," Eric said flatly, still too rattled to dissemble. He'd managed to pick up a number of the courtly arts with which the Elvenborn wiled away their time Underhill, but the whole business of saying one thing while meaning another—all in the most elliptical fashion—had eluded him completely, to Kory and even Beth's amusement.

"You were very good," Ria said. "That solo piece at the end—your own work?—was most impressive. And all done without magic. That somehow makes it even more exceptional."

"You didn't call me up just to congratulate me," Eric said, sinking down into the chair in front of the stereo with the phone cradled on his lap.

"No. Not really. I called to see if you'd be my guest for dinner this evening."

There was a long silence. When Ria spoke again, her voice in his ear was just a shade less confident.

"Eric?"

"I'm still here." He was thinking fast, trying to figure out what she *meant*, not just what she was telling him. In all of his experience with Ria, she'd never been absolutely underhanded. She might try to influence him, overshadow his power with her own, but she wouldn't lure him into a blatant trap. "Yeah, sure. I'd love to." *Almost as much as I'd love to know what you're really up to, lady.* "Just let me know the time and place."

Candlemas was the new hot restaurant in the Triangle District. What had formerly been the Meat-Packing District was gentrifying rapidly, high-priced boutiques and luxury condos driving out the artists, drug dealers, and fetish clubs that had flourished here in low-rent days. The restaurant and its five-star CIA[5]-trained chef had recently been anointed by Gotham's reigning foodies, and as a result, even on this raw Saturday night there were people lined up halfway down the block waiting for tables.

Eric had dressed carefully for this meeting. Fashion was, after all, just another form of warfare . . . and if this wasn't precisely a war, it bore more than a passing resemblance to that gentle art. Back before he really knew what either Power or Bardcraft were, Ria'd frightened him into lashing out at her—and that had terrified them both. She'd

---

[5] Culinary Institute of America, Hyde Park, New York.

seen him as an enemy and driven him away. He hadn't seen her again until Beth had broken a guitar over her head at the final battle, destroying Perenor's access to her power and gaining the day for the Sun-Descending elves.

And now she was back, pushing her way into his life once more.

Why?

Like the man says about the afterlife: sooner or later you will KNOW. So let's see what the lady has to say for herself.

Ria must have been approaching their "reunion" in much the same spirit—why else pick a place like this to meet? A venue more calculated to put the old Eric nicely off-balance could hardly have been better chosen.

Too bad I'm not the same guy she used to know. Eric grinned wolfishly. Beneath his duster-length topcoat he was wearing one of the suits Beth had helped him choose—wild silk, in a shade just this side of true black, paired with a collarless linen shirt in a deep rich cream. Instead of a tie, he wore a small elvenmade brooch at his throat: silver, set with a large, almost transparent opal. A clasp of the same design held his hair back from his face.

Once, Eric would have completely distrusted such an outfit, seeing it as somehow dishonest. Now he wore it as if it were second nature, knowing fashion for what it was: a tool, nothing more.

Which is great. But how am I going to get past that crowd at the door or find Ria once I do? I could be standing out here for hours.

As he hesitated on the curb—the weather was bad enough that he'd come in a cab instead of bringing Lady Day—a man in a chauffeur's uniform came up to him.

"Mr. Banyon?"

"That's me," Eric said a little warily.

"Ms. Llewellyn's compliments, sir. She asked me to tell you to go on in. She's already seated."

"Thanks," Eric said. *If she wants to overawe me with an ostentatious display of wealth and power . . . well, let's say I appreciate the show.*

The chauffeur retreated to the fender of a glorious vintage maroon and cream Rolls Royce Silver Ghost—a stand-out ride even by New York standards—and Eric made his way to the door of Candlemas. Getting inside was a bit like swimming upstream to spawn, but he finally made it. The next obstacle was the official greeter, a slender black man who advanced upon Eric with an openly disdainful expression.

"Good evening, sir. Welcome to Candlemas. Do you have a reservation?"

"I'm joining someone," Eric said. "Ria Llewellyn?"

The man's demeanor changed at once from arrogance to subservience, though the change was so subtle as to qualify as magery in its own right.

"Yes sir. Right this way. May I have someone take your coat?"

Eric handed the garment over, and received a discreet coat-check token in return, before following the maitre'd farther into the restaurant.

The interior of Candlemas made no concessions to currently-voguish Manhattan industrial chic. Whatever this space had been last month, it now gave the impression of being an out-take from a particularly decadent Tuscan chateau. The lighting was fashionably low, and the walls were hung with a pleated amber-colored velvet a few shades lighter than the deep-pile carpet. Gilt medallions anchored the fabric, and light spilled out from behind them in sunburst patterns, drawing a faint shimmer from the deep nap of the fabric. The velvet walls softened the ambient noise to a muted background, like ocean surf. The tables on the service floor were swathed in a creamy brocade and set far enough apart to give the diners at least the illusion of privacy.

Around the edge of the room there were half a dozen recessed alcoves, like the private boxes at the opera. They were even curtained to give the diners more privacy. Somehow Eric wasn't surprised to be escorted toward one of them. Ria always traveled first class.

She was waiting for him at the table. Her eyes widened slightly as she saw him, and Eric smiled to himself. He might have been Underhill, but time hadn't stood still for him . . . though it seemed to have for Ria. She was still the woman he'd first spotted in a crowd in L.A.—pale blond hair, cat-green eyes, ruthless mouth. Whatever injuries she'd suffered from her coma weren't evident tonight, and Eric looked carefully, his shields warily in place against any magic—though the magic Ria was deploying was of a far older and more fascinating sort.

She was wearing a dark-green dress with an old-fashioned portrait neckline, with a necklace of cloudy green stones around her throat—jade?—that only served to accentuate the flawless whiteness of her skin.

Eric felt his throat close in a purely masculine acknowledgement of her beauty. She was as fair and fey as the unfading moonlilies that bloomed in Underhill.

"Satisfied?" she asked, and Eric only just stopped himself from blushing. The maitre'd seated him, giving him a moment to recover.

"You've . . . changed," Ria said, favoring him with a sphinx-like smile.

"This is my cue to say you haven't. But I know you've got a mirror. And I remember that you hate people being obvious," Eric said boldly.

"I'm easily bored," Ria admitted, with a throaty mock-seductive purr in her voice. If you could put what she had in a bottle, Eric decided, there wouldn't be any reason for anybody to ever be lonely again.

"So—without being obvious—it's good to see you. You're obviously well." He was surprised to find that, when he spoke them, the words were true. Seeing Ria again was like . . . was like having the answer to a question he'd been asking for a very long time. "You gave me quite a start when I saw you in the audience last night. If you'd called ahead, I would've gotten you tickets."

"You concealed it admirably. Your performance was wonderful. Shall we order? Or would you like a drink first?"

There was a glass of white wine in front of her, in one of those huge tulip-shaped glasses that restaurants used for everything from Chardonnay to frozen daiquiris. Eric shook his head.

"Just water for me, thanks. Evian if they have it." Ria raised an eyebrow, but made no comment.

She must have signalled somehow, because a hovering waitperson instantly appeared to take Eric's drink order and bestow upon both of them leather-backed menus only slightly smaller than the surface of a coffee table.

"Have you eaten here before?" he asked, scanning the menu. Candlemas seemed to run to Continental Fusion fare—Eric hesitated over the medallions of venison with kiwi and mango, smirking faintly. But what the heck—if people wanted to put stuff like that in their bodies, at least it was better than drugs.

"No. My assistant suggested the place. These days, my idea of dining out is usually takeout at my desk. And I don't get to New York that often."

But you're here now, Ria. Why?

"There are a lot of good restaurants here," Eric said noncommittally. He decided on the chicken in balsamic vinaigrette as being a safe choice, one that wouldn't offer too many surprises. Ria would be surprise enough this evening.

"Oh, I don't deny that New York has its attractions. Some of the best schools in the world are here, for example."

Eric sipped at his water. If this was Ria's opening gambit, it was an awfully mild one. They both already knew he was attending Juilliard.

"Yes. I didn't appreciate it much the last time, but I think formal training has a lot to offer, don't you?"

Her eyes widened slightly as she took his double meaning. When they'd last clashed, Ria was an accomplished sorceress, and Eric barely knew what magic was. Now he was a Bard . . . and Ria had always been a political animal, raised amid Perenor's plotting. He didn't know what contacts with the elves she still had . . . or wanted.

In fact, he decided, they'd both changed a great deal. And suddenly it was very important to Eric to know who Ria had become.

"So. Tell me everything. How are Kayla and Elizabet?"

"Well, when last I saw them," Ria said, accepting the change of subject smoothly. "Kayla will be going away to school, soon. She won't have to worry about tuition—I'll see to that—but neither Elizabet nor I feel that the child needs a free ride through life. And she can't earn her living as a Healer. The medical establishment doesn't take kindly to people working miracles without a license. And Healers need a lot of downtime in order to function without burning out, so it isn't likely she's going to go for an M.D."

"Computer programming, maybe? Or web-designer?" Eric suggested, thinking of Paul Kern. If anyone needed a flexible schedule, it was a Guardian. "Those are both professions with a lot of built-in privacy. I've got a friend who could suggest some good places to study."

"We may take you up on that. I know she wants to come to New York. Says the San Fernando Valley's too quiet for her tastes."

Eric laughed, thinking of the scrappy little punkette he'd met at the Dunkin Donuts' the morning of the battle for Elfhame Sun-Descending. A greater contrast with the stately, dignified Elizabet could hardly be imagined, but Elizabet's apprentice had the true Healer's gift—as well as more street-smarts than anyone Eric had ever known, and a tongue that could strip paint off a wall at sixty paces.

Now it was Ria's turn to change the subject, and she did, asking Eric about his work at Juilliard. Eric answered readily enough—he had nothing to hide in that regard, at least from Ria, and the two of them continued sparring verbally all through the meal—appetizer, salad, entree, and dessert. Without being evasive, Ria didn't talk about anything that really mattered—Eric gathered that she was essentially making a tour of her holdings, reconsolidating her position as head of LlewellCo after a long absence. But that hardly explained her appearance at Juilliard . . . or her dinner invitation.

"I was surprised to see you surface after so long," she finally admitted over coffee. Ria's half-human heritage saved her from the poisonous effects of caffeine on her system, and Eric had surprised her once again by ordering coffee himself. The hit of the unaccustomed caffeine made his heart race, giving him a feeling as if he were riding Lady Day down a very long straightaway.

"No reason I shouldn't," Eric said. That much was true: the Feds had always really been after Bethie, not him or Kory, and besides, the Eric Banyon they were looking for would be older than he was by enough years to fool a casual inspection, even if there were anyone working the case who still remembered him.

Not that he was completely convinced they'd been legitimate Feds in the first place. . . . "And as I said, I had some business here."

"The music school."

The next obvious question would have been why Eric, with Bardcraft at his command, would even bother with something so mundane as a Juilliard degree, but Ria didn't ask it. She hadn't asked any hard questions at all over the course of dinner, Eric realized. It was as if it were enough, from her point of view, simply to be *in* view, displaying herself.

And it very nearly was. Eric had almost forgotten how downright *desirable* Ria was, in a way that had nothing (well, almost nothing) to do with sex. It was almost as if she were somehow *realer* than everyone else. She drew the eye to her automatically, like the focus of a painting.

But what the hell does she WANT?

If she wanted to kill him, they wouldn't be sitting here discussing mutual friends. If she wanted information, sooner or later she was going to have to ask some questions. If she wanted to *use* him in some way, well, those days were long past, and Eric was pretty sure that she knew it by now. But she hadn't made an excuse and left, so that wasn't it. She was still here, sitting across the table, regarding him with that steady gaze with a hint of challenge in it.

The waiter came with the check, and Ria pulled out her card to pay. Nothing as paltry as a platinum AmEx for Ria Llewellyn: what she placed on the server tray was an indigo-and-black Centurion AmEx. The user fees alone for the card were over ten thousand dollars a year, with all charges due in full at the end of each month.

Okay. Color me a little impressed. I knew back in L.A. that LlewellCo had money. I just didn't think it was quite this much. And you know what

*they say: money will get you through times of no
magic better than magic will get you through times
of no money. . . .*

"So I'm a corporate expense?" Eric asked, glancing at the card.

"You might be," Ria answered enigmatically. The waiter returned with the charge slip in record time. Ria signed it, tucked her card back out of sight, and rose to her feet.

"I don't feel we've quite said all we have to say to each other, Eric. Why not come back to my hotel and we can continue this conversation? I promise, no harm will come to you."

That's what you said the last time, Eric thought, the ghosts of old memory stirring. Just then inspiration struck.

"I've got a better idea. Why don't you come back to *my* place?" he said, standing in his turn. "I'm sure you want to see it. And good burglars don't come cheap these days." *Especially once they got a look at the building's security system.*

If he'd expected to embarrass her, Eric was disappointed. She threw back her head and laughed—a full-throated, *joyous* laugh—and smiled at him, eyes sparkling.

"Quite right. I'm not sure what market price for housebreaking is these days, but I'm sure there isn't a line item in my budget to cover it. Lead on," she added, almost gaily, laying her hand on his arm.

The sensation of the contact sent a thrill of heat up his arm and straight to his groin. He'd better stop kidding himself now: Ria Llewellyn was still an enormously attractive woman, and she used that beauty like a weapon. Once he would have been felled by its effects like a clubbed seal. He still felt its pull, tempting him.

But things, as they'd both said over the course of the evening, had changed.

It was rising eleven when they left the restaurant. Ria's limousine waited patiently at the corner. When he spotted them, the chauffeur jumped out from behind the wheel to open the passenger door for them.

The luxury of Underhill was exotic, often strange beyond his imagination, and certainly beyond his achievement here in the World Above. Bardic magic and Elven magic fit together like gloved hands, touching, but separate. Eric could reweave the fabric of Reality, open gates between worlds. But much of Elven magic was species-specific, far beyond his ability and his understanding.

This was different.

The door of the car closed behind them with the solidity of a bank vault. Eric could smell the leather of the seats, the better-than-new-car scent of the fine materials, the engineering and craftsmanship that had gone into the car's construction. And there was nothing magical about it. All of it was a creation of human hands and minds. It was certainly the most decadent thing he'd experienced since he'd come back to human lands. The inside of the Rolls was almost like walking into a small room: there were fresh flowers in matching crystal vases on the cabin walls, a table, and a sleek bulkhead panelled in mahogany burl, from which jumpseats could be folded down. There was enough floor space for two people to lie full-length—though as he settled into the deep bench seat, Eric thought there was plenty of room here, too, for the kind of things Ria's presence made him think about.

Ria settled into her seat and leaned forward to tap at the black glass partition separating them from the driver as soon as Eric was settled. They'd picked up their coats at the door, though in Ria's case the coat was a deep-hooded evening cloak, lined in satin the color of the dawn. As she moved, it fell open. The movement did interesting things to that portrait neckline. The car moved off, sleek and powerful. Eric could feel the vibration of the engine in his bones.

"Shall I tell him the address, or would you like to?" Ria asked mischievously. "The intercom button is right there, in the wall."

Eric pressed the button and gave his address. The powerful car swept uptown through the rain-slicked streets.

The clouds had broken by the time they arrived at Guardian House, and the temperature had dropped several degrees, promising snow before morning, though at this time of year the flurries should melt by noon. Eric shivered as he got out of the car. He watched as Ria looked around, mentally assessing the desirability of the neighborhood with a cold realtor's gaze. Whatever answer she came up with, it seemed to please her.

"You've moved up in the world, Eric."

"Yeah, well, nothing ever stays the same. What about your car?"

She turned back to the chauffeur, still standing alertly beside the car. "He'll wait."

She turned back to Eric. He only hoped Ria wasn't going to be back on the street again in the next ten seconds. He had no real idea of how Guardian House would respond to one of the half-elven, especially one of Ria's ambiguous loyalties.

But isn't that what you brought her here to find out?

It was, of course, but it had just now occurred to him that anything that would rouse Greystone would probably land the Guardians in his lap as well, and with all they had to worry about right now, they probably wouldn't be grateful for the interruption. He wasn't looking forward to the explanations he'd have to make if it came to that. *Still, it's always easier to get forgiveness than permission.*

He tapped out the entry code on the front door and ushered Ria through the lobby.

She was silent on the ride up, but it didn't take Bardic magic to see that Ria was thinking furiously. Eric wondered if he'd ever know the real reason she'd wanted to track him down, and thought he wouldn't. They had one new thing in common, though. Each of them was having to adjust to a world they'd been away from for several years. He wondered if the new millennium was as much of a shock to Ria as it sometimes was to him.

"Very nice," Ria said, looking around the hushed and carpeted corridor that led to Eric's apartment. "No wonder Claire thought you must be some kind of Mafia drug lord."

"I like it," Eric said, refusing to take the bait she so temptingly dangled. He punched the keycode to unlock his door. "Enter freely and of your own will."

In the living room, Ria swirled off her cloak with a practiced gesture and laid it over the back of the couch, making Eric glad he'd gone to the trouble of cleaning the place up before he left. He was really going to have to see about that house-brownie, though.

"Here, let me hang that up for you," Eric said, picking it up. He walked through to the bedroom to hang up her cloak and his coat. The unmade bed, still rumpled from his nightmare, invited his thoughts down pathways he'd rather not take just now, thank you very much. He realized he was tense, waiting for Guardian House to sound an alarm, though surely if it had been going to, it would have done it already. Ria's presence didn't seem to even be a blip on its psychic radar.

Figures. If I can't figure out what she's up to, what chance does a building have?

He came back out to find Ria inspecting his CD collection.

"You must have bought out the store," she commented, turning to him.

"Pretty much," Eric agreed. "I've got to say, these things are a lot easier to store than vinyl."

"Cheaper to produce, too," Ria agreed. "And when the cost comes down, a lot of music that was marginal before has the chance to get out there and find its audience."

Trust Ria to find a way to think of everything in economic terms, Eric thought with an inward grin.

"I promised you coffee. Will espresso do? I've got one of those fancy machines. It was a house-warming present. It even works most of the time."

Ria smiled with what seemed like genuine warmth. "Then you're more technologically advanced than I am. If I didn't have Jonathan to make the coffee, I'd go into caffeine withdrawal."

She followed him into the tiny kitchen, where Eric navigated the intricacies of the bright-orange Italian espresso maker Caity had given him without too much difficulty. Ria's presence—her warmth, her perfume—were even more distracting in this small intimate space.

Is she coming on to me? Unbidden tactile memories rose up strongly in Eric's mind. He controlled his blush with an effort. *Or is she just trying to get me so aroused I'll stop thinking?* To cover his momentary confusion, he grabbed a tray from the shelf and arranged a box of assorted biscotti on a plate. When the espresso had brewed, he drew off two cups and carried the tray back out into the living room.

"So why don't you tell me what you're really doing here?" Eric said bluntly, once they were both seated. He didn't expect her to tell him, but his question should bring the answers to the surface of her mind for Greystone to read.

"You invited me," Ria pointed out, sipping her espresso. She nibbled delicately at a biscotti with sharp white teeth. "And frankly, isn't that question the least bit insulting? Next you'll be offering to leave the money on the dresser."

Eric grinned in spite of himself at her bold words. *The best defense is always a good attack.* "I don't think it's an unreasonable question, given who we both are," Eric responded. "We didn't part on the best of terms."

"That was my fault, I suppose," Ria said graciously. "I'm not the most trusting person in the world. And you frightened me. It doesn't hurt to admit that. My father has—had—many powerful enemies. I thought you might be one of them."

"But Perenor's dead."

Ria inclined her head. "But the elvenkind has long memories. I sought you out because I was certain it was only a matter of time before you did the same to me. I have no interest in taking up my late father's feuds . . . but I will defend myself."

Was that a warning or a threat?

"I haven't got any quarrel with you, Ria." As he said the words, Eric knew they were true. "I came back to finish at Juilliard. That's all. So I'm still asking: why are *you* here?"

She wasn't convinced—he could see that in her expression. But would he have been convinced if he was the one who'd been raised amid a Sidhe Lord's intrigues? Ria's entire existence, her magical training, had been shaped to one end, to make her into a living battery from which Perenor could draw power at will. That didn't make for a trusting nature.

"Tell me who trained you in Bardcraft. Tell me he didn't send you back into the world of Men to kill me," Ria said in a low intense voice.

"*Dharinel?*" Eric said in surprise. Dharinel disliked humans and despised the half-blood, it was true, but his contempt was meted out with a fine evenhandedness. It would be completely beneath his dignity as Magus Major and Elven Bard of Elfhame Misthold to acknowledge any particular human enough to want to destroy them.

Ria was about to reply when there was a scrabbling on the fire escape. She set down her cup quickly, and glanced from Eric to the window behind her.

The sash raised, and Greystone climbed down into the room. Ria got slowly to her feet, staring at the gargoyle.

"She's okay, boyo," Greystone said to Eric. "I admit I had me doubts about you bringing her here an' all, but t'is copacetic. She's levelling with you, laddybuck."

Ria stared down at the squat, misshapen creature in speechless shock. It had a fanged doglike face and curling horns. Its arms were long and apelike, and its hindquarters like a satyr's, right down to the cloven hooves. Great bat wings lay against its back like furled umbrellas. And despite the fact that it lived and moved and talked, it seemed to be made of solid stone.

"So," she heard it say, "how'd your night out go? Or should I say going? Any o' that high-powered coffee left? It's a cold night out, and no mistake. I could use a wee bit of a jolt."

"Sure," Eric answered easily. "I'll get you a cup. Ria, this is Greystone. Greystone, meet Ria Llewellyn. I've told you about her."

With a distant part of her mind, Ria registered that Eric seemed to be on very good terms with this creature—and that he had brought her to it as a sort of test. She found it hard to be angry with Eric for showing such caution. She'd been wary herself.

She stood perfectly still as the gargoyle waddled

up to her. Though if it could stand completely upright it might be as tall as she was, its crouched position made it several inches shorter.

"You've nothin' to fear from me, Blondie. As for meself, there's more things in heaven an' earth, as I'm sure you know," Greystone said, and winked at her.

"I'm finding that out," Ria said levelly.

Eric returned from the kitchen with a mug of espresso and handed it to Greystone. The gargoyle slurped it down with evident relish, then reached out a long simian arm to grab a handful of biscotti. The talons on its fingertips would have done credit to an eagle with their sharpness, for all that they seemed to be made of stone. It set the empty cup down on the table, and, still clutching the handful of cookies, headed for the window once more.

"Well, I've gotta be going. No rest for the wicked, an' all that. You kids behave yourselves, now." He favored both of them with one last toothy grin and made his exit, closing the window carefully behind him.

Eric was looking at her, obviously waiting for her reaction.

"Well," Ria finally managed. "I see you still have interesting friends."

Eric laughed. "I seem to have a knack for that."

Cautiously they both sat down once more.

"So . . ." Ria said finally, returning to the earlier conversation. "Master Dharinel trained you?"

"Even he had to admit that everybody was better off if I knew how to use what I had. But he didn't send me after you, Ria. I swear it. I don't think most of the elves really care one way or the other about you now that Perenor's dead."

"I hope you're right. But I do know that your friends blame me for a lot of what happened at Sun-Descending and the Fairegrove . . . Beth Kentraine, for example?"

She knew she was fishing now, but if Claire MacLaren's PI report hadn't mentioned talking gargoyles, it was even less likely to have included mention of elves and their friends. Beth Kentraine was not somebody she wanted to have appear unexpectedly in her life. From what Ria remembered, Kentraine had a fiery temper and a wicked right cross.

"Oh, you won't be seeing her. She and Kory mostly live Underhill these days. It's not like they'd be dropping by unexpectedly. We're still close, but it's . . . not like it was."

When to scratch one of the three of you made the other two bleed, Ria finished silently. The way Eric spoke of them—as a couple—made Ria cheer inwardly. So little Bethie had thrown her lot in with the elven lover, had she? That was the best news Ria'd had in a long time.

"I suppose I ought to offer my condolences," Ria said politely. "Or . . . not?"

"Not," Eric said cheerfully. "Things just worked out the way they had to. The only thing is . . . I'd like to be able to think of some way to help them out. Because they want kids, and—with elves and humans—it's hard to arrange. I don't know if I ought to be asking you this, but . . . do you know anything that could help? Some kind of spell or magic, I mean. I mean, *you're* here."

Half-Blood children were incredibly rare occurrences between Sidhe and mortalkin. In most cases the unfortunate children were ostracized by their father's and mother's people both, so perhaps it was a blessing that such half-Blood children rarely inherited the immortality of their elven parent. Immortality had been the bribe Perenor had held out to his half-breed daughter, but lately Ria had come to wonder if he had meant to give it to her as a blessing . . . or as a curse? She shook her head slowly.

"Not in the way you mean, I think. Believe me, Eric. What Perenor did to create me is nothing your friends would ever want any part of," Ria said with quiet intensity. "It nearly killed my mother. It *did* drive her mad. And it cost the lives of several other people—he drained their essences to fuel his magic."

Eric sat back, a look of surprise and, oddly, pity on his face. "That's a helluva thing to have to live with. To know you're here only because a bunch of other people gave their lives—or had them taken away."

"Survivor's guilt, they call it," Ria said with a crooked smile. "It's not the only way, of course, just the quickest and easiest if you have no conscience and no scruples. If you'd like, though, I'll see what I can find about the other methods. I *am* uniquely placed for that kind of research." *And we'll see whether the high and mighty Beth Kentraine is willing to let bygones be bygones if I can offer her her heart's desire on a silver tray.*

"I'd like that," Eric said. "I'm sorry I was so hard on you before. . . ."

"But you didn't trust me. And considering how we parted, you had every right not to. That wasn't one of my best calls, Eric. If I'd been thinking clearly, I would have realized it at the time. I should have trusted what I knew of you. If you were out to get someone, you wouldn't pretend to be their friend first."

She could tell by his expression that he knew she was telling him the truth. Truth-sense was one of the oldest of the Bardic gifts; she supposed she'd just been lucky he hadn't developed it the last time they'd met.

"Is that all we were? Friends?" Eric asked. "Funny, but I remember the relationship as being somewhat . . . warmer."

This is moving a little too fast for me. Ria got to her feet. "And it might be again. I won't lie to you, Eric. As a boy you were pretty. As a man you're devastating. But I think that right now it's time for me to go."

He looked disappointed—her pride was grateful for that—but got to his feet without complaint. "I'll get your cape."

Eric walked her to the curb and the waiting Rolls. The chauffeur opened the passenger door and stood waiting like a well-oiled automaton.

Eric opened his mouth to speak, and Ria touched him lightly on the lips with her fingers. "I'll be in New York for several more days. There's no hurry. I hope we can see each other again. I'd like to get to know you."

And before Eric could assemble an answer to *that,* Ria had stepped into the car, and it was moving silently away.

❖   ❖   ❖

There was someone standing outside his apartment door when Eric got back upstairs.

"Toni?"

The Latina woman spun around when she heard him. "Blessed saints! Greystone said you were here, but I called and no one answered, so I came up."

Must be pretty important. She looks kind of worried.

"I was just walking a friend out. Do you want to come inside?"

"No. I mean, I'd like you to come outside. We've . . . found something, and none of us has seen anything like it before. Jimmie said— So I thought . . . you've had a certain amount of experience in this sort of thing, and I was hoping I could get you to come take a look. Maybe it's . . . what you were talking about."

Christ, I hope not! Eric thought fervently.

"Sure," Eric said. "Just let me get my coat and I'll be right with you. Do I have time to change?"

For the first time Toni seemed to notice what he was wearing. A slow smile crossed her face. "Sure. We wouldn't want to scare the Ungodly with your great beauty. Heavy date tonight, eh?"

"You might say," Eric said with a smile.

He dressed quickly in sweater, jeans, leather jacket and boots. He hesitated, then picked up his flute case and swung it over his shoulder. Toni hadn't said what she wanted him to look at, but if it was capable of spooking a Guardian, he wanted to go loaded for bear.

Toni's Toyota was waiting on the street—a side benefit of Guardianship seemed to be never lacking for a parking space—and in a few moments they were moving. Toni Hernandez drove like a New York cabbie, zipping into spaces almost before they opened, weaving through a deadly dance with the fleet of trucks that took over the New York streets after-hours. The traffic lightened as they headed east, and Eric realized they were going toward Central Park.

"Want to tell me what's going on?" Eric asked, catching his breath after one particularly spectacular maneuver. *She drives the way Bethie does—or did.*

"Not really. I think we'd rather see what you come up with on your own. Paul and Jimmie are already there."

The park was closed to street traffic at this time of night, and the gates were down across the road. Toni swerved into a parking space right outside and bounced out of the car before Eric had finished unbuckling his seat belt.

"I'm afraid it's a bit of a hike from here," she said. "Good thing you changed your shoes."

He felt it long before he reached the spot where Jimmie and Paul were standing. Jimmie Youngblood was in her uniform, looking shuttered and forbidding, hand on her gun, though her expression lightened with something like relief when she saw him. Paul looked like an escaped university professor, Norfolk tweed jacket with leather elbow patches and all. Eric almost expected him to pull out a pipe and light it.

The stench of magic was everywhere, a sort of palpable wrongness that made his hair stand on

end. Eric's steps slowed as he approached the
Guardians. Outside of a few burned patches on the
grass there wasn't much to see with normal vision.
Eric stopped where he was, closed his eyes, and
looked again.

He could see it now. A sketchy shape in the air,
as though the night was a different color here. He
turned slowly around in a circle, trying to pin it
down further. He felt a chill that had nothing to
do with winter, and a crawling feeling along his
spine.

"You already know this is magic, right?" he said
at last, trying for a light tone in the midst of this
incredible *wrongness*.

"Ah, but what *kind* of magic?" Paul asked, as
if this were just some sort of academic exercise.

"I told you before how a lot of people've gone
missing in the last couple of days, Eric," Jimmie
said. "People you wouldn't ordinarily miss, except
that so damn many of them are just dropping out
of sight. Or turning up dead. What we need to
know is, is this a part of that?"

Yes, there was death here, and pain, and darkness. Eric thought again of the bonewood and
goblin tower of his dream.

"This feels like Unseleighe Sidhe," he said reluctantly. "Mind, I've never had any direct contact
with them, but it's Sidhe magic, but twisted, so I
suppose that's what it feels like. . . ." He hesitated
before saying more. "And there's a lot of death
here. Human death. Beyond that. . . ." His voice
trailed off again.

"So what you told me about really is happening," Jimmie said unhappily. "But why? And how,

especially here? Don't the Dark Elves have to follow the same rules as the Light?"

"They've got the same limitations," Eric agreed. The taint of inside-out magic was starting to make his head hurt. "But I kind of think the Unseleighe Sidhe would like the City, if they could stand to be here."

"Can you tell what kind of working this is?" Jimmie asked urgently. "Its purpose?"

"It's a Gateway," Eric answered slowly. "It isn't finished. If nobody messes with it for a few days it'll probably fade away. But someone was here—an elf-mage or another human Bard—trying to open a Gateway between Underhill and the world."

He explained what he could about Nexuses—how they gave elvenkind a way to tap the power of Underhill that was life itself to them, how many of the Elven Court, especially the Lesser Sidhe, could not survive away from a Nexus, and that even the High Elves needed frequent access to one in order to replenish their magic. And that someone, apparently, was building one here.

"Well, that's something to go on with, anyway," Jimmie said when he was finished talking. She shook her head. "Now we just have to figure out what to do about it. I wonder what you bait Sidhe-traps with?"

"Power," Eric said bleakly. "At least in this case. Not your kind, though. That's at least partly learned, I'm guessing, and pretty well shielded. He isn't really interested in that. He wants the raw stuff, the innate Gift some people are born with and don't know they have."

"Well, that's a relief," Paul said dourly, then

forced himself to smile. "At least we know more than we did before. Thanks for coming out on such short notice, Eric."

"Why don't you let me get rid of it for you?" Eric offered, reaching for his flute.

"No!" Paul and Jimmie spoke at once. There was real pain on Jimmie's face—and more. Fear. He remembered their conversation at the bakery: *If anybody takes a bullet, it should be me.*

Was that what she was worrying about? Him?

Paul held up a hand. "No, that's okay. Now that we know what it is, we can keep an eye on it. It's more important to stop who's doing it rather than scare them off."

If you think you can scare off the Unseleighe Sidhe, you haven't met many of them, Eric thought. "I still think I should—"

"C'mon, Eric. I'll drive you home," Toni said briskly, taking charge of the situation before it could degenerate into an argument. "Paul, you want a lift?"

"No," Paul said. "I think I'll stay out here a little while. You two go on ahead. Jimmie can drop me when she heads back to the station house."

"I still think I ought to do something about it," Eric said. Most people wouldn't notice anything out of the ordinary here, but anybody with any amount of Talent would have a natural aversion to the place. Or an attraction to it. . . .

"I'm not bringing any more civilians onto the fireline. Do what your friends told you, Eric. Stay out of this one, for your own sake," Jimmie said urgently.

There was a world of pain—and bitter self-recrimination—in Jimmie's voice, and Toni was hovering over him as if she were about to pick him up and carry him. Reluctantly, Eric allowed himself to be led back to the car. He couldn't force his help on them if they didn't want to accept it, and Dharinel had all but ordered him to stay uninvolved. He let himself be led out of the park and deposited back on his own doorstep after another hair-raising ride in the Toyota.

But the sense of unfinished business, layered on top of the unsettling evening with Ria, made sleep particularly hard to find that night.

EIGHT:

THE CITY OF
DREADFUL NIGHT

Chesley Kurland did not believe in miracles, even though he was holding one in his hands right now. Free samples. Hell, he hadn't seen anything like that since the Sixties, and unlike most of the crowd on the streets these days, Chesley had been there for the Summer of Love and retained fond memories of it today. As dark and grey and unfriendly as the world had gotten, there were times when the memories were all that kept him going.

Chesley made his living as a free-lance mechanic. He could repair any kind of engine, the more complicated the better. Anything mechanical just talked to him, always had, the same way some people knew what horses wanted just by looking. He was a man of no fixed address, and currently lived in the back of an old Ford van parked in the back of Ralph's Niteowl Garage up in Inwood. Ralph paid him in cash, and Chesley liked to say that he was taking his retirement in installments, a line from an old book that he'd particularly liked.

Earlier this evening he'd been hanging out down at the old Peacock Coffeehouse on the edge of the Village, and this dude who looked like he'd wandered out of the last *Terminator* movie had made the scene, offering little bundles of joy to anyone with a sense of adventure. And if there was one thing Chesley still had, it was a sense of adventure.

The garage was fairly quiet as he walked across the floor. Despite the optimism of its name, there wasn't often enough work to occupy a full crew 24/7, and tonight was one of those times. He saw no one as he made his way to the van and climbed in through the back.

Most of all, he didn't see the dealer who had been offering free samples, and who now stood concealed in the shadows with another man beside him, both of them watching Chesley as he climbed into his mobile home.

Inside the van was everything Chesley needed in this world: a mattress to sleep on, his toolcase, his stashbox, and a towering blue glass bong. You could buy them on Main Street in the bad old days, Chesley remembered. What had happened to the world since he was a kid? It seemed as if all the joy were slowly draining away from everything, like somebody'd pulled out the plug in the Bathtub of the World. Well, in a few moments they'd see if modern chemistry was there to meet the challenge.

Sitting cross-legged on the floor, he prepared the bong for use with the ease of long practice. He filled the upper half of the pipe with bottled water and packed the bowl with pipe tobacco and slivers shaved from a block of Turkish Blonde. Over that, he sprinkled the contents of the little packet. The powder glistened brightly, like a fresh fall of Vermont snow. "T-Stroke." That was what the guy at the Peacock had called it. Well, the proof was in the smoking, he'd always said. When the mixture was smoldering brightly, Chesley picked up the mouthpiece and took a deep drag.

The iron all around him made his skin crawl and put him in a foul temper, but Aerune was not to be deterred from his quest. He had chosen to follow the chief of the underlings that bore the Bardmaking elixir himself, and watched as the humans succumbed to its lure one by one. Two so far tonight had not died immediately nor manifested the insensate fury that not even Aerune could shape to his own purposes. But he had not been quick enough to seize either of them, and so they had both been spirited away by his great enemy.

It had puzzled him for a short while why these men wasted their time giving their elixir to so many who would simply die, until he realized that he could see what they could not—the blue light, so feeble as to be nearly invisible, that crowned those who possessed gifts that could be aroused by the elixir. That faint flame burned above the head of the grey-haired mortal whom he had followed here, and Aerune was determined that the mortal men should not have this prize. To his elf-sight, the corners of the garage were not dark, and he could plainly see the two men lurking there. From Urla's thoughts, he recognized one of them as the man in the black chariot who had first stolen Urla's prey.

"There is your quarry, my fine hunter," Aerune said softly, his fingers brushing the redcap's head. "Take him as you will."

Just then there was a flash of the blue light invisible to mortals from within the van, and the sharp ears of the Unseleighe Sidhe heard a stifled cry.

Urla darted forward, its long arms swinging, lips spread in a toothy grin. It bounced toward its victim, its expression vacuous and innocent.

"What the hell? You— Kid— Get outta heeeere—!" one of the men shouted. Aerune turned away. There was a sound of gunfire. The man's words faded into a scream as Urla seized him.

Aerune hesitated at the door of the van. A modern car would not have given him nearly as much trouble, but the old van's panels were of heavy sheet steel, perilous to touch. He would have no more than a moment's grace, he knew, before the surviving mortal minion was upon him.

Aerune grasped the door handle and wrenched it from its hinges with inhuman strength. His gauntlets smoked as they touched Cold Iron, but they were dwarf-forged, and his skin did not burn. Within the fetid kennel lay the prize he sought— a skinny, unlovely mortal man, his face distorted with the ravages of age. The dark lord seized him, lips drawn back in a snarl of distaste, and flung the human over his shoulder. His elvensteed was waiting in the street outside. With one leap, Aerune gained the saddle and galloped away, toward the place he had chosen for his Nexus.

Michael knew he was in trouble. He and Keith had followed Geezerboy back to this chop shop from the coffeehouse where Keith had been doing his candyman imitation. The two guys who were there— waiting for tonight's shipment of Gone In Sixty Seconds, Michael had no doubt—had been easily persuaded to go in the closet and stay there, and the decks were clear for a sweet little snatch-and-grab. They'd been about to make their move when everything went wonky. Some kid wandered in from somewhere and made a beeline toward Keith.

Only it wasn't a kid. It was . . . something else. It'd bitten Keith's throat open with one chomp. It bathed in his blood, and it laughed, a high terrible sound like broken glass on a blackboard. Michael had emptied half his Glock into it with no effect, though he knew the Teflon-coated bullets hit it.

Then he saw the other guy.

Tall. Dark like Darth Vader was dark. Menace radiating off him like chill off a chunk of dry ice. And Michael had made a command decision, right then and there. He'd run for his life. Out the side door, up the hill onto Riverside, yelping at every shadow.

But he wasn't followed.

His hands shook as he got his Star-Tac open and dialled the private number they'd been given for emergencies.

"Boss? Boss! We've got a situation here—"

It was not much of a greenwood, but it was all these mortal drones deserved. Aerune reined in and dropped his burden ungently to the ground before vaulting down himself. A moment later he crouched on the turf beside the mortal.

The human creature twitched and muttered, still caught in a web of the elixir's spinning. Aerune could see the nimbus of power grow brighter around him as the tiny guttering spark of the human's innate magic grew and flowered under the effect of the draught he had imbibed.

Here is power indeed. Aerune basked in its presence as the mortal might bask in the warmth of a fire. It purged the Sidhe's cold bones of the ache of Cold Iron all around him, and fed Aerune's resolve with the siren song of power ripe for the taking.

It was a simple thing for one of the Dark Court to drain the vital essence of a mortal, though few of them had enough Power to make it worthwhile. This one was different. Aerune bent his head low and sealed the mortal's doom with a kiss. *Spin for me, little Singer. Weave the web of your race's doom.*

The veil between the worlds began to thin, and the lattice that would anchor Aerune's Nexus began to take shape on the midnight air. First the pattern must be completed, then the veil itself

pierced, and then Aerune and his Court would be
able to call up the power of Elfhame into the
World of Iron with no more than a thought. The
power poured through him from its mortal wellspring: intoxicating, vast. . . .

And then it stopped.

Aerune roared his displeasure, turning on the
mortal in a fury. But the man was dead beneath
his hands, his body wasted away, his skin and bones
crackling like a handful of autumn leaves in
Aerune's grip.

Dead. And of no more use to me, Aerune realized, choking back his rage. The mortal alchemist's
elixir gave them access to their Power, he realized,
but no way to replenish it from Underhill's eternal wellspring, and so they burned out quickly,
their bodies feeding on their own life-force.

The ghost of the Gateway, less than a shimmer
on the winter air even to Aerune's Sight, mocked
him with its incompletion. *But there are others.
They are mine of right, and I will have them.
Aerete, beloved, soon they will repay your death
in the last full measure!*

He whistled for his mount and was away again,
in a clatter of hoofbeats so swift they sounded like
one long drum roll.

Four of the containment cells in the underground warren at Threshold were full. It had been
a busy—and potentially profitable—Saturday night,
and Jeanette felt an excitement that had little to
do with Robert's glorious future.

Her drug was working. Not as well as she'd
hoped, but working. She'd tweaked the last batch

a little, hoping to shorten the time the subjects spent unconscious, and that yielded a kind of sorting mechanism. Ninety percent of those who received T-Stroke still died, two-thirds of them instantly. The thirty percent of the Survivors that were going to manifest berserker rage came up out of the drug within minutes. But the ones who were going to manifest some kind of useful Talent slept for an hour or so, and Jeanette had decided that the deep sleep was necessary to allow the neural pathways for handling the Gift to be reconfigured without the interference of outside stimulus.

And we have four: telepathy, teleportation, psychokinesis, and I wonder what this one is going to be?

Intently, she watched the monitors for the containment cells. The telepath, Vicky Moon, had been the first to awaken, screaming at the voices inside her head and begging them to stop. Jeanette had her lightly sedated, and at least the screaming had stopped, though she doubted the voices had. The PK and the teleport—Plummer and Langford— were less trouble. Langford had gotten out of his cell four times before they figured out what he could do, but he hadn't been able to 'port far and the effort had left him exhausted. He was sleeping now; no action there.

Jeanette watched in fascination as Plummer played with the test objects in her cell, a set of child's building blocks. Lost in a world of her own imagination, the PK talent made the brightly-colored cubes swoop and dance through the air like a flock of strange butterflies, perfectly content.

The alarm began to beep as the fourth subject

returned to consciousness, and Jeanette waited to see what he'd do, her mind wandering over the evening's harvest. Four, out of how many doses handed out in Soho and the East Village tonight? At least two hundred, and even assuming the sweepers missed half of them, there should be ten bodies down here in the cells, not four. She knew she'd been generalizing from pitifully inadequate data—was her viability rate closer to 5% than 10%?

Or were the others going . . . somewhere else?

Just then a scream riveted her attention on Cell Four, and Jeanette uttered a startled yelp of disbelief at what the monitors showed her.

There were *things* in the cell with Hancock. Coiling, horrible, impossible things. Things that glowed with their own light. Things that dripped blood. Things that moaned and mewed in the voices of tortured children, pressing up against the door and beginning to flow under it as if they had no bones.

Jeanette's heart hammered in terror, and for a moment all she could think of was flight. But wherever she ran, these things would find her, find her and hurt her, hurt her, *hurt* her. . . .

Unable to tear her eyes from the screen, Jeanette fumbled for the row of covered buttons, scrabbling blindly to release the safety cover. More of the *things* were sliding under the door now, creeping and slithering down the corridor, drooling blood and pus and other, less nameable fluids. They twittered like birds and mewed like kittens, and some of them were speaking words that in moments she was terrified she would begin to understand. *Please, God, I have to be right about this, please, please, please. . . .*

The guard at the end of the corridor saw them too. His eyes bulged with disbelieving terror, and he dragged at his sidearm, firing wildly and without effect into the mass of nightmare moving toward him as he screamed for mercy.

She found the button for Cell Four and stabbed down at it hard enough to break a nail. The display above it turned from green to red and began to flash; she could see it pulse out of the corner of her eye.

The guard in the corridor shot himself just before the first of the *things* reached him.

And then the gas with which Jeanette had flooded Hancock's cell did its work. Hancock slumped to the floor, unconscious, and all the nightmares began to fade away.

I was right. Oh, thank God, I was right. Jeanette blinked back tears, furious with her own weakness as the crippling terror receded. An illusionist, that was all. Some kind of mental projections, and a really sick mind behind them all.

She turned and picked up a handset on one of the other consoles. She needed to clear her throat several times before it would work. "Housekeeping. This is Campbell. I need you down on Level Three to pick up a body. And send Beirkoff down with some euphorics—strong ones." *I want Hancock thinking about nothing but white fleecy clouds and little pink bunnies until the T-Stroke has worn off.*

"What are you doing here?" Robert demanded abruptly from behind her.

Jeanette spun her chair around with a strangled shriek, her nerves still raw from the brush with Hancock's mind.

"My job, Robert," she said in a harsh voice. "We've got three usables from tonight's trials. Cell Four's no good unless you want to drop him behind enemy lines to drive the bad guys mad. I'm wondering if my original model is off, though. There should be at least a dozen more Talents from tonight's sweep."

Robert grimaced in impatience. "That's what I'm trying to tell you, you stupid bitch. Michael just called in. There's someone—some*thing*—out there that's stealing our Talents."

His words dovetailed so neatly with her earlier thoughts that Jeanette was startled. "What? *How?*" *I barely know about this project—how can anyone else have figured it out so fast? Not to mention picking off the Survivors with that kind of accuracy.*

"I don't know and I don't care," Robert snarled. "What I do know is, we're going to catch the bastard and make him sorrier than he's ever been in his life. Come on."

Having touched one such Empowered life, Aerune knew the scent of his prey now. He whistled up his pack of red-eared, red-eyed hounds, and set them on the hunt. With each of the Crowned Ones he found and took, his wrath increased, for the power in each of them flickered and guttered in moments, its mortal vehicle consumed by the body's own fires before the work of building the Gateway to anchor the Nexus could be well begun. Each desiccated shell Aerune cast aside with the others, filled with a ravening lust for victory, now that victory seemed so close. The night had been long and its rewards meager. It was nearing dawn now, and in his diminished condition, the light of the sun was as much the Unseleighe Sidhe's enemy as Cold Iron was.

But there was time enough to take one more of the Crowned Ones tonight before retiring to plan his assault upon the stronghold from which that power flowed.

His hounds took the scent and began to give tongue. In the sleeping city around him, animals and even insects fled in terror, and the pent-up hounds of the mortals barked and howled in a frenzy of helpless terror at the presence of their ancient enemy. But no mortal could see him as he rode, unless he wished it.

Somewhere ahead, Aerune sensed several of the Crowned Ones gathered together, but saw only one. His prey sat alone upon a bench in one of the city's many open spaces, his head bowed in sleep or submission. Aerune whistled his dogs to his side, and dismounted from his elvensteed, dropping his cloak of confusion and shadow. He stepped forward. . . .

And all the world was filled with blinding light.

"Freeze, bastard! We've got you covered!" a mortal voice ordered.

Who dares to command the Lord of Death and Pain?

Oh, my God, Jeanette thought numbly.

Caught in the blaze of the handheld searchlights

was something off the cover of one of the books she'd read in high school.

He was tall and slender, with skin as white as an Anne Rice vampire's. He was wearing some kind of medieval costume—black chain mail and plate armor that glinted like hematite, and his long black hair was held back by a silver circlet that plainly revealed a pair of long pointed ears. He looked like Frank Langella done up as a Vulcan in a really bad mood.

"Moon!" She pinched the arm of the handcuffed woman standing at her side. "Read his mind! Now!"

The girl whimpered. Jeanette slapped her, hard.

"Aerune. His name is Aerune. He's—" Moon broke off, moaning. "It hurts!"

"*Do it,* or I'll lock you in Bellevue and give you something to whine about!" Jeanette snarled.

Moon cringed away from her anger. "The Lord of Death and Pain," she moaned.

"You!" Robert strode through the ring of armed men toward the . . . elf. Jeanette watched him in horror. Robert had been so convinced that it was the Feds who were hijacking their project that the stranger's exotic appearance didn't even slow him down. "Who are you, and just what the *hell* do you think you're doing here?"

The stranger—Aerune—drew himself up to his full height. His black cloak billowed in the wind.

"I am the Lord Aerune mac Audelaine of the Dark Court, and this man is mine. Contest with me at your peril, mortal lordling."

He turned his back on Robert, and reached for Hancock again.

Jeanette saw the glitter of the .45 in Robert's

hand and stifled a cry of warning, though she wasn't completely sure who she wanted to warn. Robert jammed the barrel into Aerune's back, and even from where she was, Jeanette could see a curl of smoke rise up from Aerune's cloak, as if the pistol barrel were red-hot.

"It burns! It burns!" Moon cried, as Aerune whirled around with a roar, his face twisted in an inhuman mask of fury. He lashed out at Robert with a backhand blow.

"You will pay dearly for that insult!" he snarled in a voice like broken music. Robert jumped back, motioning his troops forward to deal with the intruder.

But Aerune wasn't there.

"Fan out! Find him!" Robert shouted, sounding too furious to be rattled. "I want him alive!"

You won't find him, Jeanette thought. "Moon," she said gently. "Moon, what happened? Can you tell me who he is? What he wants?"

The girl looked at her, and now there was something almost serene in her expression. "He's what you think he is, Jeanette. He's a lord of the Unseleighe Court. He wants all the Crowned Ones—us—the ones you call Survivors. He needs us. . . ." She sighed, her head lolling on her shoulders as if exhaustion had suddenly overwhelmed her. "He needs us to kill you all."

Jeanette led her over to the bench and let her sit down beside Hancock. Moon curled up, instantly asleep. Her face looked haggard, and there were dark bruises of exhaustion beneath her eyes.

This one isn't going to last long either, Jeanette thought clinically. Something about T-Stroke worked like putting a penny in an old-fashioned fusebox: people could access their hidden potential, but it burned them right out within a matter of minutes. She was glad she'd brought Moon along anyway. This was probably as close to a field trial as they were going to be able to manage with any of the Survivors. Their Gifts made them too unpredictable to let out of their cells.

She glanced warily at Hancock, but the projective telepath was still in the Land of Nod, happily quiescent under the influence of the euphorics Beirkoff had given him. That was one good thing out of this whole mess. They didn't need any Monsters From The Id cluttering up the place.

She sighed, running a hand through her hair. An elf. She'd never believed she'd see one. She'd stopped believing in them years ago—forced herself to stop believing, because it just hurt too damned much. But looking into Aerune's fallen-angel eyes, skepticism was impossible. He'd been here. He was real. He burned at the touch of Cold Iron, just like all the books said.

And boy, was he mad. Madder than Jeanette had ever seen anyone get, in a serious career devoted to shining people on.

No, she had no problem believing in his reality. She had another problem entirely. Elves were supposed to be magic, and she'd certainly seen Aerune do magic, just now.

So what did an elf want with her retread junkies?

She blinked, blinded by the headlights of the big truck that pulled up, driving across the grass of the park. Robert jumped out of the passenger seat.

"Come on! We've got to get back to the lab—and hire some decent help," Robert added, his voice hoarse with disappointment. "These losers couldn't find a pig in a one-room schoolhouse. The target gave them all the slip." For the first time, he seemed to notice Moon. "What did she get? Did she read his mind?" he demanded eagerly.

"Yes, she got something," Jeanette answered, busy unlocking Hancock's handcuffs. "And no, you're not going to like it." She glanced up at the sky. It was already turning light. She glared back at Robert. "What do you want me to do, carry them? Get me some help here. And once we get back, you and I have got to talk."

"An elf. Jesus, Campbell, you been sampling your own stuff? Elves! Next you're going to be telling me the Smurfs are after us."

Robert paced back and forth in front of Jeanette's desk in her office down in Threshold's Black Labs. It was a little after six A.M. Saturday morning. The Talents—the four they'd managed to keep—were all back in their cells sleeping off the last of their T-Stroke, and everything was tidied away before the city was fairly awake. And now Robert was looking for someone to blame for tonight's fiasco.

"An elf," Jeanette repeated patiently. "That's what Vicky Moon said. That's what Aerune is." Somehow she thought it was very important to convince Robert of that fact. She'd read a lot about elves when she was a kid. They weren't the twee little Disneyfied things that Robert seemed to be thinking of. When mankind was still living in caves, they'd ruled the

world, until Cold Iron had driven them Underhill.
Even then, they were still formidable enemies.

"Or thinks he is," Robert said, still unconvinced.
"Campbell, there's no such thing as elves, so this
guy can't be one. Q.E.D." He smiled at her patron-
izingly. Jeanette sighed.

"Well, *he* thinks he is. You want to argue with
him? What else fits the facts? You burned him.
With your gun barrel, because it was steel. Didn't
you see the smoke?"

"It was . . . it could be some kind of psycho-
somatic reaction. Or an allergy of some kind," Robert said, floundering just a little.

"The only thing with an allergy to iron is an elf,"
Jeanette repeated in a dull voice. "And besides, he
vanished right in front of us. So either we've got
ourselves an elf, or David Copperfield is looking
for outside work."

"Yeah, okay, this Aerune's an elf," Robert said
hastily, unwilling to bother continuing the argument. "If he's allergic to iron, that's good. It'll give
us some way of handling him. The important thing
is to get him back. He's obviously found some way
to use his psi powers without burning out the way
your test subjects keep doing. Do you think there
are more of them? There has to be. If we can get
our hands on them we could stop wasting our time
with these trials and go right to the source."

Jeanette stared at him blankly. Did Robert
actually think Threshold had the faintest chance
of controlling someone like Aerune? His voice echoed again through her mind: *I am the Lord
Aerune mac Audelaine of the Dark Court—contest
with me at your peril.*

The Lord of Death and Pain, Moon had said. *Oh, yeah, definitely somebody I want mad at ME.*

"And how are you planning to do that, Robert?" she asked, just to be asking.

"We'll set another trap for him tonight," Robert said in a crisp managerial style. "If he's after our Talents, you can shoot them up again so they'll attract him, and this time we'll be ready for him. No pointy-eared mutant is going to thumb his nose at me!"

Great. I'm now living in an X-Files *LARP. Mutants are so much more realistic than elves, right?* Jeanette thought. She made one more attempt to get through to him.

"But we've got something he wants, Robert—and he has something we want. We could summon him, yes, but then we could talk to him, strike a bargain. . . ." *Elves were always making bargains,* Jeanette remembered. It could work. And he could teach them so much. . . .

"We don't have to bargain. We hold all the high cards, and after tonight, we'll have this Aerune mac Whasis too. This *Highlander* reject won't be so high and mighty once he's got an iron collar around his neck. In fact, I think he'll tell me everything I want to know," Robert gloated.

"Uh-huh." Robert's refusal to negotiate frustrated her. Aerune was pure power—and Robert was talking like he was some kind of special effect that could be captured between commercial breaks. All Robert could see was what he *wanted* to see—not what was there.

This was not going to end well. It was time to cut her losses.

"Look, I've got to finish up some reports on our lab rats and tweak the T-Stroke mix before I go home and grab some Z's. What time should I meet you back here tonight?" she asked brightly.

Robert smiled, sure he'd won his point. "Be back here around nine. We'll set things up in the Park this time—after midnight there's nobody there but the muggers. We'll have plenty of elbow room and plenty of peace and quiet. And a few surprises for our mutie friend."

"Sounds good." Jeanette forced another smile. "See you then."

After Robert left, Jeanette spent a long time staring at her reflection in the black mirror of her office wall, making up her mind for sure. She'd always known that someday it would be time to leave this little party Robert was throwing, and actually, she'd been here longer than she thought she'd be. But she could smell disaster ahead, and with her own survivor instincts, Jeanette decided she didn't want to be here when it hit.

Aerune haunted her thoughts. Power. Promise. Danger. She felt the temptation to stay just to see him again beckon to her, and quashed it firmly. *It's time to go.*

She'd always known that someday it'd be time, and planned accordingly. Jeanette opened her guitar case and felt around in the lining until she found what she was looking for—a red plastic diskette with a smiley-face sticker on it. She loaded its contents to her computer and hesitated for a moment before pressing "Send."

Has to be done. She pressed the button. The

virus began working its way through the system, erasing every hint of her presence—and her work.

Next she went through her desk, pulling all her paper files and shredding them. She took the bags to the incinerator herself—in her outlaw days, Jeanette had never relied on anyone else to cover her tracks: when you wanted something done right, you did it yourself.

When that was done, she took a last look around. The office where she'd spent so much of her time was completely sanitized. No trace of her presence remained, except for her guitar and sound system, a rack of CDs, and a few posters on the walls. She wasn't going to take anything but the guitar with her, but she couldn't leave the other stuff down here. This place wasn't supposed to exist.

Because it was Saturday, most of the day staff wouldn't be coming in at all. She commandeered a cart from the laundry and loaded the rest of her personal gear into it, and took it upstairs where it belonged.

Her "official" office cubicle looked strangely virginal, since she was almost never there. She took a few minutes to set up the stereo, scatter the personal things she was abandoning around it, and hang her posters on the walls. She took the cart back down to the laundry (details were important when you were planning to vanish) and came back up to the office to turn on her computer.

She tested her worm by logging in with her Black Projects user code, and was relieved to see the message "No Such User." She reset the time on her computer to a date last week and logged in under her rarely-used official, abovestairs account. Then she spent a few minutes writing memos that would "prove" she'd gone on vacation a week ago, and wouldn't be back for two more.

Let Robert start a war with Faerie. I hope Lord Aerune makes hash of him. And either way, I'm covered, and he's left holding the bag. Bye-bye, Lintel. I can't say it's been fun, because it hasn't.

When everything was arranged to her satisfaction, she took her guitar and went home. Her apartment had always been just a place to store her stuff, and Jeanette wasn't the kind of person who accumulated a lot of stuff she really cared about—she'd learned that lesson early and too well. She threw a couple of pairs of jeans and some T-shirts on the bed, and pulled her studded leather jacket and engineer boots out of the back of the closet. She took a moment to strip the vest with the Sinner Saints colors off the jacket—it'd been years since she'd worn her colors, and she didn't want to run into any old friends now—before diving back into the closet for her saddlebags. She packed quickly—clothes, music, and cash, lots of that—before putting on her boots and jacket.

Time to go. If that idiot wants to commit suicide, he can do it without me—and if he manages to survive, he'll still need me and maybe we'll do the dance. But I'm not taking any falls for him. Survival of the fittest. I'm sure Robert would agree.

Her Harley was waiting for her in the garage below—a cream and maroon touring beauty she'd named Mystery, on which she'd blown most of her first paychecks when she'd come to Threshold. She

stripped off the protective cover and slung her
saddlebags over Mystery's back, buckling them into
place before lashing her guitar down to the pil-
lion seat. It would make an awkward load, and she
might have been willing to leave the instrument
behind if she'd been sure she was coming back.

But she wasn't.

She wheeled slowly out of the underground
garage, blinking owlishly at the winter sunlight even
through the tinted face-shield of her full-coverage
helmet. She debated where to go for a moment,
but given her mode of transport, it was pretty
much a no-brainer.

*South. Somewhere warm, with no snow and
fewer questions.*

Campbell didn't show up at the lab at nine
o'clock. At nine-thirty Robert checked her downstairs office, found it stripped, and called her
house. At nine-forty-five he let himself into her
apartment with a passkey he didn't think she knew
he had, and looked around. The place looked like
a hotel room that had been trashed by gypsies.

*God, how can anyone live like this? You can take
the girl off the street, but you can't take the street
out of the girl,* he thought in disgust.

She wasn't here either. He looked around. There
were signs of hasty packing, and the ice-cream
carton in the back of the fridge where Campbell
kept her stash of ready cash was empty. He felt
a wave of smug disdain. *So she's bolted. Da widdle
girly got scared and ran. Jesus, isn't that just like
a woman?*

But did this really change anything? Robert

thought about that for a moment, making up his mind. It wasn't like she'd be going to the police, not with what he had on her. Actually, Campbell's bailout wasn't entirely a bad thing. Ever since the drug trials had started panning out, Campbell had been acting pretty skittish, and that mutant-guy from last night showing up had obviously been more than she could handle. *After all,* Robert Lintel thought sagely, *it's one thing to read about psychic powers in a fiction book and another altogether to see them in front of your face.*

He'd probably scared her into running by talking about setting a trap for the guy tonight. Women just weren't any good in military situations. Oh, she faked it better than most, but Robert had seen the flash of fear in her eyes when the guy in the cloak had showed up. She'd just lost her head and panicked. How typical. Women were all like that.

But I don't need her anymore. I've got more than enough T-Stroke to turn a sample over to a good research chemist and find out the proportions—and more than enough to finish the trials without her.

And once he'd done that, he could write his own ticket anywhere in the world and kiss Threshold good-bye.

In fact, maybe it's better to wait a day or two before trying to trap this Aerune again. He'll be sweating, and I'll have time to rope in a few more pieces of bait.

Pleased with his conclusions, Robert Lintel left the apartment.

Everything's going to work out just fine. . . .

NINE:

A GAME OF CHESS

Though his dreams were only dreams, they were haunted by the Unseleighe taint Eric had felt in Central Park and the nagging sense that there was something he was missing. He woke up late on Sunday morning, rumpled and disgruntled and aware that somehow he'd blown most of the weekend without getting his coursework done. His mind felt fuzzy—the mental equivalent of indigestion—and he badly wanted someone to talk it out with. But Greystone wasn't available— when he looked, the gargoyle wasn't even on its perch outside his window—and Toni and Jimmie had both made it pretty clear last night that the Guardians wouldn't welcome his involvement in the situation.

But the more he thought about it, the more Eric was convinced there was something back there in the Park that they'd all missed. Something important.

Well, if they won't talk to me about it, I know someone who'll at least listen.

Even the most avaricious capitalists took Sundays off, and Ria Llewellyn knew from long experience that you got better work out of people if you didn't ask them to give 110 percent all the time. She'd been on everybody's back most of the week, getting a feel for her New York companies and finishing up with dinner with Eric last night—which, while fun, could not by any stretch of the imagination be called restful—and today Ria was looking forward to a leisurely day of shopping and sightseeing. Maybe she'd even succumb to the impulse to go down and see the giant Christmas tree at Rockefeller Center. She'd forgotten how much she liked New York—it was such a human city, so un-elvish, that she actually found herself preferring it to L.A., where not even the special effects were real, let alone the people. Too many bad associations there: tragedy and betrayal and her long painful climb back to life.

Besides, Eric will be here for at least another year. . . .

That was certainly one of the attractions. They'd made a good start last night. He wasn't as indifferent to her as he'd tried to pretend. And he wasn't out to kill her, either on his own behalf or someone else's. In Ria's opinion, both of those things made a good start to a relationship.

The windows of her sitting room at the top of the Sherry gave her a magnificent view over the Park, an unexpected oasis of green in the steel and concrete forest of the City. The trees were winter-bare, the grass a faded brown-green, but at night the lights shining down into the park gave it an air of mystery—a man-made fairyland, in sharp contrast to the inhuman beauty of Underhill. Ria preferred it.

She was lingering over a last cup of coffee, a legal pad on her lap, when her phone rang. Few enough people knew where she was that she had no hesitation about picking up the phone instead of letting the front desk take the call.

"Hello?"

"Ria? It's Eric!"

Eric! She allowed herself a small smile of triumph. The first one to pick up the phone lost. *And your loss is my gain.*

"Eric," she purred. "How wonderful to hear from you so soon. Did you sleep well?" she asked, layering a double meaning into the innocent phrase.

She heard a rueful chuckle on the other end of the line. "Not really. I'd like to talk to you."

And do more than talk, I'll wager. Should she lead him on for awhile to demonstrate her power? Or would immediately giving him what he wanted be more effective? *Decisions, decisions.*

"Of course. Why don't you come over here? I'm at the Sherry-Netherland. The view of the Park is spectacular. I'll order a fresh pot of coffee. Or would you prefer tea?"

"Central Park?" For a moment Eric sounded

completely nonplussed. Then: "Sure. Give me about forty minutes."

"I'll be waiting." *And to hell with the coffee.*

Eric hung up the phone, staring at it as if it were about to do something strange and unusual. He didn't know what he'd expected when he decided to call Ria, but it wasn't this, well, *blatant* an invitation. What was she up to this time? *Other than the obvious, and if there's one thing you can say about Ria, it's that she isn't.* Anyway, he was committed now. And there couldn't be any harm in going up to her place to talk, now, could there? Besides, if he went there, he wouldn't have to risk stirring up the Guardians by poking his nose into their business. He thought the best thing might be to stay out of their way if they'd stay out of his.

Time to get dressed, but in something a little less warlike than what he'd worn to their last encounter.

He pulled out a chunky oatmeal-colored fisherman's sweater, and hesitated for a moment between slacks and jeans. Ria wasn't a jeans kind of person, he decided, and went for a pair of dark grey slacks. He grabbed the leather jacket he'd worn last night, and dumped the contents of his messenger bag out on his bed to make room for the flute. He gave the books and notebooks a resigned glance. Rector wouldn't cut him any slack; he'd better get his paper—or at least, *some* kind of paper—done before 2 P.M. tomorrow.

Somehow.

❖   ❖   ❖

He'd been past the Sherry-Netherland a few times in his rambles, but he'd never been inside. It was an imposing structure, like something out of an Edith Wharton novel: very repressed, very Old New York. He almost expected the gaudily uniformed doorman to refuse to let him in.

He made his way across the lobby to the elevators, found the one that serviced Ria's floor, and got in. The elevator was an express, and took off with a *swoosh!* that left Eric's stomach far behind, though it mercifully released him a few moments later. The corridor outside its doors was painted a tasteful rose-beige that reminded Eric of something you might find at a mortician's. Ria's penthouse suite was at the end of the hallway, and as he approached it, Ria opened the door.

She was wearing a man-tailored blouse of heavy white silk that she'd wrapped, kimono-style, instead of buttoning, and it was pretty obvious that there was nothing under it. It was tucked into the waistband of a pair of wide-legged cuffed and pleated pants of bronze hammered silk, and on her feet she wore a pair of high-heeled gold mules. Eric could see that her toenails were painted Jungle Red. With her blond hair hanging loose in a Veronica Lake sweep, Ria looked like the Bad Girl from every film noir ever made.

"Nice to see you again," she said briskly. Spoiling the illusion? Or breaking a deliberate spell? With any other woman, he'd know. "Come on in."

Eric followed her into the main room of the suite. Her perfume hung in the air, the same subtle understated floral she'd worn last night at dinner. He tried to ignore it. He'd come here to talk over a problem, not be a slave to his raging hormones.

There was a coffee service set out on a low table bordered on three sides by loveseats in a pale shadow stripe. As Ria had said, there was also a splendid view of Central Park. Eric tried to locate the spot where he'd stood last night and failed. It wouldn't be hard to find again, though.

"Coffee?" Ria asked, and when Eric nodded she poured. He still found something deliciously perverse about drinking coffee, since what was harmless to him was so deadly to Kory and his other elven friends.

"I didn't mean to interrupt your day," Eric began, "but something pretty weird happened last night, and, well, I wanted to talk about it to someone who'd understand. You see—well, to begin with, the place I live isn't an ordinary apartment building." *Lame, Banyon, really lame!*

But Ria didn't zing him on it, the way Beth or some of the Sidhe would have.

"So I gathered, after I met your stony friend," she commented, sipping her own coffee. She regarded him over the rim of the cup with steady emerald-green eyes, their vivid color one of the many legacies of her mixed blood.

"Well, Greystone's just the tip of the iceberg," Eric said glumly, belatedly realizing how much he'd have to explain before he got to the Unseleighe Nexus, and how little Ria was probably going to like any of it. "You see, there are these folks called Guardians. . . ."

Quickly he sketched out as much as he knew of the Guardians and their mission to protect the average run of humankind from the Dark Powers. He told her about Dharinel and Kory's warning of Unseleighe activity in the city, and of his own strange, possibly prophetic, dream about the goblin tower overshadowing Central Park amid the ruins of Manhattan.

"I told Jimmie about it, but with the Sidhe you never know *when*. Right now? Next year? Next century? But last night after you left, Toni came to see me because the Guardians had run into something funky out in the Park that they wanted my opinion on. When I took a look, I found that the whole place is lousy with Unseleighe magic—and something else I couldn't quite put my finger on—and it looked to me like somebody was trying to open a Nexus."

"In Central Park?" Ria's voice was rich with disbelief. "Using what for a Bard? And leaving aside the question of what kind of Sidhe maniac would want to open up a Nexus in the middle of one of the biggest cities in the world? Sidhe magic would be almost worthless with all the iron and steel—and man-made electro-magnetic fields—around, even if they lived long enough to use it. Even a human sorcerer has trouble in a big city, with all those minds around clogging up the Ethereal Plane."

"Seleighe magic wouldn't work here," Eric admitted. "At least not consistently. But Unseleighe power runs a little differently, doesn't it?" He knew Perenor had been acting pretty much as a lone wolf in his vendetta against Terenil, but someone that ruthless must have made overtures to the Dark Court at some point.

Ria considered, worrying at her lower lip with her teeth as she thought. "I don't know that much about the Dark Court, but I'd have to say that most of the power they use isn't that different. Not in kind, anyway, or ultimate source. But in degree, yes—the Dark Court isn't squeamish about feeding off other peoples' life-force. And in a city this size, I'd have to say there'd be enough prey available to take the edge off any discomfort Cold Iron would give them. Enough deaths would allow them to punch through any kind of interference, at least for a short time. But whoever it is that's trying to put up a Nexus here, he'd have to know he couldn't just maraud around and not expect to be stopped—by your Guardians, or the police at the very least. And for all that either of us knows, there's some alphabet agency out there like the Men In Black to save the world from the scum of Faerie. This isn't the Stone Age!"

Eric grinned slightly, savoring the mental image of a posse of sunglasses-wearing Feds in Lincoln Green Armani suits armed with high-tech wizard's staves and magnetized steel sword-phones. *It's almost weird enough to happen....* Then he turned serious again.

"Maybe whoever it is doesn't realize what he's actually up against. If you're Sidhe—and practically immortal—and living Underhill anyway—you might not really have noticed the last two or three centuries go by, even though it's made a helluva lot of difference here in the world. Meanwhile, you can't deny he could do a lot of damage before someone stopped him—and what would happen if the Feds got real concrete proof that the Sidhe existed? I tried to warn Jimmie and the others, but those Guardians are way in over their heads—and they won't even consider the possibility that this is something they can't handle. Quietly, I mean." *Or at all. Guardians die as easily as anyone else, and the Dark Court can put a lot of resources into the field.*

But Ria's attitude had changed while he was making his point. She looked almost disapproving, now.

"I'm flattered that you'd want to use me as a sounding board," Ria said, sitting back in her seat and regarding him with an unreadable expression. "But frankly, Eric, I don't see what this has to do with you or me, other than meaning we ought to get out of here before the fireworks start."

Eric stared at Ria in disbelief. He'd just naturally assumed that once he'd told her what the problem was, she'd immediately have some suggestions for what to do next to take care of it.

"If a Sidhe Great Lord starts a war with the United States, we're going to be drawn into it no matter what," he finally pointed out. "This is entirely leaving out the people who'll get killed, or hurt, or sucked dry before he's stopped."

"The Guardians think they can handle it. You said yourself they'll probably stop him eventually. And you're the one who's living here, not me," Ria said. "Besides, there's a faint possibility you've misread the situation. Maybe a few disappointments will change your Nexus-builder's mind about moving here before he throws down for a full-scale war. So why not let these Guardians do what they're here for? You said it was their full-time job. They probably have lots of experience."

"Not with this," Eric said stubbornly. "They don't get many Sidhe here in the city. They've never seen this kind of magic before. You have, and so have I. You know what kind of damage a situation like this can do." He leaned forward, willing her to understand how important this was. But even before she spoke, he knew he'd failed.

"Eric, people are dying horribly every day, all over the world. Even if I devoted my every waking moment to making things better for them, it'd be a drop in the bucket compared to what they're doing to themselves. I have responsibilities closer to home—to my employees, to my staff, to the people who depend on me personally to be there, and not go haring off on some kind of damnfool idealistic crusade designed to get someone close to me out of a midterm exam."

"Is *that* what you think this is about?" Eric demanded, recoiling in hurt. Ria of all people knew how much trouble a Nexus in the wrong hands could be. He'd been sure that the moment he explained things to her she'd be ready to help.

Ria smiled gently. "No, Eric, not entirely. But I think it is part of the reason you're trying so hard to push yourself into someplace you're obviously not wanted. Dharinel told you to stay out of it. These Guardians told you the same thing. Why not listen to somebody for a change?"

I've already been doing too much of that! Eric felt a stubborn anger rising inside him, and tried to push it aside. He'd been open and honest with Ria, and she seemed to be treating this as if it were all some sort of meaningless game!

"Okay. All right. I guess I deserve some of that.

But at least come and look at the place in the Park with me. Make up your own mind about how bad this could be. And if you don't want to get involved then, I'll respect that."

He leaned forward, willing her to say yes. To that much, at least.

Ria sighed. "Okay, Eric, you've won me over. I'll come and look. But I can't do it today, and Monday's looking pretty full, too. I have companies to run; give me a few days. I'll clear a space in my schedule."

A few days could be too late! Eric took a deep breath and regained control of himself with an effort. He felt oddly disappointed—in Ria, in himself—as if a door that might lead to something wonderful had just been unexpectedly slammed in his face. He'd thought—well, maybe he hadn't actually *thought*. He'd been upset about what happened at the Park last night, he'd wanted to see Ria again, and he guessed he'd let his hormones do at least some of the thinking.

"Okay," he said grudgingly, hating how hurt, how *betrayed* he felt. "I guess that's fair. Why don't you give me a call when you've got some free time?" He got to his feet. "I won't bother you any more. I'm sure we've both got a lot of things to do."

Ria rose gracefully, her face a cool social mask of politeness. Bard or not, Truth-sense or not, he couldn't get a peek at anything behind her shields to judge her feelings. "I'll see you later, then, Eric."

With as much dignity as he felt he could muster under the circumstances, Eric left.

❖   ❖   ❖

Out on the street again, Eric took a few moments to catch his mental breath. Those mis-cues just now had been at least partly his fault—and more than partly, if he were being totally honest with himself. He realized that he'd been thinking of Ria as a sort of natural ally against the Guardians who'd fall in with anything he proposed—well, she'd disabused him of that notion pretty quick.

Then I'll do it myself, said the Little Red Hen. He managed a smile. It would have been nice to have company and a little backup, but he was a Bard, after all. He could do his own investigating. *And I'm right here, and the Park is pretty safe during the day. All the muggers are probably out Christmas shopping, too.*

And it wasn't really going against Dharinel's advice. Not yet. Whoever'd put up the Nexus didn't seem to be around during the day, and Eric would be sure not to leave any trail that could lead an Unfriendly back to his doorstep. The guy was after Talents, and Eric didn't fool himself about the fact that his own power made him a pretty enticing mouthful. And he wasn't interested in being anybody's lunch, thank you ma'am.

But a little looking around wouldn't hurt. And Ria was right about one thing. With a quick glance in the dark and a bunch of other people around, he *might* have misjudged how serious the situation was. He waited for a break in the traffic and crossed the street, heading into the Park.

From the window high above, Ria watched him go. She felt an irritated mixture of anger and regret over what had just happened.

Just who the hell did Eric Banyon think he was, anyway? The Lone Ranger?

Not the old Eric Banyon, that's for sure. The old Eric, the one she'd kept as an intriguing pet, wouldn't have thrown himself into things this way. That Eric had waited to be led, or told what to do. This one made his own choices, and his own rules.

But I'm not going to play by them. He can be the Lone Ranger if he wants, but he'll have to find another faithful Indian companion!

She respected him enough to send him away today, rather than teasing him into bed. It would have been a sweet sort of triumph to distract him that thoroughly—Eric had always been a generous lover, and this new maturity made him even more interesting as a potential bed partner—but she wanted him as an equal, not a conquest. And that meant equality on both sides. If she didn't want Eric as a submissive follower, then he was going to have to learn that he wasn't automatically the leader, either. Living in the real world meant negotiating for what you wanted—and if Eric wanted her as much as she wanted him, he was going to have to learn that little lesson. *And hope it doesn't kill either of us.*

That didn't mean she was going to hang him out to dry, either. He'd been right about one thing: she knew this enemy better than he did. She hesitated a moment, coming to a decision, and then picked up the phone.

"Jonathan? Ria. Look, I've run into a little something out here that needs looking into, and I'm going to need some backup. Yes. Armed and *very* discreet. Who do we use in New York? Call me back when you have the number. I want to make the call myself."

About an hour later there was a knock on her door. She checked through the peephole, and then opened the door.

"Gotham Security," the man said, holding open a photo ID for her to look at. *Raine Logan*, read the name below the photo.

He was only a few inches taller than she was, but he carried himself as if he were six feet tall. He wore a dark blue nylon bomber jacket and jeans, with an army surplus duffle slung over his shoulder. His black hair was brushed straight back from a deep widow's peak, there was a day's worth of black stubble on his jaw, and beneath his bulky clothing, he had the trim, sculpted body of someone who worked out with weights for more than show. When she'd called the service, she'd specified needing someone who could keep her safe anywhere in New York—and blend in on the street. The man they'd sent more than fit the bill. You wouldn't give him a second glance anywhere from Spanish Harlem to Crown Point.

"Come in, Mr. Logan," she said, closing the door behind him.

"Just Logan. And you're Ria," he said. "These are for you." He held out the bag. "The service has your size and your profile; you've used our West Coast service in the past."

She opened the duffle and pulled out the contents. Worn jeans with the extra gusset at the crotch that would give them as much flexibility as a pair of dance tights, a tight black T-shirt, and a jacket. It looked like a cheap vinyl imitation of a black leather jacket, but when she lifted it, it was heavier than she expected. She checked the lining, and found it was lined in Kevlar—enough to stop anything up to a Black Talon cop-killer.

"The dispatcher said you'd be going into some rough neighborhoods. You don't want to go looking like money," Logan said.

"Thanks," Ria said, meaning it. Gotham Security was the best. They turned down more clients than they accepted, and the reason they still accepted her commissions was because she never argued with their decisions once she'd set the parameters. Ria respected competence in any field. When you hired an expert to keep you safe, there was no point in telling him how to do his job.

"Help yourself to some coffee. I'll go change."

She'd worn running shoes on the plane, but they weren't some expensive brand someone would try to kill her for. She stripped off the seduction outfit she'd worn for Eric and changed into the street clothes the bodyguard had brought, then braided her hair severely back and pinned it into a tight bun. She looked in the mirror, frowned, and then went into the bathroom to scrub off every trace of makeup. There were thin gloves in the pocket of the jacket, and she put them on. Satisfied at last, she came back into the sitting room of the suite.

Logan was standing where he could watch both the doors and the windows, a cup of coffee in his hand. He regarded her impassively, and then gave a short nod of approval.

"Let's go." He held out a black watch cap. "Wear this. Blondes aren't that common in some parts of town."

Eric hadn't told Ria exactly where the unfinished Nexus was, but once she got into the Park, the trail of Unseleighe taint was fairly obvious. Logan followed her like a silent shadow as she cast around, working her way into the center of the magic.

Here.

The partial Nexus shimmered in the dry winter air, invisible unless you were Gifted *and* knew what you were looking for. Its twisted magic made even Ria shudder inwardly. This was Unseleighe work, fuelled by death, *human* death. She could still see the faint smudges of levin bolts on the grass where the Sidhe Lord had destroyed the bodies of his victims.

The surrounding trees looked faintly haunted. If the Nexus came fully into being, this would become a bonewood, the trees taking on a malicious life of their own in imitation of their dark master.

So he—whoever he is—was here. But where did he come from, and where did he go? In and out of Underhill, of course. She wouldn't be able to track his movements Underhill from here, and even if she'd had the power to force an entry into Underhill from a standing start, she knew too little about her foe to make it a good idea. She turned her attention to another part of the problem. Eric had been here as well, and recently. Had he seen what she saw, she wondered? And if he had, where was he now?

Not chasing the Unseleighe, that's for sure. There's nothing to track.

She circled the area, frowning faintly. This wasn't Unseleighe Sidhe work alone. There was something else here as well.

Her hands wove small patterns through the air as she called upon her magic—not the Gift that was the birthright of the Sidhe, but sorcery that she'd learned painstakingly over the years. She worked slowly and carefully, and at last she had banished everything that was wholly of Underhill from her perceptions.

But something remained, the human taint she had noticed at first.

And *that* left a trail she could follow.

An hour before Ria left her hotel room with Logan, Eric headed into Central Park. He stopped just inside the grounds to dig his flute out of his bag and put it together. He blew a soft note into the mouthpiece to warm the cold silver, and seemed to feel the trees around him shiver in response. More proof, not that he needed it, that someone had been using major magic here— enough magic to wake the trees, let alone the dead.

Carrying his flute in his hand, Eric walked deeper into the park, back to the place Toni had brought him to last night. The scorch marks were still there, and in the daylight he saw something he'd missed the night before—the deep cuts of horses' hooves in the frozen turf.

And sure, there are bridle paths through the park, but they're clearly marked and the riders stick to them. And these tracks sure weren't made by any New York Rent-a-Nag. Where were you going, Mister Dark Lord of the Sidhe? And who were you after?

Let's see just how you've been spending your time. . . .

He lifted his flute to his lips and began to play. A few trills and runs first, just to warm up, and then he segued into "Sidhe Beg, Sidhe Mor," letting the plaintive demand of the music speak for him.

The light seemed to shift, some colors growing brighter, others vanishing entirely. The hard brightness of the afternoon sun became muted, fading almost into the unchanging silvery light of Underhill, while the latticework of the unfinished Nexus burned bright and clear, like a sculpture of purest purple-black neon. The constant background noise of New York—sirens, traffic, and the hum of a thousand conversations all taking place at once—faded to silence. Now Eric could see the magic plainly, yet he himself was as invisible to mortal eyes as magic normally was. Cloaked in his music, Eric could pass through the city unseen, even by his quarry. He turned, casting about.

The whole park was dotted with hoofprints that glowed with a deep scarlet light—the Unseleighe Lord, whoever he was, had been making himself right at home, him and his elvensteed. The creature's glowing scarlet trail crisscrossed the grass from a dozen directions, giving the dry winter grass a spuriously festive look.

I can't follow all of these! Eric shifted his bag higher on his shoulder. He had to pick one—but which?

At last he saw one set of hoofprints of a slightly different color than the rest—almost maroon, instead of the bright vermilion of the others. As he stepped into them, he caught a faint whiff of something . . . something almost raw and primitive next to the ancient malice of the Unseleighe Sidhe.

As good a way to make a choice as any, Eric decided, and began to follow the dark track.

The track quickly took him across town and out of the high-priced spread. He could see splashes of magic along the way—as if someone had been carrying it in a bucket that kept slopping over, staining the sidewalks and buildings. When he got further downtown, a fine red mist seemed to hang in the air like a fog of magic—too thin to really have any effect, but more evidence that its source—or even many sources—had passed through here, all leaking magic like a sieve.

What is this? A mage's convention? And if so, why wasn't I invited? he thought whimsically.

The odd thing was, the "splashes"—for lack of a better word—seemed to be concentrated around the street people. None of them seemed to be the source, but somehow they'd been *near* the source, and not very long ago. Eric guessed the Nexus point in the Park hadn't been started more than a day or so—the timing of its building coincided perfectly with his dream—and the traces he was following would fade away completely in another day or so.

Cold weather to be on the streets, Eric thought, watching an old man pushing along a grocery cart full of bits and pieces of unnameable junk. *A Sidhe Lord down here. Now THAT's culture clash.*

The contrast between the busy, purposeful shoppers—all of whom had homes to go to—and the shabby homeless that cowered back from them like hungry ghosts was jarring. He didn't remember there being so many street people the last time he'd been in New York—hell, he didn't remember there being any, but the Upper East Side tended to run them out of the area pretty rigorously. He'd gotten used to seeing them in the last few weeks—as used as you could get, anyway— but as he headed east, he realized that the ones in his neighborhood were just the tip of the iceberg. As he left Yuppieland and entered the area of clinics, flophouses, and SROs[6] the tribe of the disenfranchised seemed to multiply, and for the first time Eric realized how very many people in this city had no other home than the streets. Not hundreds. *Thousands.*

And not just people living in slums or in welfare housing, but people who didn't have any place to go at night at all. He walked past a man in a tattered overcoat who might have been any age from forty to seventy and was carrying on an angry, animated conversation with the empty air. His hands were covered with small unhealed sores, and there were flecks of spittle on his cheeks. Greyish stubble covered his cheeks, and even in the cold he stank of urine, unwashed body, and illness.

Isn't anybody helping these people? That guy shouldn't be out on the street. But even as he wondered, Eric knew the answer. These were the "borderline" people, the ones who'd been dumped

---

[6] Single-Room Occupancies, aka welfare hotels.

out onto the streets from the institutions where many of them had spent their entire lives to make their way as best they could in the world. The idea was that they'd have caseworkers and live in supervised housing, but there weren't enough beds or caseworkers to go around, and so most of these walking wounded ended up alone on the streets. Add to that the junkies who stayed away from social services for fear they'd be jailed, the street kids damaged by predators or the homes they'd run from, and you had thousands and tens of thousands of people living on the streets—the population of an entire shadow city living invisibly in the cracks of the city most people saw.

A bright flare caught his attention out of the corner of his eye. Magic—the same magic he'd been following. It ended at a brick wall, the glare of it so bright it nearly hurt his eyes. He touched the flaking brickwork, and recoiled when his fingers came away sticky and dark. He rubbed his fingers together. It was blood. Old, but not that old.

This wasn't Unseleighe magic he'd been following, but human magic. Eric blinked, bringing up the image of the human city to overlay his magesight, and bent over to inspect the wall and the sidewalk. Now he could see that there were bloody handprints on the concrete. The wall itself was covered with blood, great arcing gouts of blood, as if somebody had tried to batter his way through the bricks with his body.

And I'm betting that's exactly what happened, Eric thought grimly, straightening up. He felt nauseated. Echoing through his mind, preserved in the stone, were ghostly screams of fury, as if the raging spirit were still trapped here. He scrubbed his hand on his jeans and raised the flute to his lips, playing the first tune that came to mind, an old folk tune called "She Moved Through The Fair," the sweet wistful lament seemed to soothe the energies here, sending the spirit on its way in peace, washing away the death-fury that had happened here.

"Mister? Hey, mister?"

Eric lowered his flute. He'd put so much of himself into the music that he'd lost his cloak of magic, and with it, his invisibility. He turned in the direction of the voice. There was a man watching him, a man only a few years older than Eric with haunted, lost eyes. *That could be me*, Eric realized in pitying horror. *A little more bad luck, a few more missed chances . . . not meeting Beth, or Kory. Missing out on the Faire-circuit. That could be me.*

"That's pretty music," the man said, when he had Eric's attention. "I'm Gary."

"Hello, Gary," Eric said quietly, so as not to startle his new friend. Though his body was full grown, it was clear that the mind behind the eyes was much younger. "Do you know what happened here?"

Gary's face turned sad, as transparently as a child's. "Fury died. We always used to call him that. He got sick and yelled at everybody, and then he started to fight with the wall." Easy tears glinted in Gary's eyes. "Nobody fights a wall," he said sadly.

Not with any chance of winning, Eric thought, glancing at the bloodstains. He was tempted to slip back into his magic and leave, but he'd already seen enough to know that he had a lot of urgent questions without answers. Maybe Gary had some of the answers.

"Have a lot of people died lately? In just the last couple days? People like Fury?"

Gary stared at him blankly, a sudden sourceless fear growing in his haunted eyes. "The angels take them—the night angels. I have to go," he said suddenly.

"Hey—wait! I didn't mean to—"

Gary turned away and scuttled quickly down an alleyway, vanishing from sight.

"—scare you," Eric finished, gazing at the empty street.

He could run after the homeless man, but he didn't think Gary had any more to tell him. Fury's death hadn't fed the Nexus—those deaths had occurred back in the Park. And what were the night angels? Unseleighe Sidhe? If the Dark Court was using Manhattan as a hunting ground, there should be unadulterated traces of their magic all over, but the only thing he'd found here was the magic he'd followed.

Nothing was adding up. It was as if he had all the puzzle pieces—and they all turned out to be from different puzzles. He sighed and looked around. At the end of the block a blue neon cross shone into the night. Eric raised his flute to his lips again, gathering his cloak of invisibility around him once more. The light at the wall was gone now, thanks to Eric's music, but somehow the neon cross shone even brighter in his Shifted sight. It was a sign for a mission, one of the places that tried to feed and shelter New York's rising tide of homeless. Reluctantly, Eric turned toward it. He didn't want to see any more horrors, any more forgotten men and women, but he needed to find out why Sidhe magic was tangled up with the homeless here.

The inside of the mission was warm and welcoming. Tables were set up where men—and women, some with children—sat spooning up soup. At the kitchen in the back, volunteer workers doled out more soup, sandwiches, and chunks of bread to a long line of those patiently waiting. They were talking among themselves in low voices where the diners couldn't here. Eric crept closer.

"Not a lot of people here tonight," a woman said. Her companion sighed, rolling his shoulders to take the kinks out.

"There's something bad out there on the streets. A lot of our regulars are afraid to come in. I heard Johnnie Rags talking to Lindy earlier. They think we might be poisoning them."

"*Poisoning* them?" The woman recoiled in shock.

The man shook his head grimly. "I've heard from some of the other soup kitchens and flops. A lot of people are dead. And more have just . . . vanished. All in the last seventy-two hours. I thought at first that a shipment of bad drugs might have reached the street—but where would our guys get the money for drugs? They can't even afford beds, most of them."

"Unless the dealers have started handing out free samples like the tobacco companies." The two of them laughed together in disbelief, sharing the bitter joke.

"And what are the cops going to do? A lot of people die down here every day," the woman went on.

"Not like this," the man said grimly, shaking his head. "Not like this."

Eric turned away. The answers he wanted weren't here, but he couldn't escape the feeling that he'd just been handed another clue . . . if he could only understand it.

Even Shielded as he was, Eric was reluctant to leave the light and warmth of the mission for the cold gloom outside, but he knew he had to move on, see if he could follow this trail to where it began . . . or ended.

As he turned to go, a young woman sitting at one of the tables got to her feet, heading for the door. She was skeleton-thin, but she'd made some attempt at looking pretty. She wore a down jacket a dozen seasons out of date and a thin bright summery dress. Her legs were bare.

"Where you going, Annie?" the man behind the soup cauldron called.

"Got me a date," Annie said belligerently. Eric could see they wanted to stop her, to call her back, but before they could do anything she was outside, hurrying up the street.

Eric followed her. She didn't go far. There was an alleyway a few doors down from the mission. Annie ducked into it with an ease borne of long familiarity. There was a crude shelter there, made of flattened cardboard boxes, and Annie scuttled inside, squatting down and digging into her jacket.

"Got me a free sample, got me a free sample," she sing-songed under her breath. Eric could see the glitter of a small packet of white powder in her hands. It radiated a kind of non-magical malignity that made Eric blink.

"Hey—don't do that," he protested, making himself visible again. He dug in his pocket for his wallet. "Don't take that. Here—I'll buy it from you. Okay?"

Seeing him, Annie crouched back with a feral cry of alarm. Before Eric could react, she'd torn open the packet and poured the contents into her mouth.

Its effect was immediate and drastic. Her eyes rolled up in her head and she slumped down, unconscious.

Oh . . . God. Eric stared at her, sure for a moment that she was dead. *I've got to help her.*

He pulled out his flute. The people at the mission knew her. They'd know what to do. But their help wouldn't be any good to Annie if she was dead.

He let the magic flow down into him, reaching out to the flicker of magic—Eric experienced it as music—that every living thing had. Her song was faint, the contents of the envelope poisoning her nearly to death. It was as if two songs were playing at once, creating a jangling discord. Imposing a third one wouldn't help much.

He listened as hard as he could for the original tune, there in the cold alleyway, and slowly began improvising a counterpoint around it, strengthening it without overwhelming it. The music became stronger—he could almost identify the tune—when suddenly he was knocked off balance by a blast of . . . music?

It reverberated through his head, soundless yet loud enough to make his teeth ache, overwhelming all other sounds. The music wanted him to follow—it was a call, a command, dark and powerful and magical. Resisting it was like trying to stand still in the path of a cyclone. Annie still needed help, but Eric couldn't "hear" his own magic against the howl of the magestorm. He ran toward the mission. He could at least summon worldly aid. The pull of the Summoning grew stronger by the moment; he pushed open the door to the mission and half staggered, half fell inside.

"Hey," Eric croaked, half-deafened by the buffeting he was receiving. "Annie's out there in the alley. She's sick."

The woman who'd been talking as she served the soup ran over to him. Dizzy and battered by the dark undertow of the magical Summoning, Eric clung to her for support.

"Are you hurt? Can you tell me your name? Come over here. Sit down—"

"No," Eric gasped. "I've got to—I've got to go. Help her. She's in an alley up the street, in a box. She took something. Something bad." It was hard to get any words out against the call of the Unseleighe magic, and finally Eric abandoned the effort. He pushed the woman away and thrust himself out into the night once more, turning in the direction of the summons.

As soon as he was moving with the pull of the magic, his head cleared enough for him to throw up some stronger shields. The power of the assault had taken him off-guard, but he had his bearings now. It would be a simple thing to isolate himself from its pull entirely, but Eric wasn't sure he wanted to do that. He'd come down here looking for the source of the magic that had befouled the city—and now, it seemed, the magic was looking for *him*.

Sorry Master Dharinel. I know you wanted me to stay out of this one, but a Bard's gotta do what a Bard's gotta do. I just hope I'm around afterward to get yelled at for it.

And I think I'm glad after all that I didn't get Ria to come with me. . . .

The only way Ria could follow the magical trail was on foot, and that was a slow process. The trace was faint, and easily confused, but Ria always managed to find it again. It led her south and east, down into some of the worst neighborhoods in New York. She was glad more than once to have Logan at her back. Most folks who saw him just tended to veer off from whatever mischief they were contemplating.

Night came early in the winter, and by the time they finally crossed Houston Street it was already getting dark. Ria was footsore and hungry, but unwilling to give up the hunt just yet. She felt more alive than she had any time yet since her recovery. Ria was a born hunter, and if more of her stalks were in the world of finance than on the city streets, well, the instinct was the same.

On the Lower East Side a lot of the buildings were red brick dating back a century and more. New York had moved slowly uptown from the foot of the island since its founding, leaving behind outgrown neighborhoods to fall into decay. With taxes rising astronomically, many landlords found it more economical to let buildings rot where they stood rather than invest the money to make them livable again. The ever-growing population of those who had slipped between the cracks of what had once been touted as the Great Society had taken over the abandoned buildings, forming new tribes outside of the protection of society. As Ria and her shadow had moved downtown, out of the affluent neighborhoods, the number of homeless had increased. They huddled in doorways or crouched on the steam vents that led down into the subways, watching Ria's progress with empty eyes.

With Logan behind her, Ria headed eastward, across the Bowery. More than a hundred years ago, this had been the northernmost boundary of Manhattan, its then-cobbled streets filled with gracious ladies, fine gentlemen, and horse-drawn carriages. Of that era, only a few landmarked buildings still remained.

The trail she followed was stronger here, but her puzzlement was growing. What would a mage, human or Sidhe, be doing here, in the middle of such poverty and despair? There was nothing down here but crack houses, squats, and a few brave homesteading yuppies. Soon enough urban development would sweep through here, just as it had elsewhere, leaving a litter of Starbucks and Barnes & Nobles in its wake, but for now, the area looked like a bombed-out city in the aftermath of a war it had lost.

Yet here was where the trail began—or ended. Ria stopped in front of the old building her stalk had led her to. It didn't look particularly promising.

Even in the cold, she could smell the pervasive fug of rotting garbage and old urine. She cast around, looking for some hint that the trail continued, but there was nothing. She would have been more reassured to find a Nexus here than what she *had* found. A blank wall.

What the hell is this? Some kind of magical roach motel? "Mages check in, but they don't check out?"

It was impossible.

It was the truth.

"Lady. Hey, lady. Gimme dollar?"

A man—a boy, really, younger than Eric—came shuffling out of the alleyway to her left. He had the look so many of the homeless had, as if he'd been sucked dry of some vital component; prematurely haggard, but no less dangerous for that. There were two more behind him, obviously there to follow his lead and share in any bounty he acquired.

She held her ground. To back away would only encourage them. Most predators—including the human predator—would chase anything that ran.

"You one a' them angels. You come down here, you gotta gimme dollar. Whaddya say, angel? Gimme dollar?"

He was close enough for her to smell him now. His hands were stuck in his pockets, clutching a knife, a club, or even a gun. She knew he didn't plan to hurt her, only to take what she had, but when did life ever go according to plan?

And why had he called her an angel? The incongruity of it made her smile. Almost.

"You don't want to do that." Logan appeared

between her and the would-be predator like a drift of smoke. She couldn't see his face, but he held his hands out, open-palmed, defusing the situation with his presence and his will. The man stopped.

"She come down here, she gotta give me money," he whined, focussing on Logan. But he was hesitating now, uncertain. "She an angel. Angels take, they gotta give."

"No." Logan's voice was gentle and final. "You need to get on and take care of business somewhere else. Go on."

"Bitch. Uptown bitch." His companions had already melted back into the alleyway, discovering that Ria wasn't an easy mark. Their leader glared at Ria in frustrated disappointment. "Bitch! Angel bitch!"

"Go on," Logan said, still in the same calm voice. *As if he were dealing with a child or a lunatic,* Ria thought. *And I suppose these people qualify on both counts.* He dropped one hand to his side and flicked his fingers at her. Obedient to his signal, Ria backed away, stepping off the curb into the street. She crossed to the other side, turning her back on them reluctantly. Behind her, Ria heard a faint scuffle, and a cry, and when she turned back, the man was lying on his back on the sidewalk, and Logan was turning away.

"Let's go," he said when he reached her. "Unless you need me to take him all the way down."

"No. I'm finished here. Let's go find a cab."

A few blocks took them back to Broadway. It was like crossing into another world. Broadway was one of the city's main arteries, running all the way from the Battery at the southernmost tip of the

city, all the way into Upstate New York. It was
fairly safe even at midnight, lined with boutiques,
shops, and all-"nite" delis. Ria did a small Summoning magic, and a few moments later, a cruising cab turned the corner and stopped.

The ride uptown covered in minutes the blocks
it had taken her hours to walk. On Sixth the trees
were strung with fairy lights. The bright shops and
well-dressed shoppers were a universe away from
the war zone she'd just left.

And Ria had more questions than she had
answers to.

*A human drug addict doesn't just suddenly turn
into a magician without a cause. And an Unseleighe
lord doesn't just start building a Nexus in the
middle of one of the most densely populated human
cities on Earth without some expectation of being
able to finish it. There's a connection there, somewhere.*

So . . . find it. Find the root cause.
I think I need to do some more research.

Aerune had been patient, and now his patience
was to be rewarded. After his last defeat, he
realized he had violated the first rule of war.
Always make the enemy come to you. No longer
would he follow the human cattle into their puny
traps to gain what he needed. His prey would come
to him. And so he had woven a dark spell, a
calling-on, that would bring every creature with the
wit to hear it to a place of his own choosing. The
Crowned Ones would hear it . . . and so, he had
no doubt, would those who sought to keep his
rightful prey from him.

And then he had waited with Sidhe patience, his dark piper playing, until the prey should walk into his snare. At last he'd caught the scent he sought—the scent of raw untrained Power bleeding flagrantly into the air. This one was more powerful than any he had taken before, and Aerune needed that power to build his Gate.

And if the mortals should think to set a trap for me, then I will lesson these human upstarts well in the ways of Hunting. . . .

Drawing his horn, Aerune blew a long, deep note. It blended with the Calling-on Song, making that melody a part of itself, grew and reverberated against the buildings of the city streets, taking on a power and a life of its own, growing until it filled the world.

Come, my children! Come to your master!

The hounds came first, and then his hunters on night-black steeds of their own—the lesser Unseleighe lords who did him homage, the Lesser Sidhe to whom his magic was life itself.

Aerune lowered the horn from his lips, but its call continued to sound, filling the air. He drew his elvensilver sword and swung it in a circle over his head. "We ride!" he roared, spurring his mount.

Behind him the Hunt followed.

They'd had to work damned hard to do it in less than a day, but this time his men had prepared the perfect trap, and Robert had the perfect bait. There was no reason to wait any longer. He'd instructed the men thoroughly about what they were to do, and sent Beirkoff and Hancock out with them. When everything was in place,

Beirkoff was to give Hancock a second dose of T-Stroke—a bigger dose this time. This Aerune would come after Hancock again as soon as he smelled him. Robert was sure of it. Whatever the guy was, he wanted these Talents as much as Robert did, and Robert was making sure he had a tight grip on the only source. He'd pulled in his field-test operation. There wasn't any more T-Stroke out on the streets, so little chance of any other random Talents appearing for Aerune to poach. If he wanted what Robert had, Hancock would be his only source.

Let the games begin. . . .

"What're we doing out here?" Angel asked Elkanah.

"Waiting," Elkanah answered, out of the boundless well of patience that was (in Angel's opinion) the senior Threshold operative's singlemost irritating quality.

"Yeah, I know we're waiting," Angel echoed sarcastically. "Waiting for some nutcase on a horse to come kidnap our geek. But what's with the chain mail? The spears? Just because this guy thinks he's King Arthur doesn't mean we have to go along with it."

Angel twirled the six-foot spear with the steel head back and forth between his fingers as if it were a quarterstaff. When he shifted position, his chain mail jingled slightly. God only knew where the boss had come up with this stuff on such short notice. But he'd worn weirder things in his time.

"We've got orders. This guy shows up, we throw a net over him and switch on the generators,"

Elkanah answered. Like Angel, he wore a silvery shirt of chain mail beneath a dark sweater. Even if they were seen, there wasn't anything to ring warning bells in any civilian mind. And this deep in the Park, this late at night, there was little chance of them being seen at all.

"Like he's going to back off because of a steel and copper net and a little electricity," Angel grumbled, but fell silent.

There were twenty-four men—all of Threshold's Black-level security operatives—gathered here, though only eight of them had chain mail shirts. Four of the others were carrying longbows with quivers full of steel-tipped arrows. Most of the men and the trucks they'd come in on were concealed now by heavy camouflage netting. They'd been in place for hours, waiting, told to stay out of sight in case any stray tourists wandered past.

The bait had come in an hour ago in an unmarked car. The technician with him had shackled him to an iron stake driven deep into the frozen ground. The bait was wearing a straitjacket and a gag, and heavily sedated besides, but he didn't look like he could be much trouble. A catheter port had been inserted into his neck, and Angel watched as the lab geek stuck a needle full of something into it and rammed the plunger home. Angel was glad he wasn't the bait.

A few moments later the night began to shimmer, and Angel looked away from the bait, resting his eyes. Your eyes played funny tricks on you at night, and because of the searchlights mounted on the trucks, they hadn't been issued night goggles. There'd be plenty of light to see by once the balloon went up. They'd be as visible as a frog on a birthday cake, but Mr. Lintel had been very clear on the fact that this operation wasn't supposed to take long. They were going after the guy who'd made trouble for Mr. Lintel before, and this time he, whoever he was, was going to be way outgunned. Angel smiled. The hard men were the most fun to crack.

"Move up! Get into position!" Elkanah whispered urgently.

"Why? I don't—" Angel said.

And chaos came.

One moment the clearing was empty. The next, it was filled with men on horseback, men with dogs, shouting and screaming and blowing horns. Angel didn't waste any effort wondering how they'd gotten here. He rushed forward, his spear raised, looking for a target. If they wanted to come in like the U.S. Cavalry, he'd make sure they went out like General Custer.

A dog leapt at him, and Angel smashed it down with a Kevlar-reinforced glove. It backed off with a yelp and he hefted his spear, looking for a target. There. One of the horses.

He thrust his spear into its flank, pushing hard. There was a scream—horses screamed just like people—a flash of light, and the horse was rearing and dancing away uncontrollably, its rider shouting and flailing as he fought for control. Angel grinned, and thrust again, no longer caring who these people were or why they were here. He got to hurt them. That was all that mattered. Another rider tried to rush him. He got his spear into the horse's belly, twisted, and jerked back. Its guts spilled out onto the grass and it screamed and thrashed, adding to the noise of the battle.

Suddenly the searchlights came up, flooding the clearing with harsh white light. He could see his opponents clearly—men in fantastic armor, carrying shields and wearing swords.

The man on the horse he'd killed jumped free, dragging at his sword. He was wearing an ornate helmet, like something out of a Conan movie, and beneath it, his eyes glowed red in a bone-white face. So what? All the fancy makeup and special effects in the world wouldn't save him once Angel got close enough. All around him there were cries and screams, flashes of light when the steel drove home, and a smell in the air like ozone. Angel stepped back, momentarily worried. A heavy sword could slice his spear-haft in two, and it would take him moments he didn't have to get to his Uzi. But just then there was a hiss, and three arrows appeared in the attacker's chest. Angel had thought that archers were a dumb idea, but now, seeing the smoke billowing from the screaming man's chest, he changed his mind. Mr. Lintel had been right as usual. Iron turned these guys into wimps.

Something struck him full in the chest, burning away his shirt, but the steel mail beneath glittered unharmed. Angel laughed, and moved forward, searching for fresh targets.

As swiftly as they'd attacked, the riders pulled back. Now he and the other pikemen were between the bait and the horsemen, and the backup troops in the trucks were moving up. In the blinding light of the headlights, Angel could see fantastic armored shapes on horseback, like something out of a bad movie, and around them the turf seemed to flow like water. A mist was rising, making it difficult to see clearly. There was a scream from behind him—one of theirs—and he turned to see someone go down beneath the jaws of a dog the size of a small pony. There was another volley from the archers, and more screams. Hefting his spear, Angel ran to help.

Elkanah saw Angel run past him, shirt still smoking from one of the lightning-blasts the Bad Guys were using. As the Boss had promised, their chain mail protected them, but God help them the moment these guys figured out how few mail shirts they had. A couple of the men were already down, and there were *things* out there he didn't even want to look at. He'd seen the briefing tapes about what Hancock could do. The Boss had said he'd be on their side. Elkanah wasn't sure about that.

A dog leapt at him, taking Elkanah's spear full in the chest. It howled, smoking like it had just scarfed a doggy-treat full of napalm, no longer a threat. But the force of its attack knocked him to the ground, and its death-agonies jerked the spear out of his hands. He rolled away, fighting to clear his street-sweeper from its harness. Still supine, he yanked it up and fired. It caught one of the armored warriors full in the chest, blowing away armor and flesh with impossible force. For a moment, Elkanah could see the heart beating in the enemy's chest before he burst into flame, burning with a pale blue light. In the momentary breathing space Elkanah rolled to his feet, looking for his own lines.

"No order of battle ever survives first contact with the enemy." Got to hand it to old Clausewitz. The man knew what he was talking about.

Aerune roared his disapproval, his injured mount dancing and shying beneath him, half-blinded by the harsh white light. Try as he might, the Unseleighe Lord could not break through the ring of steel that surrounded his prey, and his magic seemed to have little effect on the humans who sought to protect it. He'd already lost too many men. There were archers at their back, their death-metal arrows taking a fearsome toll of his Hunt—and worse, the human Mage who had been the bait in the trap was summoning creatures of madness, creatures who preyed on mortal and Sidhe alike. But his attackers were few, and there were other ways to win this battle. He could make the mortals pay for their impertinence.

And he would.

"Flank them!" he shouted over the roar of battle. "Let none escape!" *In the name of Aerete the Golden, kill them all!*

TEN:

FOR ALL THE MARBLES

"Well, what do you know?" Eric muttered under his breath.

The summons was coming from within the Park.

He'd had the brainstorm to summon Lady Day as he jogged uptown, and so had managed the rest of the trip quickly. At the edge of the park he'd dismounted.

"Go home," Eric said firmly.

The elvensteed quivered, her lights flashing in disapproval. She wanted to go with him. "Home!" Eric repeated firmly. "I'll call you when I need you."

It had taken a moment to force his will on the

elvensteed, but at last she'd submitted, turning in the direction of home. The good thing about elvensteeds was that they followed orders, most of the time. And at least he wouldn't have to worry about anything happening to her.

Hostages to fortune. . . . Something Jimmie had said, about keeping innocents off the fire-line, came back to him now, and he smiled grimly. Now more than ever, he understood what she meant. He was prepared to risk his own life, but not anyone else's.

He turned back to the park. It was fully dark now, and the streetlights in the park cast faint cones of illumination around themselves. He wasn't sure what time it was, but the streets had fewer people on them than before, and the park itself was deserted.

And something was waiting for him there.

Eric thought again about turning back, catching a cab and just going home, but sheer stubbornness egged him on. The Guardians didn't want his help. Ria didn't want to help him. Underhill didn't want to get into a fight. Dharinel had told him to stay clear. But Annie's face was fresh in his mind. Whatever it was that was out there on the streets, he had to stop it.

So I'll do it myself, said the Little Red Hen.

Inside the low stone wall that bordered the Park the call was stronger, and Eric was willing to bet that it was coming from somewhere near the unfinished Nexus point. He headed toward it, more slowly now, wary of ambush from something else that might have answered this Call.

Suddenly there was a flash of light ahead of him, bright continuous light, and a sudden blast of sound as though someone had suddenly turned the volume on a television all the way up. Eric ran toward it.

:Man. Mortal man . . . :

The voice in his head stopped him halfway to the clearing. It sounded like World War Three was going on there, but Eric didn't dare go on leaving this at his back. He turned toward it.

A pool of shadow at the base of one of the trees rose up. Eric had the fleeting impression that it wanted to be a woman but didn't quite know how. It reached out for him yearningly, and Eric felt his teeth begin to chatter at the sudden sub-arctic cold as the creature sucked the last mote of warmth out of the winter air. He raised his flute to his lips, blowing a long steady low note. He let the magic flow up into the sound, caging the creature's power and letting it drain away.

She—it—vanished with a thin despairing cry. But there were more like it, heading toward him. Half-finished things that crawled and slithered and flopped along the ground, radiating fear and pain and a kind of magic he'd never sensed before. The woods were alive with them, just like the woods in his vision—filled with gibbering shadowy shapes that were all red eyes and hunger seeking his magic, his soul, and his blood. They weren't Nightflyers— thank all the odd gods for small favors—but there were more of them than he could count.

And they all wanted *him.* Eric summoned his shields, just in time as something like a wolf but six times bigger slung into the clearing, growling. The creature crouched on its haunches, unwilling to attack alone, but still far from foiled. Eric raised his flute to his lips again and blew a quick waterfall of notes. The wolf-thing sprang up onto its hind legs, twisting and howling as the magic tore it into fragments that drifted away on the air like a skirl of autumn leaves.

But there were more to take its place, an army of darkness seeping up like water out of the ground of this suddenly accursed place.

I need something to get rid of all of them at once. What? The magic creating them had a source; he could feel it, like cold and deadly sunlight. Slowly Eric began backing toward it, dropping his shields enough to lure them in. He had to stop whoever was making these things, and hope it stopped the creatures as well. They might be a part of whatever fight was going on, but plainly they had no interest in it.

Inspiration struck. He began playing the slow opening notes of a Bach cantata as the monsters gathered in a ring around him. *Come to papa, babies. It's lunchtime!* Bach was cerebral, mathematical, human—the antithesis of the nightmare Unseleighe power that he faced. Eric focused on the music, letting it fill him completely. He had time for one last coherent thought—*if any of these gets past me into the City, there's going to be a bloodbath even the Guardians can't stop*—before he let the music take him, shutting out everything but the battle before him.

As Aerune's Hunt eddied about the edges of the human warriors seeking an opening, the Unseleighe Lord suddenly heard a bright waterfall of music— Human magic, Bard magic, a thousand times more powerful than the pitiful flickering about the Crowned One before him. He turned toward the source and saw . . . a Bard.

The man walked slowly toward the tangle of human and elven warriors as if he saw neither, destroying the nightmares that had taken a heavy toll this night on mortals and Hunt alike. Here in full measure was the power Aerune sought, power to build a thousand Gates. Not crippled and half-complete like the others he'd harvested—no, here was power enough to play all of Aerune's dark dreams into reality.

The crazed Crowned One he'd sought was only an annoyance in the face of this greater prize. Raising his hand, Aerune slew him with a gesture. The levin bolt sparked and crackled through the iron the Crowned One wore, arcing and spitting in great wasteful fountains as it seared his flesh into bubbling ruin, consuming him utterly.

"Take him!" Aerune roared, gesturing toward the Bard. He blew his horn, summoning back his Hounds and lesser creatures.

The monsters he'd been fighting melted away like ice in a blast furnace and Eric stopped playing, feeling the magic he'd been following simply . . . stop. For the first time he became aware of his surroundings.

Searchlights. Gunfire. Elves on horses. Men with guns.

What the hell have I stumbled into?

The bait went up like a roman candle, dead in an instant. When Aerune turned, Elkanah took the break in the stalemate as an opportunity to move his men back toward the trucks. Their iron bodies should provide some cover, and he was still holding in mind the Eleventh Commandment: Don't Get Caught. They'd lost the bait, they'd lost half a dozen men, but if they could get the net over the guy on the horse, they still might be able to salvage something out of this mess.

The horsemen were ignoring his guys for the moment, and Elkanah was thankful for small favors. He yanked the net out of the back of one of the trucks, gesturing for those still on their feet to help him. The net hissed along the grass behind him like a metal serpent.

Then he saw what it was that had made Aerune pull back. An ordinary guy wearing street clothes, with what looked like a flute in his hand. The searchlights made the silver radiate like a chunk of burning phosphorus, but even in the brightness, the guy *glowed*, a bright blue as deep as the October sky. Instantly, Elkanah made up his mind.

If Aerune wants this guy, then so do we.

"Get him!" Elkanah shouted, gesturing toward the flute-player.

Eric heard sounds behind him and risked looking away from the Unseleighe Lord on the horse. Behind him were half a dozen guys in commando suits. Some of them were wearing chain mail and carrying spears. All of them had guns.

"Sir? Step this way, please. You're going to have to come with us," their leader said with surreal politeness.

Eric backed away again, trying to keep both

sides in sight. He couldn't imagine why the commandos hadn't run screaming—he'd never seen elves like these, but he knew what he was seeing—a Wild Hunt.

"Choose quickly, Bard!" the leader of the Hunt called to him, holding out his hand. "You will have no second chance, and I think your shields will not hold against their weaponry! Choose! Them—or us!"

The hell I will!

He had to get out of here, and knew he'd only have one shot at escape. He reached inside himself, to where the music ran like a deep underground river and pulled up a melody for which there were no earthly terms. As it filled him, he reached out for the half-created Nexus, twisting it around him as a stage magician might swirl a cape.

And he vanished.

The Bard was gone! Aerune snarled his displeasure, his breath coming in a serpent's hiss. So close! And yet the Bard had dared to defy him! He would have liked to slay all those witnesses to his humiliation, but without a Nexus to draw from, he dared not waste the power. His vengeance must wait, and be all the sweeter for being so long denied. He wheeled his steed, slashing a Portal to Underhill open in the very air. His mount staggered beneath him, energy bled from every pore—he could hold this gate for seconds only, but it would have to be enough. Wielding his sword as if it were a whip, he drove the Hunt through the Portal ahead of him, letting it seal itself behind him.

❖   ❖   ❖

Angel stared at Elkanah for a long moment in the sudden surreal silence. The guy with the flute, the guys on horses, had all gone pop like a soap bubble. The Threshold operatives were alone in Central Park, and in the distance Angel could hear the sound of sirens. Their little excursion here hadn't quite gone unnoticed.

"Does anyone have an explanation for what just happened here?" he finally asked.

"We can worry about that later," Elkanah said. There was a livid burn along the side of his face, and he looked like he'd been through the wringer. "Right now we've got to sanitize this place and get out of here before the cops show up. Get out the flamethrowers—and get the wounded into the trucks!"

Those still on their feet hurried to obey, hosing down the dry grass to eliminate bloodstains, grabbing dropped equipment as fast as they could. Someone scattered a carefully prepared litter of expended fire-crackers and beer cans to dress the site for the police. In less than five minutes they were on their way, running dark through the Park to one of its northern exits.

He was not looking forward to the report he was going to have to make.

At six o'clock this evening, Robert Lintel had been a man well-pleased with himself and the world. It was midnight now.

Things had changed.

His men had vacated Central Park moments ahead of an army of cops. They'd lost Hancock. Beirkoff was a gibbering wreck. They hadn't caught

Aerune. And when another wild card had turned up—someone Aerune wanted more than he'd wanted Hancock, by all reports—they'd lost him, too. Half his men were dead—burned by lasers or hacked to death by swords—and all the survivors could tell him were a lot of confused tales about armored men on horseback, giant wolves, and monsters.

Monsters. He'd thought better of them than that. They were supposed to be elite troops, the best soldiers of fortune that money could buy. And they ran away like a pack of frightened schoolgirls.

Robert shook his head, pacing the expensive carpet of his top-floor office. He knew they were good. They'd never failed him before. So what had *really* happened out there?

Before Campbell took off, she'd been babbling about elves and the hordes of faerie, but those things that had been in the park tonight certainly didn't act like anything Robert had ever seen in a cartoon. Still, maybe she and her stupid telepath hadn't been as crazy as he'd thought. Maybe there *was* something in what she'd been saying—maybe there were some kind of space aliens living here on earth, space aliens that had been the source for a bunch of legends about gods and elves and things, like that von Daniken guy said.

Robert relaxed, pleased to have thought his way through to the truth. That had to be it. Not elves. Space aliens. He'd have Dr. Ram turn Vickie Moon inside out to find out what else she knew.

Because whoever they are, they're poking their pointy noses in where they're not wanted, and if they can appear and disappear the way they've been doing, it won't be long before they come here.

He sat down in the cushioned leather chair behind his desk and pushed a button. "Find Beirkoff and get him up here. Bring Moon. I don't care what time it is. That's what I pay you for."

He sat back, thinking furiously. He was on the right track with T-Stroke, he knew it. That young guy who'd wandered into the middle of things— Elkanah said that this Aerune had spoken to him. If Aerune wanted him that badly, then so did Bob Lintel. The guy could obviously do everything the Survivors could do, and he didn't seem to be in any danger of shrivelling up and dying either.

If I get him and can find out how he does it, I can make more. And then I can write my own ticket. I don't know where he's gone, but he's got to come back some time. And when I've got a stable of psychic assassins who can kill with a thought, I'm not going to have to worry about the Justice Department or the SEC anymore. I'll be able to write my own ticket anywhere on the planet . . . and I think the U.S. Government would be more than interested in getting in on the bidding.

But why wait? Nobody ever made a profit sitting on their hands. It was time to take the war to the enemy. . . .

Fortunately Logan was still with Ria when all hell broke loose. She'd ordered up dinner from room service for both of them while she'd made some calls to the Coast. If junkies were turning into mages, somebody, somewhere was making the drugs that were turning them. And Ria wanted to find out who. It wasn't impossible that this was some Unseleighe plot. Some of them positively doted on working through human pawns, using long convoluted plots like something out of a James Bond novel when a simple bullet to the head would be a lot more cost-effective.

She was standing by the window, looking out over the city, when she saw the flash of light deep in the park. Seconds later the riptide of unexpected magic washed over her—Bardic, Unseleighe, and every shading in between. Ria staggered back, caught off balance by the sudden assault on her shields, and went down.

She woke up as Logan was lifting her onto a couch. His dark face was impassive and wary. "Are you all right?"

"Yes." She didn't elaborate. Her shields had gone to full strength in the second after the assault, but she could already tell that whatever it had been was gone now.

Waving Logan away, she got to her feet again and walked carefully back to the window. There were four police cars pulled up on the street outside the park, lights flashing.

"My," Ria said coolly, eyebrows raised.

Logan was already on the phone, calling his office. She heard him give his location and ask for a weather report. He listened for a moment, then hung up.

"There's been a report of shots fired inside the park and a lot of bright lights," he said tersely.

And more than shots, Ria thought. "I want to go down there. But I don't want to get involved with the police."

He glanced at her, and she saw him think the problem over.

"Let's give it a while. I'll check back with my office in a few minutes and see what the cops are reporting," Logan said.

Fifteen minutes later the police cars were gone. According to the frequencies Gotham Security monitored, the NYPD figured the disturbance was caused by some kids setting off fireworks. Ria knew better. The only question remaining was: what exactly *had* it been?

She entered the park cautiously, Logan taking point. He was wonderfully incurious about what was going on . . . but then Ria was paying good money for that. She only hoped his perfect manners weren't going to get either of them killed.

By the time they reached the spot Ria had marked from her window, there was nobody in sight. She wasn't particularly surprised to find it was the place Eric had been so interested in, but now the half-built Nexus was gone as if it had never been.

Suddenly there was a shadow above her— something big coming in for a landing. A pistol appeared in Logan's hand—a Desert Eagle .60, capable of taking down a moose with one shot or punching right through a car's engine-block.

"Wait," Ria said, raising her hand.

The creature landed, and bounded toward her, talking all the way. It was Greystone, the talking gargoyle from Eric's apartment.

"Blondie, we got trouble, big trouble—Eric just went 'poof' on us, and somebody was holding a real brawl here when he went!"

Running up behind him were a fortyish Latina woman and an exotic dark-skinned woman in a patrolman's uniform. Neither of them looked surprised to see Greystone. *So these must be the Guardians Eric told me about, showing up a day late and a dollar short. So much for the safety of the Free World.* Ria glanced toward Logan, but his Desert Eagle had vanished as if it'd never been there. His face was impassive. Like a good bodyguard, he faded back behind her, where he could watch what happened without intruding.

"Greystone, who is this? What's she doing here?" the Latina asked.

"She's Eric's ladyfriend, Ms. Hernandez," Greystone answered. "She's okay. Her name's Ria."

"What's happening? Where's Eric?" Ria demanded.

"Gone," Greystone repeated, sounding as rattled as a gargoyle ever got.

"We're friends of Eric's, too," Hernandez said. "We, um, heard he was having trouble up here, but when we got here it was all over. And what brings you here?"

"My hotel room overlooks the Park," Ria said. It didn't count as an answer, but at least it was a response. She knew what Eric had told her about the Guardians, and wondered what he'd told them about her. And, of course, how much of it they believed. . . .

"I'm going to take another sweep around," the patrolwoman said. "Nobody's done a real search of the area. Maybe there's a clue."

You certainly look like you could use one, Ria thought, but didn't say anything out loud. If this was Toni Hernandez, then her friend the cop must be Jimmie Youngblood, another of the Guardians. But even if Youngblood was no ordinary cop, it never paid to antagonize the police. When Youngblood walked away, Ria returned her attention to Hernandez. It wouldn't hurt to be sociable, especially since she wanted something from them.

"Hello," she said, holding out her hand, and smiling. "I'm Ria. Eric's told me so much about you."

"I'm Toni," the other woman said, smiling faintly at the inane exchange of social pleasantries. Ria took the proffered hand. Toni's grip was dry and warm. "Jimmie and I are trying to figure out what happened here. And just now, we wouldn't turn down any help." She studied Ria consideringly.

"I'll do what I can," Ria said, looking around. *Whether I'll tell you about it remains to be seen.* "Maybe you could start by telling me what you *do* know? I know that Eric was very interested in this . . . location."

Toni sighed. "We asked him to take a look at it last night. Let's just say there's been some weird stuff happening, and this spot seems to be the eye of the hurricane. Eric said there were Dark Elves involved, building some kind of doorway . . . would you know anything about that?"

From the look on her face, it was clear that Toni Hernandez would rather have cut off her hand than asked, but it was equally clear that she knew she was in over her head.

"Less than you'd think, but some," Ria said. "I *can* tell you right now that the doorway you're worrying about is no longer a problem. It's gone."

And Eric's gone with it, damn the man. "Let me look around a little, okay?"

"Sure," Toni said, taking a step back. "But you won't mind if Greystone keeps an eye on you, will you?"

"As long as he doesn't step on my feet," Ria said, composing her face into another pleasant but totally unmeant smile. She turned away from Toni and began walking in a slow circle around the area where the Nexus had been, frowning in concentration. Both the other women had brought flashlights, but Ria could see clearly in dimmer light than this.

The ground was cut up and torn in a wide area, almost as if someone had been trying to plow it, or to dig something up, and there were wide burn-scars defacing the grass that remained. Ria blinked, summoning up her mage-sight. Now she could see that a lot of magic had been thrown around here. There were the scars of levin bolts on the grass and the trees, and the entire place reeked of Unseleighe magics and human death.

And as if that weren't trouble enough, the Wild Hunt had been here as well. Perenor had sometimes spoken of the Unseleighe *rade*—he'd had the right to call one, but had never done so, dismissing the Hunt as too flashy and undisciplined for his needs. More to the point, Ria thought now, it would have motivated the drowsing Court of Elfhame Sun-Descending as nothing else could have, creating an opposition that Perenor hadn't wanted to face. Every Elfhame within a thousand miles must know about this one—she was only surprised that the park wasn't crawling with Highborn.

But Central Park is in the middle of New York City. No elf would come here without a damned good reason. And you walked right into the middle of it, didn't you, Eric?

The Wild Magic she'd followed down into the slums was everywhere, stronger than she'd ever seen it before. Someone with Power had died here, in addition to humans and Sidhe. Ria could still see the dead wizard's ghost, hovering like a plume of red smoke in the air. Dead, and recently, and slain by the levin bolt whose backlash she'd been hit with.

But it wasn't Eric, which was some small relief. Once she'd sorted out the Wild Talent and the Hunt, the remaining traces were easy to read. The lingering effects of very neatly done magic, all wrapped up with no loose ends, spelled Eric as plainly to her Second Sight as if it were a neon sign twelve feet high. He'd been throwing Bard-magic around as if he'd been trying to put out a fire, but even in the middle of a fight, his work was neat, disciplined, careful, the work of a fully trained Bard, confident in his skill. He hadn't killed the Wild Talent—that wasn't his style—so it had to have been the Unseleighe *rade*. But from what she'd seen before, the Wild Talent and the Unseleighe were allies of some kind.

She glanced over her shoulder. Both Toni and Logan were giving her a lot of elbow room.

Someone else wasn't.

"You gonna do a spell, Blondie?" Greystone asked hopefully.

Ria shot him a deadly look. "I haven't seen everything that's here to see, yet—something else was here besides your Dark Lord and Eric, but it wasn't magical, so it isn't leaving traces."

"Does this help?" On its stony palm, the gargoyle held out an expended shell casing. "I found it on the ground."

Ria took it from him with a gratitude she was unwilling to show. "It might." She held it in the palm of her hand, gazing intently down at the small piece of brass. *:Speak to me, smith-wrought forging. Who has touched you? Where have you been?:*

The shell casing was too small to retain much information, but Ria gained a blurry impression of men with guns—many guns—all holding shells like this one.

"There were soldiers here," she said slowly for Greystone's benefit. "Some kind of paramilitary group, anyway." She handed the casing back to Greystone.

She frowned, trying to piece the puzzle together. Eric, the Hunt, and a wild Talent had been here. So had a team of purely human mercenaries. Since she couldn't imagine Eric allying himself with either group, the best guess was that Eric had been caught between the two and needed to get out of the way fast. The half-built Nexus would have been the weakest point in local reality, so he must have used it to escape to Underhill, which would explain why it had vanished so neatly. . . .

Ria relaxed slightly. He was alive. Eric had a lot of allies in Underhill, and even enemies would treat a Bard with respect and probably be willing to ransom him back to his own people. So if he was in trouble at the moment, it wasn't urgent trouble, and she could call in a few favors to make things easier for him if it wasn't possible for her to track him down herself.

She walked back over to where Hernandez stood. She wasn't interested in the situation here any further, but she supposed she owed Toni a hint of what the Guardians were dealing with.

"Do you know what a Wild Hunt is?" Ria asked.

Toni blinked, as if she were taken off-guard by the question. "Some kind of a . . . it's when the dead ride out to hunt down the living, isn't it?"

"Close enough," Ria answered. "Except that it's usually the Unseleighe Sidhe riding, not human dead. Bottom line: a Hunt has ridden through here recently. It looks to me like they clashed with some men with guns—the police had a report of gunfire here in the park about half an hour ago, didn't they?"

"Yeah. They checked it out and didn't find anything. Decided it was kids with cherry bombs. But why would elves be fighting humans here? Or maybe that question should be asked the other way around: how did the men know the elves would be here?"

That's your problem, not mine, Ria thought. *You're the ones who didn't want Eric's help when he offered it, and I'm not a public utility.* "I don't know. But apparently Eric didn't think you were taking his warning seriously enough and decided to look into things for himself. I know he came back here today around noon, but I wasn't with him so I don't know where he went from here." *Not that I can't find out if I have to.*

Toni Hernandez looked as though she were going to press Ria for more details, and Ria was debating how much more to give her, when the other woman—Jimmie—came running back.

"Look!" she said with excited self-mockery, "a genuine clue. Somebody's been moving trucks—big trucks, heavy enough to leave tracks even with the ground being frozen—through the park. I found this near one of the sets of tracks. Someone must have dropped it while they were bailing." She held it out to Toni. Toni took it, and held it up so Ria could see it.

"It looks like one of those magnetic hotel-room keys," Toni said, turning it over in her fingers. "But there's no name on it. Just a logo."

"May I see it?" Ria said, keeping her voice even with an effort.

She schooled her face to blankness, inspecting the card. It was grey, easy to miss in the dark on a quick inspection, and anyway, the police that'd been here earlier had been looking for perpetrators, not evidence. The card had a gold logo stamped on it . . . a logo Ria had become very familiar with over the past few days.

Threshold Labs. That's a LlewellCo subsidiary! Someone is going to pay for this. Dearly.

"No, I'm sorry," she said, smiling sweetly as she handed the key-card back to Toni. "I travel a lot on business, and I thought I might recognize it, but I don't. Sorry." And with her shields at full strength, not even a telepathic gargoyle could get through them to see that she was lying through her teeth.

"Oh." Toni sounded disappointed. "Can't you tell anything else? You're one of them, aren't you? An elf?"

Ria winced slightly. "No, sorry." *Just a mongrel that neither side wants to claim.* "I'm sorry I can't be of more help, but I'm afraid I'm not on the Unseleighe Sidhe's Christmas card list, and this isn't really something I've got much experience with." She tried to keep her impatience from showing. Threshold was *her* problem, *her* responsibility. She intended to deal with it without any kind of New Age Occult Police help.

"You've been a lot of help already," Toni said meditatively. "I just wish we knew where Eric was."

Ria raised her eyebrows in surprise. "I thought I'd explained that. He took the Gate into Underhill with him. But I'm sure he'll be back as soon as he can."

"I guess you're right." Toni looked as if she had more questions to ask, so Ria spoke quickly to forestall them.

"If there's anything else you need, Eric has my number." She turned and walked quickly away, leaving the two Guardians and Greystone staring after her.

All of a sudden, everything was quiet.

Eric straightened out of his half-crouch, lowering the flute to his side and blinking in the deafening silence. The elves and the soldiers were gone, it was "day" instead of night, and it was warm enough that he was perspiring in his sweater and leather jacket. Eric was alone, somewhere Underhill. He looked around cautiously.

He stood in the middle of a primeval forest, one lit by the sourceless silvery light of Underhill. Trees that had grown unmolested since the beginning of

Time rose high into the sky, and the ground beneath his feet was carpeted with a thick pale moss filled with tiny glowing blue flowers, making it look as if the earth beneath his feet were carpeted with stars. Despite its beauty, the forest had the faintly unloved air of a theater between performances; a stage without actors. None of the High Elves were in residence here, then—only the Lesser Sidhe, the Low Court, those which could not survive except in Underhill or near a Nexus grove. The low elves were scatterbrained at best; he could expect no help there.

As if the thought had summoned them back, he began to hear faint far-off birdcalls, and slowly, the forest filled with sound once more. An enormous purple butterfly, silver crescent moons upon its wings, wafted regally past, and at Eric's feet, something small and grey and furry exploded into action, zipping into hiding before Eric could quite see it. He grinned in spite of himself.

He was better off than he'd been a moment before, and even if the terrain was unfamiliar, there was plenty of magic here to play with. Unless he ran into a High Magus in a real bad mood, Eric could handle anything this stretch of Underhill had to throw at him.

But since I'm not going to be staying, the situation isn't going to come up.

He could open a Gate right here and step back into the mortal world, but without a Nexus to anchor him—and with no idea of where "here" was—he might find himself appearing on Earth centuries in the past—or the future, or thousands of miles from where he went in. It would be better to have an experienced conductor for this little trip, and Eric knew just where to find one. Elvensteeds were created for situations like this.

But first, he had to change his clothes before he fried.

That was a lot easier here than it would have been back in New York. Here there was so much magic in the air that it was like breathing pure oxygen. Eric concentrated for a moment, considering what he should wear, and settled on just getting rid of the heavy sweater and turning his wool slacks into a pair of jeans that wouldn't get ruined so easily by a walk through the woods. He might need the jacket if he Gated to someplace colder, and besides, he was more attached to it than he was to either sweater or slacks. There was no guarantee that having once banished them, he'd ever get them back; magic was funny that way.

Having switched to cooler clothes, Eric breathed a deep sigh of relief. He rolled his shoulders, easing out the kinks.

Now to get out of here. *Maestro, a little traveling music. . . .*

He raised his flute to his lips and began to play. First a few trills to reassure the forest that he meant it no harm, then he segued into his Calling. The forest around him shivered, half-wakened by Eric's magic, and, as if from far in the distance, he heard Lady Day's faint acknowledgement inside his head. The elvensteed would find him wherever he was, and reach him as soon as she could.

Now all he had left to do was wait—which was just as well, as he had a lot of thinking to do about recent events. Eric looked around, walking through the forest a bit until he found a comfortable place to sit. One of the great trees had fallen (or more likely, a fallen tree had been created by one of the Sidhe at just this spot the way the Victorians used to build "ancient ruins" in their gardens), and its trunk provided a pleasant seat from which to think matters over—and if he got hungry waiting, he could just conjure up whatever he wanted to eat or drink from the magic in the air. While Eric hadn't mastered *kenning*, the ability to create exact duplicates of anything he knew well out of pure magic, he could certainly summon up anything within a reasonable distance to come to him.

So it's a great place to visit, but I don't think I'd actually want to live here. All things considered, Eric preferred the "real world," even though New York didn't seem to be a healthy place to be at the moment, at least for elven-trained Bards.

He'd blundered into something big and nasty back there in the Park—something even worse than Dharinel's gloomy warnings about conquest-mad Unseleighe—and if he didn't want to have his head handed to him the next time he ran into the Guys With Guns, he'd better stop and think things through now, while he had a breathing space. Dharinel always said that a moment of thought could save a year on the battlefield.

The Guardians said there was trouble in Central Park, and I found out that the Dark Sidhe was trying to put up a Nexus about where I dreamed of the goblin tower, but when I followed the trail of the magic he was using, it seemed to be all tangled up with the homeless folks downtown. At the Park, I think there was some kind of a mage with the soldiers that the Wild Hunt was trying to get at, but when the Unseleighe Lord saw me, he killed the mage, and that got rid of the monsters I was trying to take out. And I beat it out of there, but the Sidhe's already seen me. And EVERYBODY loves a Bard.

So . . . could things be any more of a mess? Maybe, Eric decided with a sigh. *But not easily. Guns and Sidhe don't mix.* He kicked at the moss beneath his sneakers. Tiny beetles glowing in a rainbow of colors scurried out of sight, and Eric watched them for a moment, fascinated. The air was filled with birdsong now, making his fingers itch for a notebook so he could try to get some of it down on paper. Whatever he wrote would be a poor copy of the original, though. Still, it might be fun to try.

At least his responsibilities in this mess were clear. He had to get back to his own time and place, and once he did, he needed to contact Elfhame Everforest and tell them about the Wild Hunt showing up in Central Park. That should be enough reason for the Seleighe Sidhe to break the truce and settle this particular Unseleighe's hash, but that wasn't the only problem. There was still the matter of all those guys playing soldier . . . the ones with the now-dead mage.

Back in San Francisco, the Feds who were chasing him and Bethie had been tangled up with a project that was trying to tap into natural psi powers. But most people didn't have much in the way of either easily tapped psi or innate Power: the Gift usually ran deep in humans, most of the time needing magic or training to bring it to the fore.

He flashed back to the packet of white powder he'd seen in Annie's hand in the alley outside the soup kitchen downtown. What if somebody had figured out a way around needing magic or years of training to make a wizard? What if they'd come up with some kind of drug that forced Talent to the surface? That would explain the twisted mage he'd been fighting, and if the bad guys had been testing their stuff on the streets, it might also explain all those deaths that the Guardians—and the people at the kitchen—had been talking about. *Magery while you wait. No wonder that nut on the horse was so interested. If that stuff can crank up a human into a mage, just imagine what it would do for an elf?*

Eric shuddered. That was something he'd just as soon not find out about. But if the soldier-boys meant that the Feds were mixed up in things again, he was in even more trouble than he'd thought. Because if they were looking for Bethie, they were looking for him as well . . . and his cover would be blown the moment anyone looked really closely.

Well, this is another fine mess you've gotten us into, Banyon. Master Dharinel was right, not that his being right would have kept me from meddling. But it doesn't really look like I've improved the situation once, and now both sides are after ME. Gee, Brain, what do we do now? Well, Pinky . . .

He needed help and advice, and from someone who was as comfortable with high-level human politics as Eric was with Bardic magic. The trouble was, he didn't know anyone who fit that particular bill but Ria. After what he could tell her about today, he was pretty sure she'd help him if she

could, but that help might come at a higher price
than he was comfortable with paying.

*Well, we can burn that bridge when we come
to it, as Mason said to Dixon.*

All of a sudden the forest fell silent. The birds
stopped singing, and the creatures scuttling through
the fallen leaves froze where they were. Eric
looked around quickly.

Trouble.

Nothing in sight, but his shoulders crawled.
There was someone behind him. He could feel it.
Eric got to his feet, turning around slowly, shields
at full, to see what had startled the forest.

He stared. It looked like a giant lawn gnome
brought to hideous life. Upright, it would probably stand almost four feet high, but it was bent
over so far it was hard for Eric to judge its size,
balancing on grimy bare feet and the knuckles of
its long, apelike arms. It was wearing human
clothes centuries out of date—calf-length leather
pants and a long grimy smock that might have been
white once but was now soiled to a grimy brown.
Its face was a caricature of a human face—almost
noseless, with tiny piggy eyes. On its head it wore
a crusty brownish-red cap that it had dipped in
some thick liquid that was flaking away now as it
dried. The creature stank of undefinable things.

When it saw Eric's face, it smiled, the grin
splitting its nightmare face impossibly wide. Its
mouth was filled with long yellow teeth.

Sharp yellow teeth.

ELEVEN:

LORD OF THE
HOLLOW HILLS

Robert Lintel regarded his temporary headquarters
with disgust. Even in December, the smell was incredible. It was filthy beyond anything he'd imagined
possible—interior walls torn down, some covered in
graffiti, whole rooms used as toilets, people sleeping
anywhere, on torn mattresses or just piles of rags. This
abandoned building was a haven for runaways. That
was why he'd picked it.

He stared at the terrified band of feral children
huddled together in the middle of the room. He
was doing these kids a favor, he realized. They

should be grateful to him for putting an end to their whole trivial sordid existence. For once in their useless lives, they'd get the chance to do something that mattered, something that would benefit people more important than they could ever be.

As far as he had been able to tell from Jeanette's notes and what he'd gotten from the Survivors back at Threshold before he'd used them up, the younger you were, the higher the initial dose, the better chance you had of surviving exposure to T-Stroke and developing the Talents that Robert Lintel needed. He didn't have any more time to mess around handing out free samples to dozens of people to get one or two Survivors. He needed broad-based success—and fast.

"Okay, you! Sabatini! Is this everyone?" he barked.

"Everyone in the building, sir," Sabatini said. Robert had brought the cream of his surviving security troops here with him. The eight of them were loyal—and smart enough to know that they were implicated in everything Threshold had done so far. They needed Robert's protection—and Robert needed what these children could provide.

"We've got all the exits sealed. Nobody goes in or out," Sabatini said.

"Good." Street hookers and runaways were no match for trained professionals. His men had taken the place over before half of them realized they were being invaded, and within minutes his operatives had searched the whole building and rounded all of the squatters up and brought them here.

The funny thing was, not one of them had fought back. Robert had seen this kind of behavior before. Most people took a certain amount of time to work themselves up to physical resistance in a traumatic situation. Often the difference between the amateur and the professional was their quickness off the starting blocks, not their martial arts skill. The amateur might be just as proficient as the professional, but it took him longer to make up his mind that the situation required violence. And that was the difference between success and failure. So to keep any would-be heroes off balance, Robert'd had his prisoners slapped around a little once he'd gained control of the squat, just to drive home who was boss now. The children huddled together like a pack of orphaned kittens, wearing lace and leather, lipstick and sequins, the tawdry finery of a pack of Lost Boys and Girls who would never live to reach Neverland. They'd seen the uniforms and the guns, collected a few bruises, and now not one of them was willing to do so much as complain, no matter what he did to them.

They might get their spunk back in a few hours, but by then it would be far too late. In fact, it was too late right about . . .

"Now. Start dosing them."

Angel and Sabatini shouldered through the circle of huddled children. Of the twenty-four men who'd been in Central Park last night, only these eight remained, but that was more than enough for his purposes. In fact, when he got what he wanted here, they'd be disposable, too.

Robert had brought one of those pressure injectors with him from the lab, and all the T-6/157 he could find. Even after the random doses they'd put out on the streets over the last two days, there were several kilos left—more than enough to build an army with. As Angel held a gun to their heads, Sabatini injected the street kids one by one with a double dose of T-Stroke. Most of them didn't even make it into a sitting position before passing out.

Robert smiled his approval as the last of the street kids dropped unconscious to the ground.

"Sir?" Elkanah asked. "What do we do with the ones that go crazy? If we put them out on the street, they might lead someone back here."

"Put them down in the basement." On his earlier reconnoitre of the building, Robert had seen that the steps to the cellar were gone. Anyone thrown down there—assuming they survived the eighteen-foot drop—would have no way of getting back out again. "Put the dead ones down there, too. They might as well have some company."

Sabatini was sorting the limp bodies now. Two thirds of the kids were still alive. *So I was right about younger subjects surviving better. All to the good. There'll be no lack of subjects. Thousands of kids vanish every year,* Robert thought.

Almost as soon as the dead bodies were cleared away, the Screamers started to awaken. They were harder to dispose of than he'd expected; supernatural strength seemed to go hand-in-hand with violent psychosis, and his operatives had to play rough. Fortunately only five of the surviving subjects needed that treatment, and with the doors between the kitchen and the front room shut, he couldn't even hear them screaming once they'd been dumped in the basement.

And if their presence lured that pointy-eared claim-jumper Aerune back again, that was all to the good. A steel knife through the gut should settle him down and make him see reason.

Soon, the Survivors started to rouse, staring around themselves with wide, disbelieving eyes. There was a skinny blonde brat who seemed to be their leader. She glared at Lintel in terrified defiance, her mascara running down her painted cheeks in thick black streaks.

It doesn't get any better than this, Robert thought gloatingly. This was always the best part, watching someone who was too terrified of him to run away. Campbell had been an exemplary employee in many respects, but she'd never been properly afraid of him. Maybe he'd look her up and change that, once he had this situation squared away to his liking. He looked around for some place to sit, found nothing, and resigned himself to standing. He wouldn't be here for more than a few hours, anyway.

After that, he'd be taking the war to the enemy.

"Now—" he said, smiling predatorially at the Survivors. "This is what I want you to do. . . ."

Ria hadn't slept all night, and neither had a lot of people in the West Coast offices. She'd dragged Jonathan out of bed with her midnight phone call, but Ria was too angry about her discovery to care: she wanted action and she wanted it now.

Jonathan delivered, gods bless him. It hadn't taken him long to get the first of the answers she wanted, and the more she found out about Threshold Labs, the worse things sounded. The company had been draining even more money from LlewellCo than she'd realized at first glance, its depredations carefully camouflaged by the bright boys and girls in Oversight and Accounting.

And as for what Threshold had done with all that LlewellCo cash . . .

"Since when does a pharmaceutical company need a private army?" she demanded into the telephone. "These invoices are ludicrous! We've been shovelling money at them for *five years* and all we've gotten have been glowing promises—I want to know *exactly* what Threshold's been doing with its time and my money and I want to know *yesterday.*"

Baker and Hardesty were behind this. Only someone high up in LlewellCo could have covered things up for this long. Well, the two of them were going to be looking for new jobs by the time the sun set in California, Ria vowed.

As for Threshold's CEO, Robert Lintel . . .

Jonathan's people in Computer Security had gotten into the Threshold computers without trouble—no surprise, as most of them were former outlaw hackers, working for LlewellCo as an alternative to jail. According to what they'd pulled out of the files so far—the data would take weeks to sift thoroughly—Lintel had been running a black books research program for almost as long as he'd been running Threshold, something about triggering psychic powers in humans through the use of psychotropic drug cocktails.

And it looks like he got far enough with it to go to field trials. I am going to crucify him for this—and anyone else I can get my hands on!

She paced furiously, but she knew there was no point in coming down on Threshold until she had absolute proof. It would be too easy for them to start dumping records at the first sign of discovery—although, to Ria's fury, someone seemed to have anticipated her there as well.

Lintel certainly hadn't been doing the research himself—not with nothing more than a Harvard MBA—but whoever the production-end brains of the outfit had been, he or she seemed to have jumped ship, because there was no evidence of him or his research notes anywhere in the Threshold mainframe. If Mr. X had gone to that much trouble to remove all trace of his former employment, it was probably because he was on the run. Which meant that he was out of the picture for the moment, and out of reach.

But I'll find you, wherever you are. And when I do, you'll wish you'd gone down with Threshold!

She glanced at her watch, then over at the man sitting silently on the couch. Logan looked like some kind of hyperrealistic sculpture of a sleeping man, not that he was asleep. From time to time she surprised him watching her, as if he were quietly assessing the situation. She wasn't sure why she'd kept him with her, but now she was glad she had.

"I'm going downtown to break into a lab," she said. "I own it, but that probably won't count for much just at the moment. I'll need some serious backup."

"How serious?" Logan asked. He got to his feet and stretched, working out the kinks of a long sleepless night.

"They won't have tanks," she thought, thinking back to the scene in the Park. "Aside from that, assume the worst."

While the team was assembled, Ria went off to change. This assault would require armor of a different sort.

They arrived at Threshold just after the morning shift. The Guardians still had the key-card someone had dropped in Central Park, but Ria didn't need it. She went in through the front door.

"Good morning. I'm Ria Llewellyn. I own this company. If you want to have a job by tonight, you'll keep your hands off that phone and buzz us through," she said, her voice dangerous.

The receptionist took one look at Ria and the five men with her and pressed the button. Ria went directly to the top floor, and forced her way past a second receptionist and Lintel's private secretary.

But all for nothing. Lintel wasn't there. And from the look of the place, he wasn't coming back.

Ria swore feelingly. She'd been sure she'd get here in time to nail the slimy bastard. Lintel had too much invested in Threshold to just go slinking off leaving his turf undefended!

"Ma'am?"

The bodyguard she'd posted outside the door to watch the secretary came inside, dragging someone by the scruff of the neck. The victim was wearing a white lab coat, and looked absolutely terrified.

"I caught him coming out of the elevator, heading for Lintel's office. When he saw me he tried to bolt."

"Bring him over here," Ria said, leaning back against Lintel's desk. Because she thought she'd be facing a corporate raider this morning, she'd dressed to match: a dark green Dior skirted suit with matching pumps. Dagger optional.

It didn't take much in the way of Talent to read the man's mind. His name was Beirkoff, and he'd been one of the group in Central Park last night. He'd also been Lintel's inside man on the black budget op that Lintel had been running, and now that he realized Lintel was gone, Beirkoff knew he'd been cut off and left to twist in the wind. He'd be willing to do anything to save his skin.

"Lose something?" Ria asked mockingly. "Your safety net, perhaps?" Beirkoff's face went grey, and for a moment, the bodyguard's fist in his collar was the only thing holding him up. The details of the project flashed through his mind—an underground testing lab, some cells, too many people dead. . . .

"Mr. Beirkoff, you have exactly one chance to save your life and your freedom," Ria said, getting to her feet and leaning toward him. "Take me down to the Black Labs and tell me everything you know about T-6/157."

There was a slot for a key-card on the inside wall of the Executive Elevator, and three unmarked buttons below it. Ria'd found the card in Lintel's desk, once she'd broken the lock. Beirkoff slid it into place and pressed the third button.

Beirkoff hadn't been good at forming coherent sentences, but Ria'd had no trouble getting most of the story by skimming the surface of his

thoughts. Unfortunately, he had no idea what had
happened after Eric had vanished from the Park,
nor what Lintel might be up to right now. Lintel
had sent him home for the night, and when he'd
come back this morning, he'd walked straight into
Ria.

The level the elevator opened onto showed every
sign of having been hastily vacated. Doors stood
open, files lay on the floor.

"Search it," Ria said crisply. Sorcerous telepathy wasn't admissible in court, and even direct
testimony wouldn't really hold up well against a
high-priced lawyer. She needed hard evidence to
hang Lintel with.

She got it when Beirkoff took her down to the
holding cells. A man in a white lab coat—Beirkoff's
thoughts identified him as Dr. Ramchandra, the
only other on-the-books Threshold employee with
Black Level clearance—lay dead in the hallway,
shot neatly through the chest. Beirkoff was hor-
rified, and Ria suspected that he'd never seen
anyone freshly dead before. Like so many yuppies,
his only encounters with death were via the media,
or perhaps the sanitized and beautified body of a
friend or relative after the mortuary professionals
had made it acceptable. Ria thought back to the
battle in Griffith Park. She'd seen violent death
in every possible aspect. Bored with his horror, she
moved on.

All of the cells were full, and all of the occu-
pants were dead as well. They looked like the
mummies from the Egyptian wing of the Metro-
politan Museum of Art. It was hard to believe
they'd ever been human.

"They were the ones who survived," Beirkoff said from behind her in a shaken voice. "If the stuff didn't kill them on the first shot and you gave them a second dose, it was like they just . . . burned out."

"There's no one here," Logan said, coming back down the hall. He glanced at Ramchandra's body and then back at Ria, his expression unchanging. "But there's a lab back there that looks like somebody used it to cook up a major batch of something that isn't there now."

"Campbell did the cooking," Beirkoff said, recovering more by the minute. "She got the stuff as far as field trials and then she took off. But Mr. Lintel made sure she made up a big batch before she split."

And Campbell was the only one who knew the recipe, though any competent chemist could probably reconstruct it from a large enough sample, Ria read in his mind. *Campbell. Jeanette Campbell. I'll remember that name. Someday soon, Jeanette Campbell, you and I are going to have a short but interesting talk.*

It was time to call the cops and bust this situation wide open. A part of her couldn't help noting that this whole thing was going to be a media bonus for LlewellCo—valiant chairwoman discovers illegal research going on in one of her subsidiaries, does a Bernstein and Woodward, and turns the results over to the cops. She'd be a Movie of the Week for sure. She'd also be tied up in red tape and meetings for the next year, and Ria had other things to do just at the moment. She turned to Lintel's flunky.

"Listen to me, Beirkoff. You'd like to stay out of prison, right?"

Beirkoff nodded, obviously more terrified right now of Ria than of the dead body lying on the floor or the wrath of the absent Robert Lintel.

"You have exactly one hope of doing that. You are going to call the cops and report what you found here, and tell them the following story: You came to me with your suspicions. I sent you down here with a security team and orders to notify the authorities if you found anything. I wasn't here today. In fact, I've never been here at all. There will be a lawyer here in an hour to handle LlewellCo's involvement, but you won't wait for him. You're going to give the police full cooperation.

"Play it this way and you come out smelling like a rose. Cross me, and I guarantee that LlewellCo—and I personally—will do everything in our power to make the brief remainder of your sordid existence a living hell."

"Yes, sir! Yes, ma'am! I mean—yes. I can do that," Beirkoff babbled.

"Good. I'm out of here. The rest of you, stay here and keep Mr. Beirkoff honest."

When she stepped out on the street again, the contrast was as great as if she'd stepped through a Portal into Underhill. It was one of those bright winter days that sometimes came in December, the kind that made you think that New York was a nice place to be after all.

But right now it wasn't a nice place for somebody. Because somewhere out there right now, Robert Lintel was trying to turn ordinary humans into mages using a drug that had a one hundred percent net fatality rate.

And he and Eric were on a collision course.

Eric drew himself up and did his level best to channel Dharinel in a bad mood. The elven mage didn't suffer fools gladly at the best of times, and that damn-your-eyes arrogance was the only thing that would save Eric now.

"It took you long enough to get here!" he snarled at the gnomish Unseleighe lackey in his best imitation of a pissed-off elven noble, leaking a little magic past his shields to reinforce the effect. "Take me to your Lord—at once, do you hear!"

And they said spending all that time at RenFaires would never be good for anything. . . .

"Yes, High Lord. Urla hears and obeys. At once, High Lord!" The creature knelt, pulling the cap from its head and kneading it between enormous gnarled hands. Its wetness left brownish smears on Urla's skin. Eric had a sick feeling that he knew what it had been soaked with. Blood.

Not one of the good guys. That's for sure.

But for once Faire shtick wasn't just a way of amusing travelers and filling his pockets. This time he was playing for his life. His bluff had worked so far—it was a safe bet that any of the Lesser creatures he encountered would owe fealty to some High Lord or another, and even the Unseleighe Lords followed certain rules—which was more than Eric could say for this Urla. He knew that Lady Day would find him eventually, no matter where he went in Underhill. But until she did, Eric was more or less trapped here, though rather less than more.

"Get up—get up!" he said haughtily, waving the hand that didn't hold his flute. "I don't have time for this nonsense!"

The redcap crawled backward submissively before springing to its feet. Bowing and gesturing, it began to lead Eric through the forest. He took the time to take his flute apart and put it back in its case in his messenger bag before following. He didn't know what he might encounter along the way, and he didn't want to lose the instrument.

Urla led him onward through the empty forest until they came to an enormous tree. Its trunk was easily thirty feet around, and like many trees this old and large, its lower trunk was hollow. Eric followed Urla through the gap in the trunk, and when they came out the other side, the forest was gone.

The place Eric found himself in now wasn't nearly as nice. For one thing, it stank. He and Urla were standing on a hummock of grass in what seemed to be the center of a large swamp. Between the hummocks, the swamp water glowed a faint toxic green, simmering languidly as bubbles of gas worked their way to the surface and popped with an evil smacking sound. The illumination here was dimmer than the light of the forest and had a reddish cast. Thick mist hung from trees festooned with fleshy pale blossoms that gave off a nauseatingly sweet scent, as if they were rotting instead of blooming. Eric's skin crawled; he was in Unseleighe territory now, and no mistake about it. He could see large bat-winged things flying slowly through the distance, and as he stood gazing around himself, a terrible scream split the air—whether of predator or prey, he didn't know.

Urla looked up at him to see his reaction, beady eyes glittering. Eric glared back as arrogantly as he could manage, and the bluff seemed to work. The redcap hurried off, bounding from island to island of dry land. The islands were yards apart, distances Eric couldn't jump, and he'd have to be crazy to step down into the water. This was obviously some kind of test.

He summoned his power—he didn't need his flute here, or even music, but unbidden, a few bars of an old Simon and Garfunkel song skirled through his brain as he wove the magic. *Like a bridge over VERY troubled waters. . . .*

Silvery mist rose out of the swamp and coalesced, following the redcap's trail. Eric stepped out onto it cautiously. It gave slightly beneath his feet, like the surface of a waterbed, but it held him comfortingly far above the surface of the swamp. He stepped out onto the bridge and followed Urla dry-footed across the bog.

The exit Portal here was in a bank of mist. Eric knew enough about Underhill geography to know that the shortest distance between two points wasn't necessarily in a straight line. Navigating Underhill was more like solving a maze, one where every turn could take you half a dozen different places. The Unseleighe were a paranoid lot, defending their territories by making them hard to find, and even harder to enter.

Urla walked into the mist and Eric followed cautiously. He didn't trust the redcap at all, and Urla would certainly think it was a great joke to lead Eric into danger, but he didn't think the creature was trying to lead him into a trap. Not yet, anyway.

This time Eric found himself in utter darkness on the far side of the Portal, and quickly summoned a ball of elf-light. By its pale bluish illumination he could see that there was grass beneath his feet, short and trampled as if herds of animals had been running across it. A chill monotonous wind blew steadily, making him shudder more than shiver as he looked around. He was in the middle of a broad and featureless plain that seemed to stretch a thousand miles in every direction. When he looked up, there were no stars.

"I'm losing patience," Eric warned, in what he hoped was the approved Unseleighe style. It seemed to be what Urla expected, because the redcap grovelled again, swearing to the Great Lord that they were almost there, indeed, their destination was mere instants away. The redcap turned away and began to trot across the plain, picking up speed until Eric was hard-pressed to keep up with it. Without the elf-light he'd summoned, he would have been unable to follow at all.

A couple of times the ground shook silently as if something huge and heavy were running across it—though Eric saw nothing—and a couple of times he almost thought he'd heard something over the droning of the ceaseless wind, but he didn't dare stop to listen for fear of losing his guide. Bard or not, he had a notion that it would not be a good idea to be lost in this particular realm at the mercy of whatever it was that lived here. The swamp had been bad, but there was something almost honest about its malignity. This was a lot creepier.

At last they came to a henge: two black rough-hewn standing stones supporting a third laid across their tops. The three stones were the size of Greyhound buses, and seemed to be made out of some fine-grained stone. *Basalt,* Eric dredged up from a dark corner of memory. *Like in H. P. Lovecraft. I just hope whoever lives here isn't a fan of the classics.*

Urla trotted between the menhirs and vanished. Having no other real choice, Eric followed. As he'd expected, the landscape changed again. Now there was light. He stopped, blinking as his eyes adjusted.

Wait. I know this place.

He stood now in the wood that he'd dreamed of before—the black and silver wood where the winter-bare trees looked as if they were made of black and polished bone, and the ground was covered with a thick treacherous white mist. Urla was obviously on familiar ground now, for he moved more slowly than before—as if he didn't relish getting to his destination. Neither did Eric. Such a direct route to his destination indicated that whoever lived here felt he had little to fear from invaders, and that much confidence meant something old, powerful . . . and dangerous.

Dangerous enough to think invading New York would be a cakewalk. Oh, boy, Banyon. You sure know how to pick your enemies. . . .

In the distance, shining through the trees like a baleful moth-green moon, was the goblin tower of Eric's vision, but oddly, instead of worrying him

further, he found himself with a treacherous desire
to laugh.

*Whoa! Who does the decorating here? Skeletor?
That place looks more like Castle Greyskull than
any place has a right to.* This place was beyond
over-the-top: it was just *too* grim and *too* gothic
for him to be able to take it seriously—as if a
Hollywood set designer had done a makeover on
Hell.

*You'd better take it seriously, Banyon. Because
THEY sure are, and I bet Unseleighe Sidhe don't
have much of a sense of humor. . . .*

As they approached, Eric saw that the front gate
of the castle was guarded by a pair of armed
knights in full ornate elvish armor that glowed like
tarnished silver. Both of them were holding long
and wickedly barbed pikes, in addition to wearing
swords. Their eyes glowed red in the cavern of
their helmets, but it was plain to see that Eric's
arrival—at least on his own two feet—was unexpected enough to disconcert them. More bad news:
that meant they were Sidhe, not some kind of
created servitors, things little better than those
white-armored guys in Star Wars. If this lord could
compel actual Sidhe to do gruntwork like this,
well . . .

Let's just say I've got a bad feeling about this.

Urla hesitated, obviously expecting some kind
of formal challenge from the guards, but Eric was
pretty sure it wouldn't be a good idea to stop for
one. He pushed past the redcap and strode through
the castle gates as if he had every right to be there.
He passed beneath the portcullis into the outer
bailey. There was a second set of guards standing

before the inner doors, as silent and rigid as the first.

The inner door swung open as he approached, and Eric strode through, Urla scurrying along behind him. Now he was in the outermost interior room, a space as vast as a performance hall. It was bare and empty, its black stone walls polished to mirror brightness and long narrow windows high upon the walls. An open gateway beckoned Eric onward.

If he hadn't already spent so much time in various parts of Underhill, he would have been lost immediately. But by now he knew enough of the interior layout of Sidhe castles—and castles in general—to have a good idea of where the throne room was. He moved quickly through the maze of corridors and chambers, working his way upward. He saw several guards, all armored the way the first sets had been, but no one challenged him. *They probably think that if I've gotten this far, I have a right to be here. One good thing about a really evil overlord is that his underlings don't tend to do a lot of thinking for themselves. . . .*

Urla seemed to have deserted him somewhere along the way, and Eric wasn't sure whether this was a good omen or not. At last he arrived at the outer chamber of the throne room, and unlike the other rooms, this one was inhabited. Fops in jewelled armor meant strictly for display lounged languidly, most holding leashes that led to doglike and less nameable things. Ladies of the court whispered and smiled, inspecting him over spread fans or beneath embroidered veils. One of them looked more like a leopardess than anything on two legs had a right to—she caught Eric staring and laughed, exposing a mouth filled with sharp carnivore fangs. Beautiful they might be, but no one who'd ever seen one of the Sidhe would mistake a member of the Dark Court for one of the Bright.

Word of his arrival had preceded him—he could tell by the whispers and glances exchanged by the elegantly dressed lords and ladies who filled the outer hall. He thought someone might try to stop him—to curry favor with their liege-lord, if nothing else—but no one did. Eric skirted the edge of the silent group, carefully keeping his back to the wall. At the far end of the outer hall, three steps led up to another set of massive doors of enamelled silver that depicted a battle between two groups of mounted elves. The red enamel drops of blood in the picture glinted as if they were backlit, as if somehow light was shining *through* the doors. It was a startling effect. *Whoever this Unseleighe Lord is,* Eric thought, *he had a helluva special effects budget.*

He skipped up the three wide steps—turning his back on the courtiers reluctantly—and gestured at the door, summoning up a simple knock-spell. For a moment he was afraid it wouldn't open, but like the first, it yielded to his power. A collective gasp went up from the watching Unseleighe Sidhe, and Eric heard the babble of conversation begin behind him as he stepped through the doors. As soon as he'd passed through them, the doors to the throne room closed behind him with the soft finality of the doors of a bank vault. Not a good sign. He bet they wouldn't open again as easily.

Still, he'd come too far to back out now. He looked around.

The throne room was enormous—far too big to have fit into the castle Eric had seen as he approached. For a moment he thought he was back outside in the bonewood, but then he realized that the walls were only carved in the semblance of a forest. The carven tree limbs spread to form a canopy far above, making the vault of the ceiling look like a blackened crown of thorns.

Nice image, Banyon.

The floor looked as if it had been poured from a single drop of liquid mercury, but Eric didn't dare break his momentum or show a moment's indecision, and to his relief, it was solid beneath his feet. At the far end of the chamber stood the same high throne he had seen in his dream. Only this time it was facing him, and occupied by the Unseleighe Eric had seen leading the Wild Hunt in Central Park. Refusing to think about what might happen next, Eric strode boldly toward the foot of the black throne and its darkling occupant.

Like his guard knights, the Unseleighe Lord wore full ornate field plate armor of a silver so dark it seemed black. On his head was a black crown set with cabochon rubies that glowed as brightly as the blood drops in the door had. Eric stopped at the foot of the throne and stared up at its occupant. He forced himself to smile nonchalantly.

"Hi. We need to talk. Now."

When Ria got back from Threshold, the package she'd asked Jonathan to send was waiting for her at the hotel desk. She was just as glad she'd left Logan with the others back at Threshold. What she had in mind now wasn't something a bodyguard could help her with, no matter how good a bodyguard he was.

She signed for the package, and carried it upstairs to her suite to open it. Bless Jonathan! Her own personal .38 snubnose revolver and a lightweight chain mail vest—steel rings as supple and flexible as heavy silk—lay inside. There was a box of steel-jacketed hollow points beside the gun, a load that would bring serious grief to anyone— Sidhe or mortal—that it hit.

There were two speed-loaders in the package with the gun. She loaded them both as well as loading the gun, but left the rest of the box where it was—any problem that eighteen bullets couldn't solve, magic probably couldn't solve either.

A distant part of her mind was amused by her preparations. Who would ever have thought that there would come a day when she'd come riding to Eric's rescue Underhill? He knew more about the Sidhe than she did, but it was equally true that he had no idea of what people like Robert Lintel were capable of in their sublime self-obsession. Lintel wouldn't give up now that he'd seen the kind of power Eric had and thought he saw a way to get it for himself. And if Lintel caught up with him, Eric would be as helpless as a child, no matter how gifted a Bard he was. Down deep, Eric was a nice guy, and that would always put him at a disadvantage when dealing with people like Lintel—or the Dark Court.

Fortunately, Ria thought, she wasn't nice.

She stripped off her executive power suit and

dressed again in the outfit Logan had brought her to go slum-crawling in. She pulled on her tightest T-shirt and slid the vest over it before slipping on the Kevlar-lined jacket and zipping it up to her throat. The combination should stop anything she might have to face, Sidhe or human. She slid the gun into her pocket and inspected herself in the mirror. Neither gun nor vest showed.

She was ready to go to war. Now all she had to do was find the battlefield.

Guardian House looked serene and untouched by recent events. In order to track Eric, Ria needed something that was his—something attuned to his personal energy that she could use as a link to him, and his apartment was the best place to look. Ria wasn't sure it'd let her in without a fight, but fortunately she didn't have to try. As she stood in the little courtyard of the apartment building, she heard the frantic racing of a motorcycle engine coming from behind the building, and over it Greystone's gravel voice pleading with someone.

"Aw, c'mon, sweetheart! Just—could you wait a minute here! Hey! Here now, *mo chidr*—"

She ran around to the tiny private parking lot in the back of the building and found Greystone standing in front of Eric's bike. The elvensteed was making frantic dashes at the gate—all by itself—but Greystone kept blocking them, wings outstretched. The bike flashed its—*her*—lights in frustration, and her attempts to get around the gargoyle grew more frantic.

"Hey! Blondie!" Greystone called when he saw

Ria. "This thing can talk. Why ain't she talkin' to me, then?"

"It's an elvensteed," Ria answered. "She won't listen to you or let anyone ride her but Eric. But elvensteeds can travel anywhere without Gates or Portals, and if he's called for her—"

"We can follow?" Greystone said, brightening.

"Exactly. Just get out of her way before she decides to bite you."

Greystone stepped aside and folded back his wings. Lady Day zipped around him like a bull avoiding the matador's cape. By the time she was halfway up the block, she was gone from sight.

But if I can follow Eric, I can certainly follow you, my dear.

"She's gone! Hey, Blondie! What do we do now?"

"We follow. And Greystone . . . ?"

The gargoyle looked at her hopefully.

"Don't call me 'Blondie.' "

Aerune stared down at the bold interloper. It had never occurred to him that the mortal Bard might dare to beard him in his stronghold.

"Kneel to me, mortal," he thundered, mantling himself with Power and stretching out his hand. A massive ring gleamed, blood-red, on his outstretched forefinger.

"I don't think so," the Bard said. "We don't do much kneeling in the World Above these days. Or hadn't you noticed? Things have changed since the last time you led a Wild Hunt there. More iron, for one thing—but that's just the tip of the iceberg. Magic's really impressive, but Cold Iron will stop it dead, and we've got a lot of that in the World Above. We've also got machines that can do things you've never even dreamed of, machines that magic can't stop. If you want a bunch of mortals to pay homage to you, you're going to have to have a lot more in your bag of tricks than a little flashy magic and some big dogs. And I don't think you do."

Infuriated by the Bard's arrogance as he was, Aerune was an honest enough tactician to see that there was much merit in what the mortal stripling had to say. The mortal *Robertlintel* had been quick to defend himself with Cold Iron when Aerune had attacked him, nor had his servants cowered at the sight of the Wild Hunt as Aerune had expected. Fear and magic were the Unseleighe's two main weapons against the mortal kind, and if those proved ineffective . . .

"And the fact that you can't take us over isn't the worst of what I've got to tell you. Those guys in the park? The ones with the chain mail and the iron spears? They're playing you, Dark Lord. I don't know who sent them after you, but I do know the kind of person he is. I've met people like him before. He's got hundreds of 'warriors' at his command, and he wants your magic. He's already killed I-don't-know-how-many innocent people to get a handle on it, and he's getting closer to figuring you out every minute.

"And once he does, he's going to be coming after you—here. If humans figure out a way into Underhill, your intramural feuds won't matter anymore. Dark Court and Light—you'll both be history."

Such audacity and ruthlessness as the Bard described was worthy of Aerune himself, but the notion of a mortal having the temerity—and the weapons—to conquer Elven Lands was a sickening thought. Aerune considered the mad wizard he'd faced in the Park, the crude-but-effective weapons that had accounted for the lives of so many of his Hunt.

No. It is not possible. They were lucky, nothing more, he decided. *Now that I have taken their measure, I will cow them utterly. For Aerete.*

But the Bard was still talking, impervious to his own immediate peril.

"So you're going to have to choose. Work with me to take this guy out and bury what he knows. Or end up serving him with an iron collar around your neck."

"You have gone too far, Bard!" Aerune shouted, rising to his feet in a swirl of black cloak. "I am the Great Lord Aerune mac Audelaine of the Unseleighe Sidhe, and before I am done with you, you will beg me for death, as will any of your kindred who dare to raise their banners against me. *Guards!* Attend me!"

He would blast this mortal where he stood, hang his body on the castle gates as a warning to other impertinent trespassers! Aerune drew back his hand, preparing to strike.

And the throne room . . . *rippled* . . . as the fabric of Aerune's realm twisted sideways with a sickening and disorienting lurch. Mage-quake! Aerune staggered, fighting for balance in the aftermath of the disruption, as his tiny kingdom was destroyed and remade itself again in obedience to his will and his magics. But the Bard who taunted him here could not claim such power. . . .

"Told you so," said the Bard sadly.

Six of Aerune's guardsmen now stood within the doorway, obedient to his summons, but they were not the only ones within Aerune's throne room, nor was the Bard now the only human interloper.

A human man wearing the ugly grey clothing Aerune had seen in the World Above stood in the middle of his throne room, staring about himself with undisguised greed. With him were four human warriors wearing black and bearing weapons of Cold Iron that glowed and smoked in the magic of Aerune's Underhill realm. At their feet lay half a dozen dead humans, their bodies withered in the fashion of those Crowned Ones who had given up their power to Aerune's needs before.

"I will deal with you after I destroy them," Aerune growled to the Bard. He gestured to his guardsmen. "Take them!"

This is not good, Eric thought, hoping his shields would hold against stray bullets as well as spells, knowing that if the bullets were steel-jacketed they probably wouldn't after the first one or two. He'd been right, not that he was very happy about it at the moment. With humans and their Cold Iron weapons down here in Underhill, Seleighe and Unseleighe kingdoms alike would go under like wheat under a harvester. And with elven magery running wild in the World Above, the outlook for humanity wasn't very good either.

The Unseleighe guardsmen started forward, seeing only spears raised to stop them. One of the black-clad goons the Suit had brought with him raised a pistol and fired, and one of Aerune's guards staggered and fell to the ground, screaming. In moments elven-fire had consumed his entire body as the steel-jacketed bullet did its work.

Unfortunately, the Dark Lord Aerune didn't seem to be sufficiently impressed by this display to call off his men. More guardsmen poured into the room, swords drawn, red eyes gleaming. The human mercenaries turned outward, putting a ring of steel around the Suit. There was a chatter of machine-pistol fire, the bright flare of disrupted shielding, and the guardsmen moved in for close-quarters work. The mercenaries lowered their spears, obviously ready for them. There was a sudden clatter of engagement.

Eric wasn't sure what elvish swords were made of, but whatever it was, in the magic-charged air of Underhill, it sizzled like an ice cube tossed into hot grease when it met the iron blades of the spears the humans were carrying. After the first time a parry sliced one of the elven swords clear through, the guardsmen were more cautious about rushing their prey. A couple of the Suit's henchmen kept firing, covering the spearmen and choosing their targets with care. The throne room echoed with the sound of gunfire, and the faint acrid scent of gunsmoke filled the air. Elves fell beneath the onslaught of Cold Iron until the silvery mirror floor of the throne room was littered with elvish bodies, and the Suit and his hardboys were still standing. Aerune sat watching the carnage as if it were a play staged for his amusement.

Because soon enough they're going to run out

of bullets, and I don't think they've got any way out of here now that they've used up their "batteries." Aerune hasn't even called up the heavy artillery yet, and he's not a very happy camper at the moment. . . . Eric didn't want to be here when Aerune decided to take out his frustrations on the interlopers—and he wasn't sure he could stop the Unseleighe Lord either. He could issue a formal Challenge—that might slow Aerune down—but the Dark Lord was on his home ground here, and magical duels had not been a major part of Eric's education.

He'd let his mind wander for a fatal instant. Suddenly there was a lull in the fighting, and Eric found himself staring down the barrel of a pistol.

"Work with me, big man, or the hippie gets it right here!" the man in the suit called cheerfully. "You've seen what our weapons can do to your people, so back off before it happens to you!"

Aerune waved a hand, and his guardsmen pulled back, forming a ring around the interlopers. The room had grown darker in just the last few moments: Eric could no longer see the walls of the throne room clearly, and it seemed to him that there were *things* lurking in the shadows outside the ring of Unseleighe knights. But despite that, the Suit was smiling, as if things were going just the way he'd planned.

"Allow me to introduce myself, Mr. mac Audelaine. My name's Bob Lintel, Threshold Labs. You've got something I want, and I believe we can work together to our mutual advantage. I have no problem with dividing territory. You help me back home, I'll help you here. If it's psi you want, I can provide you with a permanent supply. Let's pool our forces."

Whatever else Aerune mac Audelaine was, he was a realist. He leaned forward on his dark throne, fixing Lintel with a burning gaze.

"You have an odd way of asking for favors, mortal man," Aerune rumbled, "but your arguments are . . . compelling. Come here to me, and I will hear your petition. Perhaps you are right." Aerune gestured in welcome, smiling chillingly. The man in the suit smiled back, but didn't move from the safety of his mercenaries.

Aerune and Lintel stood frozen, each testing the other's resolve in a high-stakes game of "Chicken" as Eric watched in unconcealed horror. This was the last thing he wanted—two killer sharks dividing up Underhill and the World Above like an extra-large pizza, no anchovies. *What am I going to do now?*

The Unseleighe guardsmen and the human commandos watched each other intently, neither side moving. For a moment, the room was utterly silent. And in the distance, Eric heard a faint sound that had no place in Underhill.

The sound of an engine.

A motorcycle engine.

Lady Day barreled through the open doorway to the throne room, vaulting the dead and scattering the living as she headed for Eric. Here in Underhill the elvensteed seemed to flicker back and forth between bike and horse, the strobe effect making Eric's eyes hurt. Headache or not, she was the most welcome sight he'd seen in a long time. Eric started toward her—

And Aerune froze her in place with a gesture, trapping her within a cage of flickering blue light. The elvensteed, fully in horse-form now, stamped her foot, eyes flashing dangerously as she tossed her head in frustration.

"Move, hippie, and I drill you right now!" Lintel barked, oblivious to the byplay. "You aren't getting away this easily. Aerune wants you, and so do I."

"Too bad neither of you gets him," a new voice said coolly. "I'd put that down if I were you, Mr. Lintel."

Eric felt like cheering. Ria Llewellyn strode through the door, followed by Greystone. If Ria experienced any surprise at her surroundings—or the bodies all over the floor—she didn't show it. She was wearing black leather and blue jeans, and looked deadly and confident.

And she had a gun.

Almost before she'd finished speaking, Lintel swept his pistol around and rapped off three shots directly at her chest.

"Ria!" Eric shouted, aghast.

But she didn't fall. She staggered back against Greystone, and steadied herself against the gargoyle's outspread wing, but she obviously wasn't hurt. She smiled a small wintery smile at Lintel.

"I've done plenty of corporate dueling in my time, but this is a little extreme," she said. "Oh, by the way. I'm sure we haven't met. I'm Ria Llewellyn. Your boss."

Then she shot Robert Lintel neatly in the knee.

He went down screaming, dropping his gun and scattering his men in confusion. Aerune's elven guards surged forward and stopped, uncertain of whether they should try to take advantage of the moment. One of Lintel's men knelt to try to help him. Eric ran down the steps and made it across the throne room to Ria's side in the confusion.

"Glad you could make it," he gasped.

"Wouldn't miss it for worlds," Ria answered. "Get back."

Greystone lifted him out of the way just as a levin bolt flung by an enraged Aerune struck Ria full in the chest. It popped and sizzled, running all over her body like St. Elmo's fire before sinking into the floor, but Ria stood her ground, as unharmed by elven magic as by mortal bullets.

"Stainless-steel chain mail," Ria called toward Aerune. "The least of mortal defenses. Very easy to make in the World Above—I'm sure Lintel's men are wearing it."

To Eric she said: "I'm going to distract him. Can you get your steed free? We're going to need her."

"I think so," Eric answered, his voice equally low. He reached out, feeling at the edges of the spell that had trapped Lady Day. It was a simple one, the Sidhe equivalent of a locked door. *Now let's see if I can find the key.*

As he concentrated, Ria stepped forward, away from Greystone's protection, and bowed her head, a conciliating, coaxing note entering her voice.

"My Lord, your power is vast and mine is very small. I am no match for you alone, even with weapons and armor of deathmetal from the World Above. But the Bard and I together can hold you off indefinitely. He has powerful patrons among the Seleighe Court who would much resent any harm you might do to him, nor is the gargoyle entirely friendless. I pray you, of your great mercy, allow us three—four—to depart your kingdom unmolested. We wish no quarrel with you."

Aerune looked at her measuringly, resuming his seat and regarding her with bleak expressionless eyes.

"Ria!" Eric hissed. She couldn't be suggesting what he thought she was—just *abandoning* those five guys and Lintel to Aerune's mercy? He looked behind him, through the open doors, but the rest of the Unseleighe Court seemed to have vanished; the outer room was empty. "What about Lintel and the others? We can't just leave them here!"

Lintel's agonized groans seemed to fill the room, setting his teeth on edge. A shattered kneecap was just about the most painful and crippling single wound possible to inflict.

"True," Ria answered, her voice low. "I can't afford to leave Lintel to strike a bargain of his own. Saddle up as soon as you can, Eric. We may be leaving quickly. Greystone, you too."

"Check, boss lady," the gargoyle said.

Aerune spoke again, a faint admiring smile upon his face.

"Very well, halfbreed. You, the Bard and his mount, and this . . . creature . . . which accompanies you, all have my leave to depart. But the others remain. Do these terms suit you?"

The magic around Lady Day dissolved, and the elvensteed bounded toward the doorway and Eric, changing form back into a motorbike as she did so. Aerune paid no attention. Reluctantly, Eric swung his leg over Lady Day's saddle. The elvensteed thrummed her engine, impatient to be away.

"They do, My Lord, and many thanks to you for your mercy," Ria said. She raised her gun once more and fired, placing a bullet squarely between Lintel's eyes. The corporate raider slumped to the floor, silent in death, and the commando squatting beside him reached for his gun.

"No!" Eric was half off Lady Day's back—though what he could do, he wasn't sure—when the elvensteed decided she'd had enough of this part of Underhill. With a banshee scream she took off, Greystone close behind. Nothing Eric could do could slow or turn her, and at the speed she was going, he didn't dare just jump off. Eric looked back wildly over his shoulder, catching a last glimpse of the throne room before it vanished in the distance.

Ria stood alone before Lord Aerune.

"You are properly ruthless, halfling," Aerune said, getting to his feet. Though irritated by his loss, he looked intrigued as well. She'd counted more than a little on that. Elves were suckers for a grand gesture.

Not that Aerune was a sucker in any sense of the word.

He stepped down from his throne, and stood facing her across a tangle of bodies, Sidhe and human. With a wave of his hand, he banished them all to another part of his domain. No trace of the battle—or Lintel's men—remained to mar the chilly perfection of his presence chamber. The doors of the throne room closed in the same moment, sealing Ria in with him.

Aerune held out his hand to her. The black mail

gauntlet gleamed in the unchanging radiance of Underhill.

"It has been too long since I encountered anyone with such beauty who had yet the spirit to defy me. I do not think you have been properly valued by your kin, halfling, nor by the World Above. Matters could be otherwise. Have you considered—"

"And rejected, Great Lord," Ria answered steadily. This powerful Unseleighe Sidhe was offering her a seductive prize—his patronage, and with it, a place in Underhill. Once she could have asked for no greater reward.

Once.

"I want no bargain with you beyond that which I have already struck, Great Lord, though I prize your honorable offer for the tribute it is. I will go now, by your leave, and molest your realm no more. Lintel was my vassal, and he is well rewarded for his treachery. I leave you his men as my gift, to do with as you choose."

Taking a calculated risk, she turned her back on Lord Aerune and walked away. The doors of the throne room opened before her, and she walked out into the deserted castle. No one tried to stop her, but Ria didn't breathe completely easily until she'd reached the nearest Portal and taken herself beyond Aerune's reach—or at least, his immediate reach.

I know this isn't over. Now that he knows there's something of value in the World Above, Aerune won't stop until he figures out a way to get at it. But that's a problem for another day. Thank God for small favors.

TWELVE:

TO END WHERE
WE BEGAN

As soon as Ria reached the World Above, everything that had happened in Aerune's court began to take on a vague air of unreality. After passing through several Portals and nearly exhausting her store of Power, she'd come out in Sterling Forest, near the Nexus of Elfhame Everforest, and had to hike more than a mile before she found a phone she could use to call a car to take her back to the city. It was late Monday evening by the time she arrived back in New York—time ran differently in the World Above, sometimes to the World Above's benefit.

The drive back to the City gave her a lot of time to think, mostly about the look of horror on Eric's face as she shot Robert Lintel. There'd been no other choice, though. Aerune probably wouldn't have let her take Lintel without a fight anyway, and if she *had* managed to bring him back to the World Above to face charges, the New York courts would probably have let him off on a technicality. That was the way the legal system worked when you had money and influence.

Ria had always preferred justice to law, and she'd spoken no more than the truth to the Unseleighe lord. What Lintel had done was in some sense her responsibility. Threshold was a LlewellCo company. Lintel had worked for her. Ultimately, she was responsible for what he'd done. Now he'd paid the dead for their loss in the only way possible, with his own life, and that simplified matters. He'd never have the chance to use the information he'd gained at the cost of so many innocent lives.

And if she had to lose Eric's respect—and love— because of it, Ria was willing to pay that price, though it would hurt more than she liked to think.

I might as well find out now how it's going to be as soon as possible, she thought grimly. There was no point in waiting to get bad news.

"I've changed my mind," she told the driver. "I'm not going to the Sherry. There's a stop I want you to make first."

The ride from Aerune's castle to New York passed in a dizzying blur. After the first few seconds, he'd just closed his eyes and held on tight, and finally the elvensteed had stopped.

When he opened his eyes, the world spun giddily. Eric slid sideways off Lady Day's saddle and into Greystone's arms.

"Steady there, laddybuck. Strewth, that was the wildest ride I've been on since I was a gleam in the stonecarver's eye!" the gargoyle said cheerfully.

"Yeah," Eric said weakly. After a moment the world steadied, and he could stand on his own two feet.

He looked around warily. He was back in New York, behind Guardian House. It seemed strange that everything looked normal. It was dark. Eric had no idea what day it was, though from the powdered-sugar snow that fell lightly all around him, it was still December.

But what year? Not that I care right now.

"Let's get you inside," Greystone said. "If ever a man could do with a stiff drink, boyo, it's you."

"No," Eric said, feeling a little better. "Not a drink. But I wouldn't turn down a strong cup of coffee. Meet you upstairs."

Greystone bounded skyward with surprising grace, settling back into his place with a flourish and a bow.

A shower and a change of clothes helped. He was still trying to sort everything out in his mind, trying to fit the events into some kind of order. Eventually he was going to have to figure out something to tell Toni and the other Guardians. They deserved to know how the story ended.

Greystone had joined him inside, his cheerfully ugly face contorted into an expression of worry as he watched Eric move around the apartment.

Finally, coffee and sandwich in hand, Eric sat down on the couch.

"I can't believe she did that," he said, sighing. As much as he tried to avoid it, Eric's thoughts kept returning to that one image of the bullet hole in the middle of Lintel's forehead, stopping him from thinking past it. He set his sandwich down on the table untasted. She'd just shot him. No hesitation, no remorse. Bam!

Greystone shook his head in sympathy. "I can't either. Man, talk about *cold* . . . !"

"No," Eric said, grudgingly fair. Somehow Greystone's putting his own thoughts into words made Eric see Ria's side of things. "As much as I hate what she did, I think she was telling the truth. She didn't have a choice. She couldn't leave Lintel there in Underhill alive. Believe me, he and Aerune were *this* close to making a deal. Cold Iron in Underhill—humans knowing about elves—magic in the World Above—it would have been . . ."

It would have been just like my dream: New York a wasteland. Thousands—millions—dead. And Underhill . . . gone. Humans and Sidhe need each other. Our lives are too intertwined. One can't really survive without the other. But that doesn't mean most people need to know about Underhill, or magic, or the Nexuses, any more than they need to know how to build a nuclear warhead. Ria knew that. She did what had to be done. But that doesn't mean I have to like it. . . .

"She could have brought him back here!" Greystone protested. "I could'a carried him. Easy!"

Eric shook his head reluctantly and drank his coffee. The bitter warmth helped clarify his thoughts. "Then he'd be back here, alive, still knowing what he knows, with his cache of designer poison still out there somewhere. Sure, there'd be a trial, but he'd probably be out on bail while he was waiting for his court date, and that means he could escape back Underhill, strike a bargain with Aerune, or come up with something else horrible I haven't even thought of yet. And Ria would be stuck in the middle of it—if she did anything to stop him here, she'd be the one who went to prison, not him."

"Maybe," the gargoyle said grudgingly. "But I still think we should'a brought him back here and let Jimmie and the gang sort him out."

"I don't know," Eric said unhappily. Maybe that would have worked. But with the stakes so high, was it worth taking the chance? The worst of it was, he probably wasn't going to see Ria again. He still wasn't sure how she'd found him, but she had. She'd rescued him, given him all the help he'd asked her for, and he'd thrown it back in her face—and deserted her, even if that hadn't exactly been his idea. He didn't even know if she'd gotten out of Aerune's realm alive.

Good going, Banyon. So much for your vaunted leadership abilities.

"I don't even know where she is now, or if she even got out alive. Greystone, can you—"

"Well," Greystone said abruptly, "guess I'd better get back to work. No rest for the wicked, and all that. See you around, boyo. I'm going back on duty before anyone notices I'm AWOL."

"Hey," Eric said, getting to his feet as Greystone climbed out the window. Maybe Greystone hadn't wanted to be asked if he and the Guardians could find Ria, but that didn't mean he had to just run off like that!

There was a knock at the door.

He stared after the gargoyle. The knocking continued. Thinking it was Toni, knowing that Guardian House would never allow in anything that could do its inhabitants any harm, Eric opened the door.

Ria was standing there, still dressed in battered denim and leather. A few snowflakes lay on her hair and shoulders, melting slowly. She looked tired, uncertain of her reception.

A vast relief filled Eric, as if he were finally able to set down a heavy load he'd been carrying, and he smiled.

"Glad you could make it," he said simply.

Her face relaxed into a smile of sheer relief, as if she'd gotten good news she'd hoped for but hadn't expected. Eric stepped back, gesturing for her to enter.

"Wouldn't miss it for worlds," Ria answered.

Later—much later—there was time to talk it all out. Ria explained the whole story from the beginning as she'd managed to piece it together, about Threshold's black-budget project to come up with a drug that turned ordinary people into Wild Talents. How she'd tracked the project back to Threshold, found Lintel gone, and then followed Lady Day to find Eric, knowing that wherever Lintel was, he, too, would be hot on Eric's trail.

"I still don't like what you did," Eric said. "It wasn't the only solution. We could have taken him to the Seleighe Sidhe, made him *their* problem. . . ."

Ria shrugged. "I don't know that I trust them with Lintel anymore than I did Aerune. He was too much of a wild card. This was more expedient."

Eric already knew he wanted Ria to stay a part of his life. But if he let her set the terms for their relationship, they'd still be in the same situation they'd been back in L.A., and that wouldn't work for him.

"If we're going to stay together, you're going to have to promise me that if we get into any more situations, you won't do the expedient thing anymore," he said firmly, but inside he was holding his breath, waiting for her answer.

She regarded him with a raised eyebrow, for a frozen moment looking more elvish than she did human. At last she smiled faintly.

"I'll offer you a compromise, m'love. I won't do the expedient thing without consulting you and letting you have a chance to convince me otherwise. Have we a bargain, O great Sidhe Bard?"

Eric thought about it for a moment. Things had changed between them, he realized. He wasn't her pet. She wasn't his lackey. They were equal partners. He found he liked the idea very much.

"That'll work. I'll be your conscience," he answered.

"Just like Jiminy Cricket," Ria said mockingly. She kissed him lightly on the forehead and got to her feet. "Don't forget the cricket spent most of the movie as a ghost."

"I'm not worried," Eric said contentedly.

Ria smiled, looking younger and softer—and

somehow hopeful, as if she'd been offered a new beginning.

"And now, the police are probably looking for me—and I'll bet you need to come up with an explanation for playing hooky from school today. I'll probably be out of touch for a while, but don't worry. Watch for me on the news. Then give me a call and we'll have dinner. We've still got a lot of loose ends to chase down."

"It's a date," Eric answered. He knew he was grinning like a fool, but he didn't care. He walked her to the door and stood in the doorway, watching her walk down the hall, still smiling.

I can't wait to tell Kory and Beth about all this, he thought to himself. *I wonder what they'll say.*

He heard the elevator cage rattle closed, and heard the elevator start down. *Louis, something tells me this is the start of a beautiful friendship. . . .*

PRAISE FOR
LOIS McMASTER BUJOLD

What the critics say:

The Warrior's Apprentice: "Now here's a fun romp through the spaceways—not so much a space opera as space ballet.... it has all the 'right stuff.' A lot of thought and thoughtfulness stand behind the all-too-human characters. Enjoy this one, and look forward to the next." —Dean Lambe, *SF Reviews*

"The pace is breathless, the characterization thoughtful and emotionally powerful, and the author's narrative technique and command of language compelling. Highly recommended."
—*Booklist*

Brothers in Arms: "...she gives it a genuine depth of character, while reveling in the wild turnings of her tale.... Bujold is as audacious as her favorite hero, and as brilliantly (if sneakily) successful." —*Locus*

"Miles Vorkosigan is such a great character that I'll read anything Lois wants to write about him....a book to re-read on cold rainy days." —Robert Coulson, *Comic Buyer's Guide*

Borders of Infinity: "Bujold's series hero Miles Vorkosigan may be a lord by birth and an admiral by rank, but a bone disease that has left him hobbled and in frequent pain has sensitized him to the suffering of outcasts in his very hierarchical era....Playing off Miles's reserve and cleverness, Bujold draws outrageous and outlandish foils to color her high-minded adventures." —*Publishers Weekly*

Falling Free: "In *Falling Free* Lois McMaster Bujold has written her fourth straight superb novel.... How to break down a talent like Bujold's into analyzable components? Best not to try. Best to say: 'Read, or you will be missing something extraordinary.'" —Roland Green, *Chicago Sun-Times*

The Vor Game: "The chronicles of Miles Vorkosigan are far too witty to be literary junk food, but they rouse the kind of craving that makes popcorn magically vanish during a double feature." —Faren Miller, *Locus*

MORE PRAISE FOR
LOIS McMASTER BUJOLD

What the readers say:

"My copy of *Shards of Honor* is falling apart I've reread it so often. . . . I'll read whatever you write. You've certainly proved yourself a grand storyteller."

—Lisa Kolbe, Colorado Springs, CO

"I experience the stories of Miles Vorkosigan as almost viscerally uplifting. . . . But certainly, even the weightiest theme would have less impact than a cinder on snow were it not for a rousing good story, and good story-telling with it. This is the second thing I want to thank you for. . . . I suppose if you boiled down all I've said to its simplest expression, it would be that I immensely enjoy and admire your work. I submit that, as literature, your work raises the overall level of the science fiction genre, and spiritually, your work cannot avoid positively influencing all who read it."

—Glen Stonebraker, Gaithersburg, MD

" 'The Mountains of Mourning' [in *Borders of Infinity*] was one of the best-crafted, and simply best, works I'd ever read. When I finished it, I immediately turned back to the beginning and read it again, and I can't remember the last time I did that."

—Betsy Bizot, Lisle, IL

"I can only hope that you will continue to write, so that I can continue to read (and of course buy) your books, for they make me laugh and cry and think . . . rare indeed."

—Steven Knott, Major, USAF

What Do You Say?

Cordelia's Honor	57828-6 ◆	$7.99 ☐
The Warrior's Apprentice	72066-X ◆	$6.99 ☐
The Vor Game	72014-7 ◆	$6.99 ☐
Borders of Infinity	72093-7 ◆	$6.99 ☐
Young Miles (trade)	87782-8 ◆	$15.00 ☐
Cetaganda (hardcover)	87701-1 ◆	$21.00 ☐
Cetaganda (paperback)	87744-5 ◆	$6.99 ☐
Ethan of Athos	65604-X ◆	$5.99 ☐
Brothers in Arms	69799-4 ◆	$5.99 ☐
Mirror Dance	87646-5 ◆	$6.99 ☐
Memory	87845-X ◆	$6.99 ☐
Komarr (hardcover)	87877-8 ◆	$22.00 ☐
Komarr (paperback)	57808-1 ◆	$6.99 ☐
A Civil Campaign (hardcover)	57827-8 ◆	$24.00 ☐
A Civil Campaign (paperback)	57885-5 ◆	$7.99 ☐
Falling Free	57812-X ◆	$6.99 ☐
The Spirit Ring	57870-7 ◆	$6.99 ☐

LOIS McMASTER BUJOLD

 Only from Baen Books

visit our website at www.baen.com
